PUSHKIN PRESS

FOR A LITTLE WHILE

"In *For a Little While* we have a core sample of a literary titan. At last. Bass is, hands down, a master of the short form, creating in a few pages a natural world of mythic proportions . . . The greatest joy in *For a Little While* is the belief, in story after story, in the goodness of all things on this earth, including us."

NEW YORK TIMES BOOK REVIEW

"One of our best writers."

KENT HARUF

"His narration is pitch-perfect, and his writing so full of empathy for people and places that each story is a new revelation."

SAN FRANCISCO CHRONICLE

"What a gift this bountiful book is. His stories, often stunningly elemental, concern hardy and misbegotten folks, yet are suffused with a quality of tenderness for all of whom he writes and the beautiful world they inhabit."

DANIEL WOODRELL

"A sustained achievement...Bass has used the short story form to pursue a searing vision of life."

CHICAGO TRIBUNE

"*For a Little While* is nothing short of remarkable. In the powerful lyricism of his exquisitely wrought prose, Rick Bass conveys not only the ordinary thoughts and impulses of his characters but also those moments of pure sensation – convincing in every physical, mental, and emotional detail – when the intensity of life exists at a pitch almost beyond language, grace has always been the great, elusive subject of his short fiction, and the extraordinary, transcendent stories collected here pursue it in myriad and seamless ways."

JOYCE CAROL OATES

"Rick Bass's gift as a writer is that he takes you unforgettable places and shows you unforgettable sights, all real. The tone is always quiet and sharp-eyed; details are the only exclamation points. Each story in *For a Little While* is a complete hijacking of the reader's senses, accomplished with a raw and splendid subtlety."

CARL HIAASEN

"Durable and authentic . . . a writer who can both frighten and amaze."

JIM HARRISON

"Exhilarating . . . His prose produces the ache of recognition and the sense that life is indeed worth living."

DAVID GUTERSON

"What a voice! True and desperate, and full of longing. These stories glint with rough magic."

JOY WILLIAMS

"Impossible to pick a single favorite Rick Bass story, since my enthusiasm for them started with those collected in *The Watch* all those years ago."

AMY HEMPEL

"Bass's strong, moving and impulsive stories make an important world that is all his own . . . this is urgent and valuable work."

THOMAS MCGUANE

"Extravagant . . . Writing of this quality creates a stillness in the mind."

TIME

"Bass combines precision, realism, and profound imagination. A collection of enrapturing radiance and depth, a beacon and a hearth."

BOOKLIST, STARRED REVIEW

"Bass writes movingly of the land, weather, and place. Essential reading for students of the modern American short story and some of the best work of a writer who is at the top of his game."

KIRKUS, STARRED REVIEW

FOR A LITTLE WHILE

NEW AND SELECTED STORIES

RICK BASS

PUSHKIN PRESS
LONDON

Pushkin Press
71–75 Shelton Street, London WC2H 9JQ

First published by Pushkin Press in 2017

This edition published by arrangement with Little, Brown and Company, a division of Hachette Book Group, New York, New York, USA. All rights reserved.

Acknowledgment is made to the following, in which the stories in this collection first appeared, some in slightly different form: 'Fish Story' in the *Atlantic*; 'Fires' in *Big Sky Journal* and *The Quarterly*; 'The Blue Tree' in *Ecotone*; 'Redfish' in *Esquire*; 'The River in Winter' in *GQ*; 'The Canoeists,' 'Coach,' 'Goats,' 'How She Remembers It,' and 'Pagans' in the *Idaho Review*; 'The Fireman' in the *Kenyon Review*; 'An Alcoholic's Guide to Peru and Chile' in the *Missouri Review*; 'Elk' in the *New Yorker*; 'Her First Elk,' 'The Hermit's Story,' 'The Legend of Pig-Eye,' and 'Wild Horses' in the *Paris Review*; 'The History of Rodney' in *Ploughshares*; 'Field Events' and 'The Watch' in *The Quarterly*; 'Titan' in *Shenandoah*; 'Swans' in Story; and 'Lease Hound' and 'The Lives of Rocks' in *Zoetrope: All-Story*. 'In Ruth's Country,' 'Redfish,' 'The Watch,' and 'Wild Horses' from *The Watch* by Rick Bass. Copyright © 1989 by Rick Bass. Used by permission of W. W. Norton & Company, Inc. 'Field Events' from *Platte River* by Rick Bass. Copyright © 1994 by Rick Bass. Reprinted by permission of the author. 'Fires,' 'The History of Rodney,' and 'The Legend of Pig-Eye' from *In the Loyal Mountains* by Rick Bass. Copyright © 1995 by Rick Bass. Reprinted by permission of Houghton Mifflin Harcourt Publishing Company. All rights reserved. 'The Fireman,' 'The Hermit's Story,' and 'Swans' from *The Hermit's Story* by Rick Bass. Copyright © 2002 by Rick Bass. Reprinted by permission of Houghton Mifflin Harcourt Publishing Company. All rights reserved. 'The Canoeists,' 'Goats,' 'Her First Elk,' 'The Lives of Rocks,' 'Pagans,' and 'Titan' from *The Lives of Rocks* by Rick Bass. Copyright © 2006 by Rick Bass. Reprinted by permission of Houghton Mifflin Harcourt Publishing Company. All rights reserved.

ISBN 978 1 782273 04 2

10 9 8 7 6 5 4 3 2 1

Printed and bound by CPI Group (UK) Ltd, Croydon CR0 4YY

www.pushkinpress.com

For Mary Katherine and Lowry, incomparable beloveds; and for my agent, David Evans, friend and support

Contents

NEW STORIES

SELECTED STORIES

Some dive into the sea
Some toil upon the stone

—Townes Van Zandt

Wild Horses

Karen was twenty-six. She had been engaged twice, married once. Her husband had run away with another woman after only six months. It still made her angry when she thought about it, which was not often.

The second man she had loved more, the most. He was the one she had been engaged to, but had not married. His name was Henry. He had drowned in the Mississippi the day before they were to be wed. They never even found the body. He had a marker in the cemetery, but it was a sham. All her life, Karen had heard those stories about fiancés dying the day before the wedding, and then it had happened to her.

Henry and some of his friends, including his best friend, Sydney Bean, had been sitting up on the railroad trestle that ran so far and across that river, above the wide muddiness. Louisiana and trees on one side; Mississippi and trees, and some farms, on the other side. There had been a full moon and no wind, and they were sitting above the water, maybe a hundred feet above it, laughing, and drinking Psychos from the Daiquiri World over in Delta, Louisiana. The Psychos were rum and Coca-Cola and various fruit juices and blue food coloring. They came in Styrofoam cups the size of small trash cans, so large they had to be held with both hands. Sydney had had two of them; Henry, three.

Henry had stood up, beaten his chest like Tarzan, shouted, and then dived in. It had taken him forever to hit the water. The light from the moon was good, and they had been able to watch him all the way down.

Sometimes Sydney Bean still came by to visit Karen. Sydney was gentle and sad, her own age, and he worked on his farm, out past Utica, back to the east, where he also broke and sometimes trained horses.

Once a month—at the end of each month—Sydney would stay over on Karen's farm, and they would go into her big empty closet, and he would let her hit him: striking him with her fists, kicking him, kneeing him, slapping his face until his ears rang and his nose bled; slapping and swinging at him until she was crying and her hair was wild and in her eyes, and the palms of her hands hurt too much to hit him anymore.

It built up, the ache and the anger in Karen; and then, hitting Sydney, it went away for a while. He was a good friend. But the trouble was that it always came back.

Sometimes Sydney would try to help her in other ways. He would tell her that someday she was going to have to realize Henry would not be coming back. Not ever—not in any form—but to remember what she and Henry had had, to keep *that* from going away.

Sydney would stand there, in the closet, and let her strike him. But the rules were strict: she had to keep her mouth closed. He would not let her call him names while she was hitting him.

Though she wanted to.

After it was over, and she was crying, more drained than she had felt since the last time, sobbing, Sydney would help her up. He would take her into the bedroom and towel her forehead with a cool washcloth. Karen would be crying in a child's gulping sobs, and he would brush her hair, hold her hand, sometimes hold her against him, and pat her back while she moaned.

Farm sounds would come from the field, and when she looked out the window, she might see her neighbor, old Dr. Lynly, the vet, driving along in his ancient blue truck, moving along the bayou, down along the trees, with his dog, Buster, running alongside, barking, herding cows together for vaccinations.

"I can still feel the hurt," Karen would tell Sydney sometimes, when he came over not to be beaten up but to cook supper for her, or to sit on the back porch with her, and watch the fields.

4

Sydney nodded whenever Karen said she still hurt, and studied his hands.

"I could have grabbed him," he'd say, and then look up and out at the field some more. "I keep thinking that one of these years, I'm going to get a second chance." Sydney would shake his head again. "I think I could have grabbed him," he'd say.

"Or you could have dived in after him," Karen would say. "Maybe you could have dived in after him."

Her voice would trail off, and her face would be flat and weary.

On these occasions, Sydney Bean wanted the beatings to come once a week, or even daily. But they hurt, too, almost as much as the loss of his friend, and he said nothing. He still felt as if he owed Henry something. He didn't know what.

Sometimes, when he was down on his knees and Karen was kicking him or elbowing him, he felt close to it—and he almost felt angry at Karen—but he could never catch the shape of it, only the feeling.

He wanted to know what was owed, so he could go on.

On his own farm, there were cattle down in the fields, and they would get lost, separated from one another, and would low all through the night. It was a sound like soft thunder in the night, before the rain comes, and he liked it.

He raised the cattle, and saddle-broke the young horses that had never been ridden before, the one- and two-year-olds, the stallions, the wild mares. That pounding, and the evil, four-footed stamp-and-spin they went into when they could not shake him: when they began to do that, he knew he had them beaten. He charged two hundred and fifty dollars a horse, and sometimes it took him a month.

Old Dr. Lynly needed a helper but couldn't pay much, and Sydney, who had done some business with the vet, helped Karen get the job. She needed something to do besides sitting around on her back porch, waiting for the end of each month.

Dr. Lynly was older than Karen had thought he would be, when she met him up close. He had that look to him that told her it might be the last year of his life. It wasn't so much any illness or feebleness or disability. It was just a finished look.

He and Buster—his six-year-old Airedale—lived within the city limits of Vicksburg, down below the battlefield, hidden in one of the ravines. His house was up on blocks as the property flooded with almost every rain—and in his yard, in various corrals and pens, were chickens, ducks, goats, sheep, ponies, horses, cows, and an ostrich. It was illegal to keep them as pets, and the city newspaper editor was after him to get rid of them, but Dr. Lynly claimed they were all being treated by his tiny clinic.

"You're keeping these animals too long, Doc," the editor told him. Dr. Lynly would pretend to be senile and that the editor was asking for a prescription, and would begin quoting various random chemical names.

The Airedale minded Dr. Lynly exquisitely. He brought the paper, the slippers, left the room on command, and he brought the chickens' eggs, daily, into the kitchen, making several trips for his and Dr. Lynly's breakfast. Dr. Lynly would fry six eggs for himself, and Buster would get a dozen or so broken into his bowl raw. Any extras went into the refrigerator for Dr. Lynly to take on his rounds, though he no longer had many; only the very oldest people, who remembered him, and the poorest, who knew he worked for free and would charge them only for the medicine.

Buster's black-and-tan coat was glossy from the eggs, and his eyes, deep in the curls, were bright. He watched Dr. Lynly all the time.

Sometimes Karen watched Dr. Lynly play with Buster, bending down and swatting him in the chest, slapping his shoulders. She had thought the job would be mostly kittens and lambs, but she was mistaken.

Horses, the strongest creatures, were the ones that got the sickest, he said, and their pain was unspeakable when they finally did yield to it. On rounds with Dr. Lynly, Karen forgot to think about Henry at all. She was horrified by the horses' pain, almost wishing it were hers, bearing it rather than watching it.

Once, when Sydney was with her, he had reached out and taken her hand in his. When she looked down and saw it, she had at first been puzzled, not recognizing what it was, and then repulsed, as if it were a giant slug, and she threw Sydney's hand off hers and ran into her room.

Sydney stayed out on the porch. It was heavy blue twilight and the cattle down in the fields were feeding.

"I'm sorry," he called out. "But I can't bring him back!" He waited for her to answer, but could only hear her crying. It had been three years.

He knew he was wrong to have caught her off-balance like that: but he was tired of her unhappiness and frustrated that he could do nothing to end it. The sounds of her crying carried, and the cows down in the fields began to move closer. The light had dimmed: there were dark shadows, and a low gold thumbnail of a moon—a wet moon—came up over the ragged tear of trees by the bayou.

The beauty of the evening, being on Karen's back porch and in her life when it should have been Henry, flooded Sydney with a sudden guilt. He had been fighting it, and holding it back: and then, suddenly, the quiet stillness of the evening released it, and he heard himself saying a crazy thing.

"I pushed him off, you know," he said, loud enough so she could hear. "I finished my drink, and put both hands on his skinny-ass little shoulders, and said, 'Take a deep breath, Henry.' I just pushed him off."

It felt good, making up the lie. He was surprised at the relief he felt: it was as if he had control of the situation. It was like when he was on the horses, breaking them, trying to stay on.

Presently, Karen came back out with a small blue pistol, a .38, and she put it next to his head.

"Let's get in the truck," she said.

He knew where they were going.

The river was about ten miles away, and they took their time. There was fog flowing across the low parts of the road and through the fields and meadows like smoke, coming from the woods, and he was thinking about how cold and hard the water would be when he finally hit.

He felt as if he were already falling toward it, the way it had taken Henry forever to fall. But he didn't say anything, and though it didn't feel right, he wondered if perhaps it was this simple; as if this was what was owed after all.

They drove on, past the blue fields and the spills of fog. The roofs of the hay barns were bright silver polished tin, under the little moon and stars. There were small lakes, cattle stock tanks, and steam rose from them.

They drove with the windows down. It was a hot night, full of flying bugs, and about two miles from the river Karen told him to stop.

He pulled off to the side of the road, and wondered what she was going to do with his body. A cattle egret flew by, ghostly white and large, flying slowly, and Sydney was amazed that he had never recognized their beauty before, though he had seen countless numbers of them. It flew right across their windshield, from across the road, and it startled both of them.

The radiator ticked.

"You didn't really push him off, did you?" Karen asked. She still had the pistol against his head, and had switched hands.

Like frost burning off the grass in a bright morning sun, there was in his mind a sudden, sugary, watery feeling—like something dissolving. She was not going to kill him after all.

"No," he said.

"But you could have saved him," she said, for the thousandth time.

"I could have reached out and grabbed him," Sydney agreed. He was going to live. He was going to get to keep feeling things, was going to get to keep seeing things.

He kept his hands in his lap, not wanting to alarm Karen, but his eyes moved all around as he looked for more egrets. He was eager to see another one.

Karen watched him for a while, still holding the pistol against him, and then turned it around and looked at the open barrel of it, crosseyed, and held it there, right in her face, for several seconds. Then she reached out and put it in the glove box.

Sydney Bean was shuddering.

"Thank you," he said. "Thank you for not shooting yourself."

He put his head down on the steering wheel, in the moonlight, and shuddered again. There were crickets calling all around them. They sat like that for a long time, Sydney leaning against the wheel, and Karen sitting up straight, just looking out at the fields.

Then the cattle began to move up the hill toward them, thinking that Karen's old truck had come to feed them. They drifted up the hill from all over the fields, and from their nearby resting spots on the sandbars along the little dry creek that ran down into the bayou; and eventually, they all assembled around the truck.

They stood there in the moonlight, some with white faces like skulls, all about the same size, and chewed grass and watched the truck. One, bolder than the rest—a yearling black Angus—moved in close, bumped the grill of the truck with his nose, playing, and then leapt back again, scattering some of the others.

"How much would you say that one weighs?" Karen asked. "How much, Sydney?"

They drove the last two miles to the river. It was about four a.m. The yearling cow was bleating and trying to break free; Sydney had tied him up with his belt, and with jumper cables and shoelaces, and an old shirt. His lip was bloody from where the calf had butted him.

But he had wrestled larger steers than that before.

They parked at the old bridge, the one the trains still used to cross. Farther downriver, they could see an occasional car, two round spots of headlight moving steadily across the new bridge, so far above the river, going very slowly. Sydney put his shoulders under the calf's belly and lifted it with his back and legs, and like a prisoner in the stock, he carried it out to the center of the bridge. Karen followed. It took about fifteen minutes to get there, and Sydney was trembling, dripping with sweat, when they gauged they had reached the middle, the deepest part.

They sat there, soothing the frightened calf, stroking its ears, patting its flanks, and waited for the sun to come up. When it did, pale orange behind the great steaminess of the trees and river below— the fog from the river and trees a gunmetal gray, the whole world washed in gray flatness, except for the orange disk of the sun—they untied the calf, and pushed him over.

They watched him forever and forever, a black object and then a black spot against the great background of dirt-colored river, and then there was a tiny white splash, lost almost immediately in the river's current. Logs, which looked like twigs from up on the bridge, swept across the spot. Everything headed south, and there were no eddies, no pauses.

"I am halfway over him," Karen said.

And then, walking back, she said: "So that was really what it was like?"

She had a good appetite, and they stopped at the Waffle House and ate eggs and pancakes, and sausage and biscuits and bacon and orange juice. She excused herself to go to the restroom, and when she came back out, her face was washed, her hair brushed and clean-looking. Sydney paid for the meal, and when they stepped outside, the morning was growing hot.

"I have to work today," Karen said, when they got back to her house. "We have to go see about a mule."

"Me, too," said Sydney. "I've got a stallion who thinks he's a bad-ass."

She studied him for a second, and felt like telling him to be care-ful, but didn't. Something was in her, a thing like hope stirring, and she felt guilty for it.

Sydney whistled, driving home, and tapped his hands on the steer-ing wheel, though the radio did not work.

Dr. Lynly and Karen drove until the truck wouldn't go any farther, bogged down in the clay, and then they got out and walked. It was cool beneath all the big trees, and the forest seemed to be trying to press in on them. Dr. Lynly carried his heavy bag, stopping and switching arms frequently. Buster trotted ahead, between the two of them, looking left and right and up the road, and even up into the tops of the trees.

There was a sawmill, deep in the woods, where the delta farmland in the northern part of the county settled at the river and then went into dark mystery: hardwoods and muddy roads, then no roads. The men at the sawmill used mules to drag their trees to the cutting. There had never been money for bulldozers, or even tractors. The woods were quiet, and foreboding; it seemed to be a place without sound or light.

When they got near the sawmill, they could hear the sound of axes. Four men, shirtless, in muddy boots with the laces undone, were working on the biggest tree Karen had ever seen. It was a tree too big for chain saws. Had any of the men owned one, the tree would have ruined the saw.

One of the men kept swinging at the tree: putting his back into it, with rhythmic, stroking cuts. The other three stepped back, hitched their pants, and wiped their faces with their forearms.

The fourth man stopped cutting finally. There was no fat on him and he was pale, even standing in the beam of sunlight that was coming down through an opening in the trees—and he looked old: fifty, maybe, or sixty. Some of his fingers were missing.

"The mule'll be back in a minute," he said. He wasn't even breathing hard. "He's gone to bring a load up out of the bottom." He pointed with his ax, down into the swamp.

"We'll just wait," said Dr. Lynly. He bent back and tried to look up at the top of the trees. "Y'all just go right ahead with your cutting."

But the pale muscled man was already swinging again, and the other three, with another tug at their beltless pants, joined in: an odd, pausing drumbeat, as four successive whacks hit the tree; then four more again; and then, almost immediately, the cadence shortened, growing irregular, as the older man chopped faster.

All around them the soft pittings, like hail, of tree chips rained into the bushes. One of the chips hit Buster in the nose, and he rubbed it with his paw, and turned and looked up at Dr. Lynly.

They heard the mule before they saw him: he was groaning, like a person. He was coming up the hill that led out of the swamp and was heading toward them.

They could see the tops of small trees and saplings shaking as he dragged his load through them. Then they could see the tops of his ears, then his huge head, and after that they saw his chest. Veins raced against the chestnut thickness of it.

Then the tops of his legs. And then his knee. Karen stared at it and then sat down in the mud, and hugged herself—the men stopped swinging, for just a moment—and Dr. Lynly had to help her up.

It was the mule's right knee that was injured, and it had swollen to the size of a basketball. It buckled with every step he took, pulling the sled up the slick and muddy hill, but he kept his footing and did not stop. Flies buzzed around the knee, around the infections, where the loggers had pierced the skin with nails and the ends of their knives, trying to drain the pus. Dried blood ran down in streaks to the mule's hoof, to the mud.

The sawlogs on the back of the sled smelled good, fresh. They smelled like they were still alive.

Dr. Lynly walked over to the mule and touched the knee. The mule closed his eyes and trembled, as Karen had just done, or perhaps as if in ecstasy, at the chance to rest. The three younger men, plus the sledder, gathered around.

"We can't stop workin' him," the sledder said. "We can't shoot him either. We've got to keep him alive. He's all we've got. If he dies, it's us that'll have to pull them logs up here."

A cedar moth from the woods passed over the mule's ears, fluttering. It rested on the mule's forehead, and then flew off. The mule did not open his eyes. Dr. Lynly frowned and rubbed his chin. Karen felt faint again, and leaned against the mule's sweaty back to keep from falling.

"You sure you've got to keep working him?" Dr. Lynly asked.

"Yes, sir."

The pale logger was still swinging: tiny chips flying in batches.

Dr. Lynly opened his bag. He took out a needle and rag, and a bottle of alcohol. He cleaned the mule's infections. The mule drooled a little when the needle went in, but he did not open his eyes. The needle was slender, and it bent and flexed, and slowly Dr. Lynly drained the fluid.

Karen held on to the mule's wet back and vomited into the mud: both her hands on the mule as if she were being arrested against the hood of a car, and her feet spread wide. The men gripped their axes and looked away.

Dr. Lynly gave one of them a large plastic jug of pills.

"These will kill his pain," he said. "The knee will get big again, though. I'll be back out, to drain it again." He handed Karen a clean rag from his satchel, and led her away from the mule, away from the mess.

One of the ax men carried their satchel all the way back to the truck. Dr. Lynly let Karen get up into the cab first, and then Buster; then the ax man rocked and shoved, pushing on the hood of the truck as the tires spun, and helped them back it out of the mud: their pay-ment for healing the mule. A smell of burning rubber and smoke hung in the trees after they left.

They didn't talk much. Dr. Lynly was thinking about the pain-killers; how for a moment, he had almost given the death pills in-stead.

Karen was thinking how she would not let him pay her for that day's work. Also she was thinking about Sydney Bean: she would sit on the porch with him again, and maybe drink a beer and watch the fields.

He was sitting on the back porch when she got home; he was on the wooden bench next to the hammock, and he had a tray set up for her with a pitcher of cold orange juice. There was froth in the pitcher, a light creamy foaminess from where he had been stirring it, and the ice cubes were circling around. Beads of condensation slid down the pitcher, rolling slowly, then quickly, like tears. She could feel her heart giving. The field was rich summer green, and then, past the field, the dark line of trees. A long string of cattle egrets flew past, headed down to their rookery in the swamp.

Sydney poured her a small glass of orange juice. He had a metal pail of cold water and a clean washcloth. It was hot on the back porch, even for evening. He helped her get into the hammock; then he wrung the washcloth out and put it across her forehead, her eyes. Sydney smelled as if he had just gotten out of the shower, and he was wearing clean white duckcloth pants and a bright blue shirt.

She felt dizzy and leaned back in the hammock. The washcloth over her eyes felt so good. She sipped the orange juice, not looking at it, and licked the light foam of it from her lips. Owls were beginning to call, down in the swamp.

She felt as if she were younger, going back to a place, some place she had not been in a long time but could remember fondly. It felt like she was in love. She knew that she could not be, but that was what it felt like.

Sydney sat behind her and rubbed her temples.

It grew dark, and the moon came up.

"It was a rough day," she said, around ten o'clock.

But he just kept rubbing.

Around eleven o'clock, she dozed off, and he woke her, helped her from the hammock, and led her inside, not turning on any lights, and helped her get in bed.

Then he went back outside, locking the door behind him. He sat on the porch a little longer, watching the moon, so high above him, and then he drove home cautiously, as ever. Accidents were every-where; they could happen at any time, from any direction.

Sydney moved carefully, and tried to look ahead and be ready for the next one.

He really wanted her. He wanted her in his life. Sydney didn't know if the guilt was there for that—the wanting—or because he was alive, still seeing things, still feeling. He wanted someone in his life, and it didn't seem right to feel guilty about it. But he did.

Sometimes, at night, he would hear the horses running, thundering across the hard summer-baked flatness of his pasture, running wild—and he would imagine they were laughing at him for wasting his time feeling guilty, but it was a feeling he could not shake, could not ride down, and his sleep was often poor and restless.

Sydney often wondered if horses were even meant to be ridden at all.

The thing about the broncs, he realized—and he never realized it until they were rolling on top of him in the dust, or rubbing him off against a tree, or against the side of a barn, trying to break his leg—was that if the horses didn't get broken, tamed, they'd get wilder. There was nothing as wild as a horse that had never been broken. It just got meaner, each day.

So he held on. He bucked and spun and arched and twisted, shooting up and down with the mad horses' leaps; and when the horse tried to hurt itself, by running straight into something—a fence, a barn, the lake—he stayed on.

If there was, once in a blue moon, a horse not only stronger, but more stubborn than he, then he had to destroy it.

The cattle were easy to work with, would do anything for food, and once one did it, they would all follow; but working with the horses made him think ahead, and sometimes he wondered, in streaks and bits of paranoia, if perhaps all the horses in the world had some battle against him, and were destined, all of them, to pass through his corrals, each one testing him before he was allowed to stop.

Because like all bronc-busters, that was what Sydney allowed himself to consider and savor, in moments of rest: the day when he could stop. A run of successes. A string of wins so satisfying and continuous that it would seem—even though he would be sore, and tired—that a horse would never beat him again, and he would be convinced of it, and then he could quit.

Mornings in summers past, Henry used to come over and sit on the railing and watch. He had been an elementary school teacher, and frail, almost anemic: but he had loved to watch Sydney Bean ride the horses. He taught only a few classes in the summers, and he would sip coffee and grade a few papers while Sydney and the horse fought out in the center.

Sometimes Henry had set a broken bone for Sydney—Sydney had shown him how—and other times Sydney, if he was alone, would set his own bones, if he even bothered with them. Then he would wrap them up and keep riding. Dr. Lynly had set some of his bones, on the bad breaks.

Sydney was feeling old, since Henry had drowned. Not so much in the mornings, when everything was new and cool, and had promise; but in the evenings, he could feel the crooked shapes of his bones, within. He would drink beers, and watch his horses, and other people's horses in his pasture, as they ran. The horses never seemed to feel old, not even in the evenings, and he was jealous of their strength.

❋ ❋ ❋

He called Karen one weekend. "Come out and watch me break horses," he said.

He was feeling particularly sore and tired. For some reason he wanted her to see that he could always do it; that the horses were always broken. He wanted her to see what it looked like, and how it always turned out.

"Oh, I don't know," she said, after she had considered it. "I'm just so *tired*." It was a bad and crooked road, bumpy, from her house to his, and it took nearly an hour to drive it.

"I'll come get you...?" he said. He wanted to shake her. But he said nothing. He nodded, and then remembered he was on the phone and said, "I understand."

She did let him sit on the porch with her, whenever he drove over to her farm. She had to have someone.

"Do you want to hit me?" he asked one evening, almost hopefully.

But she just shook her head.

He saw that she was getting comfortable with her sorrow, was settling down into it, like an old way of life, and he wanted to shock her out of it, but felt paralyzed and mute, like the dumbest of animals.

Sydney stared at his crooked hands, with the scars from the cuts made over the years by the horses and the fencing tools. He cursed the many things he did not know. He could lift bales of hay. He could string barbed-wire fences. He could lift things. That was all he knew. He wished he were a chemist, an electrician, a poet, or a preacher. The things he had—what little of them there were—wouldn't help her.

She had never thought to ask how drunk Henry had been. Sydney thought that made a difference: whether you jumped off the bridge with one beer in you, or two, or a six-pack; or with a sea of electric blue Psychos rolling around in your stomach—but she never asked.

He admired her confidence, and doubted his ability to be as strong, as stubborn. She never considered that it might have been her fault, or Henry's; that some little spat might have prompted it, or general disillusionment.

It was his fault, Sydney's, square and simple, and she seemed comfortable, if not happy, with the fact.

Dr. Lynly treated horses, but he did not seem to love them, thought Karen.

"Stupid creatures," he would grumble, when they would not do as he wanted, when he was trying to doctor them. He and Buster and Karen would try to herd a horse into the trailer, or the corral, pulling on the reins and swatting the horse with green branches.

"Brickheads," Dr. Lynly would growl, pulling the reins and then walking around and slapping, feebly, the horse's flank. "Brickheads and fatheads." He had been loading horses for fifty years, and Karen would laugh, because the horses' stupidity always seemed to surprise, and then anger, Dr. Lynly, and she thought it was sweet.

It was as if he had not yet really learned that that was how they always were.

But Karen had seen it right away. She knew that many girls, and women, were infatuated with horses, in love with them even, for their great size and strength, and for their wildness—but Karen, as she saw more and more of the sick horses, the ailing ones, the ones most people did not see regularly, knew that all horses were simple and trusting, and that even the smartest ones could be made to do as they were told.

And they could be so dumb, so loyal, and so oblivious to pain. It was as though—even if they could feel it—they could never, ever acknowledge it.

It was sweet, she thought, and dumb.

Karen let Sydney rub her temples and brush her hair. She would go into the bathroom and wash her hair while he sat on the porch. He had taken up whittling; one of the stallions had broken Sydney's leg by throwing him into a fence and then trampling him, and the leg was in a heavy cast. So Sydney had decided to take a break for several days.

He had bought a whittling kit at the hardware store, and was going to try hard to learn how to do it. There were instructions. The kit had a square piece of balsa wood, almost the weight of nothing, and a small curved whittling knife. There was a dotted outline in the shape of a duck's head on the balsa wood that showed what the shape of his finished work would be.

After he learned to whittle, Sydney wanted to learn to play the harmonica. That was next, after whittling.

He would hear the water running, and hear Karen splashing, as she put her head under the faucet and rinsed.

She would come out in her robe, drying her hair, and then would let him sit in the hammock with her and brush her hair. It was September, and the cottonwoods were tinging, were making the skies hazy, soft and frozen-looking. Nothing seemed to move.

Her hair came down to the middle of her back. She had stopped cutting it. The robe was old and worn, the color of an old blue dish. Something about the shampoo she used reminded him of apples. She wore moccasins that had a shearling lining in them, and Sydney and Karen would rock in the hammock. Sometimes Karen would get up and bring out two Cokes from the refrigerator, and they would drink those.

"Be sure to clean up those shavings when you go," she told him. There were balsa wood curls all over the porch. Her hair, almost dry, would be light and soft. "Be sure not to leave a mess when you go."

It would be dark then, Venus out beyond them.

"Yes," he would say.

Once, before he left, she reached out from the hammock, and caught his hand. She squeezed it, and then let go.

He drove home thinking of Henry, and of how he had once taken Henry fishing for the first time. They had caught a catfish so large it had scared Henry. They drank beers, and sat in the boat, and talked.

One of Sydney Bean's headlights faltered on the drive home, then went out, and it took him an hour and a half to get home.

The days got cold and brittle. It was hard, working with the horses. Sydney's broken leg hurt all the time. Sometimes the horse would leap, and come down with all four hooves bunched in close together, and the pain and shock of it would travel all the way up Sydney's leg and into his shoulder, and down into his wrists.

He was sleeping past sun-up some days, and was being thrown, now, nearly every day; sometimes several times in the same day.

There was always a strong wind. Rains began to blow in. It was getting cold, crisp as apples, and it was the weather that in the summer everyone said they were looking forward to. One night there was a frost, and a full moon.

On her back porch, sitting in the hammock by herself with a heavy blanket around her, Karen saw a stray balsa shaving caught between the cracks of her porch floor. It was white, in the moonlight, the whole porch was, and the field was blue—the cattle stood out in the moonlight like blue statues—and she almost called Sydney.

But then the silence and absence of a thing—she presumed it was Henry, but did not know for sure—closed in around her, and the field beyond her porch, like the inside of her heart, seemed to be deathly still, and she did not call.

She thought, I can love who I want to love. But she was angry at Sydney Bean for having tried to pull her so far out, into a place she did not want to go.

She fell asleep in the hammock, and dreamed that Dr. Lynly was trying to wake her up, and was taking her blood pressure, feeling her forehead, and, craziest of all, swatting at her with green branches.

She awoke from the dream, and decided to call Sydney after all. He answered the phone as if he, too, had been awake.

"Hello?" he said. She could tell by the questioning in his voice that he did not get many phone calls.

"Hi," said Karen. "I just—wanted to call, and tell you *hello*." She paused, almost faltered. "And that I feel better. That I feel good, I mean. That's all."

"Well," said Sydney Bean. "Well, good. I mean, great."

"That's all," said Karen. "Bye," she said.

"Goodbye," said Sydney.

On Thanksgiving Day, Karen and Dr. Lynly headed back out to the swamp, to check up on the loggers' mule. It was the hardest cold of the year, and there was bright ice on the bridges, and it was not thawing, even in the sun. The inside of Dr. Lynly's old truck was no warmer than the air outside. Buster, in his wooliness, lay across Karen to keep her warm.

They turned onto a gravel road and started down into the swamp. Smoke, low and spreading, was flowing through all the woods. The men had little fires going; they were each working on a different tree, and had small warming fires where they stood and shivered when resting.

Karen found herself looking for the pale muscled logger.

He was swinging the ax, but he only had one arm. His left arm was gone, and there was a sort of a sleeve over it, like a sock, and he was swinging at the tree with his remaining arm. The man was sweating, and a small boy stepped up and quickly toweled him dry each time the pale man stepped back to take a rest.

They stopped the truck and got out and walked up to him, and he stepped back—wet, already, again; the boy toweled him off, standing on a low stool and starting with the man's neck and shoulders, and then going down his great back—and the man told them that the mule was better and that if they wanted to see him, he was lower in the swamp.

They followed the path toward the river. All around them were downed trees, and stumps, and stacks of logs, but the woods looked no different. The haze from the fires made it seem colder. Acorns popped under their feet.

About halfway down the road, they met the mule. He was coming back up toward them, and he was pulling a good load. Another small boy was in front of him, holding out a carrot, only partially eaten. The mule's knee looked much better, though it was still a little swollen, and probably always would be.

The boy stopped and let the mule take another bite of carrot, making him lean far forward in the harness. His great rubbery lips stretched and quavered and then flapped as he tried to get it, and then there was a crunch when he did.

They could smell the carrot as the mule ground it with his old teeth. It was a wild carrot, dug from the woods, and not very big, but it smelled good.

Karen had brought an apple and some sugar cubes, and she started forward to give them to the mule but instead handed them to the little boy, who ate the sugar cubes himself and put the apple in his pocket.

The mule was wearing an old straw hat, and looked casual, out-of-place. The boy switched him, and the mule shut his eyes and started up. His chest swelled, tight and sweaty, to fit the dark stained leather harness, and the big load behind him started in motion, too.

Buster whined as the mule went by.

It was spring again then, the month in which Henry had left them, and they were on the back porch. Karen had purchased a Clydesdale yearling, a great and huge animal, whose mane and fur she had shaved to keep it cool in the warming weather, and she had asked a boy from a nearby farm with time on his hands to train it, in the afternoons. The horse was already gentled, but needed to be stronger. She was having the boy walk him around in the fields, pulling a makeshift sled of stones and tree stumps and old rotten bales of hay.

In the fall, when the Clydesdale was strong enough, she and Dr. Lynly were going to trailer it out to the swamp and trade it for the mule.

Sydney Bean's leg had healed, been broken again, and was now healing once more. The stallion he was trying to break was showing signs of weakening. There was something in the whites of his eyes, Sydney thought, when he reared up, and he was not slamming himself into the barn—so it seemed to Sydney, anyway—with quite as much anger. Sydney thought that perhaps this coming summer would be the one in which he broke all of his horses, day after day, week after week.

They sat in the hammock and drank Cokes and nibbled radishes and celery, which Karen had washed and put on a tray. They watched the neighbor boy, or one of his friends, his blue shirt a tiny spot against the tree line, as he followed the big dark form of the Clydesdale. The sky was a wide spread of crimson, all along the western trees, toward the river. They couldn't tell which of the local children it was, behind the big horse; it could have been any of them.

"I really miss him," said Sydney Bean. "I really hurt."

"I know," Karen said. She put her hand on Sydney's, and rested it there. "I will help you," she said.

Out in the field, a few cattle egrets fluttered and hopped behind the horse and boy. The great young draft horse lifted his thick legs high and free of the mud with each step, the mud made soft by the rains of spring, and slowly—they could tell—he was skidding the sled forward.

The egrets hopped and danced, following at a slight distance, but neither the boy nor the horse seemed to notice. They kept their heads down, and moved forward.

In Ruth's Country

The rules for dating Mormon girls were simple.

No coffee; no long hair.

No curse words; one kiss.

That was about it. It was simple. Anyone could do it.

Utah is an odd state—the most beautiful, I think—because it is one thing but also another. It is red and hot in the desert—in the south—while the north has the cool and blue forests and mountains, which smell of fir and snow. And like so many things, when seen from a distance, they look unattainable.

My uncle and I were not Mormons. We lived in southern Utah, Uncle Mike and I and the rest of the town of Moab. In the summers, at night, thunderstorms would sometimes roll across the dry valley, illuminating the cliffs with flashes of lightning. There would be the explosions of light and for a second—beneath the cliffs—we could see the dry creeks and the town itself. The town had wide streets, like a Hollywood stagecoach town.

There would be flash floods out in the desert: water so muddy and frothy, churning, that its anger was almost obscene. But then the floods were gone quickly, and they were easy to avoid in the first place, if you knew about them and knew to stay out of their way, and out of the places where they could occur.

Tourists came through our town on their way to the national parks. They reminded me of the bloated steers I would see floating down the Colorado, sweeping along with the current, steers that had fallen over the cliffs and into the river below; but the tourists came only in the summers.

Mormons couldn't date non-Mormons. It was a logical rule. There were different values, or so it was supposed, and we chose to believe.

Among the elders of Moab there were corny handshakes, secret meeting rooms, silly passwords, but because I was young, I could move easily through the town and among the people. I could observe, as long as I made no threats against the religion's integrity, no overtures against its gene pool.

I was allowed to watch.

There was a Mormon girl, Ruth, whom I wanted to get to know. She was two years younger than I was, but I liked the way she watched things. She looked at the tourists, and it seemed to me that she too might have been thinking about the cows, the ones that sometimes went over the cliffs. She looked at the sky now and then, checking for I don't know what.

Other times I would see her watching me. I liked it, but knew better than to like it too much. I tried not to like it, and I tried not to watch back.

It did cross my mind, too, that perhaps she was just crazy, slightly off, to be looking at me for so long, so directly. Just watching.

That was how different things were. I really did not believe she could just be watching, and thinking.

Uncle Mike and I ran wild cattle in the sage for a living, scrub steers that could handle the heat and rattlesnakes and snows of winter. The country in which the cattle were turned out was too vast for fences. Instead, we used brands, or nothing.

Sometimes the cattle would be down along a salt creek in a willow flat, grazing in the dry field behind an old beaver dam. Other times they would be back up in the mesas and plateaus, hiding in the rocks.

They had all the country they wanted, and their movements seemed to be mostly whimsical. All of the cattle were about the same size, and in trying to cut yours away from the others, out of the big herd for market—for slaughter—if you got someone else's cow, it was all right to go ahead and take that one instead of the one you wanted. They were all pretty much the same.

But if you had scruples, you had to tell the person whose cow it was, when you did that, so that he could take one of yours.

It wasn't a thing Uncle Mike and I ever worried about, because we were good at cutting the cattle, and we hardly ever picked out anyone else's cattle, even by mistake. We knew what we were doing, and as long as we didn't make mistakes—if the job was done properly—there wasn't a need for rules, scruples, or morals in the first place.

What you had to remember about cutting cattle—and it was a thing Uncle Mike had often told me—was to pretend that you were capable of being in two places at once: where the cow was going, and where it wanted to go.

You had to get there ahead of it.

We cut them on foot with our barking dogs. Sometimes we'd use the jeep. It was hard work, and it seemed to need doing always. Without fences, the cattle kept trying to drift north. The blue mountains shimmered, and seemed a place to go to. The mountains looked cooler than anything we had ever seen.

So I couldn't ask Ruth out. And why would I want to? One lousy kiss? She was flat-chested, like a seven-year-old boy, and wore librarian's gold wire-rimmed glasses, grandmother glasses.

Her hair was a reddish color—the kind that you think is brown until it gets out into the sun—and it was thick. I admired her freckles, and also the old overalls she was always wearing. They looked as if they made her feel good, because she was always smiling. I imagined what the denim softness felt like, on her ankles, on her thighs, and going higher.

It was good, being out on the north end of town the way we were. At seventeen and eighteen, one expects the things that happen, I think; they do not come as a surprise. Sometimes Mike and I would sit out on the patio and drink a beer or some vodka, or gin-and-tonics, with ice and limes—limes from faraway, tropical cultures—and we would watch the purple part of dusk rising up out of the dry valley, moving toward us, covering the desert like a spill. And the lights in town be-low would come on, in the purple valley.

Ruth's old Volkswagen came up our road one evening, trailing dust from a long way off, and when she pulled up and got out she did not hesitate, but walked up to Uncle Mike and said that her car was dying on cool mornings, and also on hills, and that she needed new wind-shield wipers too.

It was unnerving, her having come up out of the valley like that and into our part of the desert, driving in such a straight line to get there. She just did it. But once she was there, I did not want her to leave. I knew it did not fit with the unspoken deal Mike and I had cut with the town, but I liked her being up there, on our plateau, and wasn't eager for her to go back down.

"This is a beautiful view," she said, looking around at the purple dusk and the lights coming on in town. I offered her my drink, which I had not tasted yet, and she sipped it, not even knowing what it was. Mike went in the garage to look at her car. I got a chair for Ruth and seated her. We didn't say anything, just watched the desert, until it was completely dark.

After a while, Mike came out of the garage with her old spark plugs, but I knew that spark plugs wouldn't make her car do what it was she said it was doing.

"Your wipers look fine," he said. "The spark plugs will be five dollars."

She took the money from her shirt pocket—some of it in bills, some in coins—and handed it to him, but seemed to have no interest in leaving.

Instead, we sat there and each had another drink, and then the wind started to blow, the way it did every night, and made the wind chimes tinkle back behind the garage.

There was lightning to the south. We saw it almost every night, but it never seemed to reach Moab. It took her a long time to finish her drink. Then she left, the long drive back to town: her brake lights, tiny and red.

There was a bishop in the church, the head bishop for all of Moab, whose name was Homer. He was an attorney, the richest man in town. He had thousands of cattle, maybe more than anyone in Utah. The way he got his cattle when he wanted them for market was to send some of his men out into the desert with rifles to shoot them.

It was lazy and simple and I thought it was wrong. The men would load the dead cattle into their trucks that way, and take them to Bishop Homer's own slaughterhouse. We had to bring ours in alive.

Uncle Mike and I did not like Bishop Homer, but we did not waste time worrying about him either.

It was my job to keep Uncle Mike's and my cattle away from the others, if I could. Every day after school that spring, Ruth and I drove out into the desert in the jeep and chased Bishop Homer's cattle with the dogs. We tried to keep his red-eyed, wormy dwarves away from our registered Hereford heifers. Bishop Homer had his men buy whatever passed through the auction circle at a low price, whether it was healthy or not—he didn't look at the quality of an animal at all—and we tried to cut Mike's and my cattle out of the big herds, and to keep them by themselves. All of the cattle gathered at the rim of the gorge, high up over the river, and they were always trying to find different trails leading down. There wasn't any way to get to the river—the cliffs went straight up and down—but the cattle watched the river daily, as if expecting that a new path might miraculously appear.

The bulls were always hopping up on our heifers. Bishop Homer had it in his mind that the bulls could survive the desert better than the heifers, and he was keen to buy any bulls that passed through the auction, no matter that he already had too many. He was too lazy to make them into steers. He just turned them out.

The dogs raced alongside the stampeding bulls, snapping and barking. We ran along and behind them, shouting and throwing rocks, whenever we found them in with our heifers. Their great testicles tangled between their legs when they tried to run too fast, and they were an easy target. It was a hot spring, and Bishop Homer's cattle began to lose weight.

Ruth and I made picnics. We carried mayonnaise jars wrapped in newspaper to keep them cool, full of lemonade with ice cubes rattling, and we took a blanket. There were sandbars down in the river gorge, and some days we would climb down the dangerous cliffs to them. There were caves along the river, dark recesses out of which small birds flew, back and forth into the sunlight. The water was cold and green and moved very fast.

"Can you swim?" Ruth asked one day.

"Yes," I told her, though I could not, and was hoping she would not ask me to show her. I would have had to try, and almost certainly would have drowned.

"I don't know if I can or not," she said. She didn't seem frightened, however.

Other days we talked about Bishop Homer as we chased his cattle. He was in charge of Ruth's ward. That was a church subdivision, like a platoon or a brigade.

Ruth had taken an after-school job that spring as Bishop Homer's secretary. He was good friends with her parents, and it was how she got the job.

"He's got three wives," she said. "The one here in town, plus one in St. George, and one up north, in Logan."

Logan was a ski town, in the very northern part of the state. It took money to live in Logan, and it was usually where the not-so-very-good Mormons went, because it was a good place to have fun. A lot of people in Moab looked at Logan wistfully, on the map. I wondered what the wife in Logan was like.

The bulls ran ahead of us at a steady trot, a sort of controlled panic; sometimes they stumbled but caught themselves.

"I'm not supposed to know that," Ruth shouted. "I'm the only one who knows."

We stopped the jeep and watched the cattle on the trail ahead, still trotting, back up into the rocks, to where there was no grass or water, not even a thin salt creek. I thought about how far we were from anything.

There was a red-tailed hawk out over the gorge, doing slow circles, and Ruth told me that Bishop Homer had touched her once.

The engine was baking in the heat, making ticks and moans, and the wind was gusting, lifting the jeep off its shocks and rocking it. We watched the hawk and were pleased when we saw it fold its wings and dive, with a shrill cry, into the gorge.

Later in the spring our heifers began dropping more calves. Wildflowers and cactus blossoms were everywhere. There were dwarf calves, red calves, ugly cream-colored calves, and stillborns. They all had to be taken away to market; not a one was worth keeping.

Mike and I had Ruth over for dinner. She had church meetings almost every day, but she skipped some of them. We drank the gin-and-tonics, and it was okay for her to sit with her head in my lap, or mine in hers. The wind on the back patio was stronger than it had been that year; it seemed to bring new scents from new places. Sometimes Ruth asked me if I was afraid of dying.

We didn't associate much in school. Being younger, she wasn't in any of my classes, and it would have been trouble for her to be seen with me too often. Her parents didn't like her spending the evenings out on my porch, but she told them she was proselytizing. So it was all right, and she kept coming out to our place to sit up there in the evenings.

And then it was summer. We had more time than we could ever have wished for.

We had all the time anyone could ever need, for anything.

Our heifers were still dropping ruinous calves, and Mike said it had to stop. So one day, knowing what we were doing, and with the dogs to help us, we ran three of Bishop Homer's woolly bulls right over the gorge. We shouted, throwing things, and chased them toward it, and their fear took care of the rest.

We stood there, dizzy, exultant, and looked at the green river below, the slow-moving spills of white that we knew were rapids. One of the bulls was broken on the rocks and two were washing through the rapids.

"How many cattle would you say he has?" Ruth asked me. She slipped her hand in mine.

I didn't know.

"What are his other two wives' names?" I asked her. She had told me Bishop Homer was still bothering her.

We watched that hawk again—it seemed to have come from nowhere, right in front of us, I could see the light brown and cream of its breast—and Ruth told me that their names were Rebecca and Rachel.

"You're going to stay here with your Uncle Mike and work on trucks and cars, and raise the wild cattle, too, aren't you, is that right?" she asked, on our way back. It was dark by then, with bright stars and the night winds starting up. The stars seemed to glimmer and flash above us, we didn't have a top on the jeep, and instead of lying to her, I told her yes, it was what I would continue to do.

We stopped wearing clothes when we were out in the desert in July, hot July: just our tennis shoes and socks. We raced the jeep, wearing our seat belts, and we set up small piles of stones, up high on the slickrock domes, where we could see forever, and we practiced racing around them, and cornering: we designed intricate, elaborate courses, through which we tried to race at the fastest possible speed.

She was starting, finally, to get her breasts, which was all right with me. Both of us were lean, from chasing the bulls. The sun felt good, on our backs, our legs. We drove fast, wearing nothing.

A bad thing was happening with the cattle, however; with Bishop Homer's cattle. They were getting used to being chased, and would not run so far; sometimes we had to ram them with the jeep to get them even to break into a grudging trot.

The desert was like a park that summer. Flowers bloomed as never before: a different batch, different colors, every couple of weeks. It stormed almost every night, the heat of the day building up and then cooling. The lightning storms rocketed up and down the cliffs of the river, and into town.

Each night we tried to get back to Mike's in time to watch the purple and then the darkness as it sank over the desert, like stage lighting, like the end of a show. But we didn't always make it, and we would watch from one of the slickrock domes, or we would hike up and sit beneath one of the eerie, looping rock arches.

Some nights there was an early moon, and we could see the cattle, grazing in the sage, and the jackrabbits moving around, too, every-thing ghostly in that light, everything coming out after dark.

But other nights the storms would wash through quickly, windy drenching downpours that soaked us, and it was fun to sit on the rocks and let the storm hit us and beat against us. The nights were always warm, though cooler after those rains, and the smells were so sharp as to make us imagine that something new was out there, something happening that had never happened to anyone before.

It was a good summer. Though there were too many cattle and too much grazing on the already spare land, the cattle did not eat the bit-ter flowers, and as a result, wild blooming blue and yellow weeds and wine-colored cactus blossoms rushed into the spots where the weak grasses had been, sprouting up out of the dried cattle droppings.

In August, the mountains to the north took on a darker blue. And the smells seemed to change. They were coming from another direc-tion. From behind us, from the north.

Occasionally, Ruth's parents would ask her how I was doing, if I was thinking about changing yet. "Converting" was the term they used, and even the thought of it terrified me.

Ruth said that she had told them I was very close: very, very close.

She watched me as she said this. We were sitting on the boulders down by the white rapids, throwing driftwood branches into the cen-ter.

Then, above us, I saw a man looking down, a man with a camera. He was on the rim. He was so far up there. He took pictures of us while we sat on the rocks, and I looked up at him but didn't move, because there was not much I could do; our clothes were up by the jeep. Ruth didn't see him, and I didn't want to alarm her. Just a lost tourist, I thought. A lost tourist with a big lens.

But it was him, of course. I found that out soon enough, though I didn't know what he looked like. When we got back up on the rim, I saw his cattle company's pale blue truck, tiny and raising dust, mov-ing slowly away to the north, and I realized that he had come into the desert for some of his cows.

Ruth didn't say much all the rest of the day, but that evening, driving home, when we stopped at a junkyard outside the city limits and pulled in and turned the lights off, she looked at all the old rusting heaps and goggle-eyed wrecks, and then, as if we had been married for fifteen years, she helped me get the picnic blanket out. The night was warm and we lay there among the wrecks, and I thought that one of us would get her soul, Homer or myself, and wasn't sure I wanted it. It seemed like a pretty big thing to take, even if she was determined to be rid of it.

I had her home before midnight, as was the rule.

We did other new things, too, after that. Some new ground was opened up, it seemed, and we had more space in which to move, more things to see and look at and study. We learned how to track Gila monsters in the sand. Their heavy tails dragged behind them like clubs and they rested in the shade of the sagebrush. We tracked them wearing nothing but our tennis shoes, following their staggering trail from shade bush to shade bush. Eventually, we would catch up with them.

They would be orange and black, beaded, motionless, and we never got too close to them once we had found them. The most beautiful thing in the desert was also the most dangerous.

We had a rule of our own. Any time we found a Gila monster, we had to kiss: slowly, and with everything we had.

We waded in the river, too, above the rapids. I was still afraid to go out into the deep and attempt swimming. But it was a game to see how close we could get to the rapids' pull. Knee-deep, for Ruth; her small behind, like a fruit, just above the current as it shuddered against the backs of her knees.

Down in the gorge like that, there was only sun, and river, and sky, and the boulders around which the river flowed. I watched for the man with the camera, but he did not come back. Ankle-deep, and then knee-deep, I would come up behind Ruth, hold her hand, and then go out a little farther. The water beat against my thighs, splashing and spraying against me. She didn't try to pull me back. She thought it was fun. And it was; but I kept expecting her to tighten her grip, and try to pull me back into the shallows.

Her hair was getting longer, more bleached, and she was just watching, laughing, holding her hand out at full arm's length for me to hold on to. But she knew to let go if I slipped and went down.

As the summer moved on, the thunderstorms that had been building after dusk were fewer and smaller; mostly it was just dry wind. Ruth had missed her period, and though I was troubled for her, worrying about her church and her parents' reaction, I didn't mind at all, not a bit. In fact, I liked it. I put my hand on it all the time, which pleased her.

But I knew that, unlike me, she had to be thinking of other things.

We still chased the cattle. Once in the jeep we ran an old stud Brangus over the edge, and got too close. A sliding swerve, gravel under our tires; we hit a rock and went up on two wheels and almost went over, all the way down.

I had names picked out. I was going to build my own house, out even farther north, away from town, away from everything, and Ruth and I would be just fine. I had names picked out, if it was a boy.

I was picturing what life would be like, and it seemed to me that it could keep on being the same. I could see it as clearly as I thought I'd ever seen anything.

I thought because she liked the gin-and-tonics, and the river wading, and chasing cows, Ruth would change. Convert. I knew she liked her church, believed in it, attended it, but I took for granted that as she grew larger, she would not remain in it, and she would come out a little north of town to live with me. That was the picture. In my mind, the picture became the truth, and I didn't worry about anything.

Tumbleweeds blew down the center of Main Street, late at night. Dry and empty, they rolled like speedballs, hopping and skipping, smashing off the sides of buildings. They rolled like an army through town. We would sit on the sidewalk and wait for them, looking down the street—the town like a ghost town, that late at night—the wind would be in our faces, and we could never hear the tumbleweeds coming, but could only watch, and wait.

Then, finally, very close to ten o'clock, their dim shapes would come blowing toward us from out of the darkness. We would jump up and run out into their midst, and, as if they were medicine balls, we would try to catch them.

They weighed nothing. We would turn and try to run along with them, running down the center of Main Street, heading south and out of town, but we could never keep up, and we would have to stop for breath somewhere around Parkinson's Drug Store. Mike had said that tumbleweeds were more like people than anything else in the world; that they always took the easiest path—always—and that the only way they would stop was if something latched on to them, or trapped them. A branch, a rock, a dead-end alley.

During the last week in August, the north winds began to grow cool, and we wore light sweaters on the back porch. Ruth sipped lemonade and kept one of her Mormon Bibles—they had five or six—in her lap, and browsed through it. She'd never carried it around like that, and I found it slightly disturbing, but there were new smells, fresher and sharper, coming from the north, and we would turn and look back in that direction, though it would be dark and we would see nothing.

But we could imagine.

The north winds made the mountains smell as beautiful as they must have looked.

Neither of us had ever been all the way up into the mountains, but we had the little things, like the smells in the wind, that told us they were there, and even what they were like. Sometimes Ruth turned her head all the way around so that the wind was directly in her face, blowing her hair back.

She would sip her drink. She would squint beneath the patio light, and read, in that cold wind.

I had told Mike about Ruth and he had just nodded. He hadn't said anything, but I felt as if he was somehow pleased; it seemed somehow, by the way he worked in the garage, to be a thing he was looking forward to seeing happen. I know that I was.

I rolled the jeep one day in August—no heat out in the desert, just a mild shimmering day, and we were clothed—and I don't re-member how I did it, exactly. There weren't any cattle around, but we were driving fast, just to feel the wind. Over rises, the jeep would leave the ground, flying, and then it would come down with a smash, shaking the frame. We went over one rise, and must have gotten too high, and came down on our side, Ruth's side.

When we came to a stop, we were hanging upside down, saved by our belts, with broken glass in our hair and the radiator steaming and tires hissing, and all sorts of fluids—strong-smelling gasoline, water, oils—dripping on us as if in a light rain. There was a lot of blood, from where Ruth's leg had scraped across the rocks, skidding beneath the jeep, and I shouted her name because she wasn't moving.

I still remember the way I screamed for her. Sometimes I think it would be possible to go out into that part of the desert and hunt the scream down, like some wild animal, track it right up into a canyon, and find it, still bouncing around off the rocks, never stopping: Ruth's name, shouted by me, as she hung upside down, swinging, arms hanging, hair swinging, glasses hanging from one ear, everything all wrong, everything all pointed the wrong way.

Mike came in his station wagon and found us with a searchlight, when I did not get in that night.

Ruth healed, but what she did next was very strange. About two weeks later she stopped seeing me. She said she had made an error and that the gulf was too wide; that she had been mistaken. She stopped driving out to Mike's and my home. She vanished.

After three weeks, I went to Bishop Homer's law office where she was working full time, and I asked to see her.

She came out into the hall, looking very different, very changed. She had on a new dress and she was holding one of the Bibles against her chest, almost clutching it. She seemed somehow frightened of me, but also almost disdainful.

"Ruth," I said, and looked at her. She was all dressed up, and wouldn't say anything. She was just looking at me: as if afraid I wanted to take something from her, and with a look that said, too, that she could kill me if I tried.

"The baby, Ruth," I said. I ran a hand through my hair. I was wearing my old cattle-chasing clothes, and I felt like a boy, out there in the hall. There was no one else around. We were in a strange building, a strange hallway, and the river seemed very far away.

"Not yours," she said suddenly. She clutched the Bible even tighter. There were tears in her eyes. "Not yours," she said again. It's the thing I think of most, when I think about it now, how hard it probably was for her to say that.

She sent the pictures and the negatives to me after she was settled in the mountains, in a town called Brigham City. It was about three hundred miles to the north.

Uncle Mike and I still cut our cattle for market. Bishop Homer still sends his men out into the desert to shoot his. Some days I still sit up in the rocks, with the old dogs and the jeep, and try to ambush his sorry bulls and chase them over the cliff; but other days, I just sit there and listen to the silence.

Sometimes the dogs and I go swimming in the water above the rapids.

I try to imagine myself as being two people, in two places at once, but I cannot do it, not as well as I used to be able to.

Mike and I work on the trucks and cars together now. I hold the light for him, peering up into the dark maw of the engine, trying to see what part has gone wrong, what part is missing. It is hard work and occasionally we make the wrong choices.

One of us was frightened, too frightened, and though I've thought about it ever since, I still can't figure out which of us it was.

I wonder how she is. I wonder what the things are that frighten her most now.

Redfish

Cuba libres are made with rum, diet Coke, and lime juice. Kirby showed them to me, and someone, I am sure, showed them to him. They've probably been around forever, the way everything has. But the first time we really drank them was late at night on the beach in Galveston. There was a high wind coming off the water, and we had a fire roaring. I think that it felt good for Kirby to be away from Tricia for a while and I know that it felt good to be away from Houston.

We were fishing for red drum — redfish — and somewhere, out in the darkness, beyond where we could see, we had hurled our hooks and sinkers, baited with live shrimp. There was a big moon and the waves blew spray into our faces and we wore heavy coats, and our faces were orange, to one another, from the light of the big driftwood fire.

It is amazing, what washes in from the ocean. Everything in the world ends up, I think, on a beach. Whales, palm trees, television sets. . . . Kirby and I were sitting on a couch in the sand drinking the Cuba libres and watching our lines, waiting for the big redfish to hit. When he did, or she, we were going to reel it in and then clean it there on the beach, rinse it off in the waves, and then we were going to grill it on the big driftwood fire.

It was our first time to drink Cuba libres, and we liked them even better than margaritas. We had never caught redfish before either, but had read about it in a book. We had bought the couch for ten dollars at a garage sale earlier in the day. We sank down deep into it, and it was easy, comfortable fishing. In the morning, when the tide started to go out, we were going to wade-fish for speckled trout. We had read about that, too, and that was the way you were supposed to do it. You were supposed to go out into the waves after them. It sounded exciting. We had bought waders and saltwater fishing licenses and saltwater stamps, as well as the couch and the rum. We were going to get into a run of speckled trout and catch our limit, and load the ice chest with them, and take them back to Tricia, because Kirby had made her mad.

But first we were going to catch a big redfish. We wouldn't tell her about the redfish, we decided. We would grill it and drink more Cuba libres and maybe take a short nap, before the tide changed, and we had our sleeping bags laid out on the sand for that purpose. They looked as if they had been washed ashore, as well. It was December, and about thirty degrees. We were on the southeast end of the bay and the wind was strong. The flames from the fire were ten or twelve feet high, but we couldn't get warm.

There was all the wood in the world, huge beams from ships and who-knows-what, and we could make the fire as large as we wanted. We kept waiting for the big redfish to seize our shrimp and run, to scoot back down into the depths. The book said they were bottom feeders.

It seemed, drinking the Cuba libres, that it would happen at any second. Kirby and Trish had gotten in a fight because Kirby had forgotten to feed the dogs that Saturday, while Trish was at work. Kirby said, drinking the Cuba libres, that he had told her that what she was really mad about was the fact that she had to work that Saturday, while he had had the day off. (They both work in a bank, different banks, and handle money, and own sports cars.) Tricia had gotten really mad at that and had refused to feed the dogs.

So Kirby fed his dog but did not feed Tricia's. That was when Tricia got the maddest. Then they got into a fight about how Kirby's dog, a German shepherd, ate so much more, about ten times more, than did Tricky Woodles, a Cocker spaniel, Tricia's dog. Good old Tricky Woo.

On the beach, Kirby had a pocketbook that identified fishes of the Gulf Coast, and after each drink we would look at it, turning to the page with the picture of the red drum. We would study it, sitting there on the couch, as if we were in high school again, and were studying for some silly exam, instead of being out in the real world, braving the elements, tackling nature, fishing for the mighty red drum. The book said they could go as much as thirty pounds.

"The elusive red drum!" Kirby shouted into the wind. We were only sipping the Cuba libres, because they were so good, but they were adding up. They were new, and we had just discovered them, and we wanted as many of them as we could get.

"Elusive *and* wily!" I shouted. "Red E. Fish!"

Kirby's eyes darted and shifted like a cartoon character's, the way they did when he was really drunk, which meant he would be passing out soon.

"We could dynamite the ocean," he said. "We could throw grenades into the waves, and stun the fish. They would come rolling in with the waves then, all the fish in the world."

He stood up, fell in the sand, and still on his knees, poured another drink. "I really want to see one," he said.

We left our poles and wandered down the beach: jumping and stamping, it was so cold. The wind tried to blow us over. We found an ancient, upright lifeguard's tower, about twenty feet tall, and tried, in our drunkenness, to pull it down, to drag it over to our fire. It was as sturdy as iron, and had barnacles on it from where it had spent some time in the sea. We cut our hands badly, but it was dark and cold, and we did not find that out until later.

We were a long way from our fire, and it looked a lot smaller from where we were. The couch looked wrong, without us in it, sitting there by the fire, empty like that. Kirby started crying and said he was going home to Tricia but I told him to buck up and be a man. I didn't know what that meant or even what I meant by saying that, but I knew that I did not want him to leave. We had come in his car, the kind everyone our age in Houston drove, if they had a job, if they had even a little money—a white BMW—and I wanted to stay and see what a red drum looked like in the flesh.

"I've an idea," I said. "Let's pull the tower down, and drag it over to the fire with the car."

"Yeah!" said Kirby. "Yeah!" Clouds were hurrying past the moon, something was blowing in quickly, but I could see that Kirby had straightened up some, and that he was not going to pass out.

It's been ten years since we were in high school. Some days, when I am with him, it seems that eternity still lies out in front of us; and other days, it seems that we've already died, somehow, and everything is over. Tricia is beautiful. She reminds me of that white sports car.

We kicked most of the sand off of our shoes, and got in the car, and it started right up, the way it always did. It was a nice car, all right, and Kirby drove it to work every day—though work was only one-point-eight miles away—and he kept his briefcase in the back seat; but in the trunk, just thrown in, were all of the things he had always kept in his car in high school, things he thought he might need in an emergency.

There was a bow and arrows, a .22 rifle, a tomahawk, binoculars, a tire inflator, a billy club, some extra fishing poles, a tool box, some barbed wire, a bull riding rope, cowboy boots, a wrinkled, oily tuxedo he had rented and never bothered to return, and there were other things, too—but it was the bull riding rope, which we attached to the tower, and to the back bumper of the little sports car, that came in handy this time.

Sand flew as the tires spun, and like some shy animal, the BMW quickly buried itself, up to the doors.

To the very end, I think Kirby believed that at any moment he was going to pull free, and break out of the sand, and pull the tower over: the engine screaming, the car shuddering and bucking...but it was sunk deep, when he gave up, and he had to crawl out through the window.

The Cuba libres, and the roar of the wind, made it seem funny; we howled, as if it was something the car had done by itself, on its own.

"Let's take a picture and send it to Tricia," he said. I laughed, and winced too, a little, because I thought it was a bad sign that he was talking about her again, so much, so often, but he was happy, so we got the camera from the trunk, and because he did not have a flash attachment, we built another fire, stacked wood there by the tower, which is what we should have done in the first place.

We went back to get the couch, and our poles and sleeping bags, and the ice chest. I had worked, for a while, for a moving company, and I knew a trick so that I could carry on my back a couch, a refrigerator, or almost anything, and I showed it to Kirby, and he screamed, laughing, as I ran down the beach with the couch on my back, not able to see where I was going, carrying the couch like an ant with a leaf, coming dangerously close to the water. Kirby ran along behind me, screaming, carrying the other things, and when we had set up a new camp, we ran back and forth, carrying the larger pieces of burning logs, transferring the fire, too. We took a picture of the car by firelight.

Our hands and arms had dried blood on them almost all the way up to the elbows, from the barnacles, and we rinsed them off in the sea, which was not as cold as we had expected.

"I wish Tricia was here to see this," he said, more than once. The wind was blowing still harder, and the moon was gone now.

We got a new fire started, and were exhausted from all the effort; we fixed more drinks and slumped into the couch and raised our poles to cast out again, but stopped, realizing the shrimp were gone, that something had stolen them.

The other shrimp were in a live well, in the trunk, so we re-baited. It was fun, reaching in the dark into the warm bubbling water of the bait bucket, and feeling the wild shrimp leap about, fishtailing, trying to escape. It didn't matter which shrimp you got; you didn't even need to look. You just reached in, and caught whichever one leapt into your hand.

We baited the hooks and cast out again. We were thirsty, so we fixed more drinks. We nodded off on the couch, and were awakened by the fire going down, and by snow, which was landing on our faces. It was just starting. We sat up, and then stood up, but didn't say anything. We reeled in and checked our hooks, and found that the shrimp were gone again.

Kirby looked out at the darkness, where surely the snowflakes were landing on the water, and he looked up at the sky, and could not stand the beauty.

"I'm going to try to hitchhike back to Houston," he said. He did not say her name but I know he was thinking of waking up with Tricia, and looking out the window, and seeing the snow, and everything being warm, inside the house, under the roof.

"No," I said. "Wait." Then I was cruel. "You'll just get in a fight again," I told him, though I knew it wasn't true: they were always wild to see each other after any kind of separation, even a day or two. I had to admit I was somewhat jealous of this.

"Wait a little longer, and we'll go out into the waves," I said.

"Yes," said Kirby. "Okay." Because we'd been thinking that would be the best part, the most fun: wade-fishing. We'd read about that, too, and Kirby had brought a throw net, with which to catch mullets for bait.

We'd read about wade-fishermen with long stringers of fish—the really successful fishermen—being followed by sharks and attacked, and so we were pretty terrified of the sharks, knowing that they could be down there among our legs, in the darkness and under water, where we could not see, following us: or that we could even walk right into the sharks. That idea of them being hidden, just beneath us—we didn't like it a bit, not knowing for sure if they were out there or not.

We fixed a new batch of Cuba libres, using a lot of lime. We stood at the shore in our waders, the snow and wind coming hard into our faces, and drank them quickly, and poured some more, raced them down. It wasn't ocean anymore, but snowdrift prairie, the Missouri breaks, or the Dakotas and beyond, and we waded out, men searching for game, holding the heavy poles high over our heads, dragging the great Bible cast-nets behind us.

The water was not very deep for a long time; for fifteen minutes it was only knee-deep, getting no deeper, and not yet time to think about sharks.

"I wish Tricia was here," said Kirby. The Cuba libres were warm in our bellies; we'd used a lot of rum in the last ones. "I wish she was riding on my shoulders, piggy-back," he said.

"Nekkid," I said.

"Yes," said Kirby, picturing it, and he was happy, and even though

I didn't really like Tricia, I thought how nice it would have been if she could have seen him then, sort of looking off and dreaming about it. I wished I had a girlfriend or wife on my back, too, then, to go along with all the other equipment I was carrying. I was thinking that she could hold the pole, and cast out, waiting for a bite, waiting for the big fight; and I could work the throw net, trying to catch fresh mullet, which we'd cut up into cubes, right there in the water, and use for fresh bait: because the bait had to be fresh.

It was like a murder or a sin, cutting the live mullet's head off, slicing the entrails out, filleting out a piece of still-barely-living meat and putting it on the hook, and then throwing the rest of the mullet away; throwing it behind you for the sharks, or whatever— head, fins, entrails, and left-over meat—casting your hook then far out into the waves and dark and snow, with that warm very fresh piece of flesh on the hook. It was like a sin, the worst of the animal kingdom, I thought, but if you caught what you were after, if you got the big redfish, then it was all right, it was possible that you were forgiven.

I wanted to catch the largest redfish in the world. I wanted to catch one so large that I might not even be able to get it in to shore.

Kirby looked tired. He had put on about twenty pounds since high school, and it was hard work, walking with the poles over our heads.

"Wait," I said. We stopped and caught our breath. It was hard to hear each other, with only the wind and waves around us; and except for the direction of the waves, splashing into our faces from the Gulf, we couldn't tell where shore was, or in which direction the ocean lay.

"I've an idea," said Kirby, still breathing heavily, looking back to where we were pretty sure the shore was. If our fire was still burning, we couldn't see it. "There's a place back up the beach that rents horses in the daytime. Some stables."

"They shoot horse thieves," I said. But I thought it was a wonderful idea. I was tired, too; I wasn't in as good shape as I'd once been either.

"I'll go get them," I said, since I wasn't breathing quite as hard as he was. It was a tremendous picture: both of us on white horses, riding out into the waves, chest-deep, neck-deep, then the magic lift and float of the horse as it began to swim, the light feeling of nothing, no resistance.

Mares, they would be, noble and strong, capable of carrying foolish, drunken men out to sea on their journey, if they so desired, and capable of bringing them back again, too.

"Yes," I said. "You stay here. I'll go find the horses."

Back on shore, walking up the beach to the stables, I stopped at a pay phone, and dialed Tricia's number. The cold wind was rocking the little phone booth, and there was a lot of static on the line.

"Tricia," I said, disguising my voice, mumbling. "This is Kirby. I love you." Then I hung up, and thought about how I really liked her after all, and I went to look for the horses. It would be perfect.

We could ride around out in the Gulf on the swimming horses until they tired, casting and drinking, searching for what we were after, pausing sometimes to lean forward and whisper kind things, encouragement, into the horses' ears, as they labored through the waves, blowing hard through their nostrils, legs kicking and churning, swimming around in wide circles out in the Gulf, in the darkness, the snow; no doubt full of their own fears of sharks, of drowning, of going down under too heavy of a load, and of all the things unseen, all the things below.

The Watch

W hen Hollingsworth's father, Buzbee, was seventy-seven years old, he was worth a thousand dollars, that summer and fall. His name was up in all the restaurants and convenience stores along the inter-state, and the indistinctions on the dark photocopies taped to doors and walls made him look distinguished, like someone else. The Xerox sheets didn't even say *Reward, Lost,* or *Missing.* They just got right to the point: *Mr. Buzbee, $1,000.*

The country Buzbee had disappeared in was piney woods, in the center of the state, away from the towns, the Mississippi—away from everything. There were swamps and ridges, and it was the hottest part of the state, and hardly anyone lived there. If they did, it was on those ridges, not down in the bottoms, and there were some-times fields that had been cleared by hand, though the soil was poor and red and could really grow nothing but tall lime-colored grass that bent in the wind like waves in a storm, and was good for horses and nothing else—no crops, no cattle, nothing worth a damn— and Hollingsworth did not doubt that Buzbee, who had just recently taken to pissing in his pants, was alive, perhaps even lying down in the deep grass somewhere, to be spiteful, like a dog.

Hollingsworth knew the reward he was offering wasn't much. He had a lot more money than that, but he read the papers and knew that people in Jackson, the big town seventy miles north, offered that much every week, when their dogs ran off, or their cats went away somewhere to have kittens. Hollingsworth had offered only $1,000 for his father because $900 or some lesser figure would have seemed cheap; but some greater number would have made people think he was sad and missed the old man. It really cracked Hollingsworth up, reading about those lawyers in Jackson who would offer $1,000 for their tramp cats. He wondered how they came upon those figures— if they knew what a thing was really worth when they liked it.

It was lonely without Buzbee—it was bad, was much too quiet, especially in the evenings—and it was the first time in his life that Hollingsworth had ever heard such a silence. Sometimes cyclists would ride past his dried-out barn and country store, and there was one who would sometimes stop for a Coke; sweaty, breathing hard. He was more like some sort of draft animal than a person, so intent was he upon his speed, and he never had time to chat with Hollingsworth, to spin tales. He said his name was Jesse; he would say hello, gulp his Coke, and then this Jesse would be off, hurrying to catch up with the others.

Hollingsworth tried to guess the names of the other cyclists. He felt he had a secret over them: giving them names they didn't know they had. He felt as if he owned them, as if he had them on some invisible string and could pull them back in just by muttering their names. He called all the others by French names—François, Pierre, Jacques—as they all rode French bicycles with an unpronounceable name—and he thought they were pansies, delicate, for having been given such soft and fluttering names—but he liked Jesse, and even more, he liked Jesse's bike, which was a black Schwinn, a heavy old bike that Hollingsworth saw made Jesse struggle hard to stay up with the Frenchmen.

Hollingsworth watched them ride, like a pack of animals, up and down the weedy, abandoned roads in the heat, disappearing into the shimmer that came up out of the road and the fields. The cyclists disappeared into the mirages, tracking a straight line, and then, later in the day—sitting on his porch, waiting—Hollingsworth would see them again when they came riding back out of the mirages.

The very first time that Jesse had peeled off from the rest of the pack and stopped by Hollingsworth's ratty-ass grocery for a Coke—the sound the old bottle made, sliding down the chute, Hollingsworth still had the old formula Cokes, as no one ever came to his old leaning barn of a store, set back on the hill off the deserted road—that first time, Hollingsworth was so excited at having a visitor that he couldn't speak. He just kept swallowing, filling his stomach fuller and fuller with air—and the sound the old bottle made sliding down the chute made Hollingsworth feel as if he had been struck in the head with it, as if he had been waiting at the bottom of the chute. No one had been out to his place since his father ran away: just the sheriff, once.

The road past Hollingsworth's store was the road of a ghost town. There had once been a good community, a big one, back at the turn of the century, down in the bottom, below his store—across the road, across the wide fields, with rich growing grasses from the river's flooding—and down in the tall hardwoods, with trees so thick that three men, holding arms, could not circle them, there had been a colony, a fair-sized town actually, that shipped cotton down the bayou in the fall, when the waters started to rise again.

The town had been called Hollingsworth.

But in 1903 the last residents had died of yellow fever, as had happened in almost every other town in the state—strangely enough, those lying closest to swamps and bayous, where yellow fever had always been a problem, were the last towns to go under, the most resistant—and then in the years that followed, the new towns that re-established themselves in the state did not choose to locate near Hollingsworth again. Buzbee's father had been one of the few who left before the town died, though he had contracted it, the yellow fever, and both Buzbee's parents died shortly after Buzbee was born.

Yellow fever came again in the 1930s, as well as malaria, and got Buzbee's wife—Hollingsworth's mother—when Hollingsworth was born, but Buzbee and his new son stayed, dug in and refused to leave the store. When Hollingsworth was fifteen, they both caught it again, but fought it down, together, as it was the kind that attacked only every other day—a different strain than before—and their days of fever alternated, so that they were able to take care of each other: cleaning up the spitting and the vomiting of black blood; covering each other with blankets when the chills started, and building fires in the fireplace, even in summer. And they tried all the roots in the area, all the plants, and somehow—for they did not keep track of what they ate, only sampled everything, anything that grew: pine boughs, cattails, wild carrots—they escaped being buried. Cemeteries were scattered throughout the woods and fields; nearly every place that was high and windy had one.

So the fact that no one ever came to their store, that there never had been any business, was nothing for Buzbee and Hollingsworth; everything would always be a secondary calamity after the two years of fever, and burying everyone, everything. Waking up in the night with a mosquito biting them and wondering if it had the fever. There were cans of milk on the shelves in their store that were forty years old; bags of potato chips that were twenty years old, because neither of them liked potato chips.

Hollingsworth would sit on his heels on the steps and tremble whenever Jesse and the others rode past, and on the times when Jesse turned in and came up to the store, so great was Hollingsworth's hurry to light his cigarette and then talk, slowly, the way it was supposed to be done in the country, the way he had seen it in his imagination, when he thought about how he would like his life to really be—that he spilled two cigarettes, and had barely gotten the third lit and drawn one puff when Jesse finished his Coke and then stood back up, and put the wet empty bottle back in the wire rack, waved, and rode off, the great backs of his calves and hamstrings working up and down in swallowing shapes, like things trapped in a sack. So Hollingsworth had to wait again for Jesse to come back, and by the next time, he had decided for certain that Buzbee was just being spiteful.

Before Buzbee had run away, sometimes Hollingsworth and Buzbee had cooked their dinners in the evenings, and other times they had driven into a town and ordered something, and looked around at people, and talked to the waitresses—but now, in the evenings, Hollingsworth stayed around, so as not to miss Jesse should he come by, and he ate sparingly from his stocks on the shelves: dusty cans of Vienna sausage, sardines, and rock crackers. Warm beer, brands that had gone out of business a decade earlier, two decades. Holding out against time was difficult, but was also nothing after holding out against death. In cheating death, Hollingsworth and Buzbee had continued to live, had survived, but also, curiously, had lost an edge of some sort: nothing would ever be quite as intense, nothing would ever really matter, after the biggest struggle.

The old cans of food didn't have any taste, but Hollingsworth didn't mind. He didn't see that it mattered much. Jesse said the other bikers wouldn't stop because they thought the Cokes were bad for them: cut their wind, slowed them down.

Hollingsworth had to fight down the feelings of wildness sometimes, now that his father was gone. Hollingsworth had never married, never had a friend other than his father. He had everything brought to him by the grocery truck, on the rarest of orders, and by the mail. He subscribed to *The Wall Street Journal*. It was eight days late by the time he received it, but he read it; and before Buzbee had run away they used to tell each other stories. They would start at sundown and talk until ten o'clock, Buzbee relating the ancient things, and Hollingsworth telling about everything that was in the paper. Buzbee's stories were always better. They were things that had happened two, three miles away.

As heirs to the town, Hollingsworth and Buzbee had once owned, back in the thirties, over two thousand acres of cypress and water oak, down in the swamp, and great thick bull pines, on the ridges, but they'd sold almost all of it to the timber companies, a forty- or eighty-acre tract every few years, and now they had almost no land left, just the shack in which they lived.

But they had bushels and bushels of money, kept in peach bushel baskets in their closet, stacked high. They didn't miss the land they had sold, but wished they had more, so the pulp-wood cutters would return: they had enjoyed the sound of the chain saws.

Back when they'd been selling their land to be cut, they would sit on their porch in the evenings and listen to the far-off cutting as if it were music: picturing the great trees falling, and feeling satisfied, somehow, each time they heard one hit.

✧   ✧   ✧

The first thing Jesse did in the mornings when he woke up was to check the sky, and then, stepping out onto the back porch, naked, the wind. If there wasn't any, he would be relaxed and happy with his life. If it was windy—even the faintest stir against his shaved ankles, up and over his round legs—he would scowl, a grimace of concentration, and go in and fix his coffee. There couldn't be any letting up on windy days, and if there was a breeze in the morning, it would build to true and hard wind for sure by afternoon: the heat of the fields rising, cooling, falling back down: blocks of air as slippery as his biking suit, sliding up and down the roads, twisting through trees, looking for places to blow, paths of least resistance.

There was so much Hollingsworth wanted to tell someone! Jesse, or even François, Jacques, Pierre! Buzbee was gone! He and Buzbee had told each other all the old stories, again and again. There wasn't anything new, not really, not of worth, and hadn't been for a long time. Hollingsworth had even had to resort to fabricating things, pretending he was reading them in the paper, to match Buzbee during the last few years of storytelling. And now, alone, his imagination was turning in on itself, and growing, like the most uncontrollable kind of cancer, with nowhere to go, and in the evenings he went out on the porch and looked across the empty highway, into the waving fields in the ebbing winds, and beyond, down to the blue line of trees along the bayou, where he knew Buzbee was hiding out, and Hollingsworth would ring the dinner bell, with a grim anger, and he would hope, scanning the fields, that Buzbee would stand up and wave, and come back in.

Jesse came by for another Coke in the second week of July. There was such heat. Hollingsworth had called in to Crystal Springs and had the asphalt truck come out and grade and level his gravel, pour hot slick tar down over it, and smooth it out: it cooled slowly, and was beautiful, almost iridescent, like a black snake in the bright green grass; it glowed its way across the yard as if it were made of glass, a path straight to the store, coming in off the road. It beckoned.

"So you got a new driveway," Jesse said, looking down at his feet.

The bottle was already in his hand; he was already taking the first sip. Nothing lasted; nothing!

Hollingsworth clawed at his chest, his shirt pocket, for cigarettes. He pulled them out and got one and lit it, and then sat down and said, slowly, "Yes." He looked out at the fields and couldn't remember a single damn story.

He groped, and faltered.

"You may have noticed there's a sudden abundance of old coins, especially quarters, say, 1964, 1965, the ones that have still got some silver in them," Hollingsworth said casually, but it wasn't the story in his heart.

"This is nice," Jesse said. "This is like what I race on sometimes." The little tar strip leading in to the Coke machine and Hollingsworth's porch was black and smooth and new. Hollingsworth had been sweeping it twice a day, to keep twigs off it, and waiting.

It was soft and comfortable to stand on; Jesse was testing it with his foot—pressing down on it, admiring the surface and firmness, yet also the give of it.

"The Russians hoarded them, is my theory, got millions of them from our mints in the sixties, during the Cold War," Hollingsworth said quickly. Jesse was halfway through with his Coke. This wasn't the way it was with Buzbee at all. "They've since subjected them to radiation—planted them amongst our populace."

Jesse's calves looked like whales going away; his legs, like things from another world. They were grotesque when they moved and pumped.

"I saw a man who looked like you," Jesse told Hollingsworth in August.

Jesse's legs and deep chest were taking on a hardness and slickness that hadn't been there before. He was drinking only half his Coke, and then slowly pouring the rest of it on the ground, while Hollingsworth watched, crestfallen: the visit already over, cut in half by dieting, and the mania for speed and distance.

"Except he was real old," Jesse said. "I think he was the man they're looking for." Jesse didn't know Hollingsworth's first or last name; he had never stopped to consider it.

Hollingsworth couldn't speak. The Coke had made a puddle and was fizzing, popping quietly in the dry grass. The sun was big and orange across the fields, going down behind the blue trees. It was beginning to cool. Doves were flying past, far over their heads, fat from the fields and late-summer grain. Hollingsworth wondered what Buzbee was eating, where he was living, why he had run away.

"He was fixing to cross the road," said Jesse.

Jesse was standing up: balancing carefully, in the little cleat shoes that would skid out from underneath him from time to time when he tried to walk in them. He didn't use a stopwatch the way other cyclists did, but knew he was getting faster, because just recently he had gotten the quiet, almost silent sensation—just a soft hushing—of falling, the one that athletes, and sometimes other people, get when they push deeper and deeper into their sport, until—like pushing through one final restraining layer of tissue, the last and thinnest, easiest one—they are falling, slowly, and there is nothing left in their life to stop them, no work is necessary, things are just happening, and they suddenly have all the time in the world to perfect their sport, because that's all there is, one day, finally.

"I tried to lay the bike down and get off and chase him," Jesse said. "But my legs cramped up."

He put the Coke bottle in the rack.

The sun was in Hollingsworth's eyes; it was as if he were being struck blind. He could smell only Jesse's heavy body odor, and could feel only the heat still radiating from his legs, like thick andirons taken from a fire: legs like a horse's, standing there, with veins wrapping them, spidery, beneath the thin browned skin.

"He was wearing dirty old overalls and no shirt," said Jesse. "And listen to this. He had a live carp tucked under one arm, and it didn't have a tail left on it. I had the thought that he had been eating on that fish's tail, chewing on it."

Jesse was giving a speech. Hollingsworth felt himself twisting down and inside with pleasure, like he was swooning. Jesse kept talking, nailing home the facts.

"He turned and ran like a deer, back down through the field, down toward the creek, and into those trees, still holding on to the fish." Jesse turned and pointed. "I was thinking that if we could catch him on your tractor, run him down and lasso him, I'd split the reward money with you." Jesse looked down at his legs: the round swell of them so ballooned and great that they hid completely his view of the tiny shoes below him. "I could never catch him by myself, on foot, I don't think," he said, almost apologetically. "For an old fucker, he's fast. There's no telling what he thinks he's running from."

"Hogson, the farmer over on Green Gable Road, has got himself some hounds," Hollingsworth heard himself saying, in a whisper. "He bought them from the penitentiary, when they turned mean, for five hundred dollars. They can track anything. They'll run the old man to Florida, if they catch his scent; they won't ever let up."

Hollingsworth was remembering the hounds: black and tan, the colors of late frozen night and cold honey in the sun, in the morning, and he was picturing the dogs moving through the forest, with Jesse and himself behind them. The dogs straining on their heavy leashes! Buzbee, slightly ahead of them, on the run, leaping logs, crashing through the undergrowth, splashing through the bends and loops in the bayou: savage swamp birds, rafts of them, darkening the air as they rose in their fright, leaping up in entire rookeries...cries in the forest, it would be like the jungle....It might take days! Stories around the campfire! He would tear off a greasy leg of chicken, roasted on the fire, reach across to hand it to Jesse, and tell him about anything, everything.

"We should try the tractor first," Jesse said, thinking ahead. It was hard to think about a thing other than bicycling, and he was frowning and felt awkward, exposed, and, also, trapped: cut off from the escape route. "But if he gets down into the woods, we'll probably have to use the dogs."

Hollingsworth was rolling up his pants leg, cigarette still in hand, to show Jesse the scar from the hunting accident when he was twelve—his father had said he thought he was a deer, and had shot him. Buzbee had been twenty-six.

"I'm like you," Hollingsworth said faithfully. "I can't run worth a damn either." But Jesse had already mounted his bike: he was moving away, down the thin black strip, like a pilot taking a plane down a runway to lift off, or like a fish running to sea. He entered the dead highway, which had patches of weeds growing up even in its center, and he stood up in his toe clips and accelerated away, down through the trees, with the wind at his back, going home.

He was gone almost immediately.

Hollingsworth did not want to go back inside. The store had turned dark; the sun was down behind the trees. Hollingsworth sat on the porch and watched the empty road. His mother had died when he was born. She, like his father, had been fourteen. He and his father had always been more like brothers to each other than anything else. Hollingsworth could remember playing a game with his father, perhaps when he was seven or eight, and his father would run out into the field and hide, on their old homestead—racing down the hill, arms windmilling, and disappearing suddenly, diving down into the tall grass, while Hollingsworth—Quirter, Quirt—tried to find him. They played that game again and again, more than any other game in the world, and at all times of the year, not just in the summer.

Buzbee had a favorite tree, and he sat up in the low branch of it often and looked back in the direction from which he had come. He saw the bikers every day. There weren't ever cars on the road. The cyclists sometimes picnicked at a little roadside table, oranges and bottles of warm water and candy bars by the dozens—he had snuck out there in the evenings, before, right at dusk, and sorted through their garbage, nibbled some of the orange peelings—and he was nervous, in his tree, whenever they stopped for any reason.

Buzbee had not in the least considered going back to his maddened son. He shifted on the branch and watched the cyclists eat their oranges. His back was slick with sweat, and he was rank, like the worst of animals. He and all the women bathed in the evenings in the bayou, in the shallows, rolling around in the mud. The women wouldn't go out any deeper. Snakes swam in evil S-shapes, back and forth, as if patrolling. He was starting to learn the women well, and many of them were like his son, in that they always wanted to talk, it seemed—this compulsion to communicate, as if it could be used to keep something else away, something big and threatening. He thought about what the cold weather would be like, November and beyond, himself trapped, as it were, in the abandoned palmetto shack, with all of the women around the fireplace, talking, for four months.

He slid down from the tree and started out into the field, toward the cyclists—the women watched him go—and in the heat, in the long walk across the field, he became dizzy, started to fall several times, and for the briefest fragments of time he kept forgetting where he was, imagined that one of the cyclists was his son, that he was coming back in from the game that they used to play, and he stopped, knelt down in the grass and pretended to hide. Eventually, though, the cyclists finished eating, got up and rode away, down the road again. Buzbee watched them go, then stood up and turned and raced back down into the woods, to the women. He had become frightened, for no reason, out in the field like that.

Buzbee had found the old settlement after wandering around in the woods for a week. There were carp in the bayou, and gar, and catfish, and he wrestled the large ones out of the shallow oxbows that had been cut off from the rest of the water. He caught alligators, too, the small ones.

He kept a fire going continuously, to keep the mosquitoes away, and as he caught more and more of the big fish, he hung them from the branches in his clearing, looped vine through their huge jaws and hung them like villains in his little clearing, like the most ancient of burial grounds; all these vertical fish, out of the water, mouths gaping in silent death, as if preparing to ascend: they were all pointing up.

The new pleasure of being alone sometimes stirred Buzbee so that he ran from errand to errand. He was getting ready for this new life, and with fall and winter coming on, he felt young.

After a couple of weeks, he had followed the bayou upstream, toward town, backtracking the water's sluggishness. He slept under the large logs that had fallen across it like netting, and he swatted at the mosquitoes that swarmed him in the evenings whenever he stopped moving, and he had kept going, even at night. The moon came down through the bare limbs of the swamp-rotted ghost trees, skeleton-white, disease-killed, but as he got higher above the swamp and closer to the town, near daylight, the water moved faster, had some circulation, and the mosquitoes were not a threat.

He lay under a boxcar on the railroad tracks and looked across the road at the tired women going in and out of the washateria: moving so slowly, as if old. They were in their twenties, their thirties, their forties: they carried their baskets of clothes in front of them with a bumping, side-to-side motion, as if they were going to quit living on the very next step. Their forearms sweated, glistened, and the sandals on their wide feet made flopping sounds, and he wanted to tell them about his settlement. He wanted five or six, ten or twenty of them. He wanted them walking around barefooted on the dark earth beneath his trees, beneath his hanging catfish and alligators, by the water, in the swamp.

He stole four chickens and a rooster that night, hooded their eyes, and put them in a burlap sack, put three eggs in each of his shirt pockets, too, after sucking ten eggs dry, gulping them in the almost wet brilliance of the moon, behind a chicken farm back west of town, along the bayou—and then he continued on down its banks, the burlap sack thrown over his back, the chickens and rooster warm against his damp body, calm, waiting.

He stopped when he came out of the green thick woods, over a little ridge, and looked down into the country where the bayous slowed to heavy swamp and where the white and dead trees were and the bad mosquitoes lived. He sat down and leaned his old back against a tree, and watched the moon and its blue light shining on the swamp, with his chickens. He waited until the sun came up and it got hot, and the mosquitoes had gone away, before starting down toward the last part of his journey, back to his camp.

The rest of the day he gathered seeds and grain from the little raised hummocks and grassy spots in the woods, openings in the forest, to use for feed for the chickens, which moved in small crooked shapes of white, like little ghosts in the woods, all through his camp, but they did not leave it. The rooster flew up into a low tree and stared wildly, golden-eyed, down into the bayou. For weeks Buzbee had been hunting the quinine bushes said to have been planted there during the big epidemic, and on that day he found them, because the chickens went straight to them and began pecking at them as Buzbee had never seen chickens peck: they flew up into the leaves, smothered their bodies against the bushes as if mating with them, so wild were they to get to the berries.

Buzbee's father had planted the bushes, had received the seeds from South America on a freighter that he met in New Orleans the third year of the epidemic, and he had returned with them to the settlement, that third year, when everyone went down finally.

The plants had not done well; they kept rotting, and never, in Buzbee's father's time, bore fruit or made berries. Buzbee had listened to his father tell the story about how they rotted—but also how, briefly, they had lived, even flourished, for a week or two, and how the settlement had celebrated and danced, and cooked alligators and cattle, and prayed; and everyone in the settlement had planted quinine seeds, all over the woods, for miles, in every conceivable location, and Buzbee realized, when the chickens began to cluck and feed, that it was the quinine berries, which they knew instinctively they must eat, and he went and gathered all the berries, and finally, he was certain, he was safe.

The smoke from his fire, down in the low bottom, had spread through the swamp, and from above would have looked as if that portion of the bayou, going into the tangled dead trees, had simply disappeared—a large spill of white, a fuzzy, milky spot—and then, on the other side of the spill, coming out again, bayou once more.

Buzbee was relieved to have the berries, and he let the fire go down, let it die. He sat against his favorite tree by the water and watched for small alligators. When he saw one, he leapt into the water, splashed and swam across to meet it, and wrestled it out of the shallows and into the mud, where he killed it savagely.

But the days were long, and he did not see that many alligators, and many of the ones he did see were a little too large, sometimes far too large. Still, he had almost enough for winter, as it stood: those hanging from the trees, along with the gaping catfish, spun in the breeze of fall coming, and if he waited and watched, eventually he would see an alligator. He sat against the tree and watched, and ate berries, chewed them slowly, pleasuring in their sour taste.

He imagined that they soured his blood: that they made him taste bad to the mosquitoes, and kept them away. Though he noticed they were still biting him, more even, now that the smoke was gone. But he got used to it.

A chicken had disappeared, probably to a snake, but also possibly to anything.

The berries would keep him safe.

He watched the water. Sometimes there would be the tiniest string of bubbles rising, from where an alligator was stirring in the mud below.

Two of the women from the laundry came out to the woods, tentatively, having left their homes, following the bayou, to see if what they had heard was true. It was dusk, and their clothes were torn and their faces wild. Buzbee looked up and could see the fear, and he wanted to comfort them. He did not ask what had happened at their homes, what fear could make the woods and the bayou journey seem less frightening. They stayed back in the trees, frozen, and would not come with him, even when he took each by the hand, until he saw what it was that was horrifying them: the grinning reptiles, the dried fish, spinning from the trees—and he explained to them that he had put them there to smoke, for food, for the winter.

"They smell good," said the shorter one, heavier than her friend, her skin a deep black, like some poisonous berry. Her face was shiny.

Her friend slapped at a mosquito.

"Here," said Buzbee, handing them some berries. "Eat these."

But they made faces and spat them out when they tasted the bitterness.

Buzbee frowned. "You'll get sick if you don't eat them," he said. "You won't make it otherwise."

They walked past him, over to the alligators, and reached out to the horned, hard skin, and touched them fearfully, ready to run, making sure the alligators were truly harmless.

"Don't you ever, you know, get lonely for girls?" Hollingsworth asked, like a child. It was only four days later, but Jesse was back for another half-Coke. The other bikers had ridden past almost an hour earlier: a fast rip-rip-rip, and then, much later, Jesse had come up the hill, pedaling hard, but moving slower.

He was trying, but he couldn't stay up with them. He had thrown his bike down angrily, and glowered at Hollingsworth when he stalked up to the Coke machine, scowled at him as if it was Hollingsworth's fault.

"I got a whore," Jesse said, looking behind him and out across the road. The pasture was green and wet, and mist hung over it, steaming from a rain earlier in the day. Jesse was lying; he didn't have anyone, hadn't had anyone in over a year, and Jesse felt as if he was getting further and further away from ever wanting anyone, or anything. He felt like everything was a blur: such was the speed at which he imagined he was trying to travel. Beyond the fog in the pasture were the trees, clear and dark and washed from the rain, and smelling good, even at this distance. Hollingsworth wished he had a whore. He wondered if Jesse would let him use his. He wondered if maybe she would be available if Jesse was to get fast and go off to the Olympics, or something.

"What does she cost?" Hollingsworth asked timidly.

Jesse looked at him in disgust. "I didn't mean it *that* way," he said. He looked tired, as if he was holding back, just a few seconds, from having to go back out on the road. Hollingsworth leaned closer, eagerly, sensing weakness, tasting hesitation. His senses were sharp from deprivation; he could tell, even before Jesse could, that Jesse was feeling thick, laggard, dulled. He knew Jesse was going to quit. He knew it the way a farmer might see that rain was coming.

"I mean," said Jesse, "that I got an old lady. A woman friend. A girl."

"What's her name?" Hollingsworth said quickly. He would make Jesse so tired that he would never ride again. They would sit around on the porch and talk forever, all of the days.

"Jemima."

Hollingsworth wanted her, just for her name.

"That's nice," he said, in a smaller voice.

It seemed to Hollingsworth that Jesse was getting his energy back. But he had felt the tiredness, and maybe, Hollingsworth hoped, it would come back.

"I found out the old man is your father," said Jesse. He was looking out at the road. He still wasn't making any move toward it. Hollingsworth realized, as if he had been tricked, that perhaps Jesse was just waiting for the roads to dry up a little, to finish steaming.

"Yes," said Hollingsworth, "he has run away."

They looked at the fields together.

"He is not right," Hollingsworth said.

"The black women in town, the ones that do everyone's wash at the Laundromat, say he's living down in the old yellow-fever community," Jesse said. "They say he means to stay, and that some of them have thought about going down there with him: the ones with bad husbands and too much work. He's been sneaking around the laundry late in the evenings and promising he'll cook for them, if any of them want to move down there with him. He says there aren't any snakes. They're scared the fever will come back, but he promises there aren't any snakes, that he killed them all, and a lot of them are considering it." Jesse related all this in a monotone, still watching the road, as if waiting for energy. The sun was burning the steam off. Hollingsworth felt damp, weak, unsteady, as if his mind was sweating with condensation from the knowledge, the way glasses suddenly fog up when you are walking into a humid setting.

"Sounds like he's getting lonely," Jesse said.

The steam was almost gone.

"He'll freeze this winter," Hollingsworth said, hopefully.

Jesse shook his head. "Sounds like he's got a plan. I suspect he'll have those women cutting firewood for him; fanning him with leaves; fishing, running traps, bearing children. Washing clothes."

"We'll catch him," Hollingsworth said, making a fist and smacking it in his palm. "And anyway, those women won't go down into those woods. Those woods are dark, and the yellow fever's still down there.

I'll go into town, and tell them it is. I'll tell them Buzbee's spitting up black blood and shivering, and is crazy. Those women won't go down into those woods."

Jesse shook his head. He put the bottle into the rack. The road was dry; it looked clean, scrubbed by the quick thunderstorm. "A lot of those women have got bruises on their arms, their faces, have got teeth missing, and their lives are too hard and without hope," Jesse said, as if just for the first time seeing it. "Myself, I think they'll go down there in great numbers. I don't think yellow fever means anything compared to what they have, or will have." He turned to Hollingsworth and slipped a leg over his bike, got on, put his feet in the clips, steadied himself against the porch railing. "I bet by June next year you're going to have about twenty half brothers and half sisters."

When Jesse rode off, thickly, as if the simple heat of the air were a thing holding him back, there was no question, Hollingsworth realized, Jesse was exhausted, and fall was coming. Jesse was getting tired. He, Hollingsworth, and Buzbee, and the colored women at the washhouse, and other people would get tired, too. The temperatures would be getting cooler, milder, in a month or so, and the bikers would be riding harder than ever. There would be the smoke from fires, hunters down on the river, and at night the stars would be brighter, and people's sleep would be heavier, and deeper. Hollingsworth wondered just how fast those bikers wanted to go. Surely, he thought, they were already going fast enough. He didn't understand them. Surely, he thought, they didn't know what they were doing.

The speeds that the end of June and the beginning of July brought, Jesse had never felt before, and he didn't trust them to last, didn't know if they could: and he tried to stay with the other riders, but didn't know if there was anything he could do to make the little speed he had last, in the curves, and that feeling, pounding up the hills; his heart working strong and smooth, like the wildest, easiest, most volatile thing ever invented. He tried to stay with them.

Hollingsworth, the old faggot, was running out into the road some days, trying to flag him down for some piece of bullshit, but there wasn't time, and he rode past, not even looking at him, only staring straight ahead.

The doves started to fly. The year was moving along. A newspaper reporter wandered down to do a short piece on the still-missing Buzbee. It was rumored he was living in an abandoned, rotting shack, deep into the darkest, lowest heart of the swamp. It was said that he had started taking old colored women, maids and such, women from the Laundromat, away from town; that they were going back down into the woods with him and living there, and that he had them in a corral, like a herd of wild horses. The reporter's story slipped further from the truth. It was all very mysterious, all rumor, and the reward was increased to $1,200 by Hollingsworth, as the days grew shorter after the solstice, and lonelier.

Jesse stopped racing. He just didn't go out one day; and when the Frenchmen came by for him, he pretended not to be in. He slept late and began to eat vast quantities of oatmeal. Sometimes, around noon, he would stop eating and get on his bike and ride slowly up the road to Hollingsworth's—sometimes the other bikers would pass him, moving as ever at great speed, all of them, and they would jeer at him, shout yah-yah, and then they were quickly gone; and he willed them to wreck, shut his eyes and tried to make it happen— picturing the whole pack of them getting tangled up, falling over one another, the way they tended to do, riding so close together.

The next week he allowed himself a whole Coca-Cola, with Hollingsworth, on the steps of the store's porch. The old man swooned, and had to steady himself against the porch railing when he saw it was his true love. It was a dry summer. They talked more about Buzbee.

"He's probably averse to being captured," Hollingsworth said. "He probably won't go easy."

Jesse looked at his shoes, watched them, as if thinking about where they were made.

"If you were to help me catch him, I would give you my half of it," Hollingsworth said generously. Jesse watched his shoes.

Hollingsworth got up and went in the store, and came back out with a hank of calf-rope lariat, heavy, gold as a fable, and corded.

"I been practicing," he said. There was a sawhorse standing across the drive, up on two legs, like a man, with a hat on it, and a coat, and Hollingsworth said nothing else, but twirled the lariat over his head and then flung it at the sawhorse, a mean heavy whistle over their heads, and the loop settled over the sawhorse, and Hollingsworth stepped back and tugged, cinched the loop shut. The sawhorse fell over and Hollingsworth began dragging it across the gravel, reeling it in as fast as he could.

"I could lasso you off that road if I wanted," Hollingsworth said.

Jesse thought about how the money would be nice. He thought about how it was in a wreck, too, when he wasn't able to get his feet free of the clips and had to stay with the bike, and roll over with it, still wrapped up in it. It was just the way his sport was.

"I've got to be going," he told Hollingsworth. When he stood up, though, he had been still too long, and his blood stayed down in his legs, and he saw spots and almost fell.

"Easy now, hoss," Hollingsworth cautioned; watching him eagerly, eyes narrowed, hoping for an accident and no more riding.

The moonlight came in through Hollingsworth's window, onto his bed, all night—it was silver. It made things look different: ghostly. Hollingsworth lay on his back, looking up at the ceiling.

We'll get him, he thought. We'll find his ass. But he couldn't sleep, and the sound of his heart, the movement of his blood pulsing, was the roar of an ocean, and it wasn't right. His father did not belong down in those woods. No one did. There was nothing down there that Hollingsworth could see but reptiles and danger.

The moon was so bright that it washed out all stars. Hollingsworth listened to the old house. There was a blister on the inside of his finger from practicing with the lariat, and he fingered it and looked at the ceiling.

"Let's go hunt that old dog," Hollingsworth said—it was the first thing he said, after Jesse had gotten his bottle out of the machine and opened it—and like a molester, a crooner, Hollingsworth seemed to be drifting toward Jesse without moving his feet: just leaning forward, swaying closer and closer, as if moving in to smell blossoms. His eyes were a believer's blue, and for a moment, Jesse had no idea what he was talking about, and felt dizzy. He looked into Hollingsworth's eyes, such a pale wash of light, such a pale blue that he knew those eyes had never seen anything factual, nothing of substance—and he laughed, thinking of Hollingsworth trying to catch Buzbee, or anything, on his own.

"We can split the reward money," Hollingsworth said again. He was grinning, trying as hard as he could to show all his teeth and yet keep them close together, uppers and lowers touching. He breathed through the cracks in them in a low, pulsing whistle: in and out. He had never in his life drunk anything but water, and his teeth were a startling white; they were just whittled down, was all, and puny from aging and time. He closed his eyes, squeezed them shut as if trying to remember something simple, like speech, or balance, or even breathing. He was like a turtle sunning on a log.

Jesse couldn't believe he was speaking. "Give me all of it," he heard himself say.

"All of it," Hollingsworth agreed, his eyes still shut, and then he opened them and reached in his pocket and handed the money to Jesse ceremoniously, like a child paying for something at a store counter for the first time.

Jesse unlaced his shoes, folded the bills in half and slid them down into the soles, putting bills in both shoes. He unlaced the drawstring to his pants and slid some down into the black dampness of his racing silks: down in the crotch, and padding the buttocks, and in front, high on the flatness of his abdomen, like a girdle, directly below the cinching lace of the drawstring, which he then tied again, tighter than it had been before.

Then he got on the bike and rode home, slowly, not racing anymore, not at all; through the late-day heat that had built up, but with fall in the air, the leaves on the trees hanging differently. There was some stillness everywhere. He rode on.

When he got home he carried the bike inside, as was his custom, and then undressed, peeling his suit off, with the damp bills fluttering slowly to the old rug, unfolding when they landed, and it surprised him at first to see them falling away from him like that, all around him, for he had forgotten they were down there as he rode.

Buzbee was like a field general. The women were tasting freedom, and seemed to be like circus strongmen, muscled with great strength suddenly from not being told what to do, from not being beaten or yelled at. They laughed and talked, and were kind to Buzbee. He sat up in the tree in his old khaki pants and watched, and whenever it looked like his feeble son and the ex-biker might be coming, he leapt down from the tree, and like monkeys they scattered into the woods, back to another, deeper, temporary camp they had built.

They splashed across the river like wild things, but they were laughing, there was no fear, not like there would have been in animals.

They knew they could get away. They knew that as long as they ran fast, they would make it.

Buzbee grinned too, panting, his eyes bright, and he watched the women's breasts float and bounce, riding high as they charged across; ankle-deep, knee-deep, waist-deep; hurrying to get away from his mad, lonely son: moving fast and shrieking, because they were all afraid of the alligators.

Buzbee had a knife in one hand and a sharpened stick in the other, and he almost wished there would be an attack, so that he could be a hero.

The second camp was about two miles down into the swamp. No one had ever been that far into it, not ever. The mosquitoes were worse, too. There wasn't any dry land, not even a patch, so they sat on the branches, and dangled their feet, and waited. Sometimes they saw black bears splashing after fish, and turtles. There were more snakes, too, deeper back, but the women were still bruised, and some of them fingered their bruises and scars as they watched the snakes, but no one went back.

They made up songs, with which they pretended to make the snakes go away.

It wasn't too bad.

They sat through the night listening to the cries of birds, and when the woods began to grow light again, so faintly at first that they doubted it was happening, they would ease down into the water and start back toward their dry camp.

Hollingsworth would be gone, chased away by the mosquitoes, by the emptiness, and they would feel righteous, as if they'd won something: a victory.

None of them had a watch. They never knew what time it was, what day even.

"Gone," said Hollingsworth.

He was out of breath, out of shape. His shoelaces were untied, and there were burrs in his socks. The camp was empty. Just chickens. And the god-awful reptiles, twisting from the trees.

"Shit almighty," said Jesse. His legs were cramping and he was bent over, massaging them; he wasn't used to walking.

Hollingsworth poked around in the little grass-and-wood shacks. He was quivering and kept saying, alternately, "Gone" and "Damn."

Jesse had to sit down, the pain in his legs was so bad. He put his feet together like a bear in the zoo and held them there and rocked, trying to stretch them back out. He was frightened of the alligators, and felt helpless, in his cramps, knowing that Buzbee could come up from behind with a club and rap him on the head, like one of the chickens, and he, Jesse, wouldn't even be able to get up to stop him or run.

Buzbee was in control.

"Shit. Damn. Gone," said Hollingsworth. He was running a hand through his thinning hair. He kicked a few halfhearted times at the shacks, but they were kicks of sorrow, not rage yet, and did no damage.

"We could eat the chickens," Jesse suggested, from his sitting position. "We could cook them on his fire and leave the bones all over camp." Jesse still had his appetite from his riding days, and was getting fat fast. He was eating all the time since he had stopped riding.

Hollingsworth turned to him, slightly insulted. "They belong to my father," he said.

Jesse continued to rock, but thought, My God, what a madman.

He rubbed his legs and rocked. The pain was getting worse.

There was a breeze stirring. They could hear the leather and rope creaking as some of the smaller alligators moved. There was a big alligator hanging from a beech tree, about ten feet off the ground, and as they watched it, the leather cord snapped from the friction, and the weight of the alligator crashed to the ground.

"The mosquitoes are getting bad," said Jesse, rising: hobbled, bent over. "We'd better be going."

But Hollingsworth was already scrambling through the brush, up toward the brightness of sky above the field. He could see the sky, the space, through the trees, and knew the field was out there. He was frantic to get out of the woods; there was a burning in his chest, in his throat, and he couldn't breathe.

Jesse helped him across the field and got him home. He offered to ride into Crystal Springs, thirty miles, and make a call for an ambulance, but Hollingsworth waved him away.

"Just stay with me a little while," he said. "I'll be okay."

But the thought was terrifying to Jesse—of being in the same room with Hollingsworth, contained, and listening to him talk, forever, all day and through the night, doubtless.

"I have to go," Jesse said, and hurried out the door.

He got on his bike and started for home. His knees were bumping against his belly, such was the quickness of his becoming fat, but the relief of being away from Hollingsworth was so great that he didn't mind.

Part of him wanted to be as he had been, briefly: iron, and fast, racing with the fastest people in the world, it seemed—he couldn't remember anything about them, only the blaze and rip of their speed, the *whish-whish* cutting sound they made, as a pack, tucking and sailing down around corners—but also, he was tired of that, and it felt good to be away from it, for just a little while.

He could always go back.

His legs were still strong. He could start again any time. The sport of it, the road, would have him back. The other bikers would have him back, they would be happy to see him.

He thought all these things as he trundled fatly up the minor hills, the gradual rises: then coasting—with relief—on the down sides.

Shortly before he got to the gravel turnoff, the little tree-lined road that led to his house, the other bikers passed him, coming from out of the west, and they screamed and howled at him, passing, and jabbed their thumbs down at him, as if they were trying to unplug a drain or poke a hole in something; they shrieked, and then they were gone, so quickly.

He wanted to hide somewhere, he was so ashamed of what he had lost, but there was nowhere to hide, for in a way it was still in him: the memory of it.

Later, he dreamed of going down into the woods, of joining Buzbee and starting over, wrestling alligators; but he only dreamed it—and in the morning, when he woke up, he was still heavy and slow, grounded.

He went into the kitchen, looked in the refrigerator, and began taking things out. Maybe, he thought, Hollingsworth would up the reward money.

Buzbee enjoyed cooking for the women. It was going to be an early fall, and dry; they got to where they hardly noticed the mosquitoes that were always whining around them—a tiny buzzing—and they had stopped wearing clothes long ago. Buzbee pulled down hickory branches and climbed up in trees, often—and he sat hunkered above the women, looking down, just watching them move around in their lives, naked and happy, talking. More had come down the bayou since the first two, and they were shoring up the old shelter: pulling up palmetto plants from the hummocks and dragging logs across the clearing, fixing the largest of the abandoned cabins into a place that was livable for all of them.

He liked the way they began to look at him, on about the twentieth day of their being there, and he did not feel seventy-seven. He slid down out of the tree, walked across the clearing toward the largest woman, the one he had had his eye on, and took her hand, hugged her, felt her broad fat back, the backs of her legs, which were sweaty, and then her behind, while she giggled.

All that week, as the weather changed, they came drifting in, women from town, sometimes carrying lawn chairs, always wild-eyed and tentative when they saw the alligators and catfish, the others moving around naked in camp, brown as the earth itself—but then they would recognize someone, and would move out into the clearing with wonder, and a disbelief at having escaped. A breeze might be stirring, and dry colored hardwood leaves—ash, hickory, oak and beech, orange and gold—would tumble into the clearing and spill around their ankles. The leaves made empty scraping sounds when the women walked through them, shuffling, looking up at the spinning fish.

At night they would sit around the fire and eat the dripping juicy alligators, roasted; fat, from the tails, sweet, glistened on their hands, their faces, running down to their elbows. They smeared it on their backs, their breasts, to keep the mosquitoes away. Nights smelled of wood smoke. They could see the stars above their trees, above the shadows of Buzbee's catches.

The women had all screamed and run into the woods, in different directions, the first time Buzbee leapt into the water after an alligator; but now they gathered close and they applauded and chanted an alligator-catching song they had made up that had few vowels.

That first time, however, they thought he had lost his mind. He had rolled around and around in the thick gray-white mud, down by the bank, jabbing the young alligator with his pocketknife again and again, perforating it and muttering savage dog noises, until they could no longer tell which was which, except for the jets of blood that spurted out of the alligator's fat belly. But after he had killed the reptile and rinsed off in the shallows, and come back across the oxbow, wading in knee-deep water, carrying it in his arms, a four-footer, his largest ever, he was smiling, gap-toothed, having lost two in the fight, but he was also erect, proud, and ready for love. It was the first time they had seen that.

The one he had hugged went into the hut after him.

The other women walked around the alligator carefully and poked sticks at it, but also glanced toward the hut and listened, for the brief and final end of the small thrashings, the little pleasure, that was going on inside, the confirmation, and presently it came: Buzbee's goatish bleats, and the girl's too, which made them look at one another with surprise, wonder, interest, and speculation.

"It's those berries he's eatin'," said one, whose name was Onessimius. Oney.

"They tastes bad," said Tasha.

"They makes your pee turn black," said Oney.

They looked at her with caution.

Jesse didn't have the money for a car, or even for an old tractor.

He bought a used lawn-mower engine instead, for fifteen dollars; he found some old plywood in a dry abandoned barn. He scrounged some wheels, and stole a fan belt from a car rotting in a field, with bright wildflowers growing out from under the hood and mice in the back seat. He made a go-cart, and put a long plastic antenna with an orange flag, a banner, on the back of it that reached high into the sky, so any motorists coming would see it.

But there was never any traffic. He sputtered and coughed up the hills, going one, two miles an hour, then coasting down, a slight breeze in his face. He didn't wear his biking helmet, and the breeze felt good.

It took him an hour to get to Hollingsworth's sometimes; he carried a sack lunch with him, apples and potato chips, and ate, happily, as he drove.

He started out going over to Hollingsworth's in the mid-morning, and always tried to come back in the early afternoon, so that the bikers would not see him; but it got more and more to where he didn't care, and finally, he just came and went as he pleased, waving happily when he saw them. But they never waved back. Sometimes the one who had replaced him, the trailing one, would spit water from his thermos bottle onto the top of Jesse's head as he rushed past; but they were gone quickly, almost as fast as they had appeared, and soon he was no longer thinking about them. They were gone.

Cottonwoods. Rabbits. Fields. It was still summer, it seemed it would always be summer; the smell of hay was good, and dry. All summer, they cut hay in the fields around him.

The go-cart rumbled along, carrying him; threatening to stop on the hill, but struggling on. He was a slow movement of color going up the hills, with everything else in his world motionless; down in the fields, black Angus grazed, and cattle egrets stood behind them and on their backs. Crows sat in the dead limbs of trees, back in the woods, watching him, watching the cows, waiting for fall.

He would reach Hollingsworth's, and the old man would be waiting, like a child: wanting his father back. It was a ritual. Hollingsworth would wave, tiredly: hiding in his heart the delight at seeing another person.

Jesse would wave back as he drove up into the black tar road. He would grunt and pull himself up out of the little go-cart, and go over to the Coke machine.

The long slide of the bottle down the chute; the rattle, and *clunk*.

They'd sit on the porch, and Hollingsworth would begin to talk.

"I saw one of those explode in a man's hand," he said, pointing to the bottle Jesse was drinking. "Shot a sliver of glass as long as a knife up into his forearm, all the way. He didn't feel a thing; he just looked at it, and then walked around, pointing to it, showing everybody."

Hollingsworth remembered everything that had ever happened to him. He told Jesse everything.

Jesse would stir after the second or third story. He couldn't figure it out; he couldn't stand to be too close to Hollingsworth, to listen to him for more than twenty or thirty minutes—he hated it after that point—but always, he went back, every day.

It was as if he got full, almost to the point of vomiting; but then he got hungry again.

He sat on the porch and drank Cokes, and ate cans and cans of whatever Hollingsworth had on the shelf: yams, mushrooms, pickles, deviled ham—and he knew, as if it were an equation on a blackboard, that his life had gone to hell. He could see it in the size of his belly resting between his soft legs, but he didn't know what to do.

There was a thing that was not in him anymore, and he did not know where to go to find it.

❊   ❊   ❊

Oney was twenty-two and had had a bad husband. She still had the stitches in her forehead; he had thrown a chair at her, because she had called him a lard-ass, which he was. The stitches in the center of her head looked like a third eyebrow, with the eye missing. She hadn't heard about the old days of yellow fever and what it could do to one person, or everyone.

One night, even though she slept in Buzbee's arms, and even though the night was still and warm, she began to shiver wildly. And then two days later, again, she shivered and shook all night, her teeth rattling, and then two days later, a third time. It was coming every forty-eight hours, which was how it had been when Buzbee and Hollingsworth had had it.

Oney had been pale to begin with, and was turning, as if with the leaves, yellow, right in front of them: a brighter yellow each day. All of the women began to eat the berries, slowly at first, and then wolfishly, watching Oney as they ate.

They had built a palmetto coop for their remaining chickens, which were laying regularly, and they turned them out, three small white magicians moving through the woods in search of bugs, seeds, and berries. The chickens split up and wandered in different directions, and Buzbee and all the women split up too, and followed them single file, at a distance, waiting for the chickens to find more berries, but somehow two of the chickens got away from them, escaped, and when they came back to camp with the one remaining white chicken, a large corn snake was in the rooster's cage and was swallowing him, with only his thrashing feet showing: the snake's mouth hideous and wide, eyes wide and unblinking, mouth stretched into a laugh, as if he was enjoying the meal. Buzbee killed the snake, but the rooster died shortly after being pulled back out.

Oney screamed and cried and shook until she was spitting up more black blood, when they told her they were going to take her back into town, and she took Buzbee's pocketknife and pointed it between her breasts and swore she would kill herself if they tried to make her go back to Luscious. And so they let her stay, and fed her their dwindling berry supply, and watched the stars, the sunset, and hoped for a hard and cold winter and an early freeze, but the days stayed warm, though the leaves were changing on schedule, and always, they looked for berries, and began experimenting, too, with the things Buzbee and Hollingsworth had tried so many years ago: juniper berries, mushrooms, hickory nuts, acorns. They smeared grease from the fish and alligators over every inch of their bodies, and kept a fire going at all times.

None of the women would go back to town. And none of them other than Oney had started spitting up blood or shivering yet. Ozzie, Buzbee's first woman, had missed her time.

And Buzbee sat up in the trees and looked down on them often, and stopped eating his berries, unbeknownst to them, so that there would be more for them. The alligators hung from the trees like dead insurgents, traitors to a way of life. They weren't seeing any more in the bayou, and he wasn't catching nearly as many fish. The fall was coming, and winter beyond that. The animals knew it first. Nothing could prevent its coming, or even slow its approach: nothing they could do would matter. Buzbee felt fairly certain that he had caught enough alligators.

Hollingsworth and Jesse made another approach a week later. Hollingsworth had the lariat and was wearing cowboy boots and a hat. Jesse was licking a Fudgsicle.

Buzbee, in his tree, spotted them and jumped down.

"Shit," said Hollingsworth when they got to the camp. "He saw us coming again."

"He runs away," said Jesse, nodding. They could see the muddy slide marks where Buzbee and the women had scrambled out on the other side. The dark stand of trees, a wall.

"I've got an idea," said Hollingsworth.

They knew where Buzbee and the women were getting their firewood: a tremendous logjam, with driftwood stacked all along the banks, not far from the camp.

Hollingsworth and Jesse went and got shovels, and some old mattresses from the dump, and came back and dug pits: huge, deep holes, big enough to bury cars, big enough to hold a school bus.

"I saw it on a Tarzan show," said Hollingsworth. His heart was burning; both of the men were dripping with sweat. Down on the bayou, it was the softest, richest dirt in the world, good and loose and black and easy to move, but they were out of shape and it took them all day. They sang as they dug, to keep Buzbee and the women at bay, hemmed in, back in the trees.

Buzbee and the women sat up on their branches, swatting at mosquitoes, and listened, and wondered what was going on.

"Row, row, row your boat!" Jesse shouted as he dug, his big belly wet, and like a melon. Mopping his brow; his face streaked, with dirt and mud. He remembered the story about the pioneers who went crazy alone and dug their own graves: standing at the edge, then, and doing it.

"Oh, say—can—you—see," Hollingsworth brayed, "by the dawn's earl—lee—light?"

Back in the trees, the women looked at Buzbee for an explanation. They knew it was his son.

"He was born too early," he said weakly. "He has never been right."

"He misses you," said Oney. "That boy wants you to come home."

Buzbee scowled and looked down at his toes, hunkered on the branch, and held on, as if the tree had started to sway.

"That boy don't know *what* he wants," he said.

When Hollingsworth and Jesse had finished the pits, they spread long branches over them, then scattered leaves and twigs over the branches.

"We'll catch the whole tribe of them," Hollingsworth cackled.

Jesse nodded. He was faint, and didn't know if he could make it all the way back out or not. He wondered what Buzbee and the women would be having for supper.

The mosquitoes were vicious; the sun was going down. Owls were beginning to call.

"Come on," said Hollingsworth. "We've got to get out of here."

Jesse wanted to stay. But he felt Hollingsworth pull on his arm; he let himself be led away.

Back in the woods, up in the tree, Oney began to shiver, and closed her eyes, lost consciousness, and fell. Buzbee leapt down and gathered her up, held her tightly, and tried to warm her with his body.

"They gone," said a woman named Vesuvius. The singing had gone away when it got dark, as had the ominous sound of digging.

There was no moon, and it was hard, even though they were familiar with the woods, to find their way back to camp.

They built fires around Oney, and two days later she was better.

But they knew it would come again.

"Look at what that fool boy of yours has done," Tasha said the next day. A deer had fallen into one of the pits and was leaping about, uninjured, trying to get free.

Buzbee said his favorite curse word, a new one that Oney had told him, "Fuckarama," and they tried to rope the deer, but it was too wild: it would not let them get near.

"We could stone it," Tasha said, but not with much certainty; they all knew they could not harm the deer, trapped as it was, so helpless.

Then at dusk they saw Oney's husband moving through the woods, perilously close to their camp, moving through the gray trees, stalking their woods with a shotgun.

They hid in their huts and watched, hoping he would not look down the hill and see their camp, not see the alligators hanging.

Oney was whimpering. Her husband's dark shape moved cautiously, but the light was going fast: that darkness of purple, all the light being drawn away. He faded; he disappeared, and it was dark. Then, in the night, they heard a yell and a blast, and then the quietest silence they had ever known.

It was a simple matter burying him in the morning. They hadn't thought of letting the deer out that way. They had not thought of filling in the pit partially, so that the deer could walk out.

"You will get better," they told Oney. She believed them. On the days in which she did not have the fever, she believed them. There was still, though, the memory of it.

It was escapable. Some people lived through it and survived. It didn't get everyone. They didn't all just lie down and die, those who got it.

She loved old Buzbee, on her good days. She laughed, and slept with him, rolled with him, and put into the back of her mind what had happened before, and what would be happening again.

Her teeth, white and huge, when she was laughing, pressing against him, clutching him, shutting her eyes. She would fight to keep it in the back of her mind, and to keep it behind her.

Jesse rode out to Hollingsworth's in the go-cart. He took a back road, a different route. The air was cooler, it seemed that summer could be ending after all, and he felt like just getting out and seeing the country again. It was a road he had always liked to ride on, with or without the pack, back when he had been racing, and he had forgotten how fresh it had been, how it had tasted, just to look at it. He drove through a tunnel of trees; a pasture, on the other side of the trees, a stretch of pastel green, a smear of green, with charcoal cattle standing in it, and white egrets at their sides, pressed an image into the sides of his slow-moving vision. It was almost cold down in the creek bottom, going through the shade, so slowly.

He smiled and gave a small whoop, and waved a fist in the air. The light on the other side of the trees, coming down onto the field, was the color of gold smoke.

He had a sack of groceries with him, behind the engine, and he reached back and got a sandwich and a canned drink.

They went to check the traps, the pits, flushing Buzbee's troops back into the swamp, as ever.

"I'd hoped we could have caught them all," said Hollingsworth. His eyes were pale, mad, and he wanted to dig more holes.

"Look," he said. "They buried my mattress." He bent down on the fresh mound and began digging at it with his hands; but he gave up soon, and looked around blankly, as if forgetting why he had been digging in the first place.

Buzbee and the women were getting angry at being chased so often, so regularly. They sat in the trees and waited. Some of the women said nothing, but hoped to themselves that Hollingsworth and Jesse would forget where some of the pits lay, and would stumble in.

❊   ❊   ❊

Jesse and Hollingsworth sat on Hollingsworth's porch.

"You don't talk much," Hollingsworth said, as if noticing for the first time.

Jesse said nothing. It was getting near the twenty-minute mark. He had had two Cokes and a package of Twinkies. He was thinking about how it had been, when he had been in shape, and riding with the others, the pack: how his old iron bike had been a traitor some days, and his legs had laid down and died, and he had run out of wind, but how he had kept going anyway, and how eventually it had gotten better.

The bikers rode by. They were moving so fast. Hills were nothing to them. They had light bikes, expensive ones, and the climbs were only excuses to use the great strength of their legs. The wind in their faces, and pressing back against their chests, was but a reason and a direction, for a feeling; it was something to rail against, and defeat, or be defeated by—but it was tangible. Compared to some things, the wind was actually tangible.

They shouted encouragement to one another as they jockeyed back and forth, sharing turns, breaking the wind for each other.

"I'm ready," Hollingsworth told Jesse on his next visit, a few days later.

He was jumping up and down like a child.

"I'm ready, I'm ready," Hollingsworth sang. "Ready for anything."

He had a new plan. All he had been doing was thinking: trying to figure out a way to get something back.

So Jesse rode his bike to town to get the supplies they would need: an extra lariat and rope for trussing him up with; they figured he would be senile and wild. Muzzles for the dogs. Jesse rode hard, for a fat man.

The wind was coming up. It was the first week in September. The hay was baled, stood in tall rolls, and the fields looked tame, civilized, smoothed: flattened.

They muzzled the dogs and put heavy leashes on their collars, then started out across the field with a kerosene lantern and some food and water.

When they had crossed the field—half running, half being dragged by the big dogs' eagerness—and came to the edge of the woods, they were halted by the mosquitoes, which rose in a noisy dark cloud and fell upon them like soft fingers. The dogs turned back, whining in their muzzles, yelping, instinct warning them of the danger of these particular mosquitoes, and they kept backing away, retreating to the field, and would not go down into the swamp.

So Hollingsworth and Jesse camped back in the wind of the pasture, in the cool grass, and waited for daylight. They could smell the smoke from Buzbee's camp, but could see nothing, the woods were so dark. There was a quarter-moon, and it came up so close to them, over the trees, that they could see the craters.

Hollingsworth talked. He talked about the space program. He asked Jesse if this wasn't better than riding his old bike. They shared a can of Vienna sausage. Hollingsworth talked all night. Chuck-will's-widows called and bullbats thumped around in the grass, not far from their small fire, flinging themselves into the grass and flopping around as if mourning; rising again, flying past, and then twisting and slamming hard, without a cry, as if pulled down by a sudden force. As if their time was up. All around them, the bullbats flew like this, twisting and then diving into the ground, until it seemed to Jesse that they were trying to send a message: Go back, go back.

And he imagined, as he tried not to listen to Hollingsworth, that the bikers he had ridden with, the Frenchmen, were asleep, or making love to soft women, or eating ice-cream cones.

A drizzle woke Hollingsworth and Jesse and the dogs in the morning, and they stood up and stretched, and then moved on the camp. Crickets were chirping quietly in the soft rain, and the field was steaming. There wasn't any more smoke from the fire. The dogs had been smelling Buzbee and his camp all night, and were nearly crazed: their chests swelled and strained like barrels of apples, like hearts of anger, and they jumped and twisted and tugged against their leashes, pulling Hollingsworth and Jesse behind them in a stumbling run through the wet grasses.

Froth came from their muzzles, their rubbery lips. Their eyes were wild. They were too hard to hold. They pulled free of their leashes, and raced, silently, like the fastest thing in the world, accelerating across the field and into the woods, straight for the camp, the straightest thing that ever was.

Jesse bought a bike with the reward money: a French bicycle, a racer, with tires that were thinner than a person's finger held sideways. It could fly. It was light blue, like an old man's eyes.

Hollingsworth had chained Buzbee to the porch: had padlocked the clasp around his ankle with thirty feet of chain. It disgusted Jesse, but he was even more disgusted by his own part in the capture, and by the size of his stomach, his loss of muscle.

He began to ride again: not with the pack, but by himself.

He got fast again, as he had thought he could. He got faster than he had been before, faster than he had ever imagined, and bought a stopwatch and raced against himself, timing himself, riding up and down the same roads over and over again.

Sometimes, riding, he would look up and see Buzbee out on the porch, standing, with Hollingsworth sitting behind him, talking. Hollingsworth would wave wildly.

One night, when Jesse got in from his ride, the wind had shifted out of the warm west and was from the north, and it felt serious, and in it, after Jesse had bathed and gotten in bed, was the thing, not for the first time, but the most insistent that year, that made Jesse get back out of bed, where he was reading, and go outside and sit on the steps beneath his porch light. He tried to read.

Moths fell down off the porch light's bulb, brushed his shoulders, landed on the pages of his book, spun, and flew off, leaving traces of magic. And the wind began to stir harder. Stars were all above him, and they glittered and flashed in the wind. They seemed to be challenging him, daring him to see what was true.

Two miles away, up on the hill, back in the trees, the A.M.E. congregation was singing. He couldn't see the church lights, but for the first time that year he could hear the people singing, the way he could in the winter, when there were no leaves on the trees and when the air was colder, more brittle, and sounds carried. He could never hear the words, just the sad moaning that sometimes, finally, fell away into pleasure.

He stood up on the porch and walked out into the yard, the cool grass, and tried some sit-ups. When he was through, he lay back, sweating slightly, breathing harder, and he watched the stars, but they weren't as bright, it seemed, and he felt as if he had somehow failed them, had not done the thing expected or, rather, the thing demanded.

When he woke up in the morning, turned on his side in the yard, lying out in the grass like an animal, the breeze was still blowing and the light of the day was gold, coming out of the pines on the east edge of his field.

He sat up stiffly, and for a moment forgot who he was, what he did, where he was—it was the breeze moving across him, so much cooler suddenly—and then he remembered, it was so simple, that he was supposed to ride.

It was early November. It was impossible to look at the sky, at the trees, at the cattle in the fields, and not know that it was November. The clasp around Buzbee's ankle was cold; his legs were getting stronger from pulling the chain around with him. He stood out on the porch, and the air, when he breathed deeply, went all the way down into his chest. He felt good. He felt like wrestling an alligator.

He had knocked Hollingsworth to the ground, tried to get him to tell him where the key was. But Hollingsworth, giggling, with his arm twisted behind his back—the older man riding him, breathing hard but steadily, pushing his son's face into the floor—had told Buzbee that he had thrown the key away. And Buzbee, knowing his son, his poisoned loneliness, knew that it was so.

The chain was too big to break or smash.

Sometimes Buzbee cried, looking at it. He felt as if he could not breathe; it was as if he were being smothered. It was like a thing was about to come to a stop.

He watched the field all the time. Jesse raced by, out on the road, checking his watch, looking at it, holding it in one hand, pedaling hard—flying, it seemed.

Buzbee heard Hollingsworth moving behind him, coming out to gab. It was like being in a cell.

Buzbee could see the trees, the watery blur of them, on the other side of the field.

"Pop," said Hollingsworth, ready with a story.

Pop, my ass, thought Buzbee bitterly. He wanted to strangle his own son.

He had so wanted to make a getaway—to have an escape, clean and free.

He looked out at the field, remembering what it had been like with the women, and the alligators, and he thought how he would be breaking free again, shortly, for good.

This time, he knew, he would get completely away.

The blue line of trees, where he had been with the women, wavered and flowed, in watercolor blotches, and there was a dizziness high in his forehead. He closed his eyes and listened to his mad son babble, and he prepared, and made his plans.

When he opened his eyes, the road was empty in front of him. Jesse was gone—a streak, a flash: already gone.

It was as if he had never been there.

Buzbee narrowed his eyes and gripped the porch railing, squinted at the trees, scowled, and tried to figure another way out.

The Legend of Pig-Eye

We used to go to bars, the really seedy ones, to find our fights. It excited Don. He loved going into the dark old dives, ducking under the doorway and following me in, me with my robe on, my boxing gloves tied around my neck, and all the customers in the bar turning on their stools, as if someday someone special might be walking in, someone who could even help them out. But Don and I were not there to help them out.

Don had always trained his fighters this way: in dimly lit bars, with a hostile hometown crowd. We would get in his old red truck on Friday afternoons—Don and Betty, his wife, and Jason, their teenage son, and my two hounds, Homer and Ann—and head for the coast—Biloxi, Ocean Springs, Pascagoula—or the woods, to the Wagon Wheel in Utica. If enough time had passed for the men to have forgotten the speed of the punches, the force and snap of them, we'd go into Jackson, to the rotting, sawdust-floor bars like the Body Shop or the Tall Low Man. That was where the most money could be made, and it was sometimes where the best fighters could be found.

Jason waited in the truck with the dogs. Occasionally Betty would wait with him, with the windows rolled down so they could tell how the fight was going. But there were times when she went with us into the bar, because that raised the stakes: a woman, who was there only for the fight. We'd make anywhere from five hundred to a thousand dollars a night.

"Mack'll fight anybody, of any size or any age, man or woman," Don would say, standing behind the bar with his notepad, taking bets, though of course I never fought a woman. The people in the bar would pick their best fighter, and then watch that fighter, or Betty, or Don. Strangely, they never paid much attention to me. Don kept a set of gloves looped around his neck as he collected the bets. I would look around, wish for better lighting, and then I'd take my robe off. I'd have my gold trunks on underneath. A few customers, drunk or sober, would begin to realize that they had done the wrong thing. But by that time things were in motion, the bets had already been made, and there was nothing to do but play it out.

Don said that when I had won a hundred bar fights I could go to New York. He knew a promoter there to whom he sent his best fighters. Don, who was forty-four, trained only one fighter at a time. He himself hadn't boxed in twenty years. Betty had made him promise, swear on all sorts of things, to stop once they got married. He had been very good, but he'd started seeing double after one fight, a fight he'd won but had been knocked down in three times, and he still saw double, twenty years later, whenever he got tired.

We'd leave the bar with the money tucked into a cigar box. In the summer there might be fog or a light mist falling, and Don would hold my robe over Betty's head to keep her dry as we hurried away. We used the old beat-up truck so that when the drunks, angry that their fighter had lost, came out to the parking lot, throwing bottles and rocks at us as we drove away, it wouldn't matter too much if they hit it.

Whenever we talked about the fights, after they were over, Don always used words like "us," "we," and "ours." My parents thought fighting was the worst thing a person could do, and so I liked the way Don said "we": it sounded as though I wasn't misbehaving all by myself.

"How'd it go?" Jason would ask.

"We smoked 'em," Don would say. "We had a straight counter-puncher, a good man, but we kept our gloves up, worked on his body, and then got him with an overhand right. He didn't know what hit him. When he came to, he wanted to check our gloves to see if we had put *lead* in them."

Jason would squeal, smack his forehead, and wish that he'd been old enough to see the bout for himself.

We'd put the dogs, black-and-tan pups, in the back of the truck. The faithful Homer, frantic at having been separated from me, usually scrambled around, howling and pawing; but fat Ann curled up on a burlap sack and fell quickly asleep. We'd go out for pizza then, or to a drive-through hamburger place, and we'd talk about the fight as we waited for our order. We counted the money to make sure it was all there, though if it wasn't, we sure weren't going back after it.

We could tell just by looking at the outside what a place was going to be like, if it was the kind of place where we would have to leave Betty in the truck with Jason, sometimes with the engine running, and where we didn't know for sure if we would win or lose.

We looked for the backwoods nightspots, more gathering places than bars, which were frequented by huge, angry men—men who either worked hard for a living and hated their jobs or did not work and hated that too, or who hated everything. These were the kinds of men we wanted to find, because they presented as much of a challenge as did any pro fighter.

Some nights we didn't find the right kind of bar until almost midnight, and during the lull Betty would fall asleep with her head in Don's lap and Jason would drive so I could rest. The dogs curled up on the floorboard. Finally, though, there would be the glow of lights in the fog, the crunch of a crushed-shell parking lot beneath our tires, and the cinder-block tavern, sometimes near the Alabama state line and set back in the woods, with loud music coming through the doors, seeping through the roof and into the night. Between songs we could hear the clack of pool balls. When we went in the front door, the noise would come upon us like a wild dog. It was a furious caged sound, and we'd feel a little fear. Hostility, the smell of beer, and anger would swallow us up. It would be just perfect.

"We'll be out in a while," Don would tell Jason. "Pistol's in the glove box. Leave the engine running. Watch after your mother."

We kept a tag hanging from the truck's rear-view mirror that told us how many fights in a row we had won, what the magic number was, and after each fight it was Jason's job to take down the old tag and put a new one up.

Eighty-six. Eighty-seven. Eighty-eight.

❀   ❀   ❀

Driving home, back to Don's little farm in the woods, Jason would turn the radio on and steer the truck with one hand, keeping the other arm on the seat beside him, like a farmer driving into town on a Saturday. He was a good driver. We kept rocking chairs in the back of the truck for the long drives, and sometimes after a fight Don and I would lean back in them and look up at the stars and the tops of big trees that formed tunnels over the lonely back roads. We'd whistle down the road as Jason drove hard, with the windows down and his mother asleep in the front.

When a road dipped down into a creek bottom, the fog made it hard to see beyond the short beam of our headlights, as if we were underwater. The air was warm and sticky. Here Jason slowed slightly, but soon we'd be going fast again, driving sixty, seventy miles an hour into the hills, where the air was clean and cool, and the stars visible once more.

I wondered what it would be like to drive my father and mother around like that, to be able to do something for them, something right. My parents lived in Chickasha, Oklahoma, and raised cattle and owned a store. I was twenty years old.

I wanted to win the one hundred fights and go to New York and turn pro and send my parents money. Don got to keep all of the bar-fight money, and he was going to get to keep a quarter of the New York money, if there ever was any. I wanted to buy my parents a new house or some more cattle or something, the way I read other athletes did once they made it big. My childhood had been wonderful; already I was beginning to miss it, and I wanted to give them something in return.

When I took the robe off and moved in on the bar fighter, there was Don and Betty and Jason to think of too. They were just making expenses, nothing more. I could not bear to think of letting them down. I did not know what my parents wanted from me, but I did know what Don and Jason and Betty wanted, so that made it easier, and after a while it became easier to pretend that it was all the same, that everyone wanted the same thing, and all I had to do was go out there and fight.

Don had been a chemist once for the coroner's lab in Jackson. He knew about chemicals, drugs. He knew how to dope my blood, days before a fight, so I would feel clean and strong, a new man. He knew how to give me smelling salts, sniffs of ammonia vials broken under my nose when I was fighting sloppily, sniffs that made my eyes water and my nose and lungs burn, but it focused me. And even in training, Don would sometimes feint and spar without gloves and catch me off guard, going one way when I should have been going the other. He would slip in and clasp a chloroform handkerchief over my face. I'd see a mixed field of black and sparkling, night-rushing stars, and then I'd be down, collapsed in the pine needles by the lake where we did our sparring. I'd feel a delicious sense of rest, lying there, and I'd want to stay down forever, but I'd hear Don shouting, "...Three! Four! Five!" and I'd have to roll over, get my feet beneath me, and rise, stagger-kneed, the lake a hard glimmer of heat all around me. Don would be dancing around me like a demon, moving in and slapping me with that tremendous reach of his and then dancing back. I had to get my gloves up and stay up, had to follow the blur of him with that backdrop of deep woods and lake, with everything looking new and different suddenly, making no sense; and that, Don said, was what it was like to get knocked out. He wanted me to practice it occasionally, so I would know what to do when it finally happened, in New York, or Philadelphia, or even in a bar.

My body hair was shaved before each fight. I'd sit on a chair by the lake in my shorts while the three of them, with razors and buckets of soapy water, shaved my legs, back, chest, and arms so the blows would slide away from me rather than cut in, and so I would move faster, or at least *feel* faster—that new feeling, the feeling of being someone else, newer, younger, and with a fresher start.

When they had me all shaved, I would walk out on the dock and dive into the lake, plunging deep, ripping the water with my new slipperiness. I would swim a few easy strokes out to the middle, where I would tread water, feeling how unbelievably smooth I was, how free and unattached, and then I would swim back in. Some days, walking with Don and Betty and Jason back to the house, my hair slicked back and dripping, with the woods smelling good in the summer and the pine needles dry and warm beneath my bare feet—some days, then, with the lake behind me, and feeling changed, I could almost tell what it was that everyone wanted, which was nothing, and I was very happy.

After our bar fights, we'd get home around two or three in the morning. I'd nap on the way, in the rocker in the back of the truck, rocking slightly, pleasantly, whenever we hit a bump. Between bumps I would half dream, with my robe wrapped around me and the wind whipping my hair, relaxed dreams, cleansed dreams—but whenever I woke up and looked at Don, he would be awake.

He'd be looking back at where we'd come from, the stars spread out behind us, the trees sliding behind our taillights, filling in behind us as if sealing off the road. Jason would be driving like a bat out of hell, and coffee cups and gum wrappers swirled around in the truck's cab.

Sometimes Don turned his chair around to face the cab, looking in over Jason's shoulder and watching him drive, watching his wife sleep. Don had been a good boxer but the headaches and double vision had gotten too bad. I wondered what it would take for me to stop. I could not imagine anything would. It was the only thing I could do well.

On the long, narrow gravel road leading to Don's farm, with the smell of honeysuckle and the calls of chuck-will's-widows, Jason slowed the truck and drove carefully, respecting the value of home and the sanctity of the place. At the crest of the hill he turned the engine and lights off and coasted the rest of the way to the house, pumping the squeaky brakes, and in silence we'd glide down the hill. From here the dogs could smell the lake. They scrambled to their feet, leapt over the sides of the truck, and raced to the water to inspect it and hunt for frogs.

I slept in a little bunkhouse by the lake, a guest cottage they had built for their boxers. Their own place was up on the hill. It had a picnic table out front and a garage—it was a regular-looking house, a cabin. But I liked my cottage. I didn't even have a phone. I had stopped telling my parents about the fights. There was not much else to tell them about other than the fights, but I tried to think of things that might interest them. Nights, after Don and Betty and Jason had gone to bed, I liked to swim to the middle of the lake, and with the moon burning bright above me, almost like a sun, I'd float on my back and fill my lungs with air. I'd float there for a long time.

The dogs swam around me, loyal and panting, paddling in frantic but determined circles, sneezing water. I could feel the changing currents beneath and around me as the dogs stirred the water, and could see the wakes they made, glistening beneath the moon—oily-black and mint-white swirls. I loved the way they stayed with me, not knowing how to float and instead always paddling. I felt like I was their father or mother. I felt strangely like an old man, but with a young man's health.

I'd float like that until I felt ready again, until I felt as if I'd never won a fight in my life—in fact, as if I'd never even fought one, as if it was all new and I was just starting out and had everything still to prove. I floated there until I believed that that was how it really was.

I was free then, and I would break for shore, swimming again in long, slow strokes. I'd get out and walk through the trees to my cottage with the dogs following, shaking water from their coats and rattling their collars, and I knew the air felt as cool on them as it did on me. We couldn't see the stars, down in the trees like that, and it felt very safe.

I'd walk through the woods, born again in my love for a thing, the hard passion of it, and I'd snap on my yellow porch light as I went into the cottage. The light seemed to pull in every moth in the county. Homer and Ann would stand on their hind legs and dance, snapping at the moths. Down at the lake the bullfrogs drummed all night, and from the woods came the sound of crickets and katydids. The noise was like that at a baseball game on a hot day, always some insistent noises above others, rising and falling. I could hear the dogs crunching June bugs as they caught them.

Just before daylight, Betty would ring a bell to wake me for breakfast. Don and I ate at the picnic table, a light breakfast, because we were about to run, me on foot and Don on horseback.

"You'll miss me when you get up to New York," he said. "They'll lock you in a gym and work on your technique. You'll never see the light of day. But you'll have to do it."

I did not want to leave Betty and Jason, did not even want to leave Don, despite the tough training sessions. It would be fun to fight in a real ring, with paying spectators, a canvas mat, a referee, and ropes, safety ropes to hold you in. I would not mind leaving the bar fights behind at all, but I could not tell Don about my fears. I was half horrified that a hundred wins in Mississippi would mean nothing, and that I would be unable to win even one fight in New York.

Don said I was "a fighter, not a boxer."

He'd had other fighters who had gone on to New York, who had done well, who had won many fights. One of them, his best before me, Pig-Eye Reeves, had been ranked as high as fifth as a WBA heavyweight. Pig-Eye was a legend, and everywhere in Mississippi tales were told about him. Don knew all of them.

Pig-Eye had swum in the lake I swam in, ate at the same picnic table, lived in my cottage. Pig-Eye had run the trails I ran daily, the ones Don chased me down, riding his big black stallion, Killer, and cracking his bullwhip.

That was how we trained. After breakfast Don headed for the barn to saddle Killer, and I whistled the dogs up and started down toward the lake. The sun would be coming up on the other side of the woods, burning steam off the lake, and the air slowly got clearer. I could pick out individual trees through the mist on the far side. I'd be walking, feeling good and healthy, at least briefly, as if I would never let anyone down. Then I would hear the horse running down the hill through the trees, coming after me, snorting, and I'd hear his hooves and the saddle creaking, with Don riding silently, posting. When he spotted me, he'd crack the whip once—that short, mean *pop!*—and I would have to run.

Don made me wear leg weights and wrist weights. The dogs, running beside me, thought it was a game. It was not. For punishment, when I didn't run fast enough and Killer got too close to me, Don caught my shoulder with the tip of the whip. It cut a small strip into my sweaty back, which I could feel in the form of heat. I knew this meant nothing, because he was only doing it to protect me, to make me run faster, to keep me from being trampled by the horse.

Don wore spurs, big Mexican rowels he'd bought in an antiques store, and he rode Killer hard. I left the trail sometimes, jumping over logs and dodging around trees and reversing my direction, but Killer stayed with me, leaping the same logs, galloping through the same brush, though I was better at turning corners and could stay ahead of him that way.

This would go on for an hour or so, until the sun was over the trees and the sky bright and warm. When Don figured the horse was getting too tired, too bloody from the spurs, he would shout "Swim!" and that meant it was over, and I could go into the lake.

"The Lake of Peace!" Don roared, snapping the whip and spurring Killer, and the dogs and I splashed out into the shallows. I ran awkwardly, high-stepping the way you do going into the waves at the beach. I leaned forward and dropped into the warm water, felt the weeds brushing my knees. Killer was right behind us, still coming, but we would be swimming hard, the dogs whining and rolling their eyes back like Chinese dragons, paddling furiously, trying to see behind them. By now Killer was swimming too, blowing hard through his nostrils and grunting, much too close to us, trying to swim right over the top of us, but the dogs stayed with me, as if they thought they could protect me, and with the leg weights trying to weigh me down and pull me under, I'd near the deepest part of the lake, where the water turned cold.

I swam to the dark cold center, and that was where the horse, frightened, slowed down, panicking at the water's coldness and swimming in circles rather than pushing on. The chase was forgotten then, but the dogs and I kept swimming, with the other side of the lake drawing closer at last, and Jason and Betty standing on the shore, jumping and cheering. The water began to get shallow again, and I came crawling out of the lake. Betty handed me a towel, Jason dried off the dogs, and then we walked up the hill to the cabin for lunch, which was spread out on a checkered tablecloth and waiting for me as if there had never been any doubt that I would make it.

Don would still be laboring in the water, shouting and cursing at the horse now, cracking the whip and giving him muted, underwater jabs with his spurs, trying to rein Killer out of the angry, confused circles he was still swimming, until finally, with his last breath, Killer recognized that the far shore was as good as the near one, and they'd make it in, struggling, twenty or thirty minutes behind the dogs and me.

Killer would lie on his side, gasping, coughing up weeds, ribs rising and falling, and Don would come up the hill to join us for lunch: fried chicken, cream gravy, hot biscuits with honey, string beans from the garden, great wet chunks of watermelon, and a pitcher of iced tea for each of us. We ate shirtless, barefoot, and threw the rinds to the dogs, who wrestled and fought over them like wolves.

At straight-up noon, the sun would press down through the trees, glinting off the Lake of Peace. We'd change into bathing suits, all of us, and inflate air mattresses and carry them down to the lake. We'd wade in up to our chests and float in the sun, our arms trailing in the water. We'd nap as if stunned after the heavy meal, while the dogs whined and paced the shore, afraid we might not come back.

Killer, lying on the shore, would stare glassy-eyed at nothing, ribs still heaving. He would stay like that until mid-afternoon, when he would finally roll over and get to his feet, and then he would trot up the hill as if nothing had happened.

We drifted all over the lake in our half stupor, our sated summer-day sleep. My parents wanted me to come home and take over the hardware store. But there was nothing in the world that could make me stop fighting. I wished there was, because I liked the store, but that was simply how it was. I felt that if I could not fight, I might stop breathing, or I might go down: I imagined that it was like drowning, like floating in the lake, and then exhaling all my air, and sinking, and never being heard from again. I could not see myself ever giving up fighting, and I wondered how Don had done it.

We floated and lazed, dreaming, each of us spinning in different directions whenever a small breeze blew, eventually drifting farther and farther apart, but on the shore the dogs followed only me, tracking me around the lake, staying with me, whining for me to come back to shore.

On these afternoons, following an especially good run and an exhausting swim, I would be unable to lift my arms. Nothing mattered in those suspended, floating times. This is how I can give up, I'd think. This is how I can never fight again. I can drop out, raise a family, and float in the bright sun all day, on the Lake of Peace. This is how I can do it, I'd think. Perhaps my son could be a boxer.

Fights eighty-nine, ninety, ninety-one: I tore a guy's jaw off in the Body Shop. I felt it give way and then detach, heard the ripping sound as if it came from somewhere else, and it was sickening—we left without any of the betting money, gave it all to his family for the hospital bill, but it certainly did not stop me from fighting, or even from hitting hard. I was very angry about something, but did not know what. I'd sit in the back of the truck on the rides home, and I'd know I wanted something, but did not know what.

Sometimes Don had to lean forward and massage his temples, his head hurt so bad. He ate handfuls of aspirin, ate them like M&M's, chasing them down with beer. I panicked when he did that, and thought he was dying. I wondered if that was where my anger came from, if I fought so wildly and viciously in an attempt, somehow and with no logic, to keep things from changing.

On the nights we didn't have a fight, we would spar a little in the barn. Killer watched us wild-eyed from his stall, waiting to get to me. Don made me throw a bucket of lake water on him each time I went into the barn, to make sure that his hate for me did not wane. Killer screamed whenever I did this, and Jason howled and blew into a noise-maker and banged two garbage can lids together, a deafening sound inside the barn. Killer screamed and reared on his hind legs and tried to break free. After sparring we went into the house, and Betty fixed us supper.

We had grilled corn from Betty's garden and a huge porterhouse steak from a steer Don had slaughtered, and lima beans and Irish potatoes, also from the garden. It felt like I was family. We ate at the picnic table as fog moved in from the woods, making the lake steamy. It was as if everyone could see what I was thinking then; my thoughts were bare and exposed, but it didn't matter, because

Don and Betty and Jason cared for me, and also because I was not going to fail.

After dinner we watched old fight films. For a screen we used a bedsheet strung between two pine trees. Don set up the projector on the picnic table and used a crooked branch for a pointer. Some of the films were of past champions, but some were old movies of Don fighting. He could make the film go in slow motion, to show the combinations that led to knockdowns, and Betty always got up and left whenever we watched one of the old splintery films of Don's fights. It wasn't any fun for her, even though she knew he was going to win, or was going to get up again after going down.

I had seen all of Don's fights a hundred times and had watched all the films of the greatest fighters a thousand times, and I was bored with it. Fighting is not films, it's experience. I knew what to do and when to do it. I'd look past the bedsheet, past the flickering washes of light, while Jason and Don leaned forward, breathless, watching young Don stalk his victim, everything silent except for the clicking of the projector, the crickets, the frogs, and sometimes the owls. In the dark I wondered what New York was going to be like, if it was going to be anything like this.

Some nights, after the movies had ended, we would talk about Pig-Eye Reeves. It had been several years ago, but even Jason remembered him. We were so familiar with the stories that it seemed to all of us—even to me, who had never met him—that we remembered him clearly.

Pig-Eye knocked out one of the fighters Don had trained, in a bar up in the Delta one night, the Green Frog. That was how Don found Pig-Eye—he had beaten Don's challenger, had just stepped up out of the crowd. Don's fighter, whose name Don always pretended he couldn't remember, threw the first punch, a wicked, winging right, not even bothering to set it up with a jab—Don says he covered his face with his hands and groaned, knowing what was going to happen. Pig-Eye, full of beer, was still able to duck it, evidently, because Don heard nothing but the rip of air and then, a little delayed, the sound of another glove hitting a nose, then a grunt, and the sound of a body falling in the sawdust.

Don and Jason and Betty left the semiconscious fighter there in the Green Frog, with a broken nose and blood all over his chest and trunks. They drove home with no money and Pig-Eye.

They changed the number on the truck mirror from whatever it had been before—forty-five or fifty—back to one. Pig-Eye had won one fight.

"You just left your other fighter sitting there?" I asked the first time I heard the story, though I knew better than to ask now.

Don had seemed confused by the question. "He wasn't my fighter anymore," he said finally.

Sometimes Jason would ask the question for me, so I didn't have to, and I could pretend it didn't matter, as if I weren't even thinking about it.

"Is Mack a better fighter than Pig-Eye?" he'd ask after watching the movies.

Don answered like a trainer every time. He was wonderful, the best. "Mack is better than Pig-Eye ever dreamed of being," he'd say, clapping a big hand on my neck and giving it the death squeeze, his hand the size of a license plate.

"Tell him about the balloon," Jason would cry when Don had reached a fever pitch for Pig-Eye stories.

Don leaned back against a tree and smiled at his son. The lights were off in the house. Betty had gone to bed. Moths fluttered around the porch light, and down below us in the Lake of Peace, bullfrogs drummed. There was no other sound.

"Pig-Eye won his last five fights down here with one hand tied behind his back," Don said, closing his eyes. I wondered if I could do that, wondered if I'd *have* to do that, to ride down the legend of Pig-Eye, and pass over it.

"We sent him up to New York, to a promoter I knew"—Don looked at me quickly—"the same one we'll be sending Mack to if he wins the rest of his fights. This promoter, Big Al Wilson, set him up in a penthouse in Manhattan, had all Pig-Eye's meals catered to him. He had masseurs, everything. He was the *champ*. Everyone was excited about him."

"Tell him about the scars," Jason said. He moved next to his dad, so that his back was against the same tree, and it was as if they were both telling me the story now, though I knew it already, we all knew it.

"Pig-Eye had all these scars from his bar fights," Don said. "He'd been in Vietnam too, and had got wounded there. He flew those crazy hot-air balloons for a hobby, once he started winning some fights and making some money, and he was always having rough landings, always crashing the balloons and getting cut up that way."

"Helium balloons," Jason said.

"It was a very disturbing thing to Pig-Eye's opponents when he first stepped in the ring against them. They'd all heard about him, but he really had to be seen to be believed."

"Like a zipper," Jason said sleepily, but delighted. "He looked like a zipper. I remember."

"Pig-Eye won fourteen fights in New York. He was ranked fifth and was fighting well. I went to a few of his fights, but then he changed."

"He got different," Jason cautioned.

"He stopped calling, stopped writing, and he started getting a little fat, a little slow. No one else could tell it, but I could."

"He needed Dad for a trainer," said Jason. In the distance I heard Killer nicker in his stall.

"He lost," Don said, shaking his head. "He was fighting a nobody, some kid from Japan, and that night he just didn't have it. He got knocked down three times. I saw tapes of it later. He was sitting up like one of those bears in a zoo, still trying to get on his feet for a third time, but he couldn't do it. It was like he didn't know where his legs were, didn't know what his feet were for. He couldn't remember how to do it."

I thought about the ammonia and the chloroform handkerchiefs Don would sometimes place over my face when we were sparring. I wondered if every time he did that to me, he was remembering how Pig-Eye couldn't stand up—how he had forgotten how to get back up. I thought that I surely knew how Pig-Eye had felt.

"The balloon," Jason said. There was a wind in the trees, many nights, and so often those winds reminded me of that strange feeling of being both old and young, someplace in the middle, and for the first time, with no turning back.

"The balloon," Jason said again, punching his father on the shoulder. "This is the best part."

"Pig-Eye was crushed," Don said, sleepy, detached, as if it were no longer Pig-Eye he was talking about. I thought again of how they had walked off and left that other fighter up in the Delta, the nameless one, sitting in the sawdust holding his broken nose. "It was the only time Pig-Eye had ever been knocked out, the only time he'd ever lost, and it devastated him."

"A hundred and fifteen fights," Jason said, "and he'd only lost one."

"But it was my fault," Don said. "It was how I trained him. It was wrong."

"The balloon," Jason said.

"He rented one," Don said, looking up at the stars, speaking to the night. "He went out over the countryside the next day, his face all bandaged up, with a bottle of wine and his girlfriend, and then he took it up as high as it could go, and then he cut the strings to the gondola."

"He was good," Jason said solemnly.

"He was too good," Don said.

All that summer I trained hard for New York. I knew I would win my hundred fights. I knew I could win them with one arm tied behind my back, either arm, if Don and Jason wanted that. But I wasn't worried about my one hundred bar fights. I was worried about going up to New York, to a strange place, someplace different. Sometimes I did not want to fight anymore, but I never let anyone see that.

Jason was getting older, filling out, and sometimes Don let him ride Killer. We'd all have breakfast as usual, then Jason would saddle Killer. I'd wake the dogs and we'd start down toward the lake, moving lazily through the trees but knowing that in a minute or two we'd be running.

Don would sit in a chair by the shore and follow us with his binoculars. He had a whistle he'd blow to warn me when I was about to be trampled.

When the dogs and I heard the horse, the hard, fast hooves coming straight down the hill, we'd start to run. It would be almost six o'clock then. The sun would just be coming up, and we'd see things as we raced through the woods: deer slipping back into the trees, cottontails diving into the brush. The dogs would break off and chase all of these things, and sometimes they'd rejoin me later on the other side of the lake with a rabbit hanging from their jaws. They'd fight over it, really wrestling and growling.

All of this would be going past at what seemed like ninety miles an hour: trees, vines, logs; greens, browns, blacks, and blues—flashes of the lake, flashes of sky, flashes of logs on the trail. I knew the course well, knew when to jump, when to dodge. It's said that a healthy man can outrun a horse, over enough distance, but that first mile was the hardest, all that dodging.

Jason shouted, imitating his father, cracking the whip; the sun rose orange over the tops of the trees, the start of another day of perfection. And then the cry, "The Lake of Peace!" And it would be over, and I'd rush out into the shallows, a dog on either side of me, tripping and falling, the lake at my ankles, at my knees, coming up around my waist, and we'd be swimming, with Killer plunging in after us, and Jason still cracking the whip.

Actually, there were two stories about Pig-Eye Reeves. I was the only person Don told about the second one. I did not know which one was true.

In the other story, Pig-Eye recovered, survived. Still distraught over losing, he went south, tried to go back to Don, to start all over again. But Don had already taken on another fighter and would not train Pig-Eye anymore.

Don rubs his temples when he tells me this. He is not sure if this is how it went or not.

So Pig-Eye despaired even more and began drinking bottles of wine, sitting out on the dock and drinking them down the way a thirsty man might drink water. He drank far into the night, singing at the top of his lungs. Don and Betty had to put pillows over their heads to get to sleep, after first locking the doors.

Then Don woke up around midnight—he never could sleep through the night—and he heard splashing. He went outside and saw that Pig-Eye had on his wrist and ankle weights and was swimming out to the middle of the lake.

Don said he could see Pig-Eye's wake, could see Pig-Eye at the end of it, stretching it out, splitting the lake in two—and then he disappeared. The lake became smooth again.

Don said that he sleepwalked, and thought perhaps what he'd seen wasn't real. They had the sheriff's department come out and drag the lake, but the body was never found. Perhaps he was still down there, and would be forever.

Sometimes, as Jason and the horse chased me across the lake, I would think about a game I used to play as a child, in the small town in Oklahoma where I grew up.

When I was in the municipal swimming pool, I would hold my breath, pinch my nose, duck under the water, and shove off from the pale blue side of the pool. Like a frog breast-stroking, eyes wide and reddening from the chlorine, I would try to make it all the way to the other side without having to come up for air.

That was the trick, to get all the way to the other side. Halfway across, as the water deepened, there'd be a pounding in the back of my head, and a sinister whine in my ears, my heart and throat clenching.

I thought about that game, as I swam with Jason and Killer close behind me. I seemed to remember my dogs being with me then, swimming in front of me, as if trying to show me the way, half pulling me across. But it was not that way at all, because this was many years before their time. I knew nothing then about dogs, or boxing, or living, or of trying to hold on to a thing you loved, and letting go of other things to do it.

I only understood what it was like to swim through deeper and deeper water, trying as hard as I could to keep from losing my breath, and trying, still, to make it to the deep end.

The History of Rodney

It rains in Rodney in the winter. But we have history; even for Mississippi, we have that. Out front there's a sweet olive tree that grows all the way up to the third story, where Elizabeth's sun porch is. Through the summer, butterflies swarm in the front yard, drunk on the smell of the tree. But in the winter it rains.

The other people in the town of Rodney are the daughters, sons, and granddaughters of slaves. Sixteen thousand people lived in Rodney before and during the Civil War. Now there are a dozen of us.

This old house I rent costs fifty dollars a month. Electricity sizzles and arcs from the fuse box on the back porch and tumbles to the ground in bouncing blue sparks. The house has thirty-five rooms, some of which are rotting—one has a tree growing through the floor—and the ceilings are all high, though not as high as the trees outside.

Here in the ghost town of Rodney there is a pig, a murderer, that lives under my house, and she has killed several dogs. The pig had twenty piglets this winter, and like the bad toughs in a western, they own the town. When we hear or see them coming, we run. We could shoot them down in the middle of the dusty lane that used to be a street, but we don't: we're waiting for them to fatten up on their mother's milk.

We're also waiting for Preacher to come back. He's Daisy's boyfriend, and he's been gone for forty years.

Back in the trees, loose peafowl scream in the night. It is like the jungle out there. The river that used to run past Rodney—the

Mississippi, almost a mile wide—shifted course exactly one hundred years ago.

It happened overnight. The earthen bulge of an oxbow, a bend upstream, was torn by the force of the water. Instead of making its taken-for-granted way through the swamp—the slow wind of northern water down from Minnesota—the river pressed, like sex, and broke through.

I've been reading about this in the old newspapers. And Daisy, who lives across the street, has been telling me about it. She says that the first day after it happened, the townspeople could do nothing but blink and gape at the wide sea of mud. Rodney then was the second-largest port in the South, second only to New Orleans.

Boats full of cotton were stranded in the flats. Alligators and snakes wriggled in the deep brown as the townspeople waited for a rain to come and fill the big river back up. Giant turtles crept through the mud and moved on, but the great fish could do nothing but die. Anchors and massive logs lay strewn on the river bottom. Birds gathered overhead and circled the dying fish, then landed in the fetid mud. When the fish began to smell bad, the people in Rodney packed what belongings they could and hiked into the bluffs and jungle above the river to escape the rot and disease.

When the mud had dried and grown over with lush tall grass, the townspeople moved back. Some of the men tracked the river, hunting it as if it were a wounded animal, and they found it seven miles away, running big and strong, as wide as it had ever been. It was flowing like a person's heart. It had only shifted.

Daisy didn't see the river leave, but her mother did. Daisy says that the pigs in Rodney are descended from Union soldiers. The townspeople marched the soldiers into the Presbyterian church one Sunday, boarded up the doors and windows, and then Daisy's mother turned them all into pigs.

The mother pig is the size of a small Volkswagen; her babies are the color and shape of footballs. They grunt and snort at night beneath Elizabeth's and my house.

Daisy has a TV antenna rising a hundred and fifty feet into the air, above the trees. Daisy can cure thrash, tuberculosis, snakebite, ulcers, anything as long as it does not affect someone she loves. She's powerless then; she told me so. She cooks sometimes for Elizabeth and me. We buy the food and give her some money and she cooks: fried eggs, chicken, okra. Sometimes Elizabeth isn't hungry—she'll be lying on the bed up in the sun room, wearing just her underpants and sunglasses, reading a book—so I'll go over to Daisy's by myself.

We live so far from civilization. The mail comes only once a week, from Natchez. The mailman is frightened of the pigs. Sometimes they chase his jeep up the steep hill, up the gravel road that leads out of town. Their squeals of rage are a high, mad sound, and they run out of breath easily.

Daisy never gets mail. We let her come over and read ours.

"This used to be a big town," she said when she came over to introduce herself. She gestured out to the cotton field behind her house. "A port town. The river used to lay right out there."

"Why did it leave?" Elizabeth asked.

Daisy shook her head and wouldn't answer.

"Will you take us to the river?" I asked. "Will you show it to us?"

Daisy shook her head again. "Nope," she said, drawing circles in the dust with her toe. "You got to be in *love* to see the river," she said, looking at me and then at Elizabeth.

"Oh, but we are," Elizabeth cried, taking my arm. "That's why we're here!"

"Well," Daisy said. "Maybe."

Daisy likes to tell us about Preacher; she talks about him all the time. He was twenty, she was nineteen. Once there was a Confederate gunboat in the cotton field. The boat has since rusted away to nothing, but it was still in fair shape when Preacher and Daisy lived on it, out in the middle of the field, still rich and growing green with cotton, the color of which is heat-hazy in the fall. They slept in the captain's quarters on a striped mattress with no sheets. They rubbed vanilla on their bodies to keep the bugs from biting.

There were skeletons in the boat and in the field, skeletons of sailors who had drowned when the ship burned and sank from cannon fire to the bow. But these were old bones and no more harmful than, say, a cow's skull, or a horse's.

She and Preacher made love on the tilted deck, Daisy said, through the blazing afternoons. Small breezes cooled them. They made love at night, too, with coal-oil lamps burning around the gunwales. Their cries were so loud, she said, that birds roosting in the swamp took flight into the darkness and circled overhead.

"All we were going to do was live out on that boat and make love mostly all day," she said. "Preacher wasn't hurtin' anybody. We had a garden, and we went fishing. We skimmed the river in our wood canoe. One day he caught a porpoise. It had come all the way up from the Gulf after a rainstorm and was confused by the fresh water. It pulled us all over the river for a whole afternoon."

A whole afternoon. I could see the porpoise leaping, and I could see Daisy as she was then, with a straw hat low around her brow. I could see Preacher leaning forward, battling the big fish.

"It got away," Daisy said. "It broke the line." She was sitting on the porch, shelling peas from her garden, remembering. "Oh, we both cried," she said. "Oh, we wanted that fish."

Elizabeth and I live here quietly, smoothing things over, making the country tame again; but it is like walking on ice. Sometimes I imagine I can hear echoes, noises and sounds from a long time ago.

"This place isn't on the map, right?" Elizabeth will ask. It's a game we play. We're frightened of cities, of other people.

"It might as well not even exist," I'll tell her.

She seems reassured.

The seasons mix and swirl. Except for the winter rains and the brutality of August, it's easy to confuse one season with the next. Sometimes wild turkeys gobble and fan in the dust of the road, courting. Their lusty gobbles awaken us at daylight—a watery, rushing sound. That means it is April, and the floodwaters will not be coming back. Every sight, every small scent and sound, lies still, its own thing, as if there are no seasons. As if there is only one season.

I'm glad Elizabeth and I have found this place. We have not done well in other places. Cities—we can't understand them. In a city everything seems as though it is over so fast: minutes, hours, days, lives.

Daisy keeps her yard very neat; she cuts it with the push mower weekly. Tulips and roses line the edges of it. She's got two little beagle pups, and they roll and wrestle in the front yard and on her porch. Daisy conducts church services in the abandoned Mount Zion Baptist Church, and sometimes we go. Daisy's a good preacher. The church used to be on the river bank, but now it looks out on a cotton field.

Daisy's sister, Maggie, lives in Rodney too. She used to have a crush on Preacher when he was a little boy. She says he used to sleep, curled up in a blanket, in a big empty cardboard box at the top of a long playground slide in front of the church. The slide is still there, beneath some pecan trees. It's a magnificent slide, the kind you find in big city parks. Mostly wood, it's tall and steep, rubbed shiny and smooth. It's got a little cabin or booth at the top, and that's where Preacher used to sleep, Maggie says. He didn't have any parents.

The cabin kept the rain off. Sometimes the two girls sat up there with him and played cards. They'd take turns sliding down in the cardboard box, and they'd watch as white chickens walked past, pecking at the dust and clucking.

"Maybe he always wanted one for a pet," Maggie says, trying to figure it out.

Daisy says they can put you away in Whitfield for forty years for being a chicken chaser. That was what the social workers saw when they happened to pass through Rodney once: Preacher chasing chickens down the street like a crazy man. He was just doing it for fun—well, he might have been a little hungry, Daisy owns up—but they took him away.

Daisy says she's been keeping track on her calendars. There are old ones tacked to every wall in her house, beginning with the year they hauled Preacher away. The forty years will be up this fall. She expects he'll be back after that; he'll be coming back any day.

Forty years—all for maybe what was just a mistake. Maybe he only wanted one for a pet.

✿   ✿   ✿

Toward dark the mother pig lures dogs into the swamp. She runs down the middle of what used to be Main Street in a funny high-backed hobble, as if she's wounded, with all the little runt piglets running ahead of her, protected. A foolish dog follows, slavering at the thought of fresh and easy meat.

When the pig reaches the woods, she disappears into the heavy leafiness and undergrowth, and the dog goes in after her. Then we hear the squalls and yelps of the dog being killed.

The sow sometimes kills dogs in the middle of the day. She simply tramples them, the way a horse would. I'd say she weighs about six or seven hundred pounds, maybe more. Elizabeth carries a rifle when we go for our walks, an old seven-millimeter Mauser, slung over her shoulder on a sling, a relic from the First World War, which never affected Rodney. If that pig charged us, it would rue the day. Elizabeth is a crack shot.

"Are the pigs really cursed people?" Elizabeth asks one evening. We're over on Daisy's porch. Maggie is there too, shelling peas. Fireflies are blinking, floating out in the field as if searching with lanterns for something.

"Oh my, yes," Maggie says. "That big one is a general."

"I want to see the river," Elizabeth says for the one hundredth time, and Daisy and Maggie laugh.

Daisy leans forward and jabs Elizabeth's leg. "How you know there even *is* a river?" she asks. "How you know we're not foolin' you?"

"I can smell it," Elizabeth says. She places her hand over her heart and closes her eyes. "I can *feel* it."

Elizabeth and I put fireflies in empty mayonnaise jars, screw the lids on tight, and punch holes in the tops. We decorate our porch with them at night, or we line the bed with them, and then laugh as we love, with their blinking green bellies going on and off like soft, harmless firecrackers, as if they are applauding. It's as though we have become Preacher and Daisy. The firefly bottle-lights seem like the coal-oil lamps that lined the sides of their boat in the field. Sometimes we, too, shout out into the night.

The bed: buying it for this old house is one of the best things we've ever done. It's huge, a four-poster, and looks as if it came straight off the set of *The Bride of Frankenstein*. It has a lace canopy and is sturdy enough to weather our shaking. We have to climb three wooden steps to get into it, and sleeping in it is like going off on some final voyage, so deep is our slumber, so quiet are the woods around us and what is left of the town. The birds will not scream until further into the night, so they are part of our dreams, but comforting. Nothing troubles our sleep, nothing.

Before falling into that exhausted, peaceful sleep, I slip over to the window and unscrew the lids of the jars, releasing the groggy, oxygen-deprived fireflies into the fresh night air. I shake each bottle to make sure I get them all out. They float feebly down into the bushes, blinking. Wounded paratroopers, they return to their world, looking for something, searching for the world they own and know. If you keep them in a bottle too long, they won't blink anymore.

Elizabeth loves to read. She has books stacked on all the shelves in her sun room, and in all corners, books rise stacked to the ceiling. Sometimes I take iced tea up to her in a pitcher, with lemons and sugar. I don't go in with it; I just peek through the keyhole. When she's not near naked from the heat, she sometimes puts on a white dress with lace as she reads. Her hair's dark, but there by the window it looks washed with light, and she becomes someone entirely different. She disappears when she goes into those books. She disappears and that strange, solitary light seals and bathes her escape. I knock on the door to let her know the iced tea is ready whenever she feels like getting it. Then I go back down the stairs.

After a while I hear the click of the door and the scrape of the tray as she picks it up and carries it to her table. She shuts the door with the back of her foot, or so I imagine, before she goes back to reading, holding the book in one hand while fanning herself with a cardboard fan in the other hand. I'll go out and sit on the front steps and picture her drinking the tea, and think that I can taste its coolness and freshness.

In summer, even beneath the sweet olive tree, I sweat, but not the way she does in the oven of her upstairs room. There's no air conditioner, no ceiling fan, and late in the afternoon each day, when she takes off the white lacy dress, it is soaking wet. She rinses it out in the sink and hangs it on the porch to dry in the night breezes. The dress smells of sweet olive the next morning.

"We were going to have a baby," Daisy says. "We were just about ready to start when they took him away. We were going to start that week so the baby would be born in the summer."

The slow summer. The time when nothing moves forward, when everything pauses, and then stops. It's a good idea.

In August men come from all over this part of the state to pick cotton. The men pick by hand. They do not leave much behind. It's like a circus. Old white horses appear—perhaps they belong to the pickers, though perhaps they come from somewhere deep in the woods—and they stand out in the cotton and watch. Behind them, red tractor-trailers rise against blue sky, and behind them, the trees. Behind that is the river, which we cannot see but have been told is there.

Then the men are gone, almost all of the cotton is gone, and there are leaves on the roofs of the houses, leaves in our yards. They're brown and dried up and curled, and the street is covered with them like a carpet. The sweet olive tree doesn't lose its leaves, but the other trees do. You can hear the pigs rustling in the leaves at night, snuffling for acorns. In the daytime you can hear Daisy moving through them, her slow, heavy steps and the crunching of those leaves. Daisy and Maggie burn their leaves in wire baskets by the side of the old road.

Something about the fall makes us want to go to Daisy's church services. They last about thirty minutes, and mostly she recites Bible verses, sometimes making a few up, but they sound right. Then she sings for a while. She's got a good voice.

We sing too. In the early fall when everything is changing, the air takes on a stillness, and we feel like singing to liven things up.

They're old slave songs that Daisy sings, and you just hum and sway. You can close your eyes and forget about leaving the town of Rodney.

❖   ❖   ❖

The owl calls at night. He's big and lives in our attic. There's a hole in the bedroom ceiling, and we can hear him scrabbling around at ten or eleven o'clock each night. When the moon gets full, it lights the rooms, and the owl emerges from the trees, flies through one of our open windows. We hear him claw-scratch out to the banister, and with a grunt he launches himself. We hear the flapping of wings and then silence. He makes no sound as he flies.

He zooms through the house—third floor, second floor, first— looking for mice. He shrieks when he spots one. He nearly always catches them.

We have watched him from the corner in the big kitchen. Elizabeth was frightened at first, but she isn't now. The longer we live down here, the less frightened she is of anything. She is growing braver with age, as if bravery is a thing she will be needing more of.

Elizabeth and I want to build something that won't go away. We're not sure how to go about it, but some nights we run naked in the moonlight. We catch the old white plugs, the horses, as they wander loose in the cotton fields. We ride them across the fields toward where we think the river is, riding through the fog amid the tracings of the fireflies. But when we get down into the swamp, we get turned around, lost, and we have to turn back.

Daisy's standing out on her porch sometimes when we come galloping back. "You can't go to it," she says, laughing in the night. "It's got to come to you!"

Afternoons, in the fall, we pick up pecans in front of the old church. We fix grilled cheese sandwiches for supper and share a bottle of wine. We sit on the porch in the frayed wicker swing and watch the moon crest the trees, watch it slide across and over the sky, and we can hear Maggie down the street, humming, weeding in her garden.

One night I awaken from sleep and Elizabeth isn't in bed with me. I look all over the house for her, and a slight, illogical panic grows as I move through each empty room.

The moon is up and everything is bathed in hard silver. She is sitting on the back porch in her white dress, which is still damp from the wash. She's barefoot, with her feet hanging over the edge. She's swinging them back and forth. In the yard the pigs are feeding, the huge mother and the little ones, small dirigibles now, all around her. There's a warm wind blowing from the south. I can taste the salt in it from the coast. Elizabeth has a book in her lap; she's reading by the light of the moon.

A dog barks a long way off, and I feel that I should not be watching. So I climb back up the stairs and get into the big bed and try to sleep.

But I want to hold on to something.

Luther, an old blind man who lived down the street, and whom we hardly ever saw, has passed on. Elizabeth and I are the only ones with backs strong enough to dig the grave; we bury him in the cemetery on the bluff. There are toppled gravestones from the 1850s, gravestones from the war with C.S.A. cut in the stone. Some of the people buried there were named Emancipation—it was a common name then.

We dig the hole without much trouble. It's soft, rich earth. Daisy says words as we fill the hole back up. That rain of earth, shovels of it, covering the box with him in it. I had to build the coffin out of old lumber. Sometimes in the spring, and in the fall too, rattlesnakes come out of the cane and lie on the flat gravestones for warmth. Because of the snakes, hardly anyone goes to the cemetery now.

A few years ago one of Daisy and Maggie's half sisters died and they buried her up here. Her grave has since grown over with brambles and vines. Now there is the skeleton of a deer impaled high on the iron spikes of the fence that surrounds the graveyard. Dogs, maybe, had been chasing it, and the deer had tried to leap over the high fence. The skull seems to be opening its mouth in a scream.

I remember that we piled stones over the mound of fresh earth to keep the pigs from rooting.

Daisy has a salve, made from some sort of root, that she smears over her eyelids at night. It's supposed to help her fading vision, maybe even bring it back, I don't know. Whenever she comes over to read our mail, she just holds the letters and runs her hand over them, doesn't really look at the words. I think she imagines what each letter is saying, what history lies behind it, what chain of circumstances.

Daisy and Preacher used to go up onto the bluffs overlooking Rodney and walk among the trees. Then they would climb one of the tallest trees so they could see the river. They'd sit on a branch, Daisy says, and have a picnic. They'd feel the river breezes and the tree swaying beneath them. They would watch the faraway river for the longest time.

Afterward they would climb down and move through the woods some more, looking for old battle things—rusted rifles, bayonets, canteens. They would sell these relics to the museum in Jackson for a dollar apiece, boxing them up for the mailman, tying the boxes shut with twine, and sending them COD. There was always enough money to get by on.

Those nights that they came down off the bluff, they might go out onto their tilted ship, out in the deep river grass, or they might go to the river itself and swim. Or sometimes they would sit on a sandbar and look up, listening to the sounds of the water. Once in a while a barge would go by. In the night, in the dark, its silhouette would look like a huge gunboat.

Wild grapes grew along the riverbank, tart purple grapes, cool in the night, and they would pick and eat those as they watched the river.

"It can go just like that," Daisy says, snapping her fingers. "It can go that fast."

The pigs are growing fat. They're not piglets anymore; they are pigs. One morning a shot awakens us, and we sit up and look out the window.

Daisy is straddling one of the pigs and gutting it with a huge knife. She pulls out the pig's entrails and feeds them to her beagles. The other pigs have run off into the woods, but they will be back. It's a cool morning, almost cold, and steam is rising from the pig's open chest. Later, in the afternoon, there's the good smell of fresh meat cooking.

Maggie shoots a pig at dusk, for herself, and two of the old men from the other side of town get theirs the next day.

"I don't want any," Elizabeth says after she's slid down the banister. Her eyes are magic, she's shivering and holding herself, dancing up and down, goose-pimply. She's happy to be so young. "I feel as if I'll be jinxed," she says. "I mean, those pigs lived under our house."

The smell of pork, of frying bacon, hangs heavy over the town, like the blue haze from cannon fire.

Coyotes at night, and the peacocks howling. Pecans underfoot. A full moon and the gleam of night cotton. We mount an old white plug and ride in the cotton field. It's mostly stripped, ragged and picked over, forgotten-looking. Only a few stray white bolls remain, perfect snowy blossoms, untouched by the pickers. The scraggly bushes scrape against the bottoms of our bare feet as we ride. It has been four years we've been down here in the town of Rodney.

"I'm happy," Elizabeth says, squeezing my arm from behind on the horse. She taps the horse's ribs with her heels. The smell of wood smoke, and overhead the nasal, far-off cries of geese going south. The horse plods along in the dust.

Daisy will be starting her church services again, and once more we'll be going. I'm glad Elizabeth's happy living in such a little one-horse shell of an ex-town. We'll hold hands, carry our Bible, and walk slowly down the road to Daisy's church. There will be a few lazy fireflies at dusk. We'll go in and sit on the bench and listen to Daisy rant and howl.

Then the moaning songs will start, the ones about being slaves. I'll shut my eyes and sway, and try not to think of other places and moving on.

And then this is what Elizabeth might say: "You'd better love me"—an order, an ultimatum. But she'll be teasing, playful, as she knows that's near all we can do here.

The air will be stuffy and warm in the little church, and for a moment we might feel dizzy, lightheaded, but the songs are what's important, what matters. The songs about being slaves.

There aren't any words. You just close your eyes and sway.

Maybe Preacher isn't coming, and maybe the river isn't coming back either. But I do not say these things to Daisy when she sits on the porch and waits for him. She remembers being our age and in love with him. She remembers all the things they did, so much time they had, all that time.

She throws bread crumbs in the middle of the road and stakes the white chickens inside the yard for him. We try to learn from her every day. We still have some time left.

The days go by. I think that we will have just exactly enough time to build what Elizabeth and I want to build—to make a thing that will last, and will not leave.

Fires

Some years the heat comes in April. There is always wind in April, but with luck there is warmth too. When the wind is from the south, the fields turn dry and everyone in the valley moves their seedlings outdoors. Root crops are what do best up here. The soil is rich from all the many fires, and potatoes from this valley taste like candy. Carrots pull free of the dark earth and taste like crisp sun. Strawberries do well here if they're kept watered.

The snow has left the valley by April, has moved up into the surrounding woods, and then by July the snow is above the woods, retreating to the cooler, shadier places in the mountains. But small oval patches of it remain behind. As the snow moves up into the mountains, snowshoe hares, gaunt but still white, descend on gardens' fresh berry plants. You can see the rabbits, white as Persian cats, from a mile away, coming after your plants, hopping through sun-filled woods and over rotting logs, following centuries-old game trails of black earth.

The rabbits come straight for my outside garden like relentless zombies, and I sit on the back porch and sight in on them. But they are too beautiful to kill in great numbers. I shoot only one every month or so, just to warn them. I clean the one I shoot and fry it in a skillet with onions and half a piece of bacon.

At night when I'm restless, I go from my bed to the window and look out. In spring I see the rabbits standing at attention around the greenhouse, aching to get inside. Several of them will dig at the earth, trying to tunnel in, while others sit there waiting.

Once the snow is gone, the rabbits begin to lose their white fur— or rather, they do not lose it, but it begins to turn the mottled brown of decaying leaves. Finally the hares are completely brown, and safe again, indistinguishable from the world around them.

I haven't lived with a woman for a long time. Whenever one does move in with me, it feels as if I've tricked her, caught her in a trap, as if the gate has been closed behind her, and she doesn't yet realize it. It's very remote up here.

One April a runner came to the valley to train at altitude. She was the sister of my friend Tom. Her name was Glenda, and she was from Washington State. Glenda had run races in Italy, France, and Switzerland. She told everyone, including the rough loggers and their wives, that this was the most beautiful place she had ever seen, and we believed her. Very few of us had ever been anywhere else to be able to question her.

We often sat at the picnic tables in front of the saloon, ten or twelve of us at a time, half of the town, and watched the river. Ducks and geese, heading north, stopped in our valley to breed, build nests, and raise their young. Ravens, with their wings and backs shining greasy in the sun, were always flying across the valley, from one side of the mountains to the other. Anyone who needed to make a little money could always do so in April by planting seedlings for the Forest Service, and it was an easier time because of that fact, a time of no bad tempers, of worries put aside for a while. I did not need much money, in April or in any other month, and I sat at the picnic table with Glenda and Tom and Nancy, Tom's wife, and drank beer. Glenda had yellow hair that was cut short, and lake-blue eyes, a pale face, and a big grin, not unlike Tom's, that belied her seriousness, though now that she is gone, I remember her always being able to grin *because* of her seriousness. Like the rest of us, Glenda had no worries, not in April and certainly not later on, in the summer. She had only to run. She was separated from her boyfriend, who lived in California, and she didn't seem to miss him, didn't ever seem to think about him.

Before planting the seedlings, the Forest Service burned the slopes they had cut the previous summer and fall. In the afternoons there would be a sweet-smelling haze that started about halfway up the valley walls, then rose into the mountains and spilled over them, moving north into Canada, riding on the south winds. The fires' haze never settled in our valley, but hung just above us, turning the sunlight a smoky blue and making things, when seen across the valley— a barn in another pasture or a fence line—seem much farther away than they really were. It made things seem softer, too.

Glenda had a long scar on the inside of her leg that ran from the ankle all the way up to mid-thigh. She had injured her knee when she was seventeen. This was before arthroscopic surgery, and she'd had to have the knee rebuilt the old-fashioned way, with blades and scissors, but the scar only seemed to make her legs, both of them, look even more beautiful. The scar had a graceful curve to it as it ran some distance up her leg.

Glenda wore green nylon shorts and a small white T-shirt when she ran, and a headband. Her running shoes were dirty white, the color of the road dust during the dry season.

"I'm thirty-two and have six or seven more good years of running," she said whenever anyone asked her what her plans were, why she ran so much, and why she had come to our valley to train. Mostly it was the men who asked, the ones who sat with us in front of the saloon watching the river, watching the spring winds move across the water. We were all glad that winter was over. Except for Nancy, I do not think the women liked Glenda very much.

It was not well known in the valley what a great runner Glenda was. And I think it gave Glenda pleasure that it wasn't.

"I'd like you to follow Glenda on a bicycle," Tom said the first time I met her. He'd invited me over for dinner a short time after she'd arrived. "There's money available from her sponsor to pay you for it," he said, handing me some money, or trying to, finally putting it in my shirt pocket. He had been drinking, and seemed as happy as I had seen him in a long time. After stuffing the bills into my pocket, he put one arm around Nancy, who looked embarrassed for me, and the other arm around Glenda, who did not, and so I had to keep the money, which was not that much anyway.

"You just ride along behind her with a pistol." Tom had a gun holstered on his belt, a big one, and he took it off and handed it to me. "And you make sure nothing happens to her, the way it did to that Ocherson woman."

The woman named Ocherson had been walking home along the river road after visiting friends when a bear evidently charged out of the willows and dragged her across the river. She had disappeared the previous spring, and at first everyone thought she had run away. Her husband had gone around all summer making a fool of himself, bad-mouthing her. Then hunters found her body in the fall, right before the first snow. Every valley had its bear stories, but we thought our story was the worst, because the victim had been a woman.

"It'll be good exercise for me," I said to Tom, and then I said to Glenda, "Do you run fast?"

It wasn't a bad job. I was able to keep up with her most of the time. Some days Glenda ran only a few miles, very fast, and on other days it seemed she ran forever. There was hardly ever any traffic—not a single car or truck—and I daydreamed as I rode along behind her.

Early in the morning we'd leave the meadow in front of Tom's place and head up the mountain on the South Fork road, above the river and into the woods, going past my cabin. Near the summit, the sun would be up and burning through the haze of the planting fires. Everything would look foggy and old, as if we had gone back in time and not everything had been decided yet.

By the time we reached the summit, Glenda's shirt and shorts were drenched, her hair damp and sticking to the sides of her face; her socks and even her running shoes were wet. But she always said that the people she would be racing against would be training even harder than she was.

There were lakes around the summit, and the air was cooler. On the north slope the lakes still had a thin crust of ice over them, a crust that thawed each afternoon but froze again at night. What Glenda liked to do after she'd reached the summit—her face flushed and her wrists limp and loose, so great was the heat and her exhaustion— was to leave the road and run down the game trail, tripping, stumbling, running downhill again. I would have to throw the bike down and hurry after her. She'd pull her shirt off and run into the shallows of the first lake she saw, her feet breaking through the thin ice. Then she'd sit down in the cold water like an animal chased there by hounds.

"This feels good!" she said the first time she did that. She leaned her head back on the shelf of ice behind her and spread her arms as if she were resting on a cross. She looked up through the haze at the empty sky above the tree line.

"Come over here," she said. "Come feel this."

I waded out, following her trail through the ice, and sat down next to her.

She took my hand and put it on her chest.

What I felt was like nothing I had ever imagined. It was like lifting up the hood of a car with the engine on and seeing all the cables and belts and fan blades still running. Right away, I wanted to get her to a doctor. I wondered, if she were going to die, whether I would be held responsible. I wanted to pull my hand away, but she made me keep it there, and gradually the drumming slowed, became steadier, and still she made me keep my hand there, until we could both feel the water's coldness. Then we got out. I had to help her up because her damaged knee was stiff. We spread out our clothes and lay down on flat rocks to dry in the wind and the sun. She'd said that she had come to the mountains to run because it would strengthen her knee. But there was something that made me believe that that was not the truth, though I cannot tell you what other reason there might have been.

On every hot day we went into the lake after her run. It felt wonderful, and lying in the sun afterward was wonderful too. Once we were dry, our hair smelled like the smoke from the planting fires. There were times when I thought that Glenda might be dying, and had come here to live out her last days, to run in a country of great beauty.

By the time we started our journey home, there'd be a slow wind coming off the river. The wind cleared a path through the haze, moving it to either side, and beneath it, in that space between, we could see the valley, green and soft. Midway up the north slope, the ragged fires would still be burning. Wavering smoke rose from behind the trees.

The temptation to get on the bike and coast all the way down was always strong, but I knew what my job was; we both did. It was the time when bears came out of hibernation, and the safety of winter was not to be confused with the seriousness of summer, with the way things were changing.

Walking back, we would come upon ruffed grouse, the males courting and fanning in the middle of the road, spinning in a dance, their throat sacs inflated and pulsing bright orange-red. The grouse did not want to let us go past: they stamped their feet and blocked our way, trying to protect some small certain area they had staked out for themselves. Glenda stiffened whenever she saw the fanning males, and shrieked when they rushed in and tried to peck at her ankles.

We'd stop at my cabin for lunch, and I'd open all the windows. By then the sun would have heated the log walls, and inside was a rich dry smell, as there is when you have been away from your house for a long time. We would sit at the breakfast room table and look out the window at the weedy chicken house I'd never used and at the woods going up the mountain behind the chicken house. We drank coffee and ate whitefish, which I had caught and smoked the previous winter.

I had planted a few young apple trees in the backyard that spring, and the nursery that sold them to me said these trees could withstand even the coldest winters, though I wasn't sure I believed it. They were small trees and would not bear fruit for four years, and that had sounded to me like such a long time that I really had to think about it before buying them. But I bought them anyway, without really knowing why. I also didn't know what would make a person run as much as Glenda did. I liked riding alongside her, though, and having coffee with her after the runs, and I knew I would be sad to see her leave the valley. I think that was what kept up the distance between us, a nice distance—the fact that both of us knew she would stay only a short time, until the end of August. Knowing this seemed to take away any danger, any wildness. It was a certainty; there was a wonderful sense of control.

I had a couple of dogs in the backyard, Texas hounds I'd brought up north with me a few years before. I kept them penned up in the winter so they wouldn't chase deer, but in the spring and summer I let them lie around in the grass, dozing. There was one thing they would chase, though, in the summer. It lived under the chicken house, and I don't know what it was; it ran too fast for me to ever get a good look at it. It was small and dark with fur, but it wasn't a bear cub. Perhaps it was some rare animal, something from Canada— maybe something no one had ever seen before. Whatever it was, it never grew from year to year, yet it seemed young somehow, as if it might someday grow. It would rip out of the woods, a fleet blur headed for its burrow, and as soon as the dogs saw it, they would be up and baying, right on its tail, but the thing always reached its burrow under the chicken house just ahead of them.

Glenda and I would sit at the window and watch for it every day. But it kept no timetable, and there was no telling when it would come, or even if it would. We called it a hedgehog, because that was the closest thing it might have resembled.

Some nights Glenda would call me on the shortwave radio. She would key the mike a few times to make it crackle and wake me up, and then I would hear a mysterious voice floating in static through my cabin. "Have you seen the hedgehog?" she would ask sleepily, but it was never her real voice there in the dark with me. "Did you see the hedgehog?" she'd want to know, and I'd wish she were with me at that moment. But it would be no good; Glenda was leaving in August, or September at the latest.

"No," I'd say in the dark. "No hedgehog today. Maybe it's gone away." Though I had thought that many times, I would always see it again, just when I thought I never would.

"How are the dogs?" she'd ask.

"They're asleep."

"Good night," she'd say.

"Good night."

* * *

One Thursday night I had Tom and Nancy and Glenda over for dinner. Friday was Glenda's day off from running, so she allowed herself to drink and stay up late on Thursdays. Before dinner, we started out drinking at the saloon. Around dusk we went down to my cabin, and Glenda and I fixed dinner while Tom and Nancy sat on the front porch, watching the elk appear in the meadow across the road as the light faded.

"Where's this famous hedgehog?" Tom bellowed, puffing a cigar, blowing smoke rings into the night, big perfect Os. The elk lifted their heads, chewing the summer grass like cattle, the bulls' antlers glowing with velvet.

"In the backyard," Glenda said as she washed the salad greens. "But you can only see him in the daytime."

"Aww, bullshit!" Tom roared, standing up with his bottle of Jack Daniel's. He took off down the steps, stumbling, and the three of us put down what we were doing to get flashlights and run after him to make sure he was all right. Tom was a trapper, and it riled him to think there was an animal he did not know, could not trap, could not even see. Out by the chicken house, he got down on his hands and knees, breathing hard, and we crowded around him to shine the flashlights into the deep, dusty hole. He made grunting noises that were designed, I suppose, to make the animal want to come out, but we never saw anything. It was cold under the stars. Far off, the planting fires burned, but they were held in check, controlled by back fires.

I had a propane fish fryer, and we put it on the front porch and cut trout into cubes, rolled them in flour, then dropped them in hot spattering grease. We fixed about a hundred trout cubes, and when we finished eating there were none left. Glenda had a tremendous appetite, and ate almost as many as Tom. She licked her fingers afterward, and asked if there were any more.

After dinner we took our drinks and sat on the steep roof of my cabin, above the second-floor dormer. Tom sat out on the end of the dormer as if it were a saddle, and Glenda sat next to me for warmth, and we watched the fires spread across the mountainside, burning but contained. Below us, in the backyard, those few rabbits that still had not turned completely brown began coming out of the woods. Dozens of them approached the greenhouse, then stopped and lined up around it, wanting to get into the tender young carrots and the Simpson lettuce. I had put sheets down on the ground to trick them, and we laughed as the rabbits shifted nervously from sheet to sheet, several of them huddling together on one sheet at a time, imagining they were protected.

"Turn back, you bastards!" Tom shouted. That woke the ducks on the pond nearby, and they began clucking among themselves. It was a reassuring sound. Nancy made Tom tie a rope around his waist and tie the other end around the chimney, in case he fell. But Tom said he wasn't afraid of anything, and was going to live forever.

Glenda weighed herself before and after each run. I had to remind myself not to get too close to her; I only wanted to be her friend. We ran and rode in silence. We never saw any bears. But she was frightened of them, even as the summer went on without us seeing any, and so I always carried the pistol. We had gotten tan from lying out by the lake up at the summit. Glenda took long naps at my cabin after her runs; we both did, Glenda sleeping on my couch. I'd cover her with a blanket and lie down on the floor next to her. The sun would pour in through the window. There was no longer any other world beyond our valley—only here, only now. But still, I could feel my heart pounding.

It turned drier than ever in August, and the loggers began cutting again. The days were windy, and the fields and meadows turned to crisp hay. Everyone was terrified of sparks, especially the old people, because they'd seen big fires rush through the valley, moving through like an army: the big fire in 1910, and then again in 1930, which burned up every tree except for the luckiest ones, so that for years afterward the entire valley was barren and scorched.

One afternoon in early August Glenda and I went to the saloon. She lay down on top of a picnic table and looked up at the clouds.

She would be going back to Washington in three weeks, she said, and then down to California. Almost all of the men would be off logging in the woods by then, and if she stayed, we would have the whole valley to ourselves. Tom and Nancy had been calling us "the lovebirds" since July, hoping for something to happen—something other than what was, or wasn't—but they'd stopped in August. Glenda was running harder than ever, really improving, so that I was having trouble keeping up with her.

There was no ice left anywhere, no snow, not even in the darkest, coolest parts of the forest, but the lakes and rivers were still ice cold when we waded into them. Glenda continued to press my hand to her breast until I could feel her heart calming, and then almost stopping, as the waters worked on her.

"Don't you ever leave this place," she said as she watched the clouds. "You've got it really good here."

I stroked her knee with my fingers, running them along the inside scar. The wind tossed her hair around. She closed her eyes, and though it was hot, there were goose bumps on her tanned legs and arms.

"No, I wouldn't do that," I said.

I thought about her heart, hammering in her chest after those long runs. At the top of the summit, I'd wonder how anything could ever be so *alive*.

The afternoon she set fire to the field across the road from my cabin was a still day, windless, and I suppose that Glenda thought it would do no harm—and she was right, though I did not know it then. I was at my window when I saw her out in the field lighting matches, bending down and cupping her hands until a small blaze appeared at her feet. Then she came running across the field.

At first I could hardly believe my eyes. The smoke in front of the fire made it look as if I were seeing something from memory, or something that had happened in another time. The fire seemed to be secondary, even inconsequential. What mattered was that she was running, coming across the field toward my cabin.

I loved to watch her run. I did not know why she had set the fire, and I was very afraid that it might cross the road and burn up my hay barn, even my cabin. But I was not as frightened as I might have been. It was the day before Glenda was going to leave, and mostly I was delighted to see her.

She ran up the steps, pounded on my door, and came inside, breathless, having run a dead sprint all the way. The fire was spreading fast, even without a wind, because the grass was so dry, and red-winged blackbirds were flying out of the grass ahead of it. I could see rabbits and mice scurrying across the road, heading for my yard. It was late in the afternoon, not quite dusk. An elk bounded across the meadow. There was a lot of smoke. Glenda pulled me by the hand, taking me back outside and down the steps, back out toward the fire, toward the pond on the far side of the field.

It was a large pond, large enough to protect us, I hoped. We ran hard across the field, and a new wind suddenly picked up, a wind created by the flames. We got to the pond and kicked our shoes off, pulled off our shirts and jeans, and splashed into the water. We waited for the flames to reach us, and then work their way around us.

It was just a grass fire. But the heat was intense as it rushed toward us, blasting our faces with hot wind.

It was terrifying.

We ducked our heads under the water to cool our drying faces and threw water on each other's shoulders. Birds flew past us, and grasshoppers dived into the pond with us, where hungry trout rose and snapped at them, swallowing them like corn. It was growing dark and there were flames all around us. We could only wait and see whether the grass was going to burn itself up as it swept past.

"Please, love," Glenda was saying, and I did not understand at first that she was speaking to me. "Please."

We had moved out into the deepest part of the pond, chest deep, and kept having to duck beneath the surface because of the heat. Our lips and faces were scorched. Pieces of ash were floating down to the water like snow. It was not until nightfall that the flames died, leaving just a few orange ones flickering here and there. But the rest of the small field was black and smoldering.

It turned suddenly cold, and we held on to each other tightly, because we were shivering. I thought about luck and about chance. I thought about fears, all the different ones, and the things that could make a person run.

She left at daylight. She would not let me drive her home—she said she wanted to run instead, and she did. Her feet raised puffs of dust in the road.

Field Events

But the young one, the man, as if he were
the son of a neck and a nun: taut and powerfully filled
with muscles and innocence.

—Rilke, "The Fifth Elegy"

It was summer, and the two brothers had been down on a gravel bar washing their car with river water and sponges when the big man came around the bend, swimming upstream, doing the butterfly stroke. He was pulling a canoe behind him, and it was loaded with darkened cast-iron statues. The brothers, John and Jerry, had hidden behind a rock and watched as the big man leapt free of the water with each sweep of his arms, arching into the air like a fish and then crashing back down into the rapids, lunging his way up the river, with the canoe following him.

The brothers thought they'd hidden before the big man had spotted them—how could he have known they were there?—but he altered his course as he drew closer, until he was swimming straight for the big rock they were hiding behind. When it became apparent he was heading for them, they stepped out from behind the rock, a bit embarrassed at having hidden. It was the Sacandaga River, which ran past the brothers' town, Glens Falls, in northeastern New York.

The brothers were strength men themselves, discus throwers and shot-putters, but even so, they were unprepared for the size of the man as he emerged from the water, dripping and completely naked save for the rope around his waist, to which the canoe was tied.

Jerry, the younger—eighteen that summer—said, "Lose your briefs in the rapids?"

The big man smiled, looked down, and quivered like a dog, shaking the water free one leg at a time, one arm at a time. The brothers had seen big men in the gym before, but they'd never seen anyone like this.

With the canoe still tied around his waist, and the rope still tight as the current tried to sweep the iron-laden canoe downstream, the big man crouched and with a stick drew a map in the sand of where he lived in Vermont, about fifteen miles upstream. The rapids surged against the canoe, crashed water over the bow as it bobbed in place, and the brothers saw the big man tensing against the pull of the river, saw him lean forward to keep from being drawn back in. Scratching in the sand with that stick. Two miles over the state line. An old farmhouse.

Then the man stood, said goodbye, and waded back into the shallows, holding the rope taut in his hands to keep from being dragged in. When he was in up to his knees he dived, angled out toward the center, and once more began butterfly-stroking up the river, turning his head every now and again to look back at the brothers with cold, curious eyes, like those of a raven, or a fish.

The brothers tried to follow, running along the rocky, brushy shore, calling for the big man to stop, but he continued slowly upriver, swimming hard against the crashing, funneled tongue of rapids, lifting up and over them and back down among them, lifting like a giant bat or manta ray. He swam up through a narrow canyon and left them behind.

At home in bed that night, each brother looked up at the ceiling in his room and tried to sleep. Each could feel his heart thrashing around in his chest. The brothers knew that the big man was up to something, something massive.

The beating in the brothers' hearts would not stop. They got up and met, as if by plan, in the kitchen for a beer, a sandwich. They ate almost constantly, always trying to build more muscle. Sometimes they acted like twins, thought the same thing at the same time. It was a warm night, past midnight, and when they had finished their snack, they got the tape measure and checked to see if their arms had gotten larger. And because the measurements were unchanged, they each fixed another sandwich, ate them, measured again. No change.

"It's funny how it works," said John. "How it takes such a long time."

"No shit, Sherlock," said Jerry. He slapped his flat belly and yawned.

Neither of them had mentioned the big man in the rapids. All day they'd held it like a secret, cautious of what might happen if they discussed it. Feeling that they might chase him away, that they might make it be as if he had never happened.

They went outside and stood in the middle of the street under a streetlamp and looked around like watchdogs, trying to understand why their hearts were racing.

So young, they were so young!

They drove an old blue Volkswagen beetle. When the excitement of the night and of their strength and youth was too much, they would pick up the automobile from either end like porters, or pallbearers, and carry it around the block for exercise, without having to stop and set it down and rest. But that night, the brothers' hearts were running too fast just to walk the car. They lay down beneath the trees in the cool grass in their backyard and listened to the wind that blew from the mountains on the other side of the river. Sometimes the brothers would go wake their sisters, Lory and Lindsay, and bring them outside into the night. The four of them would sit under the largest tree and tell stories or plan things.

Their father was named Heck, and their mother, Louella. Heck was the principal of the local school. Lory was thirty-four, a teacher, and beautiful: she was tiny, black-haired, with a quick, high laugh not unlike the outburst of a loon. Despite her smallness, her breasts were overly large, to the point that they were the first thing people noticed about her, and continued noticing about her. She tried always to keep moving when around new people, tried with her loon's laugh and her high-energy, almost manic actress's gestures, to shift the focus back to her, not her breasts, but it was hard, and tiring. She had long, sweeping eyelashes, but not much of a chin. The reason Lory still lived at home was that she loved her family and simply could not leave. Lindsay was sixteen, but already half a foot taller than Lory. She was red-headed, freckled, had wide shoulders, and played field hockey; the brothers called her Lindsay the Red.

Lory was not allowed to work at the school where her father was principal, so she taught in a little mountain town called Warrensburg, about thirty miles north. She hated the job. The children had no respect for her, no love; they drank and died in fiery crashes, or were abused by their parents, or got cancer—they had no luck. Lory's last name, her family's name, was Iron, and one night the boys at her school had scratched with knives onto every desktop the words "I fucked Miss Iron." Sometimes the boys touched her from behind when she was walking in the crowded halls.

The night the brothers' hearts beat so wildly, they lay in the grass for a while and then went and got their sisters. Lory was barely able to come out of her sleep but followed the brothers anyway, holding Jerry's hand as if sleepwalking. She sat down with her back against the largest tree and dozed in and out, still exhausted from the school year. Lindsay, though, was wide awake, and sat cross-legged, leaning forward, listening.

"We went down to the river today," John said, plucking at stems of grass, putting them in his mouth and chewing on them for their sweetness, like a cow grazing. Jerry was doing hurdler's stretches, had one leg extended in front of him. There was no moon, only stars through the trees.

"Summer," mumbled Lory in her half sleep. Often she talked in her sleep and had nightmares.

"Who was your first lover?" Jerry asked her, grinning, speaking in a low voice, trying to trick her.

Lindsay covered her sister's ears and whispered, "Lory, no! Wake up! Don't say it!"

The brothers were overprotective of Lory, even though she was the oldest and hadn't had any boyfriends for a long time.

"Michael," Lory mumbled uncomfortably. "No, no, Arthur. No, wait, Richard, William? No—Mack, no, Jerome, Atticus, no, that Caster boy—no, wait..."

Slowly Lory opened her eyes, smiling at Jerry. "Got you," she said.

Jerry shrugged, embarrassed. "I just want to protect you."

Lory looked at him with sleepy, narrowed eyes. "Right."

They were silent for a moment, then John said, "We saw this big man today. He was pulling a boat. He was really pulling it." John wanted to say more, but didn't dare. He reached down and plucked a blade of night grass. They sat there in the moon shadows, a family, wide awake while the rest of the town slept.

They waited a week, almost as if they had tired or depleted the big man, and as if they were now letting him gather back his whole self. John and Jerry went to the rapids every day to check on the map in the sand, and when it had finally begun to blur, almost to the point of disappearing, they realized they had to go find him soon, or risk never seeing him again.

Lindsay drove, though she did not yet have her license, and John sat in the front with her and told her the directions, navigating from memory. (To have transcribed the map onto paper, even onto a napkin, would also somehow have run the risk of diminishing the big man, if he was still out there.) Jerry sat in the back seat, wearing sunglasses like a movie star and sipping a high-protein milk shake. John's strength in the discus was his simple brute power, while Jerry's strength—he was five years younger and sixty pounds lighter—was his speed.

"*Right!*" Jerry cried every time John gave Lindsay the correct instructions. In his mind, Jerry could see the map as clear as anything, and when John gave Lindsay a bad piece of advice—a left turn, say, instead of a right—Jerry would shout out "*Wrong!—Braaapp! Sham-bam-a-LOOM!*"

Up and over hills they went, across small green valleys, around a lake and down sun-dappled lanes, as if passing through tunnels— from shade to sun, shade to sun, with wooden bridges clattering beneath them, until Lindsay was sure they were lost. But Jerry, in the back seat, kept smiling, his face content behind the dark glasses, and John was confident, too. The closer they got to the big man, the more they could tell he was out there.

The road crossed over the border into Vermont, and turned to gravel. It followed a small creek for a stretch, and the brothers wondered if this creek flowed into the Sacandaga, if the big man had swum all the way upstream before turning into this side creek to make his way home. It looked like the creek he had drawn on his map in the sand.

Blackbirds flew up out of the marsh reeds along either side of them. They could feel him getting closer. There was very much the sense that they were hunting him, that they had to somehow capture him.

Then they saw him in a pasture. A large two-story stone house stood at the end of the pasture like a castle, with the creek passing by out front, the creek shaded by elm and maple trees, and giant elms that had somehow, in this one small area, avoided or been immune to the century's blight. The pasture was deep with rich green summer hay, and they saw a few Holsteins grazing there.

Again, the man wasn't wearing anything, and he had one of the cows on his back. He was running through the tall grass with it, leaping sometimes, doing jetés and awkward but heartfelt pirouettes with the sagging cow draped across his wide shoulders. He had thick legs that jiggled as he ran, and he looked happy, as happy as they had ever seen anyone look. The rest of the cattle stood in front of the old house, grazing and watching without much interest.

"Jiminy," said Lindsay.

"Let's get him," said John, the strongest. "Let's wait until he goes to sleep and then tie him up and bring him home."

"We'll teach him to throw the discus," said Jerry.

"If he doesn't want to throw the discus, we'll let him go," said John. "We won't force him to."

"Right," said Jerry.

But force wasn't necessary. John and Jerry went into the field after him, warily, and he stopped spinning and shook hands with them. Lindsay stayed in the car, wanting to look away but unable to; she watched the man's face, watched the cow on his back. The cow had a placid but somehow engaged look on its face, as if just beginning to awaken to the realization that it was aloft.

The big man grinned and put the cow back on the ground. He told them that he had never thrown the discus, had never even seen it done, but would like to try, if that was what they wanted him to do. He left them and went into the stone house for a pair of jeans and tennis shoes and a white T-shirt. When he came back out, dressed, he looked even larger.

He was too big to fit into the car—he was as tall as John but thirty pounds heavier, and built of rock-slab muscle—so he rode standing on the back bumper, grinning, with the wind blowing his long, already thinning hair back behind him. The big man's face was young, his skin smooth and tanned.

"My name's A.C.!" he shouted to them as they puttered down the road. Lindsay leaned her head out the window and looked back at him, wanting to make sure he was all right. The little car's engine shuddered and shook beneath him, trying to manage the strain. The back bumper scraped the road.

"I'm Lindsay!" she shouted. "John's driving! Jerry's not!"

Her hair swirled around her, a nest of red. She knew what Lory would say. Her sister thought that all the muscle on her brothers was froufrou, adornment, and unnecessary. Lindsay hoped that Lory would change her mind.

"Lindsay, get back in the car!" John shouted, looking in the rear-view mirror. But she couldn't hear him. She was leaning farther out the window, reaching for A.C.'s wrist, and then higher, gripping his thick arm.

"She's mad," Jerry howled, disbelieving. "She's lost her mind."

A.C. grinned and held on to the car's roof, taking the bumps with his legs.

When they drove up to their house, Lory had awakened from her nap and was sitting on the picnic table in her shorts and a T-shirt, drinking from a bottle of red wine. She burst into laughter when she saw them approach with A.C. riding the back bumper as if he had hijacked them.

"Three peas in a pod," she cried. She danced down from the table and out to the driveway to meet him, to shake his hand.

It was as if there were three brothers.

From the kitchen window, Louella watched, horrified. The huge young man in the front yard was not hers. He might think he was, and everyone else might too, but he wasn't. She stopped drying dishes and was alarmed at the size of him, standing there among her children, shaking hands, moving around in their midst. She had had a miscarriage, twenty years ago. This man could have been that child, could even have been that comeback soul.

Louella felt the blood draining from her face and thought she was dying. She fell to the kitchen floor in a faint, breaking the coffee cup she was drying.

It was the end of June. Fields and pastures all over the Hudson Valley were green. She had been worrying about Lory's sadness all through the fall and winter, on through the rains and melting snows of spring, and even now, into the ease of green summer.

Louella sat up and adjusted her glasses. When she went outside to meet A.C., she could no longer say for sure whether she knew him or not; there was a moment's hesitancy.

She looked hard into his eyes, dried her hands on her apron, and reached out and shook his big hand. She was swayed by her children's happiness. There was a late-day breeze. A hummingbird dipped at the nectar feeder on the back porch. She let him come into their house.

"We're going to teach A.C. how to throw the discus," said Jerry.

"Thrilling," said Lory.

He had supper with the family, and they all played Monopoly that evening. Louella asked A.C. where he was from and what he did, but he would only smile and say that he was here to throw the discus. He wasn't rude, he simply wouldn't tell her where he was from. It was almost as if he did not know, or did not understand the question.

They played Monopoly until it was time for bed. The brothers took him for a walk through the neighborhood and on into town. They stopped to pick up people's cars occasionally, the three of them lifting together.

There was a statue of Nathan Hale in the town square, and, drunk on the new moon, drunk with his new friends, A.C. waded through the shrubbery, crouched below the statue, and gave the cold metal a bear hug. He began twisting back and forth, pulling the statue from the ground, groaning, squeezing and lifting with his back and legs, his face turning redder and redder, rocking until he finally worked it loose. He stood up with it, sweating, grinning, holding it against his chest as if it were a dance partner, or a dressmaker's dummy.

They walked home after that, taking turns carrying the statue on their backs, and snuck it into Lory's room and stood it in the corner by the door, so that it impeded her exit. It still smelled of fresh earth and crushed flowers. Lory was a sound sleeper, plunging into unconsciousness as an escape at every opportunity, and she never heard them.

Then A.C. went downstairs to the basement and rested, lying on a cot, looking up at the ceiling with his hands behind his head. John and Jerry stayed in the kitchen, drinking beer.

"Do you think it will happen?" Jerry asked.

John was looking out the window at the garden. "I hope so," he said. "I think it would be good for her." He finished his beer. "Maybe we shouldn't think about it, though. It might be wrong."

"Well," said Jerry, sitting down as if to think about it himself, "maybe so."

John was still looking out the window. "But who cares?" he said. He looked at Jerry.

"This guy's okay," said Jerry. "This one's good."

"But do you think he can throw the discus?"

"I don't know," Jerry said. "But I want you to go find some more statues for him. I liked that."

That first night at the Irons' house, A.C. thought about John and Jerry, about how excited he had been to see them walking up to him. He considered how they looked at each other sometimes when they were talking. They always seemed to agree.

Then he thought about John's hair, black and short, and about his heavy beard. And Jerry, he seemed so young with his green eyes. His hair was blond and curly. A.C. liked the way Jerry leaned forward and narrowed his eyes, grinning, when he talked. Jerry seemed excited about almost anything, everything, and excited to be with his older brother, following him down the same path.

Later, A.C. got up from his cot—he'd been sleeping among punching bags and exercise bikes, with dumbbells and barbells scattered about like toys—and went quietly up the stairs, past Lindsay's room, through the kitchen, and into the living room.

He sat down on the couch and looked out the big front window at the moon and clouds as if watching a play. He stayed there for a long time, dozing off for a few minutes. Around four in the morning he awoke to find Lory standing in front of him, blocking the moon. She was dark, with the moon behind her lighting only the edge of one side of her face. He could see her eyelashes on that side. She was studying him almost the way Louella had.

"Look," he said, and pointed behind her.

The clouds were moving past the moon in fast-running streams, like tidal currents, eddying, it seemed, all to the same place, all hurrying by as if late to some event.

"What is that statue doing in my room?" Lory asked. She was whispering, and he thought her voice was beautiful. A.C. hoped he could be her friend too, as he'd become a friend of her brothers. He looked at the moon, a mottled disc.

"Do you want to sit down?" he asked. He patted the side of the couch next to him.

She did, and then, after a few seconds, she leaned into his shoulder and put her head against it. She put both her hands on his arm and held on.

After a while, A.C. lifted her into his lap, holding her in both arms as if she were a small child, and slowly he rocked her. She curled against him as tightly as she could, and he rocked her like that, watching her watch him, until dawn.

When it got light, she reached up and kissed him, touching his face with her hands, and got out of his lap and hurried into the kitchen to fix coffee before anyone else was up. A few minutes later, Louella appeared in the living room, sleepy-eyed, shuffling, wearing a faded blue flannel robe and old slippers, holding the paper. She almost stepped on A.C.'s big feet. She stopped, surprised to see him up so early, and in her living room. He stood up and said, "Good morning," and she smiled in spite of herself.

Around eight o'clock John and Jerry got up, and they chased each other into the kitchen, playing some advanced form of tag. The lighter, faster Jerry stayed just ahead of John, leaping over the coffee table, spinning, tossing a footstool into his path for John to trip over. Lory shrieked, spilled some milk from the carton she was holding, and Louella shouted at them to stop it, tried to look stern, but was made young again by all the motion, and loved it—and A.C., having come meekly in from the living room, stood back and smiled. Louella glanced over at him and saw him smiling, looking at the brothers, and she thought again of how eerie the fit was, of how he seemed to glide into all the right spots and stand in exactly the right places. It was as if he had been with them all along—or even stranger, it was as if he were some sort of weight or stone placed on a scale that better balanced them now.

After breakfast—a dozen eggs each, some cantaloupes, a pound of sausage split among them, a gallon of milk, and a couple of plates of pancakes—the brothers went out to their car and tossed all their throwing equipment in it—tape measure, discs, throwing shoes—and they leaned the driver's seat forward so that A.C. could get in the back, but still he wouldn't fit.

He rode standing on the bumper again. They drove to the school, to the high, windy field where they threw. From there it seemed they could see the whole Hudson Valley and the knife-cut through the trees where the river rushed, the Sacandaga melting through the mountains, and on the other side the green walls of the Adirondacks. A.C. looked around at the new town as they drove. He thought about Lory, about how soft and light she'd been in his arms, and of how he'd been frightened by her. Riding on the back of the tiny car reminded him of being in the river, swimming up through the rapids: all that rushing force, relentless, crashing down over and around him, speeding past. Things were going by so fast. He looked around and felt dizzy at the beauty of the town.

✣   ✣   ✣

There was a ring in the center of the field, a flat, smooth, unpainted circle of cement, and that was where the brothers and A.C. set their things and began to dress. The brothers sat down like bears in a zoo and took their street shoes off. As they laced up their heavy leather throwing shoes, stretching and grasping their toes, they looked out at the wire fence running along the south end of the field, which was the point they tried to reach with their throws.

A.C. put his shoes on, too, the ones they had given him, and stood up. He felt how solid the earth was beneath him. His legs were dense and strong, and he kicked the ground a couple of times with the heavy shoes. A.C. imagined he could feel the earth shudder when he kicked. He jumped up and down a couple of times, short little hops, just to feel the shudder again.

"I hope you like this," said Jerry, still stretching, twisting his body into further unrecognizable shapes and positions. He was loosening up, his movements fluid, and to A.C. it was exactly like watching the river.

A.C. sat down next to them and tried to do some of the stretches, but it didn't work for him yet. He watched them for half an hour, as the blue air over the mountains and valley waned, turning to a sweet haze, a slow sort of shimmer that told A.C. it was June. Jerry was the one he most liked to watch.

Jerry would crouch in the ring, twisted—wound up—with his eyes closed, his mouth open, and the disc hanging back, hanging low, his knees bent. When he began to spin, it was like some magical force was being born, something that no other force on earth would be able to stop.

He stayed in the small circle, hopping from one foot to the other, crouched low, but with the hint of rising, and then he was suddenly at the other end of the small ring, out of room—if he went over the little wooden curb and into the grass, it would be a foul—and with no time or space left in which to spin, he shouted, brought his arm all the way around on the spin, his elbow locking straight out as he released the disc, and only then did the rest of his body react, starting with his head; it snapped back and then forward from the recoil, as if he'd first made the throw and then had a massive heart attack.

"Wow," said A.C., watching him unwind and recover and return, surprisingly, to a normal upright human being.

But John and Jerry were watching the disc. It was moving so fast. There was a heavy, cutting sound when it landed, far short of the fence, and it skidded a few feet after that and then stopped, as if it had never been moving.

Jerry threw two more times—they owned only three discs—and then the three of them, walking like gunslingers, like giants from another age, went out to get the discs. The brothers talked about the throws: what Jerry had done right, and what he had done wrong. His foot position had been a little off on the first throw. He hadn't kept his head back far enough going into the spin of the second throw. The third throw had been pretty good; on the bounce, it had carried to the chain-link fence.

John threw next, and then Jerry again, and then it was John's turn once again. A.C. thought he could do it himself. Surely that whip-spin dance, skip, hurl, and shout was a thing that was in everyone. It had to be the same way he felt when he picked up a cow and spun through the tall grass, holding it on his shoulders. When it was his turn to throw the discus, he tried to remember that, and he stepped into the ring, huffing.

A.C.'s first throw slammed into the center of the head-high fence and shook it. John and Jerry looked at each other, trying not to feel amazed. It was what they had thought from the beginning, after all; it was as if he had always been with them.

But A.C.'s form was spastic. It was wrong, it was nothing. He threw with his arms and shoulders—not with his legs, and not with the twist of his wide back. If he could get the spin down, the dance, he would throw it 300 feet. He would be able to throw it the length of a football field. In the discus, even 230 feet was immortality.

Again, the brothers found themselves feeling there was a danger of losing him—of having him disappear if they did or said the wrong thing, if they were not true and honest.

But the way he could throw a discus! It was as if their hearts had created him. He was all strength, no finesse. They were sure they could teach him the spin-dance. The amazing thing about a bad spin, as opposed to a good one, is how *ugly* it looks. A good spin excites the spectators, touches them all the way down and through, makes them wish they could do it—or even more, makes them feel as if they *had* done it, somehow. But a bad throw is like watching a devil monster changeling being born into the world; just one more awful thing in a world of too many, and even spectators who do not know much about the sport will turn their heads away, even before the throw is completed, when they see an awkward spin. A.C.'s was, John and Jerry had to admit, the ugliest of the ugly.

His next throw went over the fence. The one after that—before they realized what was happening, or realized it too late, as it was in the air, climbing, moving faster than any of their throws had ever gone—rose, gliding, and hit the base of the school. There was a *crack!* and the disc exploded into graphite shards. One second it was there, flying and heroic, and then it was nothing, just an echo.

"A hundred and ten bucks," Jerry said, but John cared nothing for the inconvenience it would bring them, being down to two discs, and he danced and whooped, spun around and threw imaginary discs, waved his arms and continued to jump up and down. He danced with Jerry, and then he grabbed A.C.

"If you can learn the steps..." John was saying, almost singing. The three men held one another's shoulders and danced and spun across the field like children playing snap-the-whip. John and Jerry had never seen a discus thrown that far in their lives, and A.C., though he had felt nothing special, was happy because his new friends were happy, and he hoped he could make them happy again.

Riding home on the back bumper, the air cooling his summer-damp hair and clothes, he leaned against the car and hugged it like a small child, and watched the town going past in reverse now, headed back to the Irons' house, and he hoped that maybe he could make them happy forever.

The brothers bragged about him when they got home, and everyone listened, and like John and Jerry they were half surprised, but they also felt that it confirmed something, and so that part of them was anything but surprised.

John was dating a schoolteacher named Patty. A shy-eyed Norwegian, she was as tall as he was, with freckles and a slow-spreading smile. A.C. grinned just watching her, and when she saw A.C., she would laugh for no real reason, just a happy laugh. Once when John and Jerry had gone to their rooms to nap, A.C. went outside with Lindsay and Patty to practice field hockey.

A.C. had never played any formal sports and was thrilled to be racing across the lawn, dodging the trees and the women, passing the ball along clumsily but quickly. Patty's laughs, Lindsay's red hair. If only he could live forever with this. He ran and ran, barefoot, back and forth in the large front yard, and they laughed all afternoon.

On the nights when A.C. did not stay with the family, he returned to the old stone house in Vermont. Some days he would swim all the way home, starting upstream at dusk and going on into the night— turning right where the little creek entered the Sacandaga, with fish bumping into his body and jumping around him as if a giant shark had passed through. But other nights he canoed home against the rapids, having loaded boulders into the bottom of the canoe to work his shoulders and arms harder. After he got home, he tied the canoe to the low branch of a willow, left it bobbing in the current.

Some nights in the farmhouse, A.C. would tie a rope around his waist and chest, attach the other end of it to one of the rafters, and climb up into the rafters and leap down, swinging like a pirate. He'd hang there, dangling in the darkness. He'd hold his arms and legs out as he spun around and around, and it would feel as if he were sinking, descending, and as if it would never stop.

He would tell no one where he had come from. And he would forget the woman in Colorado, the one he was supposed to have married. Everyone comes from somewhere. Everyone has made mistakes, has caused injuries, even havoc. The woman had killed herself after A.C. left her; she had hanged herself.

This is what it's like, he'd think. This is the difference between being alive and being dead. He'd hang from the rope and spin. This is the only difference, but it's so big.

Sometimes he would sleep all night dangling from the rafters:

spinning, a bit frightened, hanging like a question mark, only to awaken each morning as the sun's first light filtered through the dusty east windows. The sound of the creek running past just out front, the creek that led into the river.

There were mornings when Lory was afraid to get up. She thought it was just common depression and that it would pass with time, but some days it seemed too much. She slept as much as she could, which seemed to make it worse and worse. She tried to keep it a secret from her family, but suspected that her brothers knew, and her mother, too. It was like drowning, like going down in chains. And she felt guilty about the anguish it would cause others.

But her brothers! They anchored her and nourished her, they were like water passing through her gills. If they came down the hall and found her just sitting in the hallway, her head down between her knees, they—John or Jerry, or sometimes both of them—would gently pick her up and carry her outside to the yard, into the sun, and would rub her back and neck. Jerry would pretend to be a masseur with a foreign accent, would crack Lory's knuckles one by one, counting to ten some days in German, others in Spanish or French, mixing the languages to keep her guessing, to make her pay attention. Then he would start on her toes as John continued to knead her neck muscles and her small, strong shoulders.

"Uno, dos, *trey*," Jerry would hiss, wiggling her toes. He'd make up numbers. "Petrocci, zimbosi, bambolini, *crunk!*" he'd mutter, and then, "The little pig, he went to the market. He wanted beef—he wanted roast beef..."

He'd keep singing nonsense, keep teasing her until she smiled or laughed, until he had her attention, until he'd pulled her out of that well of sadness and numbness, and he'd shake his finger at her and say, "Pay attention!" She'd smile, back in her family's arms again, and be amazed that Jerry was only eighteen, but knew so much.

They would lie in the grass afterward and look up at the trees, at the way the light came down, and Lory would have the thought, whenever she was happy, that this was the way she really was, the way things could always be, and that that flat, vacant stretch of nothing-feeling was the aberration, not the norm; and she wanted it always to be like that, and still, even at thirty-four, believed that it could be.

When they were sure she was better, one of the brothers would walk to the nearest tree and wrap his arms around it, would grunt and lean hard against it, and then would begin to shake it until leaves began to fall. Lory would laugh and look up as they landed on her face and in her hair, and she would not pull them out of her hair, for they were a gift, and still John or Jerry would keep shaking the tree, as if trying to cover her with the green summer leaves.

A.C. and the brothers trained every day. When A.C. stayed at the farmhouse, each morning shortly before daylight he would get in his canoe and float all the way to Glens Falls, not ever having to paddle—just ruddering. As if following veins or arteries, he took all the correct turns with only a flex of his wrist, a slight change of the paddle's orientation in the water, and in the morning light he passed beneath dappled maples, flaking sycamores, listening to the cries of river birds and the sounds of summer as he slipped into the town.

Besides hurling the discus outside near the school, the brothers lifted weights in the school's basement, and went for long runs on the track. Each had his own goal, and each wanted A.C. to throw the unspeakable 300 feet. It would be a throw so far that the discus would vanish from sight.

No one believed it could be done. Only the brothers believed it. A.C. was not even sure he himself believed it. Sometimes he fell down when entering his spin, trying to emulate their grace, their precision-polished whip-and-spin and the clean release, like a birth, the discus flying wild and free into the world.

In the evenings the whole family would sit around in the den watching *M*A*S*H* or the movie of the week—*Conan the Barbarian* once—their father, Heck, sipping his gin and tonic, fresh-squeezed lime in with the ice, sitting in the big easy chair watching his huge sons sprawled on the rug, with their huge friend lying next to them. Lindsay would sit in the corner, watching only parts of the movie, spending more time watching Lory—and Lory, next to her mother on the couch, would sway a bit to her own internal rhythm, smiling, looking at the TV screen but occasionally at the brothers, and at A.C.

The nights that A.C. stayed over, Lory made sure that he had a pillow and fresh sheets. Making love to him was somehow unimaginable, and also the greatest thought of all; and he had this silly throw to make first, this long throw with the brothers.

Lovemaking was unthinkable—the waist-to-waist kind, anyway. If she gambled on it and lost, she would chase him away from the brothers as well as herself.

The idea was unthinkable. But each night she and A.C. would meet upstairs in the dark, or sit on the couch in the living room, dozing that way, with Lory in his arms, curled up in his lap, her head resting against his wide chest. That was not unimaginable.

A.C. trained all through the summer. Sometimes early in the evenings the brothers went out looking for statues with him. Their backyard was becoming filled with statues, all of them upright outside Lory's and Lindsay's windows. A.C. laid them down in the grass at daylight and covered them with tarps, but raised them again near sundown: long-ago generals, riverboat captains, composers, poets.

Louella kept her eye on him, suspecting, and believing in her heart, that he was the soul of her lost son come back in this huge body, come home finally. She did not want him to love Lory—it seemed that already he was too close—but she did not want him to go away either. Louella watched A.C. carefully, when he could not see she was watching him. What would it have been like to have three sons? What would that third son have been like? She felt both the sweetness and the anguish of it. She could not look away.

He had not been so happy in a long time. He was still throwing clumsily, but the discus was going farther and farther: 250, 255 feet; and then 260.

Each was a world-record throw, but the brothers did not tell A.C. this. They told no one else either. It was the brothers' plot to not show him off until he was consistently throwing the astonishing 300 feet. Perhaps A.C.'s first public throw of the discus would not only set a world's record; perhaps he'd hurl it so great a distance that no one would believe he was from this earth. Sportswriters and fans would clamor after him, chase him, want to take him away and lock him up and do tests on him, examine him. He would need an escape route, the brothers imagined, a way back to the Sacandaga River, never to be seen or heard from again...

The plan got fuzzy at that point. The brothers were not sure how it would go after that, and they had not yet consulted with A.C., but they were thinking that somehow Lory would figure in it.

Certainly they had told no one, not even their mother—especially not her.

A.C. was euphoric as the summer moved on. When he was back at his farmhouse, he often went out to the pasture and lifted a cow and danced around with it as if it were stuffed or inflated. Or in Glens Falls he'd roll the brothers' little Volkswagen over on its back, and then he would grab the bumper and begin running in circles with it, spinning it like a top in the deep grass. The muscles in his cheeks tensed and flexed as he spun, showing intricate striations. His veins would be visible just beneath his temples. A.C. would grin, and John and Jerry thought it great fun, too, and they'd get on either end and ride the upside-down car like a playground toy as A.C. continued to spin it.

The summer had not softened him; he was still all hard, still all marvelous. Children from the neighborhood would run up and touch him. They felt stronger, afterward.

Lately, on the nights he stayed over at the Irons' house, once everyone else was asleep, A.C. would carry Lory all through the house after she had fallen asleep in his lap. He imagined he was protecting her. He carried her down all the hallways—past her parents' room, her brothers', past Lindsay's, into the kitchen and out to the garage: it was all safe and quiet. Next he took her into the backyard, among the statues, and then into the street, walking through the neighborhood with her as she slept.

There was a street called Sweet Road that had no houses, only vacant lots, and trees, and night smells. He would lay her down in the dew-wet grass along Sweet Road and touch her robe, an old fuzzy white thing, and the side of her face. The wind would stir her hair, wind coming up out of the valley, wind coming from across the river. He owed the brothers his happiness.

Some nights, heat lightning flickered over the mountains, behind the steep ridges. She slept through it all in the cool grass. He wondered what she was dreaming.

Late in the afternoons, after practice, the brothers walked the mile and a half to the grocery store in town, and along the way they showed A.C. the proper discus steps. Lory and Lindsay followed sometimes, to watch. The brothers demonstrated to A.C., in half crouches and hops, the proper setup for a throw, the proper release, and he tried to learn: the snap forward with the throw, and then the little trail-away spin at the end, unwinding, everything finished.

Jerry brought chalk and drew dance steps on the sidewalk for the placement of A.C.'s feet so he could move down the sidewalk, practicing his throws. Like children playing hopscotch, ducking and twisting, shuffling forward and then pretending to finish the spin with great shouts at the imaginary release of each throw, they moved through the quiet neighborhood, jumping and shouting, throwing their arms at the sky. Dogs barked at them as they went past, and children ran away at first, though soon they learned to follow, once the brothers and the big man had passed, and they would imitate, in the awkward fashion of children, the brothers' and A.C.'s throws.

Lory could see the depression, the not quite old part of herself, behind her—back in June, back in the spring, and behind in winter; back into the cold fall and the previous dry-leaved summer—but she was slipping forward now, away from all that. A.C. took her to his farmhouse and showed her how to hang from the ceiling. He'd rigged the harness so that she could hang suspended and spin.

He had to get over the fear of injuring someone again. Had to hit the fear head-on and shatter it. He had run a long way to get here. He was ready to hit it head-on. It was worth it, once again. And he wanted her to be brave, too.

"It feels better naked," he said the first time he showed it to her, and so she took her clothes off. Lory closed her eyes and put her arms and legs out and spun in slow circles around and around, and

A.C. turned the light off, sat down against the wall, and watched her silhouette against the window, watched her until she fell asleep, and then he took her out of the harness and got in bed with her, where she awoke.

"We won't tell anyone," he said. She was in his arms, warm, alive. It made him dizzy to consider what being alive meant.

"No," she said. "No one will ever find out."

She fell asleep with her lips on his chest. A.C. lay there looking at the harness hanging above them, and wondered why he wanted to keep it a secret, why it had to be a secret.

He knew that this was the best way to protect her, and that he loved her.

He stayed awake all through the night, conscious of how he dwarfed her, afraid that if he fell asleep he might turn over and crush her. He rose before daylight, woke her, and they got in the canoe and drifted back to New York State, and were home before dawn. A.C. crept into the basement that first night, and every night thereafter.

Lory had not liked hanging from the ceiling. She didn't know why, only that it had frightened her. She kept the harness with her, kept it hidden in her drawer. She just wanted to love him, was all.

Many evenings the family had grilled corn for dinner, dripping with butter. They sat outside at the picnic table and ate with their hands. Night scents would drift toward them. As darkness fell, they would move into the house and watch the lazy movies, the baseball games of summer, and then they would go to sleep. But Lory and A.C. stayed up later and later as the summer went on, and made love after everyone had gone to bed, and then they would go out on their walk, A.C. still carrying Lory, though now she remained awake.

When she was not too tired—when she did not need to go to bed—they would paddle the canoe upriver to his farmhouse, with Lory sitting behind A.C. and tracing her fingers on his wide back as he paddled. The waves would splash against the bow, wetting them both. They moved up the current slowly, past hilly, night-green pastures with the moon high above or just beyond their reach. Summer haying smells rose from the fields, and they passed wild tiger lilies growing along the shore as they crossed into Vermont. Lory felt weightless and free until it was time to go back.

They lay on the old mattress in the farmhouse with holes in the roof above them, and, through the roof, the stars. No brothers, thought Lory fiercely, clutching A.C. and rolling beneath him, over him, beneath him again; she knew it was like swimming through rapids, or maybe drowning in them. Her brothers protected her and understood her, but A.C. seemed to know what was in the center of her, a place she had believed for a long while to be soft and weak.

It was exciting to believe that perhaps it was strong in there. To begin to believe she did not need protecting. It made his protection of her all the more exciting, all the more delicious—unnecessary, and therefore extravagant, luxurious.

They sat on the stone wall in front of the farmhouse afterward, some nights, before it was time to leave, and watched the cattle graze under the moon, listening to the slow strong grinding sound of their teeth being worn away as their bodies took nourishment. Lory and A.C. held hands and sat shoulder to shoulder, cold and still naked, and when it was time to go, they carried their clothes in a bundle down to the stream, the dew wetting their ankles, their knees, so that they were like the cattle as they moved through the grass—and they'd paddle home naked, Lory sitting right behind A.C. for warmth against the night.

The brothers continued to train in the daytime, and as the summer ended, there was a haze over the valley below them. They were throwing far over the fence, better than they'd ever thrown in their lives. They were tanned from the long hours of practicing shirtless. The sisters came by with a picnic lunch while the men threw. They laid out an old yellow Amish quilt that had belonged to their mother's mother, with the hexagon patterns on it looking not unlike the throwing ring in which A.C. and the brothers whirled before each heave of the discus. The sisters lay on the quilt on their stomachs, the sun warm on the backs of their legs. They ate Swiss cheese, strawberries, and apples, drank wine and watched the men throw forever, it seemed, until the sisters grew sleepy in the sun and rolled over and looked up at the big white cumulus clouds that did not seem to be going anywhere. They closed their eyes, felt the sun on their eyelids, and fell hard asleep, their mouths open, their bodies still listening to the faint tremors in the earth each time the discus landed.

A.C. had stopped sleeping altogether. There was simply too much to do.

He and Lory went for canoe rides out on Lake George, only they did not take paddles with them. Instead, A.C. had gotten the harness back from Lory, and he slipped that over himself and towed her out into the lake as if going to sea, bare to the waist, and Lory in her one-piece suit. They were both brown from the picnics, and with nothing but the great blue water before them, they appeared to glow red, as if smudged with earth. The sunlight seemed to focus on them alone, the only two moving, living figures before the expanse of all that water, out on top of all that water. Their bodies gathered that solitary light so that they were upright, ruddy planes of flesh, of muscle, dull red in the late summer light, with nothing but blue water beyond.

A.C. waded out, pulling the canoe with Lory riding inside, sitting upright like a shy stranger, a girl met on the first day of school. And then thigh-deep, and then deeper, up to his chest, his neck—he would take her out into the night.

Once they were on the lake, he would unbuckle the harness and swim circles around her and then submerge, staying under for a very long time, Lory thought. She lost track of the time. There was no way for her to bring him up; she could only wait for him. She watched the concentric ripples he'd left in the lake's surface until the water faded to smoothness again. She could feel him down there, somewhere below her, but the water was flat again, motionless. She would try to will him back to the surface, as if raising him with a rope from the bottom of a well, but he'd stay hidden below her.

For A.C., it was dark and yet so safe at the bottom of the lake. But then he would kick for the surface, up to the wavering glimmer of where she was, the glimmer becoming an explosion as he surfaced. He found her trying to pretend she wasn't worried, not even turning her head to look at him.

A.C. would get back into the harness and, like a fish or a whale, he would begin her on her journey again, taking her around and around the lake, leaving a small V behind the canoe. Lory trailed her hand in the water and looked back at the blotted tree line against the night and the restaurant-speckled shore; or she would look out ahead of her at the other shore, equally distant, where there were no lights at all.

With A.C. so close, tied to the end of a rope, pulling her and the boat through the water as if she were a toy, she wanted to stand up and call out, cupping her hands, "I love you." But she stayed seated and let her hand trail in the coolness of the lake. She was not a good swimmer, but she wanted to get in the water with him. She wanted to strip and dive in and swim out to him. He seemed so at ease that Lory would find herself—watching his wet, water-sliding back in the moonlight, the dark water—believing that he had become a sleek sea animal and was no longer a true human, mortal, and capable of mortal things.

Occasionally Lory and A.C. went out to the lake in the late afternoon, and she took a book. Between pages, as he continued to swim, she looked at the tree line, the shore, all so far away. Sometimes a boat drew near to see if she needed help, but always she waved it away, gave the people in the other boat a cheery thumbs-up signal. When dusk came, if A.C. had been swimming all afternoon, he would head back to the harbor, side-stroking and looking at her with a slow, lazy smile. But she did not want laziness or slow smiles; she wanted to reach out and hold him.

In the dark harbor he would climb into the boat, slippery and naked, as she removed her own clothes, pulling off the old sea-green sweater she wore over her swimsuit in the chill night air, then removing the yellow swimsuit itself, and then her earrings, placing all of these things in the bow, out of the way, so that there was nothing, only them. They would lie in the bottom of the cool green canoe, hold each kiss, and feel the lake pressing from beneath as they pressed back against it, riding the surface of the water. With the water so very nearly lapping at her skin but not quite—separated only by the canoe's thin shell—Lory felt like some sort of sea creature.

One or both of her arms would sometimes hang over the edge of the canoe as they made love, would trail or splash in the water, and often she didn't see why they didn't just get it over with, dive into the lake and never come back to the surface.

Later, they would get up and sit on the wicker bench seat in the stern, side by side, and lean against each other, holding hands.

They would sit in the harbor, those cool nights, steaming from their own heat. Other boats rode into the harbor, idling through the darkness back to shore, their lengths and shapes identifiable by the green and yellow running lights that lined their sides for safety, as they passed through the night, going home. At times it seemed as if one of the pleasure boats was coming right at them, and sometimes one of the boats with bright running lights would pass by so close they could see the faces of the people inside.

But they were unobserved. They watched the boats pass and let the night breezes dry their hair, dry the lake water from their bodies so that they felt human once more, and of the earth. They would make love again, invisible to all the other passing boats, all of them full of people who could not see what it was like to be in love.

A.C. and Lory would have coffee at a restaurant on the short drive back—five or six miles from home—on a deck beneath an umbrella like tourists, looking out at Highway 9A. Lory drank her coffee slowly, stirring milk and sugar into it, cup after cup, watching the black liquid turn into swirling, muddy shades of brown. A.C.'s weight was up to three hundred pounds now, more muscle than ever, but she would reach over, smiling, look into his eyes, and grip the iron breadth of his thigh and squeeze it, then pat it and say, "How are you doing, fat boy?"

She felt lake water still inside her, even though they had gone in for a quick cleaning-off swim—A.C. staying right next to her, holding her up in the water with one hand. She felt deliciously wild. They drank coffee for an hour, until their hair was completely dry. Then they drove home, to Louella's dismay and the brothers' looks of happiness, but looks that were somehow a little hurt, a little lost; home to Heck's mild wonderment and interest, looking up from his gin and tonic; home to Lindsay's impatience, for A.C. and Lory would have been gone a long time.

"We're just friends, Mom," Lory would say whenever Louella tried to corner her in the kitchen. "I'm happy, too. See? Look!" She danced, leapt, and kicked her heels together three times, spun around when she landed, then went up on her toes—an odd interpretation of the discus spin that A.C. was trying to learn.

"Well," said Louella, not knowing what to say or do. "Good. I hope so."

One morning when A.C. stayed in Glens Falls, he lifted himself from sleep and moved around the basement, examining the old weights, the rowing machines, the rust-locked exercise bikes, and the motionless death-hang of the patched and battered punching bags. A.C. ran his hand over the weights and looked at the flecks of rust that came off on his hands, and thought how the brothers were outlasting the iron and the steel. He stared at the rust in the palm of his hand and smelled the forever-still air that had always been in the basement, air in which John and Jerry had grown up, spindly kids wrestling and boxing, always fighting things, but being part of a family: eating meals together, going to church, teasing their sisters, growing larger, finding directions and interests, taking aim at things. That same air was still down there, as if in a bottle, and it confused A.C. and made him more sure that he was somehow a part of it, a part he did not know about.

He pictured pushing through the confusion, throwing the discus farther and farther, until one day he did the skip-and-glide perfectly. He would be able to spin around once more after that, twice more, and still look up after the throw in time to see the disc flying. It would make the brothers happy, but perhaps then they would not feel that he was a brother anymore.

He trained harder than ever with them, as if it were the greatest of secrets they were giving him. They put their arms around him, walking back from training. Sometimes they teased him, trying to put his great throws in perspective.

"The circumference of the earth at the equator is more than 24,000 miles," Jerry said nonchalantly, looking at his watch as if to see what time it was, as if he had forgotten an appointment. Lory had put him up to it. She'd given him the numbers to crib on his wrist. "Why, that's over 126,720,000 feet," he'd exclaim.

John looked over at A.C. and said, "How far'd you throw today, A.C.?"

A.C. would toss his head back and laugh a great, happy laugh, the laugh of someone being saved, being thrown a rope and pulled in. He would rather be their brother than anything. He wouldn't do them any harm.

Lory and A.C. took Lindsay canoeing on the Battenkill River, over in Vermont. It was almost fall. School was starting soon. Lory stayed close to A.C., held on to his arm, sometimes with both hands. She worried that the fatigue and subsequent depression would be coming on like a returning army, but she smiled thinly, moved through the cool days and laughed, grinning wider whenever their eyes met. Sometimes A.C. would blush and look away, which made Lory grin harder. She would tickle him, tease him; she knew he was frightened of leaving her. She knew he never would.

They drove through the countryside, past fields lined with crumbling stone walls and Queen Anne's lace, with the old canoe on top of the VW. They let Lindsay drive, like a chauffeur. A.C. and Lory had somehow squeezed into the back seat. Now and then Lindsay looked back at them when they kissed, and a blush came into her face, but mostly it was just shy glances at the mirror, trying to see, as if through a telescope, the pleasure that lay ahead of her.

The road turned to white gravel and dust with a clatter and clinking of pebbles, but Lory and A.C. did not notice. They looked like one huge person wedged into the back seat. Sun flashed through the windshield. It felt good to Lindsay to be driving with the window down, going faster than she ever had. Meadows passed, maples, farms, cattle. A.C. reached forward and squeezed the back of Lindsay's neck, startling her, and then began rubbing it. She relaxed, smiled, and leaned her head back. Her red hair on his wrist.

Lindsay drove down the narrow road raising dust, and brilliant goldfinches swept back and forth across the road in front of them, flying out of the cattails, alarmed at the car's speed. Lindsay hit one; it struck the hood and flew straight up above them, sailing back toward the cattails, dead, wings folded, but still a bright yellow color. Lindsay cried "Oh!" and covered her mouth, because neither A.C. nor Lory had seen it. She was ashamed and wanted to keep it a secret.

They stopped for cheeseburgers and shakes at a shady drive-in, in a small Vermont town whose name they'd never heard of. The drive-in was right by the banks of the river, where they would put the canoe in. The river was wide and shallow, cool and clear, and they sat beneath a great red oak and ate. Lindsay was delighted to be with them, but also she could not shake the oddest feeling. Again, the feeling was that there was nothing special, that it had been happening all her life, these canoe trips with A.C. and Lory, and that it could just as easily have been John or Jerry sitting with them under the tree. If anything, Lindsay felt a little hollow somehow, and cheated, as if something were missing, because A.C. had shown up only this summer.

Lindsay had never paddled before. She sat backwards and gripped the paddle wrong, like a baseball bat. And Lory did an amazing thing that her sister never understood: she fell out, twice. It was like falling out of a chair. She hadn't even been drinking. Lindsay shrieked. They had water fights.

Lindsay had baked a cake, and they ate it on a small island. When the sisters waded into the cold river to pee, A.C. laughed, turned his back, and made noise against the rocks on the shore.

"Lindsay's jealous," Lory said when they came trudging out of the river. Lindsay swung at her but missed, and fell back into the water.

The sun dried them quickly. Several times A.C. got out of the canoe and swam ahead, pulling them by a rope held in his teeth.

Lory had brought a jug of wine. They got out and walked up into a meadow and drank from it whenever they became tired of paddling, which was often. At one stop, on the riverbank, Lory ran her fingers through A.C.'s hair. In six years, she would be forty. A crow flew past, low over the river. Farther upstream, they could see trout passing beneath the canoe, could see the bottom of the river, which was deep. Stones lined the river bottom, as if an old road lay beneath them.

On the way home, with A.C. at the wheel, they stopped for more cheeseburgers and had Cokes in the bottle with straws. They kept driving with the windows down. Their faces were not sunburned, but darker.

When A.C., Lory, and Lindsay got home and went into the house, the brothers were immediately happy to see the big man again, as always, but then, like small clouds, something crossed their faces and then vanished again, something unknown, perhaps confused.

The day before school started, Lory and A.C. paddled up to the farmhouse in Vermont. They were both sad, as if one of them were leaving and not ever coming back. Lory thought about another year of school. Tired before it even began, she sat on the stone wall with him, her head on his shoulder. He let her stay that way and did not try to cheer her up with stunts or tricks or feats of strength. The cattle in the field grazed right up to the edge of the stone wall, unafraid of Lory and A.C.

He rubbed the back of Lory's neck, held her close against him. He could be kind and tender, he could be considerate and thoughtful, he could even love her, but she wanted something else. He was afraid of this, and knew he was as common as coal in that respect. He also knew he was afraid of leaving, and of being alone.

A.C. was running out of money, so he took a paper route. He had no car, so he pulled the papers on a huge scraping rickshaw, fitting himself with a harness to pull it. It had no wheels and was really only a crude travois: two long poles with a sheet of plywood nailed to them, and little guard rails so he could stack the papers high on it.

He delivered papers in the early afternoon. All through the neighborhoods he trotted, grimacing, pulling a half ton of paper slowly up the small hills, and then, like a creature from the heavens, like some cruel-eyed bird, he swooped down the hills, street gravel and rock rattling under the sled. He shouted and tossed papers like mad, glancing back over his shoulder with every throw to be sure that he was staying ahead of the weight of the sled, which was accelerating, trying to run him down. It was funny, and the people who lived at the bottom of a hill learned to listen for him, loved to watch him, to see if one day he might get caught.

But now it was lonely for A.C., with Jerry in his final year at school, playing football, and John coaching. Lindsay was back in school too, and Heck was still the principal. Only Louella stayed at home.

Usually A.C. finished his paper route by late afternoon, and then he would put the sled in the garage and hose himself off in the backyard, his chest red from where the harness had rubbed, his running shorts drenched with sweat. He'd hold the hose over his head and cool down. Louella would watch from the kitchen window, feeling lonely, but she was also cautious, a mother first.

Dripping, A.C. would turn the water off, coil the hose up, and sit at the picnic table, his back turned to the kitchen. Like a dog finished with his duties, he would wait until he could see Lory again, see all the siblings. Louella would watch him for a long time. She just couldn't be sure.

When Lory got home from school, riding on a fresh burst of energy at the idea of seeing him again, A.C. would jump up, shake sprays of water from his wet hair, and run to open the door for her. He kissed her delicately, and she would ask, teasing, "How was your day, dear?" It was all working out differently from how she had expected, but she was fresher and happier than she could ever remember.

The children at Lory's school were foul, craven, sunk without hope. She would resurrect one, get a glimmer of interest in one every now and then, but eventually it would all slide back; it had all been false—that faint progress, the improvement in attitude. Sometimes she hit her fist against the lockers after school. The desks with "I fucked Miss Iron" on them were still there, and the eyes of the male teachers were no better, saying the same thing. She was getting older, older, and each year she wondered if this was the year that the last of her youth would go away. It was a gauntlet, but she needed to stay close to Glens Falls. She had to keep going.

It was like traveling upriver at night in the canoe with him, up through the rapids, only it was like being one of the darkened iron statues rather than her live, loving self. It was like night all the time, this job, and in her dreams of it, there was never any sound, no promise, no future. She was in the wrong place, taking the wrong steps, and she knew—she could feel it as strongly as anything—that it took her too far away from him, teaching at Warrensburg each day, a place of darkness.

She was up until midnight every night, grading papers, preparing lesson plans, reading the barely legible scrawled essays of rage—"i wont to kil my sester, i wont to kil my bruthers"—and then she was up again at four or four-thirty, rousing herself from the sleepy dream of her life. But A.C. was also up by then, making coffee for her.

When they kissed in the morning she'd be wearing a tattered, dingy robe and her owlish reading glasses. His hands would slide under her robe and find her warm beneath the fuzzy cloth. He wanted nothing else for either of them. There could be no improvement. He knew she wanted more, though, that she wanted to keep going.

They would take a short walk right before she left for school. By the time they got back, John and Jerry would be up. Jerry's clock radio played hard rock. John, with no worries, no responsibilities, sorted through the refrigerator for his carton of milk (biceps drawn on it with a Magic Marker) and got Jerry's carton out (a heart with an arrow through it, and the word "Mom" inside the heart). The brothers stood around and drank, swallowing the milk in long, cold gulps.

Watching A.C. and Lory grow closer was, to Louella, like the pull of winter, or like giving birth. Always, she thought about the one she had lost. Twenty years later, she had been sent a replacement. She wanted to believe that. She had not led a martyr's life, but she had worked hard, and miracles did happen.

It was true, she realized. She could make it be true by wanting it to be true.

She looked out her kitchen window at him, sitting at the picnic table with his back to her, resting after his paper route, facing the garden, the late-season roses. Sun came through the window, and she could see hummingbirds fly into the backyard, lured by the sweetness of the nectar she had put in the feeders.

Louella watched A.C. look around at the hummingbirds, staring at them for the longest time, like a simple animal. The birds were dancing flecks of color, flashes of emerald and cobalt. Louella saw a blur of orange in the garden, the cat racing across the yard, up onto the picnic table, then leaping into the air, legs outstretched. She saw the claws, and like a ballplayer the cat caught one of the hummingbirds in midair, came down with it, and tumbled and rolled.

Louella watched as A.C. ran to the cat, squeezed its neck gently, and lifted the limp hummingbird from the cat's mouth. The cat shivered, shook, and ran back into the garden. A.C. set the limp hummingbird down on the picnic table. The other hummingbirds were gone.

Louella went into the backyard. The little bird lay still with its eyes shut, a speck of blood on its throat like a tiny ruby. The glitter of its green back like scales.

"That damn cat," Louella said, but as they watched, the hummingbird began to stir, ruffled its feathers, looked around, and flew away.

Each morning after the others had left, A.C. would sit at the picnic table a bit longer. Then he would come inside and tell Louella that he was going to Vermont for a while. Always, he asked her if she needed anything, or if she cared to go with him for the ride, and always she refused, saying she had things to do. Always, afterward, she wished she had said yes, wondered what it would be like, wondered what his stone farmhouse looked like. But there were boundaries to be maintained; she could not let go and say yes. So A.C. would lift the canoe over his head and walk through the neighborhood, out across the main road and down to the river, leaving her alone.

What A.C. was working on in Vermont was a barn, for throwing the discus during the winter months. He wanted to perfect his throw, to make John and Jerry happy. He had no money left, so he ripped down abandoned barns, saving even the nails from the old boards. He built his barn in the woods, on the side of the hill behind his farmhouse. It was more like a bowling alley than anything.

He had planned it to be 300 feet long. He climbed high into the trees to nail on the tall roof that would keep the snow out. There was not enough wood to build sides for the barn; mostly it was like a tent, a long, open-walled shed. He had built up the sides with stones about three feet high to keep the drifts from blowing in. It would be cold, but it would be free of snow.

He cut the trees down with an ax to build the throwing lane, and then cut them into lengths to be dragged away. He was building a strip of empty space in the heart of the woods; it ran for a hundred yards and then stopped. He kept it a secret from the whole family, and was greatly pleased with its progress as the fall went on.

The air inside the throwing room felt purified, denser somehow. It had the special scents of the woods: pine, moss, creek, frost. He burned all the stumps, leveled the ground with a shovel and hoe, and made a throwing ring out of river stones. The rafters overhead reminded him of the church he'd gone to once with the Irons: the high ceiling, the beams, keeping the hard rains and snows out, but also distancing them from what it was they were after.

He would work on the barn all morning, leave in time to get home and do his paper route, and still be back at the house before anyone else got there. Sometimes Louella would be out shopping or doing other errands. He would sit at the picnic table and wait for the sound of Lory's car.

Feathery snow fell on the Hudson highlands on the third of October, a Friday night. They were all walking to the movie theater in the mall, A.C. and Lory holding hands, Lindsay running ahead of them. It was too early for real snow.

The brothers were as full of spirit as they had been all year. It was as if they were fourteen. They danced, did their discus spins in crowded places, ending their imaginary releases with shouts that drew some spectators and scared others away, then all three of them spun and whooped—John's and Jerry's spins still more polished than A.C.'s, but A.C.'s impressive also, if for no reason other than his size. Soon there was a large audience, clapping and cheering as if they were Russian table dancers. (A.C. pictured it being late spring still, or early summer, before he had met them: back when he was still dancing with the cows on his back, a sport he had enjoyed, and which he secretly missed, though the brothers had asked him to stop doing it, saying it would throw his rhythm off. He missed the freedom of it, the lack of borders and rules, but did not want to hurt their feelings, did not want them to know he thought discus throwing was slightly inferior, so he'd done as they said, though still, he missed dancing and whirling with the cattle over his shoulders.)

Lory shrieked and hid her eyes with her hands, embarrassed, and Lindsay blushed her crimson color, but was petrified, unable to move, and she watched them, amazed as always. Lory's fingers were digging into Lindsay's arm; Lindsay smiled bravely through her embarrassment, and was happy for Lory. Everyone around them in the mall kept clapping and stamping their feet, while outside, the first snow came down.

A.C. gave the money from the paper route to Louella and Heck, and as he made more money, he tried to give that to them as well, but they wouldn't hear of it. So he bought things and gave them to Lory. He bought whatever he saw, if he happened to be thinking about her: a kitten, bouquets of flowers, jewelry, an NFL football, a smoked turkey.

She was flattered and excited the first few times he brought something home, but soon became alarmed at the volume of things, and asked him to stop. Then she had to explain to him what she really wanted, what really made her happy, and he was embarrassed, felt a fool for not having realized it before, for having tried to substitute. It was like throwing the discus from his hip rather than with the spin.

They went out in the canoe again that Saturday night, on Lake George. It was a still night at first, calm and chilly, and the full moon was so bright they could see the shore, even from far out on the water. They could see each other's face, each other's eyes; it was like some dream-lit daylight, hard and blue and silver, with the sound of waves lapping against the side of their small boat. They were cold, but they undressed anyway. They wanted to get close, as close as they could; they wanted to be all there was in the world, the only thing left.

He covered her with the blanket they had brought, and kept her warm with that and with himself. After making love to her he fell asleep, dreaming, in the warmth of the blanket and the roll of the boat, that he was still in her, that they were still loving, and that they always would be.

"You were smiling," she said when he woke around midnight. She'd been watching him all night. She'd held him, too, sometimes pressing him so tightly against her breast that she was sure he'd wake up, but he had slept on. "What were you smiling about?"

"You," he said sleepily. "I was thinking about you."

It was the right answer. She was so happy.

One weekend, Lory's school had a Halloween dance. A girl had been raped after the dance last year, and several of the teachers' cars had had their tires slashed and their radio antennas snapped. A small fire had been set inside the school and had scorched the walls. Lory was chaperoning this year. She went up there with John and Jerry and A.C., and stayed near them the whole time.

The brothers dwarfed Lory like bodyguards; she was almost hidden whenever she was in their midst. The young thugs and bullies did not attempt to reach out from the crowd and squeeze her breasts, as they sometimes did on dares, and the male teachers, married and unmarried, treated her with respect. The four of them sat in the bleachers and watched the dance, listening to the loud music until midnight. There was no mischief, and they were relieved when it was time to go.

They felt almost guilty, driving home to warmth and love. They rode in silence, thinking their own thoughts, back down to Glens Falls, whose lights they could see below, not twinkling as if with distance but shining steadily, a constant glow, because they were so close.

Geese, heading south late in the year, stragglers. A.C. worked on his barn during the mild sunny days of November. He could feel more snow coming, could feel it the way an animal can. The hair on his arms and legs was getting thicker, the way it had in Colorado in past autumns. The barn reminded him of the one that had been out there—the hay barn. That was where she had done it.

The throwing barn was almost finished. It was narrow, so his throws would have to be accurate. There could be no wildness, or he would wreck the place he had built. He would teach himself to throw straight.

He finished the barn in mid-November, as the big flakes arrived, the second snow of the season. Now the snows that came would not go away, not until the end of winter. He brought the brothers up to see the barn, to show them how they could keep training together, how they could keep throwing all through the winter, even with snow banked all around them, and they were delighted.

"This is the best year of my life," Jerry said.

A.C. bought a metal detector, and when throws did not travel perfectly straight—the barn was only thirty feet wide—the brothers and A.C. had to search in the snow, listening for the rapid signal that told them they were getting near. They used old metal discs now, which flew two or three feet farther in the cold air. The brothers ate more than ever, and trained harder.

There was a stone wall at the end of the barn, the 300-foot mark, stacked all the way to the rafters and chinked with mud and sand and grass. A.C. had lodged a discus in it once, had skipped a few of them against its base. Hitting that mark was magical, unimaginable; it required witchcraft, an alteration of reality.

It took the brothers and A.C. about sixty seconds to walk 300 feet. A minute away—and unobtainable, or almost.

Sometimes the throws went too far off into the woods, and the discs were lost for good. Other times, they went too high and crashed through the rafters, like cannonballs, cruel iron seeking to destroy.

"Forget it," John would say whenever A.C. threw outside the barn. They'd hear the snapping, tearing sound of branches being broken and then the *whack!* of the discus striking a tree trunk. John would already be reaching for another disc, though, handing it to him. "Come on, come on, shake it off, pal. Past history. Over and done with. Shake it off."

Past history. No harm done. These were sweet words to A.C. His eyes grew moist. He wanted to believe that. He wanted to make good this time.

✤　　✤　　✤

As the winter deepened, they set their goals harder and farther. John and Jerry wanted to throw 221 feet, and A.C. wanted to be able to throw 300 feet on any given throw, at will.

And he wanted Lory. He wanted to build fences, to take care, protect. Sometimes while everyone was at school, Louella would decide that she just couldn't keep away any longer. She would challenge herself to be brave, to accept him without really knowing whether he was hers or not. She would ride in the canoe with him up to the barn, to watch him throw. She had come over to his side, and believed in him. Louella wanted to know about his past, but A.C. simply wouldn't tell her.

A.C. built a fire for Louella in the barn, and she sat on a stump and sipped coffee while he threw. His spin was getting better. It was an imitation of her sons', she could tell, but it was starting to get some fluidity to it, some life, some creativity. Louella enjoyed watching him train. His clumsiness did not worry her, because she could tell he was working at it and overcoming it. She was even able to smile when the discus soared up through the rafters, letting a sprinkle of snow pour into the barn from above—yet another hole punched through the roof, one more hole of many, the snow sifting down like powder.

They were alarming, those wild throws, but she found herself trusting him. Secretly she liked the wild throws: she was fascinated by the strength and force behind them, the lack of control. It was like standing at the edge of a volcano, looking down. She moved a little closer to the fire. She was fifty-eight, and was seeing things she'd never seen before, feeling things she'd never felt. Life was still a mystery. He had made her daughter happy again.

"Keep your head back," Louella would caution whenever she saw that his form was too terribly off. "Keep your feet spread. Your feet were too close together." She knew enough about form to tell how it differed from her other sons'.

The whole family came for Thanksgiving: cousins and moved-away aunts, little babies, uncles and nieces. Everything flowed. A.C. was a good fit; it was as if he'd always been there. Passing the turkey, telling jokes, teasing Lindsay about a boyfriend; laughter and warmth inside the big house.

The roads iced over. There was the sound of studded snow tires outside, and of clanking chains. Football all day on television, and more pie, more cider. Then Thanksgiving passed and they were on into December, the Christmas season, with old black-and-white movies on television late at night and Lory on her holiday break from school. Everyone was home, and he was firmly in their center, her center.

He was in a spin of love and asked her to marry him. "Yes," she said, laughing, remembering last year's sadness and the crazy lost hope of it, never dreaming or knowing that he had been out there, moving toward her.

In her dreams, in the months preceding the wedding, she saw images of summer, of June coming around again. She and her mother stood in a large field, with cattle grazing near the trees. In the field were great boulders and fieldstones left over from another age, a time of glaciers and ice, of great floods.

And in the dream, she and her mother leaned into the boulders, rolling them, moving them out of the field, making the field pure and green. They built a stone wall out of the boulders, all around the field, and some were too large to move. Lory gritted her teeth and pushed harder, straining, trying to move them all. Then she would wake up and be by his side, by his warmth, and realize that she had been pushing against him, trying to get him out of bed. That could not be done, and she'd laugh, put her arms around as much of him as she could, and bury her face in him. Then she would get up after a while, unable to return to sleep.

She'd dress, put on her snow boots, go to the garage, and pick up one of the disks, holding it with both hands, feeling the worn smoothness, the coldness, and the magic of it—magic, Lory believed, because he had touched it. Certain that no one was watching, that no one could ever find out, she would go into the front yard, bundled up in woolens and a parka, and under the blue cast of the streetlight she'd crouch and then whirl, spinning around and around, and throw the discus as far as she could, in whatever direction it happened to go. She'd shout, almost roar, and watch it sink into the soft new snow, jumping up and down afterward when she threw well and was pleased with her throw.

Then she would wade out to where she had seen the discus disappear, kneel down, and dig for it with her hands. She'd carry it back to the garage, slip it into the box with the others, and finally she'd be able to sleep, growing warm again in bed with him.

In the spring, before the wedding, after the snows melted and the river began to warm—the river in which A.C. had first seen and swum up to his brothers—he began to swim again, but with Lory this year.

A.C. would fasten a rope to the harness around his chest and tie the other end of it to the bumper of her car before leaping into the river from a high rock and being washed down through the rapids.

Then he would swim upriver until his shoulders ached, until even he was too tired to lift his head, and was nearly drowning. Lory would leap into the car then, start it, and ease up the hill, pulling him like a limp wet rag through the rapids he'd been fighting, farther up the river until he was in the stone-bottomed shallows. She'd park the car, set the emergency brake, jump out, and run back down to get him.

Like a fireman, she'd pull him the rest of the way out of the river, splashing knee-deep in the water, helping him up, putting his arm around her tiny shoulders. Somehow they'd stagger up into the rocks and trees along the shore. He'd lie on his back and gasp, looking up at the sky and the tops of trees, and smelling the scent of pines. They would lie in the sun, drenched, exhausted, until their clothes were almost dry, and then they would back the car down and do it again.

He liked being saved. He needed her. And she needed him. Closer and closer she'd pull him, reeling in the wet rope, dragging him up on shore, bending over and kissing his wet lips until his eyes fluttered, bringing him back to life every time.

The Hermit's Story

An ice storm, following seven days of snow; the vast fields and drifts of snow turning to sheets of glazed ice that shine and shimmer blue in the moonlight, as if the color is being fabricated not by the bending and absorption of light but by some chemical reaction within the glossy ice; as if the source of all blueness lies somewhere up here in the north—the core of it beneath one of those frozen fields; as if blue is a thing that emerges, in some parts of the world, from the soil itself, after the sun goes down.

Blue creeping up fissures and cracks from depths of several hundred feet; blue working its way up through the gleaming ribs of Ann's buried dogs; blue trailing like smoke from the dogs' empty eye sockets and nostrils—blue rising as if from deep-dug chimneys until it reaches the surface and spreads laterally and becomes entombed, or trapped—but still alive, and drifting—within those moonstruck fields of ice.

Blue like a scent trapped in the ice, waiting for some soft release, some thawing, so that it can continue spreading.

It's Thanksgiving. Susan and I are over at Ann and Roger's house for dinner. The storm has knocked out all the power down in town— it's a clear, cold, starry night, and if you were to climb one of the mountains on snowshoes and look forty miles south toward where town lies, instead of seeing the usual small scatterings of light—like fallen stars, stars sunken to the bottom of a lake, but still glowing— you would see nothing but darkness—a bowl of silence and darkness in balance for once with the mountains up here, rather than opposing or complementing our darkness, our peace.

As it is, we do not climb up on snowshoes to look down at the dark town—the power lines dragged down by the clutches of ice—but can tell instead just by the way there is no faint glow over the mountains to the south that the power is out; that this Thanksgiving, life for those in town is the same as it always is for us in the mountains, and it is a good feeling, a familial one, coming on the holiday as it does—though doubtless too the townspeople are feeling less snug and cozy about it than we are.

We've got our lanterns and candles burning. A fire's going in the stove, as it will all winter long and into the spring. Ann's dogs are asleep in their straw nests, breathing in that same blue light that is being exhaled from the skeletons of their ancestors just beneath and all around them. There is the faint smell of cold-storage meat—slabs and slabs of it—coming from down in the basement, and we have just finished off an entire chocolate pie and three bottles of wine. Roger, who does not know how to read, is examining the empty bottles, trying to read some of the words on the labels. He recognizes the words *the* and *in* and *USA*. It may be that he will never learn to read—that he will be unable to—but we are in no rush; he has all of his life to accomplish this. I for one believe that he will learn.

Ann has a story for us. It's about a fellow named Gray Owl, up in Canada, who owned half a dozen speckled German shorthaired pointers and who hired Ann to train them all at once. It was twenty years ago, she says—her last good job.

She worked the dogs all summer and into the autumn, and finally had them ready for field trials. She took them back up to Gray Owl— way up in Saskatchewan—driving all day and night in her old truck, which was old even then, with dogs piled up on top of one another, sleeping and snoring: dogs on her lap, dogs on the seat, dogs on the floorboard.

Ann was taking the dogs up there to show Gray Owl how to work them: how to take advantage of their newfound talents. She could be a sculptor or some other kind of artist; she speaks of her work as if the dogs are rough blocks of stone whose internal form exists already and is waiting only to be chiseled free and then released by her, beautiful, into the world.

Basically, in six months the dogs had been transformed from gangling, bouncing puppies into six wonderful hunters, and she needed to show their owner which characteristics to nurture, which ones to discourage. With all dogs, Ann said, there was a tendency, upon their leaving her tutelage, for a kind of chitinous encrustation to set in, a sort of oxidation, upon the dogs leaving her hands and being returned to someone less knowledgeable and passionate, less committed than she. It was as if there were a tendency for the dogs' greatness to disappear back into the stone.

So she went up there to give both the dogs and Gray Owl a checkout session. She drove with the heater on and the windows down; the cold Canadian air was invigorating, cleaner. She could smell the scent of the damp alder and cottonwood leaves beneath the many feet of snow. We laughed at her when she said it, but she told us that up in Canada she could taste the fish in the water as she drove alongside creeks and rivers.

She got to Gray Owl's around midnight. He had a little guest cabin but had not heated it for her, uncertain as to the day of her arrival, so she and the six dogs slept together on a cold mattress beneath mounds of elk hides: their last night together. She had brought a box of quail with which to work the dogs, and she built a small fire in the stove and set the box of quail next to it.

The quail muttered and cheeped all night and the stove popped and hissed and Ann and the dogs slept for twelve hours straight, as if submerged in another time, or as if everyone else in the world were submerged in time—and as if she and the dogs were pioneers, or survivors of some kind: upright and exploring the present, alive in the world, free of that strange chitin.

She spent a week up there, showing Gray Owl how his dogs worked. She said he scarcely recognized them afield, and that it took a few days just for him to get over his amazement. They worked the dogs both individually and, as Gray Owl came to understand and appreciate what Ann had crafted, in groups. They traveled across snowy hills on snowshoes, the sky the color of snow, so that often it was like moving through a dream, and, except for the rasp of the snowshoes beneath them and the pull of gravity, they might have believed they had ascended into some sky-place where all the world was snow.

They worked into the wind—north—whenever they could. Ann would carry birds in a pouch over her shoulder and from time to time would fling a startled bird out into that dreary, icy snowscape. The quail would fly off with great haste, a dark-feathered buzz bomb disappearing quickly into the teeth of cold, and then Gray Owl and Ann and the dog, or dogs, would go find it, following it by scent only, as always.

Snot icicles would be hanging from the dogs' nostrils. They would always find the bird. The dogs would point it, Gray Owl or Ann would step forward and flush it, and the beleaguered bird would leap into the sky again, and once more they would push on after it, pursuing that bird toward the horizon as if driving it with a whip. Whenever the bird wheeled and flew downwind, they'd quarter away from it, then get a mile or so downwind from it and push it back north.

When the quail finally became too exhausted to fly, Ann would pick it up from beneath the dogs' noses as they held point staunchly, put the tired bird in her game bag, and replace it with a fresh one, and off they'd go again. They carried their lunch in Gray Owl's daypack, as well as emergency supplies—a tent and some dry clothes—in case they should become lost, and around noon each day (they could rarely see the sun, only an ice-white haze, so that they relied instead only on their internal rhythms) they would stop and make a pot of tea on the sputtering little gas stove. Sometimes one or two of the quail would die from exposure, and they would cook that on the stove and eat it out there in the tundra, tossing the feathers up into the wind as if to launch one more flight, and feeding the head, guts, and feet to the dogs.

Seen from above, their tracks might have seemed aimless and wandering rather than with the purpose, the focus that was burning hot in both their and the dogs' hearts. Perhaps someone viewing the tracks could have discerned the pattern, or perhaps not, but it did not matter, for their tracks—the patterns, direction, and tracing of them—were obscured by the drifting snow, sometimes within minutes after they were laid down.

Toward the end of the week, Ann said, they were finally running all six dogs at once, like a herd of silent wild horses through all that snow, and as she would be going home the next day there was no need to conserve any of the birds she had brought, and she was turning them loose several at a time: birds flying in all directions, and the dogs, as ever, tracking them to the ends of the earth.

It was almost a whiteout that last day, and it was hard to keep track of all the dogs. Ann was sweating from the exertion as well as the tension of trying to keep an eye on, and evaluate, each dog, and the sweat was freezing on her, an ice skin. She jokingly told Gray Owl that next time she was going to try to find a client who lived in Arizona, or even South America. Gray Owl smiled and then told her that they were lost, but no matter, the storm would clear in a day or two.

They knew it was getting near dusk—there was a faint dulling to the sheer whiteness, a kind of increasing heaviness in the air, a new density to the faint light around them—and the dogs slipped in and out of sight, working just at the edges of their vision.

The temperature was dropping as the north wind increased—"No question about which way south is," Gray Owl said, "so we'll turn around and walk south for three hours, and if we don't find a road, we'll make camp"—and now the dogs were coming back with frozen quail held gingerly in their mouths, for once the birds were dead, the dogs were allowed to retrieve them, though the dogs must have been puzzled that there had been no shots. Ann said she fired a few rounds of the cap pistol into the air to make the dogs think she had hit those birds. Surely they believed she was a goddess.

They turned and headed south—Ann with a bag of frozen birds over her shoulder, and the dogs, knowing that the hunt was over now, once again like a team of horses in harness, though wild and prancy.

After an hour of increasing discomfort—Ann's and Gray Owl's hands and feet numb, and ice beginning to form on the dogs' paws, so that the dogs were having to high-step—they came in day's last light to the edge of a wide clearing: a terrain that was remarkable and soothing for its lack of hills. It was a frozen lake, which meant—said

Gray Owl—they had drifted west (or perhaps east) by as much as ten miles.

Ann said that Gray Owl looked tired and old and guilty, as would any host who had caused his guest some unasked-for inconvenience. They knelt and began massaging the dogs' paws and then lit the little stove and held each dog's foot, one at a time, over the tiny blue flame to help it thaw out.

Gray Owl walked to the edge of the lake ice and kicked at it with his foot, hoping to find fresh water beneath for the dogs; if they ate too much snow, especially after working so hard, they'd get violent diarrhea and might then become too weak to continue home the next day, or the next, or whenever the storm quit.

Ann said that she had barely been able to see Gray Owl's outline through the swirling snow, even though he was less than twenty yards away. He kicked once at the sheet of ice, the vast plate of it, with his heel, then disappeared below the ice.

Ann wanted to believe that she had blinked and lost sight of him, or that a gust of snow had swept past and hidden him, but it had been too fast, too total: she knew that the lake had swallowed him. She was sorry for Gray Owl, she said, and worried for his dogs—afraid they would try to follow his scent down into the icy lake and be lost as well—but what she had been most upset about, she said—to be perfectly honest—was that Gray Owl had been wearing the little daypack with the tent and emergency rations. She had it in her mind to try to save Gray Owl, and to try to keep the dogs from going through the ice, but if he drowned, she was going to have to figure out how to try to get that daypack off of the drowned man and set up the wet tent in the blizzard on the snowy prairie and then crawl inside and survive. She would have to go into the water naked, so that when she came back out—if she came back out—she would have dry clothes to put on.

The dogs came galloping up, seeming as large as deer or elk in that dim landscape against which there was nothing else to give the viewer a perspective, and Ann whoaed them right at the lake's edge, where they stopped immediately, as if they had suddenly been cast with a sheet of ice.

Ann knew the dogs would stay there forever, or until she released them, and it troubled her to think that if she drowned, they too would die—that they would stand there motionless, as she had commanded them, for as long as they could, until at some point—days later, perhaps—they would lie down, trembling with exhaustion—they might lick at some snow, for moisture—but that then the snows would cover them, and still they would remain there, chins resting on their front paws, staring straight ahead and unseeing into the storm, wondering where the scent of her had gone.

Ann eased out onto the ice. She followed the tracks until she came to the jagged hole in the ice through which Gray Owl had plunged. She was almost half again lighter than he, but she could feel the ice crackling beneath her own feet. It sounded different, too, in a way she could not place—it did not have the squeaky, percussive resonance of the lake-ice back home—and she wondered if Canadian ice froze differently or just sounded different.

She got down on all fours and crept closer to the hole. It was right at dusk. She peered down into the hole and dimly saw Gray Owl standing down there, waving his arms at her. He did not appear to be swimming. Slowly, she took one glove off and eased her bare hand into the hole. She could find no water, and, tentatively, she reached deeper.

Gray Owl's hand found hers and he pulled her down in. Ice broke as she fell, but he caught her in his arms. She could smell the wood smoke in his jacket from the alder he burned in his cabin. There was no water at all, and it was warm beneath the ice.

"This happens a lot more than people realize," he said. "It's not really a phenomenon; it's just what happens. A cold snap comes in October, freezes a skin of ice over the lake—it's got to be a shallow one, almost a marsh. Then a snowfall comes, insulating the ice. The lake drains in fall and winter—percolates down through the soil"—he stamped the spongy ground beneath them—"but the ice up top remains. And nobody ever knows any different. People look out at the surface and think, *Aha, a frozen lake.*" Gray Owl laughed.

"Did you know it would be like this?" Ann asked.

"No," he said. "I was looking for water. I just got lucky."

Ann walked back to shore beneath the ice to fetch her stove and to release the dogs from their whoa command. The dry lake was only about eight feet deep, but it grew shallow quickly closer to shore, so that Ann had to crouch to keep from bumping her head on the overhead ice, and then crawl; and then there was only space to wriggle, and to emerge she had to break the ice above her by bumping and then battering it with her head and elbows, struggling like some embryonic hatchling; and when she stood up, waist-deep amid sparkling shards of ice—it was nighttime now—the dogs barked ferociously at her, but they remained where she had ordered them. She was surprised at how far off course she was when she climbed out; she had traveled only twenty feet, but already the dogs were twice that far away from her. She knew humans had a poorly evolved, almost nonexistent sense of direction, but this error—over such a short distance—shocked her. It was as if there were in us a thing—an impulse, a catalyst—that denies our ever going straight to another thing. Like dogs working left and right into the wind, she thought, before converging on the scent.

Except that the dogs would not get lost, while she could easily imagine herself and Gray Owl getting lost beneath the lake, walking in circles forever, unable to find even the simplest of things: the shore.

She gathered the stove and dogs. She was tempted to try to go back in the way she had come out—it seemed so easy—but she considered the consequences of getting lost in the other direction, and instead followed her original tracks out to where Gray Owl had first dropped through the ice. It was true night now, and the blizzard was still blowing hard, plastering snow and ice around her face like a mask. The dogs did not want to go down into the hole, so she lowered them to Gray Owl and then climbed gratefully back down into the warmth herself.

The air was a thing of its own—recognizable as air, and breathable as such, but with a taste and odor, an essence, unlike any other air they'd ever breathed. It had a different density to it, so that smaller, shallower breaths were required; there was very much the feeling that if they breathed in too much of the strange, dense air, they would drown.

They wanted to explore the lake, and were thirsty, but it felt like a victory simply to be warm—or rather, not cold—and they were so exhausted that instead they made pallets out of the dead marsh grass that rustled around their ankles, and they slept curled up on the tiniest of hammocks, to keep from getting damp in the pockets and puddles of water that still lingered here and there.

All eight of them slept as if in a nest, heads and arms draped across other ribs and hips; and it was, said Ann, the best and deepest sleep she'd ever had—the sleep of hounds, the sleep of childhood. How long they slept, she never knew, for she wasn't sure, later, how much of their subsequent time they spent wandering beneath the lake, and then up on the prairie, homeward again, but when they awoke, it was still night, or night once more, and clearing, with bright stars visible through the porthole, their point of embarkation; and even from beneath the ice, in certain places where, for whatever reasons—temperature, oxygen content, wind scour—the ice was clear rather than glazed, they could see the spangling of stars, though more dimly; and strangely, rather than seeming to distance them from the stars, this phenomenon seemed to pull them closer, as if they were up in the stars, traveling the Milky Way, or as if the stars were embedded in the ice.

It was very cold outside—up above—and there was a steady stream, a current like a river, of the night's colder, heavier air plunging down through their porthole—as if trying to fill the empty lake with that frozen air—but there was also the hot muck of the earth's massive respirations breathing out warmth and being trapped and protected beneath that ice, so that there were warm currents doing battle with the lone cold current.

The result was that it was breezy down there, and the dogs' noses twitched in their sleep as the images brought by these scents painted themselves across their sleeping brains in the language we call dreams but which, for the dogs, was reality: the scent of an owl *real*, not a dream; the scent of bear, cattail, willow, loon, *real*, even though they were sleeping, and even though those things were not visible, only over the next horizon.

The ice was contracting, groaning and cracking and squeaking up tighter, shrinking beneath the great cold—a concussive, grinding sound, as if giants were walking across the ice above—and it was this sound that awakened them. They snuggled in warmer among the rattly dried yellowing grasses and listened to the tremendous clashings, as if they were safe beneath the sea and were watching waves of starlight sweeping across their hiding place; or as if they were in some place, some position, where they could watch mountains being born.

After a while the moon came up and washed out the stars. The light was blue and silver and seemed, Ann said, to be like a living thing. It filled the sheet of ice just above their heads with a shimmering cobalt light, which again rippled as if the ice were moving, rather than the earth itself, with the moon tracking it—and like deer drawn by gravity getting up in the night to feed for an hour or so before settling back in, Gray Owl and Ann and the dogs rose from their nests of straw and began to travel.

They walked a long way. The air was damp down there, and whenever they'd get chilled, they'd stop and make a little fire out of a bundle of dry cattails. There were pockets and puddles of swamp gas pooled in place, and sometimes a spark from the cattails would ignite one of those, and the pockets of gas would light up like when you toss gas on a fire—explosions of brilliance, like flashbulbs, marsh patches igniting like falling dominoes, or like children playing hopscotch— until a large enough flash-pocket was reached—sometimes thirty or forty yards away—that the puff of flame would blow a chimney-hole through the ice, venting the other gas pockets, and the fires would crackle out, the scent of grass smoke sweet in their lungs, and they could feel gusts of warmth from the little flickering fires, and currents of the colder, heavier air sliding down through the new vent-holes and pooling around their ankles. The moonlight would strafe down through those rents in the ice, and shards of moon-ice would be glittering and spinning like diamond-motes in those newly vented columns of moonlight; and they pushed on, still lost, but so alive.

The small explosions were fun, but they frightened the dogs, so Ann and Gray Owl lit twisted bundles of cattails and used them for torches to light their way, rather than building warming fires, though occasionally they would still pass through an invisible patch of methane and a stray ember would fall from their torches, and the whole chain of fire and light would begin again, culminating once more with a vent-hole being blown open and shards of glittering ice tumbling down into their lair.

What would it have looked like, seen from above—the orange blurrings of their wandering trail beneath the ice; and what would the sheet of lake-ice itself have looked like that night—throbbing with ice-bound, subterranean blue and orange light of moon and fire? But again, there was no one to view the spectacle: only the travelers themselves, and they had no perspective, no vantage from which to view or judge themselves. They were simply pushing on from one fire to the next, carrying their tiny torches.

They knew they were getting near a shore—the southern shore, they hoped, as they followed the glazed moon's lure above—when the dogs began to encounter shore birds that had somehow found their way beneath the ice through fissures and rifts and were taking refuge in the cattails. Small winter birds—juncos, nuthatches, chickadees—skittered away from the smoky approach of their torches; only a few late-migrating (or winter-trapped) snipe held tight and steadfast; and the dogs began to race ahead of Gray Owl and Ann, working these familiar scents: blue and silver ghost-shadows of dog muscle weaving ahead through slants of moonlight.

The dogs emitted the odor of adrenaline when they worked, Ann said—a scent like damp, fresh-cut green hay—and with nowhere to vent, the odor was dense and thick around them, so that Ann wondered if it too might be flammable, like the methane; if in the dogs' passions they might literally immolate themselves.

They followed the dogs closely with their torches. The ceiling was low, about eight feet, so that the tips of their torches' flames seared the ice above them, leaving a drip behind them and transforming the milky, almost opaque cobalt and orange ice behind them, wherever they passed, into wandering ribbons of clear ice, translucent to the sky—a script of flame, or buried flame, ice-bound flame—and they hurried to keep up with the dogs.

Now the dogs had the snipe surrounded, as Ann told it, and one by one the dogs went on point, each dog freezing as it pointed to the birds' hiding places, and Gray Owl moved in to flush the birds, which launched themselves with vigor against the roof of the ice above, fluttering like bats; but the snipe were too small, not powerful enough to break through those frozen four inches of water (though they could fly four thousand miles to South America each year and then back to Canada six months later—is freedom a lateral component, or a vertical one?), and as Gray Owl kicked at the clumps of frost-bent cattails where the snipe were hiding and they burst into flight, only to hit their heads on the ice above them, they came tumbling back down, raining limp and unconscious back to their soft grassy nests.

The dogs began retrieving them, carrying them gingerly, delicately—not caring for the taste of snipe, which ate only earthworms—and Ann and Gray Owl gathered the tiny birds from the dogs, placed them in their pockets, and continued on to the shore, chasing that moon, the ceiling lowering to six feet, then four, then to a crawlspace, and after they had bashed their way out and stepped back out into the frigid air, they tucked the still-unconscious snipe into little crooks in branches, up against the trunks of trees and off the ground, out of harm's way, and passed on, south—as if late in their own migration—while the snipe rested, warm and terrified and heart-fluttering, but saved, for now, against the trunks of those trees.

Long after Ann and Gray Owl and the pack of dogs had passed through, the birds would awaken, their bright, dark eyes luminous in the moonlight, and the first sight they would see would be the frozen marsh before them, with its chain of still-steaming vent-holes stretching back across all the way to the other shore. Perhaps these were birds that had been unable to migrate owing to injuries, or some genetic absence. Perhaps they had tried to migrate in the past but had found either their winter habitat destroyed or the path so fragmented and fraught with danger that it made more sense—to these few birds—to ignore the tuggings of the stars and seasons and instead to try to carve out new lives, new ways of being, even in such a stark and severe landscape: or rather, in a stark and severe period—knowing that lushness and bounty were still retained with that landscape; that it was only a phase, that better days would come. That in fact (the snipe knowing these things with their blood, ten million years in the world) the austere times were the very thing, the very imbalance, that would summon the resurrection of that frozen richness within the soil—if indeed that richness, that magic, that hope, did yet exist beneath the ice and snow. Spring would come like its own green fire, if only the injured ones could hold on.

And what would the snipe think or remember, upon reawakening and finding themselves still in that desolate position, desolate place and time, but still alive, and with hope?

Would it seem to them that a thing like grace had passed through, as they slept—that a slender winding river of it had passed through and rewarded them for their faith and endurance?

Believing, stubbornly, that that green land beneath them would blossom once more. Maybe not soon; but again.

If the snipe survived, they would be among the first to see it. Perhaps they believed that the pack of dogs, and Gray Owl's and Ann's advancing torches, had only been one of winter's dreams. Even with the proof—the scribings—of grace's passage before them— the vent-holes still steaming—perhaps they believed it was a dream.

Gray Owl, Ann, and the dogs headed south for half a day until they reached the snow-packed, wind-scoured road on which they'd parked. The road looked different, Ann said, buried beneath snow-drifts, and they didn't know whether to turn east or west. The dogs chose west, and Gray Owl and Ann followed them. Two hours later they were back at their truck, and that night they were back at Gray Owl's cabin; by the next night Ann was home again.

She says that even now she sometimes has dreams about being be-neath the ice—about living beneath the ice—and that it seems to her as if she was down there for much longer than a day and a night; that instead she might have been gone for years.

It was twenty years ago, when it happened. Gray Owl has since died, and all those dogs are dead now, too. She is the only one who still carries—in the flesh, at any rate—the memory of that passage.

Ann would never discuss such a thing, but I suspect that it, that one day and night, helped give her a model for what things were like for her dogs when they were hunting and when they went on point: how the world must have appeared to them when they were in that trance, that blue zone, where the odors of things wrote their images across the dogs' hot brainpans. A zone where sight, and the appearance of things—*surfaces*—disappeared, and where instead their essence—the heat molecules of scent—was revealed, illuminated, circumscribed, possessed.

I suspect that she holds that knowledge—the memory of that one day and night—especially since she is now the sole possessor—as tightly, and securely, as one might clench some bright small gem in one's fist: not a gem given to one by some favored or beloved individual but, even more valuable, some gem found while out on a walk— perhaps by happenstance, or perhaps by some unavoidable rhythm of fate—and hence containing great magic, great strength.

Such is the nature of the kinds of people living, scattered here and there, in this valley.

The Fireman

They both stand on the other side of the miracle. Their marriage was bad, perhaps even rotting, but then it got better. He—the fireman, Kirby—knows what the reason is: every time they have an argument, the dispatcher's call sounds, and he must run and disappear into the flames—he is the captain—and while he is gone, his wife, Mary Ann, reorders her priorities, thinks of the children, and worries for him. Her blood cools, as does his. It seems that the dispatcher's call is always saving them. Their marriage settles in and strengthens, afterward, like some healthy, living, supple thing.

She meets him at the door when he returns, kisses him. He is grimy-black, salt-stained and smoky-smelling. They can't even remember what the argument was about. It's almost like a joke, the fact that they were upset about such a small thing—any small thing. He sheds his bunker gear in the utility room and goes straight to the shower. Later, they sit in the den by the fireplace and he drinks a few beers and tells her about the fire. He knows he is lucky—he knows they are both lucky. As long as the city keeps burning, they can avoid becoming weary and numb. Each time he leaves, is drawn away, and then returns to a second chance.

The children—a girl, four, and a boy, two—sleep soundly. It is not so much a city that they live in, but a town—a suburb on the perimeter of a city in the center of the southern half of the country—a place where it is warm more often than it is cold—a land of air conditioners—so that the residents are not overly familiar with chimney fires: the way a fire spreads from room to room; the way it takes only one small, errant thing in a house to invalidate and erase the whole structure—to bring it all down to ashes and send the building's former occupants out wandering lost and adrift into the night, poorly dressed and without direction.

They often talk until dawn, if the fire has occurred at night. She is his second wife; he is her first husband. Because they are in an unincorporated suburb, his is a volunteer department. Kirby's crew has a station with new equipment—all they could ask for—but there are no salaries, and he likes it that way; it keeps things purer. He has a day job as a computer programmer for an engineering firm that designs steel girders and columns used in industrial construction: warehouses, mills, and factories. The job means nothing to him—he slips through the long hours of it with neither excitement nor despair, his pulse never rising, and when it is over each day he says goodbye to his coworkers and leaves the office without even the faintest echo of his work lingering in his blood. He leaves it all the way behind, or lets it pass through him like some harmless silver laxative.

But after a fire—holding a can of cold beer, and sitting there next to the hearth, scrubbed clean, talking to Mary Ann, telling her what it had been like, what the cause had been, and who among his men had performed well and who had not—his eyes water with pleasure at his knowing how lucky he is to be getting a second chance with each and every fire.

He would never say anything bad about his first wife, Rhonda— and indeed, perhaps there is nothing bad to say, no failing in which they were not both complicit. It almost doesn't matter; it's almost water under the bridge.

The two children are asleep in their rooms, the swing set and jungle gym out in the backyard. The security of love and constancy— the *safety*. Mary Ann leads the children's choir in church and is as respected for her work with the children as Kirby is for his work with the fires.

It would seem like a fairy-tale story: a happy marriage, one that turned around its deadly familiar course of the mundane and the boring early on, that day six years ago when he signed up to be a volunteer for the fire department. One of those rare marriages, as rare as a jewel or a forest, that was saved by a combination of inner strength and the grace and luck of fortuitous external circumstances—*the world afire.* Who, given the chance, would not choose to leap across that chasm between a marriage that is heading toward numbness and tiredness and one that is instead strengthened, made more secure daily for its journey into the future?

And yet—even on the other side of the miracle, even on the other side of luck—a thing has been left behind: his oldest daughter, his only child from his first marriage, Jenna. She's ten, almost eleven.

There is always excitement and mystery on a fire call. It's as if these things are held in solution just beneath the skin of the earth and are then released by the flames; as if the surface of the world is some errant, artificial crust—almost like a scab—and that there are rivers of blood below, and rivers of fire, rivers of the way things used to be and might someday be again—true but mysterious, and full of power.

It does funny things to people—a fire, that burning away of the thin crust. Kirby tells Mary Ann about two young men in their thirties—lovers, he thinks—who, bewildered and bereft as their house burned, went out into the front yard and began cooking hamburgers for the firefighters as the building burned down.

He tells her about a house full of antiques that could not be salvaged. The attack crew was fighting the fire hard, deep in the building's interior—the building "fully involved" as they say when the wood becomes flame, air becomes flame, world becomes flame. It is the thing the younger firemen live for—not a smoke alarm, lost kitten, or piddly grass fire, but the real thing, a fully involved structure fire—and even the older firemen's hearts are lifted by the sight of one. Even those who have been thinking of retiring (at thirty-seven, Kirby is the oldest man on the force) are made new again by the sight of it, and by the radiant heat, which curls and browns and sometimes even ignites the oak leaves of trees across the street from the fire. The paint of cars parked too close to the fire sometimes begins to blaze spontaneously, making it look as if the cars are traveling very fast.

Bats, which have been out hunting, begin to return in swarms, dancing above the flames, and begin flying in dark, agitated funnels back down into the chimney of a house that's on fire, if it is not a winter fire—if the chimney has been dormant—trying to rescue their flightless young, which are roosting in the chimney, or sometimes the attic, or beneath the eaves. The bats return to the house as it burns down, but no one ever sees any of them come back out. People stand around on the street—their faces orange in the firelight—and marvel, hypnotized at the sight of it, not understanding what is going on with the bats, or any of it, and drawn, too, like somnambulists, to the scent of those blood-rivers, those vapors of new birth that are beginning already to leak back into the world as that skin, that crust, is burned away.

The fires almost always happen at night.

This fire that Kirby is telling Mary Ann about—the one in which the house full of antiques was being lost—was one of the great fires of the year. The men work in teams, as partners—always within sight, or one arm's length of one another, so that one can help the other if trouble is encountered: if the foundation gives way, or a burning beam crashes across the back of one of the two partners, who are not always men—more and more women are volunteering, though none has yet joined Kirby's crew. He likes the idea; of the multiple-alarm fires he's fought with other crews in which there were women firefighters, the women tended to try to out-think rather than out-muscle the fire, the former being almost always the best approach.

Kirby's partner now is a young man, Grady, just out of college. Kirby likes to use his intelligence when he fights a fire, rather than just hurling himself at it and risking getting sucked too quickly into its maw and becoming trapped—not just dying himself, but possibly causing harm or death to those members of his crew who might then try to save him—and for this reason Kirby likes to pair himself with the youngest, rawest, most adrenaline-rich trainees entrusted to his care—to act as an anchor of caution upon them, to counsel prudence and moderation even as the world burns down around them.

At the fire in the house with the antiques, Kirby and Grady had just come out to rest and to change oxygen tanks. The homeowner had at first been beside himself, shouting and trying to get back into his house, so that the fire marshal had had to restrain him—they had bound him to a tree with a canvas strap—but soon the homeowner was watching the flames almost as if hypnotized. Kirby and Grady were so touched by his change in demeanor—the man wasn't struggling any longer, was instead only leaning out slightly away from the tree, like the figurehead on a ship's prow, and sagging slightly—that they cut him loose so he could watch the spectacle in freedom, unencumbered.

He made no more moves to reenter his burning house, only stood there with watery eyes—whether tears of anguish, or irritation from the smoke, they could not tell—and, taking pity, Kirby and Grady put on new oxygen tanks, gulped down some water. And although they were supposed to rest, they went back into the burning building and began carrying out those pieces of furniture that had not yet ignited, and sometimes even those that had—burning breakfronts, flaming rolltop desks—and dropped them into the man's backyard swimming pool for safekeeping, as the tall trees in the yard crackled and flamed like giant candles, and floating embers drifted down, scorching whatever they touched.

Neighbors all around them climbed up onto their cedar-shingled roofs in their pajamas and with garden hoses began wetting down their own roofs, trying to keep the conflagration from spreading.

The business of it has made Kirby neat and precise. He and Grady crouched and lowered the dining room set into the deep end (even as some of the pieces of furniture were still flickering with flame), releasing them to sink slowly to the bottom, settling into place in the same manner and arrangement in which they had been positioned back in the burning house.

There is no room for excess, unpredictability, or recklessness; these extravagances cannot be borne, and Kirby wants Grady to see and understand this, the sooner the better. The fire hoses must always be coiled in the same pattern, so that when unrolled the male nipple is nearest the truck and the female farthest. The backup generators must always have fresh oil and gas in them and be kept in working order; the spanner wrenches must always hang in the same place.

The days go by in long stretches, twenty-three and a half hours at a time, but in the last half hour, in the moment of fire, when all the old rules melt down and the new world becomes flame, the importance of a moment, of a second, is magnified ten-thousand-fold—is magnified to almost an eternity, and there is no room for even a single mistake. Time inflates to a greater density than iron. You've got to be able to go through the last half hour, that wall of flame, on instinct alone, or by force of habit, by rote, by feel.

An interesting phenomenon happens when time catches on fire like this. It happens even to the veteran firefighters. A form of tunnel vision develops—the heart pounding almost two hundred times a minute and the pupils contracting so tightly that vision almost vanishes. The field of view becomes reduced to an area about the size of another man's helmet, or face: his partner, either in front of or behind him. If the men ever become separated by sight or sound, they are supposed to freeze instantly and then begin swinging a free arm, in all directions, and if their partner does the same, is within one or even two arms' lengths, their arms will bump each other and they can continue—they can rejoin the fight, as the walls flame vertically and the ceiling and floors melt and fall away.

The firefighters carry motion sensors on their hips, which send out piercing electronic shrieks if the men stop moving for more than thirty seconds. If one of those goes off, it means that a firefighter is down—that he has fallen and injured himself or has passed out from smoke inhalation—and all the firefighters stop what they are doing and turn and converge on the sound, if possible, centering back to it like the bats pouring back down the chimney.

A person's breathing accelerates inside a burning house, and the blood heats, as if in a purge. The mind fills with a strange music. Sense of feel, and memory of how things *ought* to be, becomes everything; it seems that even through the ponderous, fire-resistant gloves the firefighters could read Braille if they had to. As if the essence of all objects exudes a certain clarity, just before igniting.

Everything in its place; the grain, the threading of the canvas weave of the fire hoses, tapers back toward the male nipples; if lost in a house fire, you can crouch on the floor and with your bare hand— or perhaps even through the thickness of your glove, in that hyper-tactile state—follow the hose back to its source, back outside, to the beginning.

The ears—the lobes of the ear, specifically—are the most temperature-sensitive part of the body. Many times the heat is so intense that the firefighters' suits begin smoking and their helmets begin melting, while deep within the firefighters are still insulated and protected. But they are taught that if the lobes of their ears begin to feel hot, they are to get out of the building immediately, that they themselves may be about to ignite.

It's intoxicating; it's addictive as hell.

The fire does strange things to people. Kirby tells Mary Ann that it's usually the men who melt down first—they seem to lose their reason sooner than the women. During the fire in which they sank all the man's prize antiques in the swimming pool, after the man was released from the tree (the top of which began flaming, dropping ember-leaves into the yard, and even onto his shoulders, like fiery moths), he walked around into the backyard and stood next to his pool, with his back turned toward the burning house, and began busying himself with his long-handled dip net, laboriously skimming—or endeavoring to skim—the ashes from the pool's surface.

Another time—a fire in broad daylight—a man walked out of his burning house and went straight to his greenhouse, which he kept filled with flowering plants for his twenty or more hummingbirds of various species. He was afraid that the fire would spread to the greenhouse and burn up the birds, so he closed himself in there and began spraying the birds down with the hose as they flitted and whirled from him, and he kept spraying them, trying to keep their brightly colored wings wet so they would not catch fire.

Kirby tells Mary Ann all of these stories—a new one each time he returns—and they lie together on the couch until dawn. The youngest baby, a boy, has just given up nursing; Kirby and Mary Ann are just beginning to earn back moments of time together—little five- and ten-minute wedges—and Mary Ann naps with her head on his fresh-showered shoulder, though in close like that, at the skin level, she can still smell the charcoal, can taste it. Kirby has scars across his neck and back, pockmarks where embers have landed and burned through his suit, and she, like the children, likes to touch these; the small, slick feel of them reminds her of smooth stones from a river. Kirby earns several each year, and he says that before it is over he will look like a Dalmatian. She does not ask him what he means by "when it is all over," and she reins herself back, to keep from asking the question "When will you stop?"

Everyone has fire stories. Mary Ann's is that when she was a child she went into the bathroom at her grandmother's house, took off her robe, laid it over the plug-in portable electric heater, and sat on the commode. The robe quickly leapt into flame, and the peeling old wallpaper caught on fire, too—so much flame that she could not get past—and she remembers even now, twenty-five years later, how her father had to come in and lift her up and carry her back out—and how that fire was quickly, easily extinguished.

But that was a long time ago and she has her own life, needs no one to carry her in or out of anywhere. All that has gone away, vanished; her views of fire are not a child's but an adult's. Mary Ann's fire story is tame, it seems, compared to the rest of the world's.

She counts the slick small oval scars on his back: twenty-two of them, like a pox. She knows he is needed. He seems to thrive on it. She remembers both the terror and the euphoria after her father whisked her out of the bathroom, as she looked back at the dancing flames she had birthed. Is there greater power in lighting a fire or in putting one out?

He sleeps contentedly there on the couch. She will not ask him—not yet. She will hold it in for as long as she can, and watch—some part of her desirous of his stopping, but another part not.

She feels as she imagines the streetside spectators must, or even the victims of the fires themselves, the homeowners and renters: a little hypnotized, a little transfixed, and there is a confusion, as if she could not tell you nor her children—could not be sure—whether

she was watching him burn down to the ground or watching him being born and built up, standing among the flames like iron being cast
from the earth.

She sleeps, her fingers light across his back. She dreams the
twenty-two scars are a constellation in the night. She dreams that the
more fires he fights, the safer and stronger their life becomes.

She wants him to stop. She wants him to go on.

They awaken on the couch at dawn to the baby's murmurings
from the other room and the four-year-old's—the girl's—soft sleep-
breathings. The sun, orange already, rising above the city. Kirby gets
up and dresses for work. He could do it in his sleep. It means nothing
to him. It is its own form of sleep, and these moments on the couch,
and in the shells of the flaming buildings, are their own form of wake-
fulness.

Some nights, he goes over to his daughter Jenna's house—to the
house of his ex-wife. No one knows he does this: not Mary Ann, and
not his ex-wife, Rhonda, and certainly not Jenna—not unless she
knows it in her sleep and in her dreams, which he hopes she does.

He wants to breathe her air; he wants her to breathe his. It is a bi-
ological need. He climbs up on the roof and leans over the chimney,
and listens—*silence*—and inhales, and exhales.

The fires usually come about once a week. The time between them
is peaceful at first but then increasingly restless, until finally the dispatcher's radio sounds in the night and Kirby is released. He leaps
out of bed—he lives four blocks from the station—kisses Mary Ann,
kisses his daughter and son sleeping in their beds, and then is out
into the night, hurrying but not running across the lawn. He will be
the first one there, or among the first—other than the young firemen
who may already be hanging out at the station, watching movies and
playing cards, just waiting.

Kirby gets in his car—the chief's car—and cruises the neighborhood, savoring his approach. There's no need to rush and get to the
station five or ten seconds sooner, when he'll have to wait another
minute or two anyway for the other firemen to arrive.

It takes him only five seconds to slip on his bunker gear, ten seconds to start the truck and get it out of the driveway.

There used to be such anxiety, getting to a fire: the tunnel vision beginning to constrict from the moment he heard the dispatcher's voice. But now he knows how to save it, how to hold it at bay—that powerhousing of the heart, which now does not kick into life, does not come into being, until the moment Kirby comes around the corner and first sees the flames.

In her bed—in their bed—Mary Ann hears and feels the rumble of the big trucks leaving the station, hears and feels in her bones the belch of the air horns, and then the going-away sirens. She listens to the dispatcher's radio—hoping it will remain silent after the first call, will not crackle again, calling more and more stations to the blaze. Hoping it will be a small fire, and containable.

She lies there, warm and in love with her life—with the blessing of her two children asleep there in her own house, in the other room, safe and asleep—and she tries to imagine the future, tries to picture being sixty years old, seventy, and then eighty. How long—and of that space or distance ahead, what lies within it?

Kirby gets her—Jenna—on Wednesday nights and on every other weekend. On the weekends, if the weather is good, he sometimes takes her camping and lets the assistant chief cover for him. Kirby and Jenna cook over an open fire; they roast marshmallows. They sleep in sleeping bags in a meadow beneath stars. When he was a child Kirby used to camp in this meadow with his father and grandfather, and there would be lightning bugs at night, but those are gone now.

On Wednesday nights—Kirby has to have her back at Rhonda's by ten—they cook hamburgers, Jenna's favorite food, on the grill in the backyard. This one constancy: this one small sacrament. The diminishment of their lives shames him—especially for her, she for whom the whole world should be widening and opening, rather than constricting already.

She plays with the other children, the little children, afterward, all of them keeping one eye on the clock. She is quiet, inordinately so—thrilled just to be in the presence of her father, beneath his huge shadow; she smiles shyly whenever she notices that he is watching her. And how can she not be wondering why it is, when it's time to leave, the other two children get to stay?

He drives her home cheerfully, steadfastly, refusing to let her see or even sense his despair. He walks her up the sidewalk to Rhonda's like a guest. He does not go inside.

By Saturday—if it is the off-weekend in which he does not have her—he is up on the roof again, trying to catch the scent of her from the chimney; sometimes he falls asleep up there, in a brief catnap, as if watching over her and standing guard.

A million times he plays it over in his mind. Could I have saved the marriage? Did I give it absolutely every last ounce of effort? Could I have saved it?

No. Maybe. *No.*

It takes a long time to get used to the fires. It takes the young firemen, the beginners, a long time to understand what is required: that they must suit up and walk right into a burning house.

They make mistakes. They panic, breathe too fast, and use up their oxygen. It takes a long time. It takes a long time before they calm down and meet the fires on their own terms, and the fires'.

In the beginning, they all want to be heroes. Even before they enter their first fire, they will have secretly placed their helmets in the ovens at home to soften them up a bit—to dull and char and melt them slightly, so anxious are they for combat and its validations: its contract with their spirit. Kirby remembers the first house fire he entered—his initial reaction was "You mean I'm going in *that?*"—but enter it he did, fighting it from the inside out with huge volumes of water—the water sometimes doing as much damage as the fire—his new shiny suit yellow and clean amongst the work-darkened suits of the veterans.

Kirby tells Mary Ann that after that fire he drove out into the country and set a grass fire, a little pissant one that was in no danger of spreading, then put on his bunker gear and spent all afternoon walking around in it, dirtying his suit to just the right color of anonymity.

You always make mistakes, in the beginning. You can only hope they are small or insignificant enough to carry little if any price: that they harm no one. Kirby tells Mary Ann that on one of his earliest house fires, he was riding in one of the back seats of the fire engine, facing backwards. He was already packed up—bunker gear, air mask, and scuba tank—so that he couldn't hear or see well, and he was nervous as hell. When they got to the house that was on fire— a fully involved, "working" fire—the truck screeched to a stop across the street from it. The captain leapt out and yelled to Kirby that the house across the street was on fire.

Kirby could see the flames coming out of the first house, but he took the captain's orders to mean that it was the house across the street from the house on fire that he wanted Kirby to attack—that it too must be burning—and so while the main crew thrust itself into the first burning house, laying out attack lines and hoses and running up the hook-and-ladder, Kirby fastened his own hose to the other side of the truck and went storming across the yard and into the house across the street.

He assumed there was no one in it, but as he turned the knob on the front door and shoved his weight against it, the two women who lived inside opened it so that he fell inside, knocking one of them over and landing on her.

Kirby tells Mary Ann it was the worst he ever got the tunnel vision, that it was like running along a tightrope—that it was almost like being blind. They are on the couch again, in the hours before dawn; she's laughing. Kirby couldn't see flames anywhere, he tells her— his vision reduced to a space about the size of a pinhead—so he assumed the fire was up in the attic. He was confused as to why his partner was not yet there to help him haul his hose up the stairs. Kirby says the women were protesting, asking why he was bringing the hose into their house. He did not want to have to take the time to explain to them that the most efficient way to fight a fire is from the inside out. He told them to just be quiet and help him pull. This made them so angry that they pulled extra hard—so hard that Kirby, straining at the top of the stairs now, was bowled over again.

When he opened the attic door, he saw that there were no flames.

There was a dusty window in the attic, and out of it he could see the flames of the house across the street, really rocking now, going under. Kirby says that he stared at it a moment and then asked the ladies if there was a fire anywhere in their house. They replied angrily that there was not.

He had to roll the hose back up—he left sooty hose marks and footprints all over the carpet—and by this time the house across the street was so engulfed and Kirby was in so great a hurry to reach it that he began to hyperventilate, and he blacked out, there in the living room of the nonburning house.

He got better, of course—learned his craft better—learned it well, in time. No one was hurt. But there is still a clumsiness in his heart, in all of their hearts—the echo and memory of it—that is not too distant. They're all just fuckups, like anyone else, even in their uniforms: even in their fire-resistant gear. You can bet that any one of them who comes to rescue you or your home has problems that are at least as large as yours. You can count on that. There are no real rescuers.

Kirby tells her about what he thinks was his best moment—his moment of utter, breathtaking, thanks-giving luck. It happened when he was still a lieutenant, leading his men into an apartment fire. Apartments were the worst, because of the confusion; there was always a greater risk of losing an occupant in an apartment fire, simply because there were so many of them. The awe and mystery of making a rescue—the holiness of it, like a birth—in no way balances the despair of finding an occupant who's already died, a smoke or burn victim—and if that victim is a child, the firefighter is never the same and almost always has to retire after that; his or her marriage goes bad, and life is never the same, never has deep joy and wonder to it again.

The men and women spend all their time and energy fighting the enemy, *fire*—fighting the way it consumes structures, consumes air, consumes darkness—but then when it takes a life, it is as if some threshold has been crossed. It is for the firemen who discover that victim a feeling like falling down an elevator shaft, and there is sometimes guilt, too, that the thing they were so passionate about, fighting fire—a thing that could be said to bring them relief, if not plea-sure—should have this as one of its costs.

They curse stupidity, curse mankind, when they find a victim, and are almost forever after brittle.

This fire, the apartment fire, had no loss of occupants, no ca-sualties. It was fully involved by the time Kirby got his men into the structure—it was Christmas Eve—and they were doing room-to-room searches. No one ever knows how many people live in an apartment complex: how many men, women, and children, coming and going. They had to check every room.

Smoke detectors—thank God!—were squalling everywhere, though that only confused the men further—the sound slightly less piercing, but similar, to the motion sensors on their hip belts, so that they were constantly looking around in the smoke and heat to be sure they were all still together, partner with partner.

Part of the crew fought the blazes, while the others made searches: horrible searches, for many of the rooms were burning so intensely that if anyone was still inside it would be too late to do anything for them.

If you get trapped by the flames, you can activate your ceased-motion sensor. You can jab a hole in the fire hose at your feet. The water will spew up from the hose, spraying out of the knife hole like an umbrella of steam and moisture—a water shield, which will buy you ten or fifteen more seconds. You crouch low, sucking on your scuba gear, and wait, if you can't get out. They'll come and get you if they can.

This fire—the one with no casualties—had all the men stumbling with tunnel vision. There was something different about this one—they would talk about it afterward. It was almost as if the fire wanted them, had laid a trap for them.

They were all stumbling and clumsy, but still they checked the rooms. Loose electrical wires dangled from the burning walls and from crumbling, flaming ceilings. The power had been shut off, but it was every firefighter's fear that some passerby, well meaning, would see the breakers thrown and would flip them back on, unthinking.

The hanging, sagging wires trailed over the backs of the men like tentacles as they passed beneath them. The men blew out walls with their pickaxes, ventilated the ceilings with savage maulings from their lances. Trying to sense, to *feel,* amid the confusion, where someone might be—a survivor—if anyone was left.

Kirby and his partner went into the downstairs apartment of a trophy big game hunter. It was a large apartment and on the walls were the stuffed heads of various animals from all over the world. Some of the heads were already ablaze—flaming rhinos, burning gazelles— and as Kirby and his partner entered, boxes of ammunition began to go off: shotgun shells and rifle bullets, whole caseloads of them. Shots were flying in all directions, and Kirby made the decision right then to pull his men from the fire.

In thirty seconds he had them out—still the fusillade continued— and thirty seconds after that the whole upper floor collapsed: an inch-and-a-half-thick flooring of solid concrete dropped like a fallen cake down to the first floor, crushing the space where the men had been half a minute earlier, the building folding in on itself and being swallowed by itself, by its fire.

There was a grand piano in the lobby and somehow it was not entirely obliterated when the ceiling fell, so that a few crooked, clanging notes issued forth as the rubble shifted, settled, and burned; and still the shots kept firing.

No casualties. All of them went home to their families that night.

One year Rhonda tells Kirby that she is going to Paris with her new fiancé for two weeks and asks if Kirby can keep Jenna. His eyes sting with happiness. Two weeks of clean air, a gift from out of nowhere. A thing that was his and taken away, now brought back. *This must be what it feels like to be rescued,* he thinks.

Mary Ann thinks often of how hard it is for him—she thinks of it almost every time she sees him with Jenna, reading to her, or helping her with something—and they discuss it often, but even at that, even in Mary Ann's great lovingness, she underestimates it. She thinks she wants to know the full weight of it, but she has no true idea. It transcends words—spills over into his actions—and still she, Mary Ann, cannot know the whole of it.

Kirby dreams ahead to when Jenna is eighteen; he dreams of reuniting. He continues to take catnaps on the roof by her chimney. The separation from her betrays and belies his training; it is greater than an arm's length distance.

The counselors tell him never to let Jenna see this franticness—this gutted, hollow, gasping feeling.

As if wearing blinders—unsure of whether the counselors are right or not—he does as they suggest. He thinks they are probably right. He knows the horrible dangers of panic.

And in the meantime, the marriage strengthens, becomes more resilient than ever. Arguments cease to be even arguments anymore, merely differences of opinion; the marriage is reinforced by the innumerable fires and by the weave of his comings and goings. It becomes a marriage as strong as a galloping horse. His frantic attempts to keep drawing clean air are good for the body of the marriage.

Mary Ann worries about the fifteen or twenty years she's heard get cut off the back end of all firefighters' lives: all those years of sucking in chemicals—burning rags, burning asbestos, burning formaldehyde—but she does not ask him to stop.

The cinders continuing to fall across his back like meteors; twenty-four scars, twenty-five, twenty-six. She knows she could lose him. But she knows he will be lost for sure without the fires.

She prays in church for his safety. Sometimes she forgets to pay attention to the service and instead gets lost in her prayers. It's as if she's being led out of a burning building herself; as if she's trying to remain calm, as someone—her rescuer, perhaps—has instructed her to do.

She forgets to listen to the service. She finds herself instead thinking of the secrets he has told her: the things she knows about fires that no one else around her knows.

The way lightbulbs melt and lean or point toward a fire's origin—the gases in incandescent bulbs seeking, sensing that heat, so that you can often use them to tell where a fire started: the direction in which the lightbulbs first began to lean.

A baby is getting baptized up at the altar, but Mary Ann is still in some other zone—she's still praying for Kirby's safety, his survival.

The water being sprinkled on the baby's head reminds her of the men's water shields: of the umbrella-mist of spray that buys them extra time.

As he travels through town to and from his day job, he begins to define the space around him by the fires that have visited it, which he has engaged and battled. *I rescued that one, there, and that one,* he thinks. *That one.* The city becomes a tapestry, a weave of that which he has saved and that which he has not—with the rest of the city becoming simply everything between those points, waiting to burn.

He glides through his work at the office. If he were hollow inside, the work would suck something out of him—but he is not hollow, only asleep or resting, like some cast-iron statue from the century before. Whole days pass without his being able to account for them. Sometimes at night, lying there with Mary Ann—both of them listening for the dispatcher—he cannot recall whether he even went into the office that day or not.

He wonders what she is doing: what she is dreaming of. He gets up and goes in to check on their children—to simply look at them.

When you rescue a person from a burning building, the strength of their terror is unimaginable: it is enough to bend iron bars. The smallest, weakest person can strangle and overwhelm the strongest. There is a drill that the firemen go through, on their hook-and-ladder trucks—mock-rescuing someone from a window ledge, or the top of a burning building. Kirby picks the strongest fireman to go up on the ladder, and then demonstrates how easily he can make the fireman—vulnerable, up on that ladder—lose his balance. It's always staged, of course—the fireman is roped to the ladder for safety—but it makes a somber impression on the young recruits watching from below: the big man being pushed backwards by one foot, or one hand, falling and dangling by the rope; the rescuer suddenly in need of rescuing.

You can see it in their eyes, Kirby tells them—speaking of those who panic. You can see them getting all wall-eyed. The victims-to-be look almost normal, but then their eyes start to cross, just a little. It's as if they're generating such strength within—such *torque*—that it's causing their eyes to act weird. So much torque that it seems they'll snap in half—or snap you in half, if you get too close to them.

Kirby counsels distance to the younger firemen. Let the victims climb onto the ladder by themselves, when they're like that. Don't let them touch you. They'll break you in half. You can see the torque in their eyes.

Mary Ann knows all this. She knows it will always be this way for him—but she does not draw back. Twenty-seven scars, twenty-eight. He does not snap; he becomes stronger. She'll never know exactly what it's like, and for that she's glad.

Many nights he runs a fever for no apparent reason. Some nights, it is his radiant heat that awakens her. She wonders what it will be like when he is too old to go out on the fires. She wonders if she and he can survive that: the not-going.

There are days when he does not work at his computer. He turns the screen on but then goes over to the window for hours at a time and turns his back on the computer. He's up on the twentieth floor. He watches the flat horizon for smoke. The wind gives a slight sway, a slight tremor to the building.

Sometimes—if he has not been to a fire recently enough—Kirby imagines that the soles of his feet are getting hot. He allows himself to consider this sensation—he does not tune it out.

He stands motionless—still watching the horizon, looking and hoping for smoke—and feels himself igniting, but makes no movement to still or stop the flames. He simply burns, and keeps breathing in, detached, as if it is some structure other than his own that is aflame and vanishing, as if he can keep the two separate—his good life, and the other one, the one he left behind.

Swans

I got to know Billy and Amy, over the years, about as well as you get to know anybody up here, which is to say not too well.

They were my nearest neighbors. They saw me fall in and out of love three times, being rejected—abandoned—all three times.

And though that's not the story, they were good neighbors to me then, in those hard days. Amy had been a baker in Chicago, thirty years before, and even after coming out here to be with Billy she'd never stopped baking. She was the best baker who ever lived, I think: huckleberry pies and sweet rolls and the most incredible loaves of bread. I've heard it said that when you die you enter a room of bright light, and that you can smell bread baking just around the corner. I've read accounts of people who've died and come back to life, and their stories are all so similar I believe that's how it is.

And that's what this end of the valley—the south fork of it, rising against the flex of the mountains—smells like all the time, because Amy is almost always baking. The scent of her fresh loaves drifts across the green meadows and hangs along the riverbanks. Sometimes I'll be hiking in the woods, two or three miles up into the mountains, and I'll catch a whiff of bread, and I'll feel certain that she's just taken some out of the oven, miles below. I know that's a long way for a human to catch a scent, but bears can scent food at distances of nine miles, and wolves even farther. Living up here sharpens one's senses. The social senses atrophy a bit, but the wild body becomes stronger. I have seen men here lift the back ends of trucks and roll logs out of the woods that a draft horse couldn't pull.

I've seen a child chase down a runaway tractor and catch it from be-hind, climb up, and turn the ignition off before it went into the river. Several old women up here swim in the river all year round, even through the winter. Dogs live to be twenty, twenty-five years old.

And above it all—especially at this south end of the valley—Amy's bread-scents hang like the smells from heaven's kitchen.

All that rough stuff—the miracle strength, the amazing bodies—that's all fine, but also, we take it for granted; it's simply what the val-ley brings out, what it summons.

But the gentle stuff—that's what I hold in awe; that's what I like to watch.

Gentlest of all were Amy and Billy.

All his life, Billy worked in the woods, sawing down trees on his land in the bottoms, six days a week. He'd take the seventh day off—usu-ally Sunday—to rest his machinery.

There weren't any churches in the little valley, and if there had been, I don't know if he and Amy would have gone.

Instead, he would take Amy fishing on the Yaak River in their wooden canoe. I'd see them out there on the flats above the falls, fishing with cane poles and crickets for trout—ten- and fifteen-pound speckled beauties with slab bellies that lived in the deepest holes in the stillness up above the falls, waiting to intercept any nymphs that floated past. Those trout were easy to catch, would hit anything that moved. Billy and Amy wore straw hats. The canoe was green. Amy liked to fish. The hot summer days would be *ringing* with stillness, and then when Amy hooked one, it would seem that the whole valley could hear her shout.

The great trout would pull their canoe around on the river, held only by that one thin tight fly-line, spinning their canoe in circles while Amy shrieked and Billy paddled with one hand to stay up with the fish, maneuvering into position so he could try to net it with his free hand—and Amy holding on to that flexing cane pole and holler-ing.

They were as much a part of the valley, living there in the South Fork, as the trees and the river and the very soil itself, as much a part and substance of the valley as the tremulous dusk swamp-cries of the woodcock in summer.

And the swans.

Five of them, silent as gods, lived on a small pond in the woods below Billy and Amy's cabin, gliding in circles and never making a sound. Amy said they never sang like other birds—that they would remain silent all their lives, until they died, at which point they would stretch out their long necks and sing beautifully, and that that was where the phrase "swan song" came from.

And it was for the swans as much as for anyone that Amy baked her bread. She had a park bench at the pond's edge that Billy had made for her, and every evening she would take a loaf of bread there and feed it, crumb by crumb, to the elegant big birds, just as dusk began to come sliding in from out of the trees.

Amy would toss bread crumbs at the black-masked swans until it was dark, until she could see only their dim white shapes moving pale through the night, the swans lunging at the sound of the bread crumbs hitting the water. I had sat there with her on occasion.

On the very coldest nights—when the swans were able to keep the pond from freezing only by swimming in tight circles in the center, while the shelf ice kept creeping out, trying to freeze around their feet and lock them up, making them easy prey for coyotes or wolves or foxes—Amy would build warming fires all around the pond's edge. Wilder swans would have moved on, heading south for the hot-springs country around Yellowstone or western Idaho, where they could winter in splendor, as if in a sauna, but these swans had gotten used to Amy's incredible breads, I guess, and also believed— knew—that she would build fires for them if it got too cold.

They weren't tame. She was just a part of their lives. I think she must have seemed as much a natural phenomenon to these swans as the hot springs and geysers must have seemed to other swans, farther south.

From my cabin on the hill, I'd see the glow from Amy's fires begin to flicker through the woods, would see the long tree shadows dancing across the snowfields, firelight back in the timber, and because I was her neighbor, I'd help her build the fires.

Billy would be out there, too, often in his shirtsleeves, no matter how cold the weather. It was known throughout the valley that Billy slept naked with the windows open every night of the year, like an animal, so that it would help him get ready for winter—and he was famous for working shirtless in zero-degree weather, and for ignoring the cold, for liking it, even. It was nothing to see Billy walking down the road in a snowstorm, six miles to the mercantile for a bottle of milk or a beer, wearing only a light jacket and with his hands shoved down in his pockets, bareheaded, ten below, and the snow coming down like it wasn't ever going to stop.

Billy had always been precise—a perfectionist, the only one in the valley—but during this year I am telling about he seemed more that way than ever. Even his body was in perfect shape, like a mountain lion's—a narrow waist but big shoulders and arms from sawing wood all the time. But there were indications that he was human and not some forever-running animal. He was going bald, though that was no fault of his. He had brown eyes almost like a child's, and a mustache. He still had all of his teeth (except for one gold one in the front), which was unusual for a logger.

He took his various machines apart every day, in the dusty summers, and oiled and cleaned them. I think he liked to do this not just for fanatical maintenance but also to show the machines his control over them; reminding them, perhaps, every evening, that he created them each day when he took them in his hands. That his work gave them their souls—the rumbling saw, the throbbing generator, and his old red logging truck.

Even in the winter, Billy took deep care of his machines, keeping fires going night and day in the wood stoves in his garage, not to warm himself, but to keep the machines "comfortable," he said—to keep the metal from freezing and contracting.

It would make a fine story to tell, a dark and somehow delicious one, to discover at this point that all the concern and even love that Billy gave to his machines was at a cost, that perhaps it came at Amy's expense.

But that was not the case.

He had a fullness to him that we just don't often see. He was loving and gentle with Amy, and I would often marvel, over the years I knew him, at how he always seemed to be thinking of her—of how his movements seemed to be dictated by what might bring her pleasure. And I was struck, too, by the easy way he had of being with her. They seemed fresh together: untouched by the world, and as fresh as that bread.

Billy took caution to cut the lengths of stove wood to fit in Amy's various stoves for her bread-baking. He scanned the woods for dead standing or fallen trees, wood that would have the proper grain and dryness to release good and controlled steady heat—good cooking wood.

In some ways Billy was as much a part of that bread's scent hanging over the South Fork as was Amy.

But they were her swans.

So Billy and Amy had a lot of fires: for Amy's baking; for Amy's swans, along the shores of the little pond on the coldest nights; for Billy's machines. Fires in Billy and Amy's cabin, with those windows always open.

They used an incredible volume of wood. I could step on my porch at almost any hour of the day and hear Billy's saw buzzing away in the rich bottom, where trees sprouted, grew tall, became old, and fell over; and through their midst, all his life, Billy wielded a giant saw that other men would have had trouble even lifting, much less carrying and using.

He kept the woods down there neat; he cut up almost all of that which had already fallen, and carried it out. You could have picnics or ride bicycles or drive cars into those woods if you so desired, between and among the larger, healthier trees, so free of underbrush and downed trees did he keep it.

But no one ever went there. Things only came out of it.

Stove-sized pieces of wood, for Amy's bread. For the swans' bread. For the scent of the valley. The sound of the saw. Billy's huge, cross-striated chest muscles.

What it was like was a balance; Billy's (and Amy's) life was wedged—as if stuck in a chimney—between rise and fall, growth and rot. He had found some magic seam of life, a stasis in those woods, and as long as he could keep the woods the same, he and Amy would stay the same, as would his love for her—as would her love for him.

I would think—without pity—*If I had done it like him, none of them would ever have left. If I'd given it my all, I could have lodged us, wedged us, into that safe place where neither life nor death can erode a kind of harmony or peace—a spirit—but I wasn't a better man. There goes a better man,* I'd think, when I saw him driving out of the woods and down the road in his old red truck, the truck sunk nearly to the ground with its load of fresh wood. *He gave it his all, and continues to give it his all,* I'd think, *and he's going to make it. They're both going to make it.*

I would feel better to realize that—and to see it.

Somebody in this world has to attain peace, I'd think.

Baking was not all Amy knew how to do. She had gone to a music school in Chicago, had been there on a scholarship to play the piano, but then she'd met Billy, who had driven a trailer load of horses out to sell to a man near Chicago, Amy's uncle.

Amy left her bakery, and she left school, too. For thirty years after that, the only times she ever played the piano were on the irregular visits to friends' houses in town, and once or twice a year when she would go to one of the churches in town, sixty miles away, on a Wednesday, alone before God on a Wednesday afternoon in the spring or in the fall, the church dark and cool and quiet, and she would play there, ignoring the church's organ and playing their piano.

I know that loving a woman isn't about giving her things; I know that's an easy and common mistake for men to make, confusing the two. It is the way of other animals in the wild, animals with strong social bonds, to show affection for their mates by bringing in fresh-killed game—but with men and women it is needless to say a little more complex. I have watched Billy and Amy, and have watched my three lovers flee the valley—which is the same thing as fleeing me—and I know the best way for a man to love a woman, or woman to love a man, is not to bring gifts, but to simply understand that other person:

to understand as much (and with as much passion and concern) as is possible.

Nonetheless, certain presents can sometimes speak eloquently the language of this understanding, and in the last year before Billy became different, before he began to slip, he bought Amy a piano.

Billy had been cutting trees in secret for her—live trees, some of them, not just the standing or fallen dead ones.

Big, beautiful trees—mixed conifers, immense larch and spruce and fir trees, and ponderosa and white pine.

Not a lot of them—just a few every year—on the far side of the bottoms, his father's land, his cutting-ground—and Billy had been saving that money for years, he told me.

A tree cut for love is not the same as a tree cut for money, or bread-baking. But even so, Billy said, he didn't like doing it, and after he'd made the finishing cut on each piano-tree—cutting one every two or three months—his secret life—Billy said he would feel queasy, as if he were sawing off a man's thigh: the forest, and life, growth, that dear and powerful to him.

It was not that Billy did not understand death—he did. Or said he thought he did, which is, I guess, as close as you can come, until you're there.

Billy knew, he sensed, something was getting out of balance whenever he'd cut one of those ancient trees. But he'd sit and rest after the big tree leaned and then fell, crashing slowly through the leafy canopy below, stripping limbs off other trees, even taking smaller trees with it—shaking the forest when it hit, making the woods jump.

Billy would sit on a log and just breathe, he told me, and think about nothing but love, about Amy, and he would not move until he felt that balance—that strange stasis—return to the woods.

The way he put it—what he was looking for, sitting there in the woods like that, barely breathing—was that he would wait until the woods "had forgotten him again." Then he would feel safe and free to move back through their midst.

So he knew what he was doing, in this life; it wasn't just by accident that he'd holed up in this valley, wedged between the past and the future. Just him and Amy. He had a good feel for what was going on. The way he worked at sawing those logs every day was exactly the way he felt about preserving and nurturing his love for and his life with Amy, until the way he went at those logs with his saw *became* his love for Amy.

It was easy to picture Billy just sitting there, mopping his balding head, pouring a cup of water from his thermos in the after-silence of each tree felled, and watching, and listening. Drinking the water in long gulps. A flicker darting through the woods, perhaps, flying from one tree to another, looking for bugs.

Billy's eyes, watching it.

And then home in the evenings, those secret trees resting silent and new-cut, drying out in the forest, and his old red truck laboring, puttering up the hill, past my cabin, home to his wife—past the pond, past Amy in the dusk, Amy seeing the truck pass, waving, throwing a few more bread crumbs to the beautiful, silent, patient swans, and then rising and taking the shortcut through the woods up to their cabin.

Back to the other part of her life, her husband. She had her swans, and she had a husband. Children? Never. She was suspended as gracefully, as safely, between the past and the future as was Billy.

And then, when Billy had sawed enough logs, he sold them and bought the piano and built a little cabin for her next to the pond, just a tiny cabin which housed only the piano and a bench and a lantern and, of course, a stove. The little piano cabin was full of windows, and Amy would open them if it wasn't raining, and play music to the swans—beautiful classical compositions like Pachelbel's *Canon* and Mozart, but also church music. "Rock of Ages" was one of my favorites, and it carried the farthest. Sometimes I would walk through the woods at dusk and sit on a boulder on the hillside above the river and the pond and listen to the music rising from the trees below.

Other times I'd creep through the woods like an animal to get closer to the pond, and I'd look through the trees and see Amy playing by lantern-light, her face a perfect expression of serenity, playing hard (the thrown-open windows of the little cabin acting as a giant speaker, so that the sound carried across the hills, up into the mountains; and I liked to think of the mountains absorbing that music, the peace of it settling inches deep into the thin soil, to bedrock, and calming the wild mountains as darkness fell).

Sometimes Amy sang, ever so quietly. It occurred to me as I watched the swans all watch Amy (lined up, floating there on the water like children in a school recital, listening) that Amy had let go of her bakery job, and her music school, as easily as she let go of everything—tossing away all thoughts of controlling the moment (much less the wild future), as if tossing crumbs to the long-necked swans. Casting away all control, and simply being.

Billy had always taught me things. He would stop in and point to my fallen-down wandering fence (I had no livestock, and hence no need of repairing the fence) and tell me that if I'd lay it in a straighter line, that would somehow dissuade the moose from walking through and knocking it down.

"You can keep those same-sized replacement poles in your barn, too, instead of having to custom cut a new one each time a moose or elk herd walks through," he said, but again, I didn't really care if they knocked it down. I didn't really care if there was a fence or not.

Other times Billy would drive up while I was splitting wood in the side yard and point out that the head of my ax was about to fly off at any moment—that the little splinter-wedge chuck I'd used to wedge it back on the first time was getting loose again.

"Soak the handle in salt water," he said. "*Then* drive the wedges in."

Everything could be controlled. I listened to Billy, and nodded, and learned some things.

But in the evenings, I listened to Amy.

I went over to Billy and Amy's for supper about once a month. I felt safe in there, sitting at the kitchen table while Amy baked her tortes, quiches, breads, and pies—showing off, the way a person should probably do from time to time. The kitchen, and perhaps the entire valley, groaned with the bread's scent, which enveloped the deer, the elk, the swans—all living things were aware of it. Yearling wolves fell asleep dreaming of man's heaven, perhaps, not knowing what they were dreaming of, but surely just as at peace as if they had dreamed of their own.

Billy took me out to his barn at our October supper—the moon round and orange, and a breeze from the north—and we walked around in his barn looking at things while Amy baked. Billy had not yet started up the wood stoves in his barn—that would not happen until November or December, when the machines, like the animals, began to get cold. Instead, we just walked around inspecting his inventory—the rows of nuts and bolts, oil filters of various shapes and sizes, ignition coils.

Everything gleamed under the light of the shop's lanterns. The concrete floor was spotless, with none of the drip and splatter of oil stains one usually sees in such a place. He picked up a set of packed wheel bearings and spun the smooth inside hub like a toy. He had a case of a dozen—a lifetime supply, perhaps—and when one set went bad, he'd just pull them off and stick in a new set. The bearings glistened with the faintest high-grade condensate of lubrication, of earnest readiness.

"If something happened to me," he said, "you'd take care of her? Not just anybody could take my place. You'd have to learn things she doesn't know, and kind of check in on her. Kind of make sure she had *enough* of everything."

"Nobody could ever take your place, Billy."

"That's what I'm worried about," he said. The big barn was silent except for the flickering hiss of the lanterns; safe and clean and warm.

We blew out the lanterns and went back across the yard (so many stars above!) and into the warm small kitchen. We sat at the table, the three of us, said grace, and began to eat, closing our eyes in the bliss of the meal. The windows, as ever, were wide open, and the night's cool breezes stirred against our arms and faces as we ate. The wood stove creaked as the fire died down and the cabin cooled.

Night and day; day and night. There is a perfect balance, a drawn and poised moment's tension to everything. Is it peculiarly human, and perhaps wrong, to try to hang back—to try to shore up, pause, build a fortress against the inevitable snapping or release of that tension? Of trying to not allow the equation to roll forward, like riffle-water over, past, and around the river's boulders?

When things started slipping for Billy, they didn't seem like much, not at first: forgetting names, and forgetting the sequence of things—getting in the truck one morning, he told me, and not re-membering to turn the ignition on—putting it in gear, easing the clutch out, and then wondering for several moments why the truck wasn't moving. Those sorts of things were allowed up in this country and were fairly common, though I didn't know why.

Billy was coming by to visit more frequently that fall, telling me things out of the blue—giving me knowledge the way someone else might pass out old clothes he no longer had any use for. Maybe Billy knew he was losing the race and was trying to give away as much as he could before it all seeped away. I didn't know that, then. I just lis-tened, and watched, and was glad he was my neighbor.

"You can put sixteen-inch tires on your truck in bad winters," he said. "Gives you another three, four inches clearance. It won't hurt nothin'."

Later in the fall, when the larch needles turned gold and began fall-ing, flying through the air, tiny and slender, covering the road with a soft gold matting, Billy began forgetting to go into the woods.

Instead, he would come over to my place, with his empty truck and his dog, to give me advice. We'd share a glass of iced tea, and I'd just listen. I could tell he had forgotten my name—the way he looked at me strangely and never used my name anymore. I'd often be wearing my camouflage clothes from having been out in the woods hunting deer, meat for the winter, and sometimes I still had my face painted with charcoal.

Billy would stare at my face for a full minute. His mind was going, almost gone—over the next ridge—and I wonder what he must have thought, looking at me, wondering if I was a devil, or an angel. I hope that he still recognized me as his neighbor.

"Cut those lodgepole pines behind your house as soon as they die," he said, "those beetle-killed ones. Get 'em down on the ground where it's damp, so's the eggs can't hatch and spread."

Billy would stare out at my crooked, wandering fences. He'd open his mouth to say something else, but then would close it. We'd be out on my porch.

"Shit. I can't remember what I was going to say." Billy would rub his head, the side of his face. "Shit," he'd sigh, and just sit there— having forgotten, as well, that he was on his way to go cut wood.

"Let me take you to a doctor," I said once; a notion as foreign to Billy, surely, as taking him to Jamaica.

"No. No doctors. I've got to pull myself out of this one."

It was exactly like slipping, like walking down a hill pasted with damp aspen and cottonwood leaves in the fall, going down too steep a trail. Your hand reached out and grabbed a tree, and you saved yourself from falling.

Billy's body was still strong—his arms, and his saw-wielding, maul-splitting back as broad as ever—but he was talking slower, and his face looked older, and so did his eyes. They looked—*gentler*.

"Amy," is what he'd say, sometimes, as he looked out at my half-assed fence—unable to remember what it was he wanted to say.

Instead of cutting wood, he'd go back toward his cabin, park on one side of the road, get out, and wander through the woods as if drawn by lodestone (or the smell of the bread) to the pond, where Amy might be sitting on the bench reading, or writing a letter back home, or feeding the expectant swans.

Billy would sit on the bench next to her as he must have when they first met, when they were young and so far from the end of anything.

Amy would come over to my cabin sometimes, on the days that Billy did manage to find his way back into the bottom to cut still more firewood. She was a strong and content and whole woman, her own life held together as completely as Billy's, make no mistake about it, and with much more grace, much less muscle, but she was also worried, not so much for herself, but for Billy.

There is romantic nonsense these days about the beauty of death, about the terrible end becoming the lovely beginning, and I think that's wrong, a diminution of the beauty of life. Death is as terrible as birth is wonderful. The laws of physics and nature—not romance—dictate this.

It occurs to me that sometimes even nature—raw, silent, solemn, and joyous nature—fears, even if only slightly, rot, and decay.

"I'm angry at him," Amy said one day. "He's getting worse." Amy had brought a loaf of bread over and we were sitting on my porch. We could hear Billy's saw running only intermittently—long pauses between work.

"I feel guilty," Amy said. "I feel bad for being angry and afraid. I try to remember all we've had, but I can't help it. He's always been the same, and now that he's changing, I'm angry."

"Maybe he'll get better," I said.

"He's changing so fast," Amy said. "Never any change, and now so much."

The times when Billy went into the woods to cut logs for all his various fires—the times when he went past my cabin without stopping—he would often miss the turnoff for the small road that went into his woods, and he would just keep going a mile or two. Then I'd hear him stop, and he'd back up the road in reverse, the engine groaning—backing all the way to the turnoff—embarrassed, at first, and telling me about it, laughing, on my front porch the next day (as if I'd not been able to see it clearly, with my own eyes, from where I was sitting); but then, as it happened more often, he stopped talking about it.

I'd sit there every day and watch him drive past in reverse, backing the big empty truck to a spot where he could turn around and go back into the woods and down onto the land his family had owned for more than a hundred years.

It must have struck some chord in Billy—going backwards like that, with the engine straining, things falling away from him, out the front windshield, getting smaller rather than larger. He took to doing it all the time—driving backwards—even while going to the mercantile for groceries.

It was real hard watching someone I admired and respected, whom I wanted to emulate, disappear, as if being claimed by the forest itself.

Other people, however, began to shy away from Billy, in the manner that animals will sometimes avoid another of their kind when it becomes sick.

He no longer seemed to be in that secret seam between wildness and gentleness—the hidden fissure. Amy seemed as ensconced there as ever, but Billy seemed to have suddenly jumped—in the flip of a heartbeat—out to the far end, the very edge of wildness.

I don't mean he was tortured or even unhappy during this last sea change, the fluctuating tremors of the forest claiming him back; if anything, I think there was more sweetness, wildness, and pure joy in it for him than ever—lying there listening to Amy's masterful piano playing and watching out the open cabin door the ghostly shapes of the swans, watching them as if they had gathered, silently, to watch him.

The great coolness of the net of night, the safety of autumn evenings coming down on them again and again, with the days growing shorter, and less conflict, less ambition, less *trouble* in Billy's mind as the coils and loops and convolutions of his brain smoothed out and erased themselves.

The smell in the valley, as always, of her bread baking.

People in town said that whenever Billy came into the mercantile for groceries, he would walk into the store and just stand there, unable to remember what he had come for.

He would have to borrow the mercantile's radio and call Amy on the shortwave and ask her what it was she needed.

I could see the fright in Billy's eyes, every time I saw him, and in Amy's, too, as the fall progressed and the light snows began.

I remember walking one starry night after the snow was down— early November, and cold—just out walking, going down the road toward town, to the saloon for a beer or two and a breath of fresh air—and Billy's truck came over the hill, sputtering and rattling, from a direction that was away from his cabin. I was glad to see that he was not driving backwards—not at night.

I was a long way past his cabin, a long way up the road. It had been more than an hour since I had gone across the bridge over the little creek by where he lived—the swans paddling in slow circles in the creek, white in the moonlight, with the moon's blurry reflection wavering in their ripples, and ice beginning to form on the creek's edges. I imagined that the swans were waiting for Amy's next sonata, these beautiful birds for whom music was an impossibility.

I walked on farther, past the yellow lights of Billy and Amy's cabin, up the hill. I had assumed Billy was at home, that they were both at home, maybe sitting in bed and playing a hand of cards or two before going to sleep, as Amy had told me they often did—playing cards, that is, if Billy could still remember how.

So I was surprised to see him come driving slowly over the hill, his truck slipping on the fresh snow a little; and he stopped, recognizing me in the glare of his headlights—recognizing me, I could tell, but not able to remember my name.

"Hop in, bub," he said. "I was just out looking at things."

I did not believe this was so. I was certain he had forgotten which cabin was his, and I tried to think of a way to tell him when he passed it—wondering if I should say something like, "Is Amy still baking tonight?" and point up the hill toward the yellow squares of light, piecy-looking through the trees.

It was a full moon, and I was surprised to see that Billy was driving with the heater on, and that his windows were rolled up. It was hot and stuffy in the truck. A shooting star streaked in front of us and then disappeared over the trees, and Billy, who was driving with both hands on the wheel, leaning forward and watching the road carefully, looked up at it but said nothing.

Deer kept trotting across the road in front of us, red-eyed in the glare of the headlights—some with antlers, some without—and Billy would turn the lights out immediately whenever he saw a herd of them—in November and December, they were beginning to bunch up and travel together, for protection, and for warmth—and I sat in my seat and gripped the high dashboard, certain that we were going to plow right through the herd.

"What are you doing, Billy?" I said.

He drove intently, slowly, but not enough for my liking. I kept waiting to hear the thud of bodies, and to feel the jolt—and then when we were past the spot where we should have struck the deer, he would turn the lights back on, and the road in front of us would be empty.

"Sheriff told me to do that," Billy would say each time it happened. "The noise of the truck scares 'em off the road. If you leave the lights on, you blind 'em, and they can't decide which way to go—that's how you end up hittin' 'em—but if you turn your lights off, they can think straight and know to get out of the way."

I had never heard of such a thing and did not believe that he had either—and it is something that I have never heard of since—but it seemed to give him a distinct pleasure, hunched over the steering wheel and punching the lights off and gliding toward where we had last seen the herd of deer in the middle of the road. He seemed at peace, doing that, and I decided that he was not lost at all, that he just enjoyed getting out and driving at night, and so when we passed the lights of his cabin, I looked up the hill at them but said nothing.

"Take care, Billy," I said when he let me out at my place. It was dark, and I felt that he was frightened of something.

"Take care," he said back to me. "Do you need a light?" he said, rummaging through the toolbox on the seat beside him. "I've got a flashlight, if you need it."

It was only about a ten-yard walk to my cabin.

"No, thanks, I'll be all right. You take care now, Billy."

"You're sure?" he asked.

"I'm sure."

"Take care," he said again. "Take good care."

He drove in a circle in my yard, found the driveway again, and headed up the road toward his house. I stood there and watched him disappear around the bend.

I watched then as Billy's lights came back around the bend—he was driving back to my house in reverse; gears groaning.

Billy backed up in my driveway but didn't get out of his big truck, just leaned out the window. He seemed embarrassed. "Can you show me how to get home?"

He got all the way home in January. He was still trying to cut and load stove wood, as if trying to lay in a hundred years' supply for all of his and Amy's fires, on the day that he did not come back—a short winter's day, as if the apogee of waning light had finally scooped him up, had claimed him.

Amy and I went into the woods with lanterns. A light snow was falling, flakes hissing when they landed on our lanterns. Billy was lying on his side in the snow (having shut his saw off, but with his helmet still on), looking as if he had stretched out only to take a nap.

Amy crouched and brushed the snow from his face. There were lengths of firewood scattered all around, wood he had not yet loaded in his truck, but already the snow was covering it.

We lifted him carefully into my truck. I drove, and Amy rode with his head cradled in her lap. She removed his helmet and covered his bare head with her hands as if to keep it warm, or perhaps summon one last surge of force, or even the memory of force.

I glanced at the tall trees above us, tried to guess which ones would be the next to fall, and wondered if the forest felt relieved that Billy was gone now—if those trees would be free now to just rot, once they fell.

We rode past the swans' pond. It was a cold night and earlier in the day Amy had lit a few fires around the edge. The fires were beautiful in the falling snow, though diminished and not putting out much heat. The swans had moved in as close to the small ragged orange fires as they could get without leaving the pond. Their beauty was of no help to them, it seemed; they were cold.

They watched us, silent as ever, as we passed, the swans graceful and perfect in the firelight, and I rolled my window down, thinking that as we passed some of them would cry out at Billy's death. But then I remembered it was only for their own death that they sang, and only that once.

Elk

I t was Matthew who killed the elk. I was only trying to learn how it was done.

My first year in the valley, I knew next to nothing, though when only a week of hunting season remained and still I had no meat, I knew enough to ask Matthew for help. People told me he didn't like new people coming into the valley and that he wouldn't help me, wouldn't help anyone—but when I went to his cabin and asked, he said he would, just this one time, and that I would have to watch and learn: he would only hunt an elk for me once.

We canoed across the Yaak River and went into the wilderness. We found a bull's tracks, and followed the bull for three days, killing it on the fourth.

Afterward, Matthew built a fire in the woods next to the elk to warm us as we went to work. There was plenty of dry wood and it was easy to make a roaring fire; its flames grew almost as tall as we were, and lit up the woods. The light danced against the elk's hide and antlers, making it seem as if he had come back to life. In his final death leap he had gotten tangled in a gridwork of blow-down and now hung there, several feet off the ground. Matthew crawled underneath and began cutting. His knife made a rasping sound against the coarse hair and thick skin and cartilage, and from time to time he had to stop and sharpen the knife with a whet-stone.

"Nothing in the world dulls a steel blade like elk hair," he said. He was doing a neat job. "I'd like a stone knife someday, obsidian," he said. I added wood to the fire. I would not have believed you could skin such an animal. It was surely enough meat for the coming year.

By morning we had the elk skinned and the antlers sawed off. Matthew had brought a small folding saw—its blade was now ruined—and he tossed it into the fire. The bull's immense hindquarters—heavier than a man's body—were hanging from trees, as were the shoulders.

We filled our packs with the loose meat: all the neck roasts, tenderloins, neck loins, and lengths of backstrap like deep red anacondas. In lifting the hindquarters and shoulders, we became covered with blood. I was glad the bears were already in hibernation.

The fire had sprawled and wandered through the night. Ashes and charred half-lengths of timber lay in a circle thirty feet across.

We roasted some of the ribs over the coals and chewed on them for a long time. We ate a whole side of the trimmings from the elk skeleton—the bones were stripped clean and gleaming when we were done—and then broke the other side in half with the hatchet. We tied the rib cages to our packs like a frame; they would help hold in place the shifting weight of the meat, which was still warm against our backs. I gathered a few stones as we were about to leave and, not knowing why, stacked them where the elk had fallen, now a pile of hooves, shins, and hair.

Matthew carried the antlers—settled them over his shoulders upside down—and with their long tips and tines furrowing the snow behind him, he looked as if he were in a yoke, plowing the snow. I carried the wet hide atop my pack of meat, increasing the weight of my pack to well over a hundred pounds. Matthew said it was important to carry out the extraneous stuff first—the antlers, the hide—before our resolve weakened and we were tempted to leave them behind for the wolves.

It began to snow again. I wondered where the other elk were, if they knew that our hunt for them was over.

We stayed on the ridges. Under such a load, our steps were small and slow. We packed for a mile, dropped our weight, then went back to where we'd left all the other meat, and carried it to the point we'd gotten to before—each of us carrying a hindquarter on his back, or dragging it behind like a sled.

And so we moved across the valley, as if in some eternal meat relay—continuously undoing the progress we'd made, working hours to move the whole mass only one mile, at which point we then started all over again. The short winter days passed quickly, and we slept soundly through the nights.

The snow kept coming. We dropped off one ridge down into a creek and ascended another, and Matthew said he knew where we were. After the second or third day, the ravens appeared. They landed in front of us and strutted with outstretched wings, drawing little tracings in the snow, barking and cawing in voices alternately shrill and hoarse, as if hurling different languages at us. Sometimes they landed behind us, darted in and pecked at whatever section of the elk we were dragging, but usually they picked at the meat fragments in the snow.

On the third day there was a moment of startling beauty. We were walking in a fog so thick that we could see no more than a few feet in front of us. We knew to stay on the ridge. Four ravens were following us, walking behind us in their penguin strut. And then to our left, to the west, a slot appeared in the fog, a slot of pale blue sky, and through the slot there was a shaft of gold light illuminating the forest below us. The shaft was the only thing we could see in the storm. The wind was blowing north, the direction we were going, and for a while the shaft traveled with us. As it did, it kept revealing more of the same uncut, untouched forest. The impression it made was that the uncut forest would never end. In less than a minute, the shaft had moved on—the wind was about thirty miles an hour—but the sight has stayed with me, and neither Matthew nor I said anything about it to each other, though we did stop and watch it, as if unsure of what it was we were seeing.

We ate more elk as we traveled, a lot of elk, but after four days I wanted bread or potatoes. I was tired of all meat. I wanted an apple pie, dense with sugar, and a hot bath.

The antlers had sunk lower on Matthew's shoulders, and the plow they made cut deeper in the snow. Sometimes their heavy tips struck a rock beneath the snow and made a *clinking* sound. The weight of the antlers was starting to wear Matthew's skin raw, even though he had cut a strip of hide to use as a cushion. A red "Y" now ran down his back, merging just below his shoulders. The furrows in the snow behind him, wide as the antlers, looked like the boundaries of a small road, a lane, and within them we sometimes noticed the tracks of the creatures that were following us: the ravens, coyotes, and wolves.

We were descending, and were beginning to see the tracks of other animals again—deer, moose, and elk, though the elk tracks were those of cows and calves, not bulls.

We were down out of the high country now and into the dense forest. It was growing warmer at the lower elevation, so that rather than snow falling, there was a sleety drizzle that was more chilling than any storm or blizzard. We came across a dropped moose antler, resting upright on the snow—we could read his tracks leading to it, and leading away from it—and the antler, upturned, was full of water and slush from the sleet. We knelt and took turns drinking from it, without disturbing it. We were almost home. One more night, and the next day. A year's worth of meat, put away safely.

The "Y" on Matthew's back widened, but he was moving stronger again. I was shivering hard by now. I was drenched. For a long time the effort of hauling and skidding the meat had been enough to keep me warm, but that effort was no longer enough. I was cold and I needed help from the outside. My body could no longer hold off the whole mass of winter. I was without reserves.

"Do you want to stop and light a fire?" Matthew asked, watching my slowing movements, my clumsiness, my giving-upness. I nodded, still lucid enough to know that hypothermia had arrived. Matthew seemed to be a great distance away, and I felt that he was studying me, evaluating me. We were no longer partners in the hunt, brothers in the hunt—brothers in anything—and as my mind began to close down, chamber by chamber, I had the feeling that Matthew was going to let me freeze: that he had run me into the ground, had let me haul out half the elk, and now, only a day's journey from town, he was going to let winter have me. He would carry the rest of the meat out himself, leaving me to disappear beneath the snow.

He stood there waiting. I knelt and slipped out of my pack. I lost my balance and tipped over in the snow. Not thinking clearly—not thinking at all—I searched through my pack for matches, shivering. I found them, held the small box tightly in my gloved hands, then remembered that I needed wood.

Matthew continued watching me. He had not taken his pack off—as if he had no intention of stopping here anyway—and the antlers had been with him so long that they seemed to be growing out of him. I moved off into the trees and down a slope and began snapping twigs and gathering branches, dropping much of what I picked up. Matthew stayed up on the hill above, watching. The rain and sleet kept coming down. He was drenched, too—there was ice on his antlers—but he seemed to have a fire and a hardness in him I knew I didn't have.

I heaped the branches, some green and some dry, into a small pile, and began striking matches. The sodden pile of wood would not light. I tried until I was out of matches, then rose and went back to my pack to look for more. I was moving slowly and wanted to lie down. I had to keep going, but knew I wasn't going to find any more matches.

"This way," Matthew said, taking a cigarette lighter out of his pack. "Look at me," he said. "Watch." He walked down to the nearest dead tree, an old wind-blasted fir, shrouded dense with black hanging lichen. "This is what you do," he said. His words came in breaths of steam rising into the rain. He stood under the canopy of the tree's branches and moss cloak and snapped the lighter a couple of times, holding it right up against the lichen tendrils.

On the third snap the lichen caught, burned blue for a moment, then leapt into quick orange flame.

It was like something chemical—the whole tree, or the shell of lichen around it, metamorphosed into bright crackling fire, the lichen burning explosively, and the sudden shock of heat, the updraft, in turn lighting the lichen above, accelerating the rush of flame as if climbing a ladder. It was a forty foot tall tree, and it was on fire from top to bottom in about five seconds.

"That's how you do it," Matthew said, stepping back. I had stopped shivering, my blood heated by one last squeeze of adrenaline at the sight; but now, even as I watched the flames, the chill and then the shivering returned.

"You'd better get on over there," he said. "They don't burn long."

I walked over to the burning tree. There was a lot of heat, and the snow in all directions glistened. Flaming wisps of lichen separated from the tree and floated upward in curls before cooling and descending. By the time they landed on me, they were almost burnt out—charcoal skeletons of the lichen. A few of the tree's branches burned and crackled, but that was pretty much it; soon the fire was gone.

I wouldn't say I was warm, but I had stopped shivering.

"Come on," Matthew said. "Let's find another one." He set off into the rain, the antlers behind him plowing a path.

And that was how we came out of the mountains, in that last night and the next day, moving from tree to tree—looking for the right one, properly dead—through the drizzle, from one tower of flame to the next, Matthew probing the trees with his cigarette lighter, testing them, always choosing the right ones. That was how we walked through that night—the trees sizzling and steaming after we were done with them—and on into the gray rainy day. We were back into country I knew well, even underneath all the snow. We were seeing the tracks of wolves, and finding some of their kills. I had stopped shivering, though we continued lighting tree torches—leaving a crooked, wandering path of them behind us.

I suspect that in twenty years I will still be able to trace our journey backward, back up the mountain from torched tree to torched tree. Some will be fallen and rotting black husks, others might still be standing. In twenty years, I'll be able to return to where it all started—that point where we first saw the elk, and then lost him, and then found him again, and killed him. From among the stones and ferns and forest, there will be a piece of charcoal, a fire-blackened rock, an antler in a tree, a rusting saw blade, even a scabbed-over set of initials where Matthew marked his kill, although as the years go on, those initials will be harder to find, until finally you will have to know exactly where they are, or have someone who has been there before to show you.

The rut was on as we approached town the next day—the giant bucks chasing the does—and though we were exhausted, we could see that we had to shoot a deer.

As we drew nearer the village—the forest ripe with the scent of rut—we saw a swarm of antlers, dozens of bucks prowling the woods, mesmerized by sex, by creation, by the needs of the future, and we were almost home when we saw the buck we wanted.

We saw him because he had seen us, and was coming up the hill toward us—or rather, toward Matthew. He was drawn by the sight of the giant antlers strapped to Matthew's back. We were moving through dense brush and it's possible that was all he could see. He came forward with a strange aggression. He was wet from the rain. His antlers were black-brown from having lived in a dark forest and rose three feet above his head and extended beyond the tips of his outstretched ears. It did not seem possible that he could carry such a weight on his head.

Matthew dropped to his knees. The deer stopped, then came closer, still entranced by the antlers, and Matthew raised his rifle and shot the deer, now not twenty yards away, through the neck.

The deer's head snapped back, and we saw a thin pattern of blood spray across the snow behind him, but the deer did not drop. Instead it whirled and ran down the hill, hard and strong.

I wondered if Matthew could ever finish anything gracefully.

We had to track it.

The snow was deep and slushy. There was little if any blood trail to follow, and the buck's tracks merged with hundreds of others: the carnival of the rut. We stood there in the hissing, steady rain, breathing our own milky vapors.

"Fuck," Matthew said. He looked down toward the river in the direction the buck had run. He dropped his pack in the snow. The bloody "Y" on his chest was the same as the one on his back; the two together were like the delicate, world-shaped markings on the wings of some obscure tropical butterfly. I dropped my pack as well. A blood trail was beginning to form on my own back and chest.

To not be wearing a pack after having carried one for so long gave us a feeling like flight; as if, suddenly, we could have gone for another seventy-five miles. We rested a moment, then donned our packs again. The rain and slush continued to beat down on us. We kept stopping to rest, ass-whipped. We began lighting trees again—tree after tree, following the wounded buck's tracks.

A drop of blood here, a loose hair there.

We found the buck down at the river, in a backwater slough, thrashing around in six feet of water, having broken through a skin of ice as he tried to cross. We watched him for a moment as he swam in circles with only his head and the tower of antlers above the water. He was choking on his blood, coughing sprays of it across the water with each exhalation, and swallowing blood with each breath—the bullet had missed an artery, but severed a vessel—and his face was a red mask of blood.

He glared at us as he swam—a red king, defiant. It was a strange sight, those antlers going around and around in the small pond—like some new creature being born into the world. Matthew raised his rifle and waited for the deer to swim back around, closer to the edge of the shore.

The deer continued to watch us as it swam—head held high, drowning in blood. Matthew shot it in the neck again, breaking it this time, and the deer stopped swimming. The antlers sank.

We sat and stared at it for a long time—watching it motionless through the refraction of water—as if expecting it to come back to life.

Another buck, following the trail of the giant's hock musk, appeared on the other side of the pond, lowered its head, trying to decipher the cone of scent that had drifted its way.

We hiked upriver to where Matthew had left the canoe. It was under a shell of snow. We got it out and went and got the elk and loaded it, part by part, into the canoe, until the canoe was low in the water. Dusk was coming on again and we could see a few lights across the river, the lights of town. We had been gone only two weeks but it felt like a century.

I stayed behind while Matthew made two crossings with the meat, and then he came back for me. The rain had stopped and the sky was clearing and Matthew said we had to get the deer out now as the pond would freeze thick if we waited until the next day.

We waded into the pond together. The water was just warmer than the air. In the water, the deer was light, and we were able to muscle him up to the shore. Then we dragged him over to the canoe—gutted him quickly—and loaded him, and set out across one more time, riding lower than ever. Freezing seemed to be a more imminent danger than drowning, but we reached the other shore, sledded the canoe up onto the gravel, and finally we quit; left the mountain of meat for now, hundreds of pounds of it, only a short distance from home, and ran stumbling and falling up the hill toward town.

Lights were on in the bar. We went straight in and lay down next to the big wood stove, shivering and in pain. The bartenders, Artie and Charlie, came over with blankets and hides and began helping us out of our wet clothes and wrapping the hides around us. They started heating water on the stove for baths and making hot tea for us to drink. It was the first fluid we'd had in days that was neither snow nor cold creek water, and the heat of it made us vomit the instant the tea hit our stomachs. Artie looked at the meat we had spit up and said, "They got an elk."

Pagans

There once were two boys, best friends, who loved the same girl, and, in a less common variation on that ancient story, she chose neither of them but went on to meet and choose a third, and lived happily ever after.

One of the boys, Richard, nearly gambled his life on her—poured everything he had into the pursuit of her, Annie—while the other boy, Kirby, was attracted to her, intrigued by her, but not to the point where he would risk his life, or his heart, or anything else. It could have been said at the time that all three of them were fools, though no one who observed their strange courtship thought so, or said so; and even now, thirty years later, with the three of them as adrift and asunder from one another as any scattering of dust or wind, there are surely no regrets, no notions of failure or success or what-if, though among the three of them it is perhaps Richard alone who sometimes considers the past and imagines how easily things might have been different. How much labor went into the pursuit, and how close they, all three, passed to different worlds, different histories.

Richard and Kirby were seniors in high school while Annie was yet a junior, and as such they were able to get out of class easier than she was—they were both good students—and because Kirby had a car, an old Mercury with an engine like a locomotive's, he and Richard would sometimes spend their skip days traveling down to the coast, forty miles southeast of Houston, drawn by some force they neither understood nor questioned, traveling all the way to the water's lapping edge.

The boys traveled at night, too, always exploring, and on one of their trips they had found a rusting old crane half sunk near the estuary of the Sabine River, salt-bound, a derelict from gravel quarry days. They had climbed up into the crane (feeling like children playing in a sandbox) and found they could manually unspool the loopy wire cable and with great effort crank it back in. (When they did so, the giant rusting gear teeth gave such a clacking roar that the night birds roosting down in the graystick spars of dead and dying trees on the other shore took flight, egrets and kingbirds and herons, the latter rising to fly slow and gangly across the moon; and as the flecks of rust chipped from each gear tooth during that groaning resurrection, the flakes drifted down toward the river in glittering red columns, fine as sand, orange wisps and strands of iron like dust being cast onto the river by the conjurings of some midnight sorcerer.)

With such power at their fingertips, there was no way not to exercise it. Richard climbed down from the crane and muck-waded out into the gray shallows—poisoned frogs yelped and skittered from his approach, and the dancing flames of the nearby refineries wavered and belched, as if noticing his approach and beckoning him closer: as if desiring to stoke their own ceaseless burning with his own bellyfire.

Richard grabbed the massive hook of the cable's end and hauled it back up to shore and fastened it to the undercarriage of Kirby's car, then raised his hand over his head and made a twirling motion.

Kirby began cranking, and the car began to ascend in a levitation, rising slowly into the air. Loose coins, pencils, and Coke cans tumbled from the windows at first, but then all was silent save for the steady ratchet of slow gears cranking one at a time, and the boys howled with pleasure, and more birds lifted from their rookeries and flew off into the night.

It was only when the car was some twenty feet in the air—dangling, bobbing, and spinning—that Richard thought to ask if the down gears worked, imagining what a long walk home it would be if they did not—and imagining, too, what the result might be if one of the old iron teeth failed, plummeting the Detroit beast into the mud below.

The gears held. Slowly, a foot at a time in its release, the crane let the car back down toward the road.

The boom would not pivot—had long ago been petrified into its one position, arching out toward the river like some tired monument facing the direction of a long-ago, all-but-forgotten war—but there were hundreds of feet of cable, so they were able to give each other rides in the rocket car now, one of them lifting it with the crane while the other gripped the steering wheel and held on for dear life, aiming straight for the moon and praying the cable would hold.

They soon discovered that by twisting and jouncing in the passenger seat they could induce the car to sway farther and spin as it was raised—and it took all of an evening (the spinning headlights on high beam, strafing the bilious green cloudbank above, where refinery steam crept through the tops of the trees) to tire of that game, as startled birds flew past the sky-driver's windows. They began hooking on to other objects, attaching the Great Claw of Hunger, as they called it, to anything substantial they could find: pulling from the sandbank half-submerged railroad ties, the old bumpers of junked cars, twisted steel scrap, rusting slag-heaped refrigerators, washers and dryers.

As if in a game of crude pinball or some remote-controlled claw clutch game at an arcade, they were able to lurch their attachments out into the center of the river; with a little practice they learned how to disengage the hook in midair, dropping junked cars from forty feet up, landing them sometimes back on the road with a grinding clump of sparks, and other times in the river's center with a great whale plume of splash.

A sculpture soon appeared in the river's middle, a testament to machines that had been hard-used and burned out early, spring-busted not even halfway through the great century: the steel wheels of trains, cogs and pulleys, transmissions leaking rainbow sheens into the night water, iridescent sentences trailing slowly downstream.

Within a few nights they had created an island in the slow current's middle, an island of steel and chrome that gathered the bask of reptiles on the hot days, and into the evenings: turtles, little alligators, snakes, and bullfrogs.

Nights were the best. There were still fireflies back then, along the Sabine, and the fireflies would cruise along the river and across the toxic fields, swirling around the ascending car, the joy ride: and the riders, the journeyers, would imagine that they were astronauts, voyaging through the stars, cast out into some distant future.

In September the river was too low for barges to use, though when the rains of winter returned the river would rise quickly, flooding the banks and filling the cab of the crane; and the riverboat captains working at night would have to contend with the new obstacle of the junk slag island, not previously charted on their maps. They might or might not marvel at the genesis of the structure, but would tug at the brims of their caps, note the obstacle in the logbook, and pass on, un-dreaming, laboring toward the lure of the ragged refineries, ferrying more oil and chemicals, hundreds of barrels of toxins sloshing in the rusty drums stacked atop their barges, and never imagine that they were passing the fields of love.

Richard and Kirby bought an old diving bell in an army-navy sur-plus store for fifty dollars—they had to cut a new rubber gasket for the hatch's seal—and after that they were able to give each other crane rides down into the poisoned river.

For each of them it was the same, whether lowering or being lowered. The crane's operator would swing the globe out over the mercury-colored moonlit water, then lower it, with his friend inside, into that netherworld—the passenger possessing only a flashlight, which dimmed upon submersion and then disappeared—the globe tumbling with the current and its passenger not knowing whether or not the cable was still attached, bumping and tumbling, spotlight probing the black depths, with brief, bright glimpses of fish eyes, gold-rimmed and wild in fright, pale turning-away bellies flashing past, darting left and right to get out of the way of the tumbling iron ball of the bathysphere.

Soon enough, the cable would stretch taut, and shudder against the current: swaying in place but traveling no more.

Then the emergence, back up out of total darkness and into the night, with the gas flares still flickering all around them. Why, again, was the rest of the world asleep? The boys took comfort in the knowledge that they would never sleep: never.

On their afternoon school-skips together, down to the Gulf Coast, Richard, Kirby, and Annie would wander the beaches barefoot, walking beneath the strand line, studying the Gulf as if yearning to travel still farther—as if believing that, were they to catch it just right, the tide might one day pull back so far as to reveal the entire buried slope of the unseen ocean floor, wholly new territory.

Beyond the smokestack flares of the refineries, out on a windy jetty, there was an abandoned lighthouse, its base barnacle-encrusted, that they enjoyed ascending on some such trips, and once up in the glassed-in cupola they would drink hot chocolate from a thermos they had brought, sharing the one cup, and would play the board game Risk, to which they were addicted.

And, slowly, within Annie, a little green fire began to burn as she spent more and more time with the two older boys; and, more quickly, an orange fire began to flicker, then burn within Richard as he began to desire to spend even more time in her company.

Only Kirby seemed immune, his own internal light cool and blue.

They played on.

By mid-September Kirby and Richard were bringing Annie out to play the bathysphere game, and to view their slag island. They would come out on lunch break, and would skip a class before and sometimes after to buy them the time they needed. There was a bohemian French-African oceanography teacher who was retiring that year and who could see what Richard, if not Kirby, was trying to do, chasing the heart of the young girl, the junior. The teacher—Miss Countée, who wore a beret—would write hall passes for all three of them, knowing full well they would be leaving campus. She issued the passes under the stipulation they bring back specimens for her oceanography lab. They drove through the early autumn heat with the windows down and an old green canoe on top of their car. They paddled out to the new slag island and had picnics of French bread and green apples and cheese.

They piled lawn chairs atop the edifice. And even though the water was poisoned, the sound of it, as they lay there in the sun with their sleeves rolled up and their shoes and socks off, eyes closed, was the same as would be the sound of waves in the Bahamas, or a clear cold stream high in the mountains. Just because the water was ugly did not mean it had to sound ugly.

Richard knew that to the rest of the world Annie might have appeared gangly, even awkward, but that had nothing to do with how his heart leapt now each time he saw her—and after they began traveling to the river, he started to notice new things about her. Her feet pale in the sun, her shoulders rounding, her breasts lifting. A softening in her eyes as the beauty in her heart began to rise out of her. And many years later, after their lives separated, he would believe there was something about the sound, the harmonics, of that ravaged river and her ability to love it and take pleasure in it, that released something from within her; transforming in ancient alchemy the beautiful unseen into the beautifully tangible.

The water lapping against the edges of the canoe, tethered to one of the steel spars midpile. Umbrellas for parasols; crackers and cheese. Annie's pale feet browning in the sun. Perspiration at their temples, under their arms, in the smalls of their backs. Richard felt himself descending, sinking, deeper into love, or what he supposed was love. How many years, he wondered, before the two of them were married and they would browse upon each other, in similar sunlight, in another country, another life? He was content to wait forever.

It was, however, as if Annie's own fire, the quiet green one, would not or could not quite merge with his leaping, dancing orange one. As if the two fires (or three fires) needed to be in each other's company and were supported, even fed, by each other's warmth—but that they could not, or would not yet, combine.

Without true heat of conviction, Annie would sometimes try to view the two boys separately, and would even, in her girl's way, play or pretend at imagining a future. Kirby, she told herself, was more mature, more responsible. As well, there was an instinct that seemed to counsel her to both be drawn toward yet also move away from Richard's own more exposed fires and energies.

It was too much work to consider; it was all pretend anyway, or almost pretend. They had found a lazy place, a sweet place, to hang out, in the eddy between childhood and whatever came next. She told herself she would be happy to wait there forever, and, for a while, she believed that.

Occasionally the river would ignite spontaneously; other times, they found they could light it themselves by tossing matches or flaming oily rags out onto its oil and chemical slicks. None of the three of them was a church-goer, though Annie, a voracious reader, had been carrying around a Bible that autumn, reading it on their picnics while crunching an apple, the bayou breeze, river breeze, stirring her strawberry hair.

"I want to give the river a blessing," she said the first time she saw the river ignite. The snaky, wandering river fires, in various bright petrochemical colors, seemed more like a celebration than a harbinger of death or poison, and they told themselves that through such incinerations they were doing the river a favor, helping rid it of excess toxins.

They loaded their green canoe with gallon jugs of water the next day, tap water straight from their Houston faucets and hoses.

The canoe rode low in the water on their short trip out to the iron-and-chrome island, carrying the load of the three of them as well as their jugs of water. The gunwales of their green boat were no more than an inch above the murk of the river, and they sat in the canoe as still as perched birds to avoid capsizing, letting the current carry them to the island of trash.

Once there, they spent the rest of the afternoon scrubbing with steel wool and pouring the clean bright water over the encrusted, mud-slimed ornamenture of bumpers and freezers, boat hulls and car bodies. They polished the chrome appurtenances and rinsed the mountain anew.

When they had it sparkling, Annie climbed barefoot to the top and read a quote from Jeremiah: "And I brought you into the plentiful country, to eat the fruit thereof and the goodness thereof; but when ye entered, ye defiled my land and made mine heritage an abomination."

On her climb up to the top, she had gashed her foot on the rusted corner of one sharp piece or another. She paid it no mind as she stood up there in her overalls, her red-brown hair stirring in the wind, a bright trickle of blood leaking from her pale foot, and Richard had the uneasy feeling that something whole and vital and time-crafted, rare, was leaking out of her through that wound, and that he, with his strange vision of the world and his half-assed, dreamy shenanigans, was partly responsible: if not for leading her directly astray, then at least for leading her down the path to the flimsy or even unlatched gate and showing her a view beyond.

And Kirby, too, viewing her blood, felt an almost overpowering wave of tenderness, and with his bare hand quickly wiped it from her foot, then put his arm around her as if to comfort her, though she did not feel discomforted; and now the two of them began to sink down into the fields of love, like twin pistons dropping a little deeper, leaving Richard off-balance for a moment, for a day, poised above, distanced now.

There was no clean water left with which to rinse or purify themselves after the ceremony. Instead they burned twisted bunches of green Johnson grass held in their hands, wands of slow-swirling blue smoke. Like pagans, they paddled back to shore, mucked across the oily sandbar, and while Richard and Kirby were loading the canoe back onto the car, Annie went off into the tall waving grass to pee, and when she came back she was carrying a dead white egret—not one of the splendid but common yellow-legged cattle egrets but a larger and much rarer snowy egret (within their lifetime it would all but vanish), whiter than even the clouds, so white that as Annie carried it, it seemed to glow. It had died so recently that it was still limp.

She laid it in the grass for them to examine. They stroked its head, and the long crested plumes flowing from the head. Perhaps it was only sleeping. Perhaps they could resuscitate it. Kirby stretched the wings out into a flying position, then folded them back in tight against the body. Nothing. Annie's eyes watered, and again Kirby felt the overpowering wave of tenderness that was not brotherly but stronger, wilder, fiercer—as if it came from the river itself.

It seemed the obvious thing to do would be to bury the egret, but they couldn't bring themselves to give such beauty back to the earth, much less to such an oily, drippy, marred earth, and so they took the canoe and paddled back out to the island and laid the bird—fierce-eyed and thick-beaked—to rest in the crown of the island, staring downriver like a gunner in his turret, with the breeze stirring his elegant plumage and a wreath of green grass in a garland around his snowy neck.

This time on the way out they remembered their oceanography assignment and scooped up a mayonnaise jar full of water and sediment that was the approximate color and consistency of watery diarrhea, and swabbed a dip net through the grass shallows, coming up with a quick catch of crabs and bent-backed, betumored mullet minnows. Then they loaded the canoe and drove back to school through the brilliant light, the three of them riding in the front seat together.

When they got back to school, they hurried up the stairwell with their fetid bounty, late to class as usual, and placed their murky-watered bottles on the cool marble lab table at the front of the room for the rest of the class to see.

Miss Countée made clucking sounds of pleasure and then dismay while she examined the macroinvertebrates as well as the crippled vertebrates, murmuring their names in genus and species, not as if naming them but instead greeting old acquaintances, old warriors, perhaps, from another time and place—and the other students got up from their seats and crowded around the jars and bottles as if to be closer to the presence of magic.

Richard and Annie and Kirby still had the marsh scent of the river on them, and the blue smoke odor of burnt Johnson grass, and sometimes, for a moment, Miss Countée and the students would get the strange feeling that the true wildness was not the catch in the mayonnaise jars but the catchers themselves.

Miss Countée took an eyedropper and drew up a shot of the dying

Sabine, dripped it onto a slide, slid it under a microscope, and then crooned at all the violent erratica dashing about beneath her—the athleticism and diversity, the starts and stops and lunges, the silky passages, the creepings and slitherings, the throbbings and pulsings.

The river was dying, but it was still alive.

By October the leaves on the trees at water's edge were turning yellow, and Annie was riding in the bathysphere.

As the sphere tumbled, she could orient herself to the surface by the bright glare above—the bouncy, jarring ride to the bottom, the tumultuous drift downstream, and then the shuddering tautness when the cable reached full draw. Usually she was busy laughing or praying for her life, but sometimes, at full stretch, she considered sex.

Then the crane lifted the sphere free and clear of the river, back into that bright light, water cascading off the bathysphere and glittering in sheets and torrents of sun diamonds (the awful river transformed, in that moment, into something briefly beautiful). To tease her, the boys would let her remain down there just a beat or two longer, each time, just long enough for the precursor of a thought to begin to enter her mind, the image that—despite their affection for her—something had snapped within them. Not quite the thought, but the advancing shadow of the thought, of the boys, her friends, climbing down from the crane and getting in the car and driving off. Not *abandoning* her, but going off for a burger and fries. And then forgetting her, perhaps, or getting in a wreck.

Always, the boys pulled her up and reeled her back in before the thought of abandonment formed fully, and the thought beyond that—the terror of utter loneliness, utter emptiness.

None of them questioned that the crane was there for them, a relic still operating for them. They didn't question that it was tucked out of the way below a series of dunes and bluffs, away from the prying, curious eyes of man, and didn't question the grace that allowed them to run it, day or night, unobserved. They didn't question that the world, the whole world, belonged to them.

There were still a million, or maybe a hundred thousand, or at least ten thousand such places left in the world back then. Soft seams of possibility, places where no boundaries had been claimed—places where reservoirs of infinite potential lay exposed and waiting for the claimant, the discoverer, the laborer, the imaginer. Places of richness and health, even in the midst of gut-eating poisons.

For the first time, however, Richard and Kirby began to view each other as competitors. It was never a thought that lasted; always, they were ashamed of it and able to banish it at will—but for the first time, it was there.

The egret fell to pieces slowly. Sun-baked, rained-upon, wind-ruffled, ant-eaten, it deflated as if only now was its life leaving it; and then it disintegrated further until soon there were only piles of sun-bleached feathers lying in the cracks and crevices of the slag island below, and feathers loose, too, within the ghost frame of its own skeleton, still up there at the top of the machines.

As the egret decomposed, so too was revealed the quarry within—the last meal upon which it had gorged—and they could see within the bone basket of its rib cage all the tiny fish skeletons, with their piles of scale-glitter lying around like bright sand. There were bumps and tumors, misshapen bends in the fishes' skeletons, and as they rotted (flies feasting on them within that ventilated rib cage, as if trapped in a bottle, but free, also, to come and go) the toxic sludge of their lives melted to leave a bright metallic residue on the island, staining here and there like stripes of silver paint.

Sometimes they would be too restless to fool with even the magnificence of the crane. Bored with the familiar, the three of them would walk down the abandoned railroad tracks, gathering plump late-season dewberries, blackening their hands with the juice until they looked as if they had been working with oil. Kirby or Richard would take off his shirt and make a sling out of it in which to gather the berries. Their mouths, their lips, would be black-ringed like clowns'.

She beheld their bodies. They filled her dreams—first one boy, then the other—as did dreams of ghost ships and underworld rides. Dreams of a world surely different from this one—a stripping back to reveal the bones and flesh, the red muscle of a world not at all like the image of the one we believe we have crafted above.

Unsettling dreams to be shaken off, with difficulty, upon awakening. Surely all below is only imagined, she tried to tell herself, only fantasy. Surely there is only one world.

The berries they brought home were sweet and delicious, ripe and plump. The dreams of gas flares and simmering underworld fires, only images, possessed nothing of the berries' reality. Only one world, she told herself. There is nothing to be frightened of, no need to be cautious about anything.

The cracks and fissures of chance, ruptures at the earth's surface claiming the three of them, as all must be claimed—those crevasses manifesting as random occurrence but operating surely just beneath the surface in intricate balancings and alignments of fates as crafted and organic as the movements of the tides themselves. There was a school Halloween dance that autumn, which Kirby was unable to attend due to a family matter that had arisen just that week. The crack or crevice, seemingly without meaning.

It was a low-key evening filled with chaperones, and with the elementary and middle schools combining, that evening, with the high schoolers. Twister and pin the tail on the donkey, Bingo and bobbing for apples. There was a haunted house, and masked children of all ages in all manner of costumes ran laughing and shouting through the school hallways, and the high schoolers hung back for a while but then gave themselves over to the fun.

There was dancing in the basketball gym, with some of the children and adults still wearing their masks and costumes, though many of the teenagers had taken off their masks and were now only half animal—tiger, fairy, princess, gorilla. Their faces were flushed, and the discrepancy between what their hormones were telling them—*destroy, rebel*—and what the rigid bars of their culture were telling them—*no, no, no*—was for the most lively of them like a pressure cooker.

Annie was dressed as a princess, and Richard a red devil. They sat for a while and watched the other children dance. Annie waited and was aware of no pressure. It's possible that she could afford to step aside of the drumming, mounting pressure her peers were feeling because most days she had Richard and Kirby in her life, and Richard at her side, much as a young girl might have a pet bear or lion in her backyard. She turned and smiled at Richard, serene, while the music played and the little monsters ran shrieking, bumping against their legs. The scent of sugar in the air. Around them the dense aura of all the other itchy, troubled, angst-bound teenagers, wanting sex, wanting power, wanting God, wanting salvation—wanting home and hearth, and yet also wanting the open road.

There was no need yet for Annie to participate in any of that confusion. Everything else around her was swirling and tattering, but she was grounded and centered, and she was loved deeply, without reason. She smiled, watching Richard watch the dancers. She reached over and took his hand in the darkness and held it while they watched, and as they felt the palpable fretting and shifting of their peers. It was lonely, being sunk down to the bottom of the world, she thought, but comfortable, even wonderful, to have each other during such a journey.

"What do you think Kirby's doing right now?" she asked, twisting his hand in hers.

They left the party and went out for an ice cream sundae and enjoyed it leisurely, watching the rest of the city zoom by on the neon strip of Westheimer Road, a busy Friday night, hearing even in the restaurant the whooping and shouting from open car windows and the screeching of tires, and gears accelerating.

They enjoyed the meal with no conscious forethought of where they were going next—though if anyone had asked them, they would have been able to answer immediately; and after a little while Kirby drove past, finished with his family engagement. He saw Richard's car, and pulled in and joined them.

With Richard and Annie still wearing their costumes, they journeyed east, riding with the windows down as ever, and with the radio playing, but with a seriousness, a quietness, the three of them knowing with adults' wisdom they were ascending now into the world ahead, as if to some upper level, a level that would sometimes be exciting but where more frequent work would be the order of the day: less dreaming and more awareness and consciousness. Carve and scribe, hammer and haul. Almost like a war. As if this unasked-for war must be, and was, the price of all their earlier peace, and all their peace to come.

Richard and Annie held hands again in the car on the way east, and the three of them knew by the way the crane's allure was dying within them as they drew nearer to that sulfurous, wavering glow on the horizon that they would soon be moving on to other things, and in other directions. It was almost as if now—for the first time—they were pushing into a heavy headwind.

It was getting late. The city's children had finished their trick-or-treating. As they passed through a small wooded suburb sandwiched between shopping malls, they stopped and went up and gathered several stubbed candle remnants from the scorched mouths of sagging, sinking, barely glimmering pumpkins.

One pumpkin had already been taken out to the sidewalk for the garbage men to pick up the next morning, and they resurrected that one, placed it on the front seat between Annie and Kirby and fed it a new candle, coaxing it back to brightness as one might offer a cigarette to an injured or dying soldier.

They rode through the city and then east toward the refineries, with their runty candles wax-welded all over the front and back dashboards, the windows rolled almost all the way up to keep from extinguishing the little flames—the light on their faces wavering as they passed through the night (to people in passing cars and trucks, it must have seemed as if Kirby and Richard and Annie were floating, so disorienting was the sight of the big car filled with all those candles)—and they kept heading east, toward the flutterings and spumes of the refineries' fires, toward that strange glow that was like daytime at night.

That night Annie and Richard went down into the bathysphere, and into the river, together, with Kirby, above them, working the manual crank on the crane like a puppeteer. They were still wearing their costumes and there was barely room for them to squeeze in together. Annie's satin dress spread across the whole bench, and Richard's devil's tail got folded beneath them. He rode with his arm around her, and hers around him, for stability as well as courage, as the globe was lifted, swaying, from the earth—that first familiar and sickening feeling of powerlessness as the ground fell away below them—and they rode with an array of candles in front of them.

Their faces were almost touching. *This,* Richard was thinking, *this is how I want it always to be.*

They glimpsed the stars as Kirby levered them out over the river, and then there was the thrill of free fall—"Hold on!" Richard shouted, covering her with both arms and shielding her head—and the concussion of iron meeting water, the great splash. Candles went everywhere, spilling warm wax on their hands and wrists, their faces—one landed on Annie's dress and burned a small hole into it—and once underwater, the globe righted itself and settled in for the brief ride downstream.

With the candles that were still burning they relit the scattered ones and leaned forward, and cheek to cheek they studied the interior of the foul river as they tumbled through its center.

"What if the cable snapped loose," Richard asked, "when we hit the water so hard?"

Not to be outdone, Annie said, "What if some old bum, as a Halloween joke, sawed the cable down to its last fiber, so that when we reach the end it'll snap?"

There was a long silence as Richard's imagination seized and worked with that one for a while, until it became too true, and he sought to change the outcome.

"What if we were stranded on a desert island?" Richard asked.

"How about a forested island?"

"Right," Richard said. "What if? And what if we had only a little while to live?"

"The last man and woman on earth," Annie said.

"Right." *Man and woman.* The phrase sounded so foreign and distant: light-years away, still.

"Well," said Annie, "let's wait and see." But her arm tightened around his, and Richard found himself urging the cable to *break, break, break*.

The cable reached full stretch; there was a bumping, and then the globe was swept up and out, tumbling them onto their backs—as if a carpet had been pulled from beneath their feet—and again the candles fell over on them, as did the hot wax, and this time no candles stayed lit, so that they shuddered in darkness, feeling the waves, the intimate urgings of the river, washing over and around their tiny iron shell.

The force of the current made eerie sounds, murmurings and chatterings against their craft, as if it, that injured river, had been waiting to speak to them for all their life and had only now gained that opportunity—and they lay there, reclining in each other's arms, safe from the eyes of the world and its demands, its appetites for paradox and choice; and just as the air was getting stuffy and they were beginning to get a little lightheaded, they felt the surge begin: the magnificent power, the brute gears and cogs hauling them back upstream, just when they would have imagined (convinced by those fast murmurings and chatterings) that there could be no force stronger or greater than that of the river.

Gradually they broke the surface. Through their portal, still lying on their backs and arm-in-arm, but relaxed now, they could see the plumes and spray of water from their birthing back to the surface; they could see the crooked, jarring skyline of the refinery fires and, farther above, the dim stars just beyond the reach of the gold-green puffs of steam that marked the factories.

There was not much time now. Soon they would be out and free of the river, swinging, and then Kirby would land them on the beach. They were hot now, sweating, and there was barely any air left. Annie leaned over and found Richard's face with her hands and kissed him slowly, with both hands still on his face. He kissed her back, took her face in his hands and tried to shift in order to cover her with his body, but there was no room, and for a moment they became tangled, cross-elbowed and leg-locked like some human Rubik's cube. They broke off the kiss quickly, and now there was no air at all—as if they had each sucked the last of it from out of the other—but they could feel the craft settling onto the sand beach and knew that in scant moments Kirby would be climbing down and coming toward them, that there would be the rap of his knuckles on the iron door, and then the creak of the hatch being opened.

Time for one more kiss, demure and tender now, before the gritty rasp of the hatch; the counterclockwise twist, and then the lid being lifted, and Kirby's anxious face appearing before them, and beyond him, those dim stars, almost like the echoes or spent husks of stars. The cool October night sliding in over their sweaty faces.

Richard helped Annie out—her dress was a charred mess—and then climbed out behind her, marveling at how delicious even the foul refinery air tasted in their freedom. Kirby looked at them both curiously and started to speak, but then could think of nothing to say, and he felt a strange and great sorrow.

They left the bathysphere as it was, sitting with the hatch opened, still attached to the crane with its steel umbilicus. For any number of reasons, none of them would ever go back; they would never see how the crane would eventually tip over on its side, half buried in silt, or how the bathysphere would become buried, too.

They rode back into the city, still in costume, silent and strangely serious, reflective on the trip home, and with the pumpkin and candles glimmering once more, and with Annie and Richard holding hands again. The candle wax was still on their faces, and it looked molten upon them in the candlelight.

On the drive home Annie peeled the candle wax from her face and then from Richard's, and she held the pressings carefully in one hand.

When Kirby pulled up in front of her house—the living room lights still on, and one of her parents waiting up and glancing at the clock (ten minutes past eleven, but no matter; they trusted her)—Annie leaned over and gave Richard a quick peck, and gave Kirby a look of almost sultry forgiveness, then climbed out of the big old car (they had extinguished their candles upon entering the neighborhood) and hurried up the walkway to her house, holding her long silk skirt bunched up in one hand and the candle wax pressings in the other.

"Well, *fuck*," said Kirby, quietly, unsure of whether he was more upset about what seemed to him like Annie's sudden choice or about the fracturing that now existed between him and his friend. The imbalance, after so long a run, an all-but-promised run, of security.

"Shit," said Richard, "I'm sorry." He lifted his hands helplessly. "Can we...can it...?" *Stay the same,* he wanted to say, but didn't.

They both sat there, feeling poisoned, even as the other half of Richard's heart—as if hidden behind a mask—was leaping with electric joy.

"I'm sorry," Richard said again.

"The two of you deserve each other," Kirby said. "It's just that, I hate it that..." But the words failed him; there were none, only the bad burning feeling within, and after sitting there a bit longer, they pulled away from her house and drove through the night, as they used to do, back before she had begun riding with them. And for a little while they were foolish enough, and hopeful enough, to believe it would not matter, that they could get back to that old place again, and believing even that the old place would be finer than any new places lying ahead of them.

The romance lasted only a little longer than did the carcass of the egret. The three of them continued to try to do new things together—they did not return to the bathysphere—though Richard and Annie went places by themselves, too, and explored, tentatively, those new territories. Always between or beneath them, however, there seemed to be a burr. It was not that she had made the wrong choice, but rather that some choice had been required—that she had had to turn away from one thing in the turning-toward another—and that summer, even before the two boys, two young men, prepared to go off to college, while Annie readied herself to return for her senior year of high school, she informed Richard that she thought she would like a couple of weeks apart to think things over and to prepare for the pain of his departure. To prepare both of them.

"My God," Richard said, "two *weeks*?" They had been seeing each other almost every day. Their bodies had changed, their voices had changed, as had their patterns and gestures, and even the shapes of their faces, becoming leaner and more adultlike, so that now when Annie placed the old wax pressings to her face, they no longer fit.

"I want to see what it's like," she said. "Maybe everything will be just fine. Maybe we'll find out we can't live without each other, and we'll end up married and having kids and living happily ever after. But I just want to know."

"All right," he said, far more frightened than he'd ever been while dangling from the crane. "All right," he said, and it seemed to him it was as if she were climbing into the bathysphere alone, and he marveled at her bravery and curiosity, her adventurousness, and even her wisdom.

There is still a sweetness in all three of their lives now: Kirby, with his wife and four children, in a small town north of Houston; Richard, outside of Dallas with his wife and two children; and Annie, down near Galveston, with her husband and five children, and, already, her first grandchild. A reservoir of sweetness, a vast subterranean vault of it, like the treasure lair of savages—the past, hidden far away in their hearts, and held, and treasured, mythic and powerful, even still.

It was exactly like the treasure-trove of wild savages, they each realize, and for some reason—grace? simple luck?—they were able to dip down into it back then, were able to scrape out handfuls of it, gobs of it, like sugar or honey.

As if it—the discovery of that reservoir—remains with them, a power and a strength, so many years later.

And yet, they had all once been together. How can they ever be apart, particularly if that reservoir remains intact, buried, and ever-replenishing?

Even now, Richard thinks they missed each other by a hairs-breadth, that some sort of fate was deflected—though how or why or what, he cannot say. He thinks it might have been one of the closest misses in the history of the world. He has no regrets, only marvels. He wonders sometimes if there are not the ghosts or husks of their other lives living still, far back in the past, or far below, or even further out into the future—still together, and still consorting; other lives, birthed from that strange reservoir of joy and sweetness, and utter newness.

And if there are, how does he access that? Through memory? Through imagination?

Even now, he marvels at how wise they were then, and at all the paths they did not take.

The Canoeists

The two of them would go canoeing on any of the many winding creeks and rivers that braided their way through the woods and gentle hills to the north. They would drive north in Bone's old truck and put the boat on the Brazos, or the Colorado, or White Oak Creek, or even the faster-running green waters of the Guadalupe, without a care of where they might end up, and would explore those unknown seams of water and bright August light with no maps, knowing only what lay right before them as they rounded each bend.

They would take wine, and a picnic lunch, and fishing tackle, and a lantern. They drifted beneath high chalky bluffs, beneath old bridges, and past country yards where children playing tag on the hillsides among trees above the river stopped to watch them pass. They paddled on, Bone shirtless in the stern and Sissy straw-hatted in the bow, in her swimsuit. When they reached sun-scrubbed bars of white sand next to deep, dark pools, around the bend from any town or road, shaded by towering oaks, they would beach the canoe and lie on blankets in the sun like basking turtles, sweating nude, glistening, drinking wine and getting up every now and again to run down to the river and dive in, to cleanse the suntan oil and grit of sand and shine of sex from their bodies.

Hot breezes would dry their bodies quickly again, once they returned to the blankets. Their damp hair would keep them cool for a little while. They would lie perfectly still on their backs, looking up at the sun, hands clasped, and listen to the sawing buzz of the seventeen-year locusts going insane back in the forest, choking on the heat.

Later, when the day had cooled slightly, they would climb back into the green canoe and drift farther downstream, unconcerned by the notions or constraints of time and the amount of water that had passed by.

They would paddle on into dusk, and then into the night, falling deeper in love, and speaking even less, as night fell; paddling with the lantern lit and balanced on the bow, with moths following them. Fireflies would line the banks, and they passed occasionally the bright window-square blazons of farmhouses, of families tucked in for the night.

When they came to a lonely bridge or railroad trestle, they would finally relinquish the day, or that part of it, to the river, and eddy out to the bank, where Sissy would climb out with the lantern and Bone would pass her the equipment, and then he would climb out and shoulder the canoe like some shell-bound brute, and they would pick their way up the slope, clambering through brush and litter tossed from decades of the bridge's passersby, ascending to the road, while the river below kept running past.

Owls would be hooting, and heat lightning, like a pulse or an echo from the day's troubles—or like a price that must be paid for the day's bliss—would be shuddering in distant sky-flash in all directions, though it seemed like no debt or accounting to Bone and Sissy, only more blessing, as the breezes from the far-off thunderstorms stirred and cooled them as they walked through the quiet slow sounds of crickets, and through a near-total darkness, save for those glimmers of lightning, and the fireflies that dotted the meadows and swarmed around the couple as if accompanying them. They might be five miles from their truck, or they might be twenty; how to get there, they would have no idea, but neither would they be worried: Bone would not be due back at work for another twelve hours.

They would walk down the center of the dark road, Bone toting the canoe over his head like a crucifix, or some huge umbrella, and Sissy walking beside him as she would any living thing: a dog, a horse, a gentle bull, a cat. And she felt much the same herself—part human, but part other-animal, as well—and it was, again, the calmest she could ever remember being.

After a while a vehicle would approach from one direction or another, almost always an old truck in that part of the country, and the driver would give them a ride. They would lash the canoe in the bed of the truck belly-side down, as if it were still in the water, and climb up into the cab with the old farmer and ride back north into the night, though other times when there was no rope they would sit in the canoe itself, in the back, slanted skyward, gripping both the canoe's gunwales and the side of the truck to keep it from sliding out. They would ride seated in the canoe, wind rushing past them at forty, fifty miles an hour, and would be unafraid, their hair swirling and the rolls of lightning-wash flashing.

Sometimes their patron, as he crossed a county line, would want to stop at the neon red of a bar, and they would climb out of the canoe and go inside with him, to share a beer, and perhaps a sandwich or ribs. The sides of their green canoe would be smeared with the wind-crushed bodies from the swarms of fireflies they'd driven through, some of them still glowing gold but becoming dimmer, as if cooling, and it made the canoe look special, and pretty, like a float in some parade, and people in the bar would come to the doorway and stare for a moment at it thus decorated, and at Bone and Sissy.

They would drink a beer, would shoot a game or two of pool, and would visit in the dark bar, listening to the jukebox while the summer storm moved in and thundered across and past, like the nighttime passage of some huge herd of animals above. And afterward, when they went back out and climbed into their canoe to head on back north, with the driver searching for where they had left their truck, the air would be scrubbed clean and cooler, and steam would be rising from the dark roads, and the smears of fireflies would be washed from their canoe, so that all was dark around them again.

They would find their truck, eventually, and thank the old driver, and shake his hand, and for the rest of his short days he would remember having given them a ride.

They would drive home toward the city with the windows rolled down, listening to the radio. They would unload the canoe when they got to Bone's house and climb the stairs without bothering to turn on any of the lights. It might be two or three a.m. They would undress and climb into his bed, into the familiar clean sheets—warmer, upstairs—and open the windows for fresh air, and would make love again, both for the pleasure of it as well as to somehow seal or anchor their return home; and at daylight Bone would awaken and shower and dress in his suit, and head to work, leaving Sissy still asleep in his bed, their bed, swirled in white cotton sheets and asleep in a wash of morning sun.

Goats

It would be easy to say that he lured me into the fields of disrepair like Pan, calling out with his flute to come join in on the secret chaos of the world: but I already had my own disrepair within, and my own hungers, and I needed no flute call, no urging. I've read that scientists have measured the brains of adolescent boys and have determined there is a period of transformation in which the ridges of the brain swell and then flatten out, becoming smoother, like rolling hills, rather than the deep ravines and canyons of the highly intelligent, and that during this physiological metamorphosis it is for the boys as if they have received some debilitating injury, some blow to the head, so that, neurologically speaking, they glide, or perhaps stumble, through the world as if in a borderline coma, during that time.

Simple commands, much less reason and rules of consequence, are beyond their ken, and if heard at all sound perhaps like the clinking of oars or paddles against the side of a boat heard underwater, or like hard rain drumming on a tin roof: as if the boys are wearing a helmet of iron against which the world, for a while, cannot, and will not, intrude.

In this regard, Moxley and I were no different. We heard no flute calls. Indeed, we heard nothing. But we could sense the world's seams of weaknesses—or believed we could—and we moved toward them.

Moxley wanted to be a cattle baron. It wasn't about the money—we both knew we'd go on to college, Moxley to Texas A&M and me to the University of Texas, and that we'd float along in something or other. He wanted to become a veterinarian, too, in addition to a cattle baron—back then, excess did not seem incompatible with the future—and I thought I might like to study geography. But that was all eons away, and in the meantime the simple math of cattle ranching—one mother cow yielding a baby, which yielded a baby, which yielded a baby—appealed to us. All we had to do was let them eat grass. We had no expenses: we were living at home, and we just needed to find some cheap calves. The money would begin pouring in from the cattle, like coins and bills from their mouths. With each sale we planned to buy still more calves—four more from the sale of the fatted first one, then sixteen from the sale of those four, and so on.

I lived in the suburbs of Houston with both my parents (my father was a realtor, my mother a schoolteacher), neither of whom had a clue about my secret life with cattle (nor was there any trace of ranching in our family's history), while Moxley lived with his grandfather, Old Ben, on forty acres of grassland about ten miles north of what were then the Houston city limits.

Old Ben's pasture was rolling hill country, gently swelling, punctuated by brush and thorns—land that possessed only a single stock tank, a single aging tractor, and a sagging, rusting barbed-wire fence good for retaining nothing, with rotting fence posts.

Weeds grew chest high in the abandoned fields. Old Ben had fought in the first World War as a horse soldier and had been injured multiple times, and was often in and out of the V.A. clinic, having various pieces of shrapnel removed, glass and metal both, which he kept in a bloodstained gruesome collection, first on the windowsills of their little house but then, as the collection grew, on the back porch, scattered in clutter, like the collections of interesting rocks that sometimes accrue in people's yards over the course of a lifetime.

Old Ben had lost most of his hearing in the war, and some of his nerves as well, so that even on the days when he was home, he was not always fully present, and Moxley was free to navigate the rapids of adolescence unregulated.

We began to haunt the auction barns on Wednesdays and Thursdays, even before we had our driver's licenses—skipping school and walking there, or riding our bikes—and we began to scrimp and save, to buy at those auctions the cheapest cattle available: young calves, newly weaned, little multicolored lightweights of uncertain pedigree, costing seventy or eighty dollars each.

We watched the sleek velvety gray Brahma calves, so clearly superior, pass on to other bidders for $125, or $150, and longed for such an animal; but why spend that money on one animal when for the same amount we could get two?

After parting with our money we would go claim our prize. Sometimes another rancher offered to put our calf in the back of his truck or trailer and ferry it home for us, though other times we hobbled the calf with ropes and chains and led it, wild and bucking, down the side of the highway, with the deadweight of a log or creosote-soaked railroad tie attached behind it like an anchor to keep the animal—far stronger, already, than the two of us combined—from breaking loose and galloping away unowned and now unclaimed, disappearing into the countryside, our investment now no more than a kite snatched by the wind.

We gripped the calf's leash and dug in our heels, and were half hauled home by the calf itself. In the creature's terror it would be spraying and jetting algae-green plumes of excrement in all directions, which we would have to dodge, and were anyone to seek to follow us—to counsel us, perhaps, to turn away from our chosen path, still experimental at this point—the follower would have been able to track us by the scuffed-up heel marks and divots of where we had resisted the animal's pull, and by the violent fans of green-drying-to-brown diarrhea: the latter an inauspicious sign for an animal whose existence was predicated on how much weight it would be able to gain, and quite often the reason these marginal calves had been sent to the auction in the first place.

Arriving finally at Moxley's grandfather's farm, bruised and scratched, and with the calf in worse condition, we would turn it loose into the wilderness of weeds and brambles circumscribed by the sagging fence.

We had attempted, in typical adolescent half-assed fashion, to shore up the fence with loose coils of scrap wire, lacking expertise with the fence stretcher, and in some places where we had run out of wire we had used the orange nylon twine gathered from bales of hay, and lengths of odd-sorted rope, to weave a kind of cat's cradle, a spider web of thin restraint, should the calf decide to try and leave our woolly, brushy, brittle pasture.

We had woven the fence with vertical stays also, limbs and branches sawed or snapped to a height of about four feet, in the hopes that these might help to provide a visual deterrent, so that the curving, collapsing fence looked more like the boundaries of a trap or funnel constructed by Paleolithics in an attempt to veer driven game toward slaughter.

We had money only for cattle or fence, but not both. Impulsive, eager, impatient, we chose cattle, and the cattle slipped through our ramshackle fence like the wind itself—sometimes belly-wriggling beneath it, other times vaulting it like kangaroos.

Usually, the calves went straight through the weakened fence, popping loose the rusted fence staples and shattering the leaning fence posts and crude branches stacked and piled as barricades. Sometimes the calves, fresh from the terror and trauma of their drive from auction, never slowed when first released through the gate at Old Ben's farm, but kept running, galloping with their heads lowered all the way down the hill, building more speed, and they would hit the fence square on.

More often than not, they sailed right on through it like a football player charging through the paper stretched between goalposts before a football game, though occasionally they bounced back in an awkward cartwheel before scrambling to their feet and running laterally until they found a weaker seam and slipped through it not like anything of this world of flesh and bone, but like magicians, vanishing.

When that happened, we had to leap on the old red tractor, starting it with a belch and clatter that frightened the calf into even wilder flight; and with Moxley driving the old tractor flat-out in high gear, and me standing upright with a boot planted wobbily on each of the sweeping wide rear fenders, riding the tractor like a surfer and swinging a lariat (about which I knew nothing), we would go racing down the hill after the calf, out onto the highway, the tractor roaring and the calf running as if from some demon of hell that had been designed solely to pursue that one calf, and which would never relent.

We never caught the calves, and only on the rarest of occasions were we ever able to draw near enough to one—wearing it down with our relentlessness—to even attempt a throw of the rope, which was never successful.

Usually the animal would feint and weave at the last instant, as the tractor and whizzing gold lariat bore down on it, and would shoot or crash through another fence, or cross a ditch and vault a fence strung so tightly that as the calf's rear hoofs clipped the fence going over, the vibration would emit a high taut hum, which we could hear even over the sound of the tractor.

It was like the sound of a fishing line snapping, and by the time we found an unlocked gate to that pasture the calf would have escaped to yet another field, or might be down in some creek bottom, reverting to instincts more feral than those of even the deer and turkeys that frequented those creeks; and we would scour the surrounding hills for all the rest of that day—sometimes pursuing, for a short distance, a calf that might look like ours, until that calf's owner would come charging out on his own tractor, shouting and cursing, angling to intercept us like a jouster.

Old Ben fell too ill to drive and then became a problem while Moxley was in school; he had begun to wander out into the same fields in which the rogue calves had been released, and was trying to escape his lifelong home, though he was too feeble to bash or batter his way through the patchwork fence, and instead endeavored to climb over it.

Even on the instances when he made good his escape, he snagged his shirt or pants on a barb and left behind flag-size scraps of bright fabric fluttering in the breeze, and we were able to track him that way, driving the roads in his old station wagon, searching for him.

Often, Old Ben lay down in a ditch, trembling and exhausted from his travels, and pulled a piece of cardboard over him like a tent to shield him from the heat, and we would pass on by him, so that it might be a day or two before we or a neighbor could find him.

Other times, however, Old Ben became so entangled in his own fence that he would be unable to pull free, and when we came home from school we would see him down there, sometimes waving and struggling though other times motionless, spent, with his arms and legs akimbo, and his torn jacket and jeans looking like the husk from some chrysalis or other emerging insect; and we'd go pluck him from those wires, and Moxley would mend his torn jacket with the crude loops of his own self-taught sewing: but again and again Old Ben sought to flow through those fences.

There were also days, however, when Old Ben was fine, fit as a fiddle; times when the disintegrating fabric of his old war-torn mind, frayed by mustard gas and the general juices of war's horror, shifted like tiny tectonic movements, reassembling into the puzzle-piece grace his mind had possessed earlier in life—the grandfather Moxley had known and loved, and who loved him, and who had raised him. On those occasions it felt as if we had taken a step back in time. It was confusing to feel this, for it was pleasant; and yet, being young, we were eager to press on. We knew we should be enjoying the time with Old Ben—that he was not long for the world, and that our time with him, particularly Moxley's, was precious and rare, more valuable than any gold, or certainly any rogue cattle.

On the nights when the past reassembled itself in Old Ben and he was healthy again, even if only for a while, the three of us ate dinner together. We sat on the back porch feeling the Gulf breezes coming from more than a hundred miles to the southeast, watching the tall ungrazed grass before us bend in oceanic waves, with little gusts and accelerations stirring the grass in streaks and ribbons, looking briefly like the braids of a rushing river, or as if animals in hiding were running along those paths, just beneath the surface, unseen.

We grilled steaks on the barbecue, roasted golden ears of corn, and drank fresh-squeezed lemonade, to which Ben was addicted. "Are these steaks from your cattle?" he would ask us, cutting into his meat and examining each bite as if there might be some indication of ownership within; and when we lied and told him yes, he seemed pleased, as if we had amounted to something in the world, and as if we were no longer children. He would savor each bite, as if he could taste some intangible yet exceptional quality.

We kept patching and repatching the ragged-ass fence, lacing it back together with twine and scraps of rope, with ancient twists of baling wire, and with coat hangers; propping splintered shipping pallets against the gaps, stacking them and leaning them here and there in an attempt to plug the many holes. (The calves ended up merely using these pallets as ladders and springboards.)

In his own bedraggled state, however, Ben saw none of the failures. "That's what being a cattleman's about," he said—he who had never owned a cow in his life. "Ninety-five percent of it is the grunt work, and five percent is buying low and selling high. I like how you boys work at it," he said, and he never dreamed or knew that in our own half-assedness we were making much more work for ourselves than if we'd done the job right the first time.

After we got our driver's licenses we used Ben's old station wagon, and after getting him to bed, and hasping the doors shut as if stabling a wild horse, and latching the windows from the outside, we left the darkened farmhouse and headed for the lights of the city, which cast a golden half-dome high into the scudding clouds.

It was a vast glowing ball of light, seeming close enough that we could have walked or ridden our bikes to reach it: and driving Ben's big station wagon, with its power steering and gas-sucking engine, was like piloting a rocket ship. There were no shades of gray, out in the country like that: there was only the stillness of night, with crickets chirping, and fireflies, and the instrument panels on the dashboard were the only light of fixed reference as we powered through that darkness, hungry for that nearing dome of city light. The gauges and dials before us were nearly as mysterious to us as the instrument panel of a jet airplane, and neither Moxley nor I paid much attention to them. For the most part, he knew only the basics: how to aim the car, steering it crudely like the iron gunboat it was, and how to use the accelerator and the brakes.

And after but a few miles of such darkness there would suddenly be light, blazes of it hurled at us from all directions—grids and window squares and spears of light, sundials and radials of inflorescence and neon; and we were swallowed by it, were born into it, and suddenly we could see before us the hood of the old Detroit iron horse that had carried us into the city and swallowed us, as the city, and Westheimer Avenue, seemed to be swallowing the car, and we were no longer driving so much as being driven.

All-night gas stations, all-night grocery stores, movie theaters, restaurants, massage parlors, oil-change garages, floral shops, apartment complexes, dentists' offices, car dealerships—it was all jammed shoulder to shoulder, there was no zoning, and though we had seen it all before in the daytime, and were accustomed to it, it looked entirely different at night: alluring, even beautiful, rather than squalid and chaotic.

The neon strip fascinated us as might a carnival, but what most caught our imagination on these night sojourns was not the glamorous, exotic urban core but the strange seams of disintegrating roughness on the perimeters, pockets toward and around which the expanding city spilled and flowed like lava: little passed-by islands of the past, not unlike our own on the western edge. We passed through the blaze of light and strip malls, the loneliness of illuminated commerce, and came out the other side, on the poorer eastern edge, where the high-voltage power grids were clustered, and the multinational refineries.

Here the air was dense with the odor of burning plastic, vaporous benzenes and toluenes adhering to the palate with every breath, and the night-fog sky glowed with blue, pink, and orange flickers from the flares of waste gas jetting from a thousand smokestacks. The blaze of commerce faded over our shoulders and behind us, and often we found ourselves driving through neighborhoods that seemed to be sinking into the black soil, the muck of peat, as if pressed down by the immense weight of the industrial demands placed upon that spongy soil—gigantic tanks and water towers and chemical vats, strange intestinal folds and coils of tarnished aluminum towering above us, creeping through the remnant forests like nighttime serpents.

Snowy egrets and night herons passed through the flames, or so it seemed, and floated amid the puffs of pollution as serenely as if in a dream of grace; and on those back roads, totally lost, splashing through puddles axle deep and deeper, and thudding over potholes big enough to hold a bowling ball, Moxley would turn the lights off and navigate the darkened streets in that manner, passing through pools of rainbow-colored poisonous light and wisps and tatters of toxic fog as if gliding with the same grace and purpose as the egrets above us.

Many of the rotting old homes had ancient live oaks out in front, their yards bare due to the trees' complete shading of the soil. In the rainy season, the water stood a foot deep in the streets, so that driving up and down them was more like poling the canals of Venice than driving; and the heat from our car's undercarriage hissed steam as we plowed slowly up and down.

We were drawn to see these rougher, ranker places at night, and yet we wanted to see them in the full light of day also; and when we traveled to these eastern edges during school, while taking a long lunch break or cutting classes, we discovered little hanging-on businesses run out of those disintegrating houses, places where old men and women still made tortillas, or repaired leather boots and work shoes, or did drywall masonry, or made horseshoes by hand, even though there were increasingly few horses and ever more cars and trucks, especially trucks, as urban Texas began the calcification of its myths in full earnestness.

There were places where a patch of corn might exist next to a ten-story office building, places where people still hung their clothes on the line to dry, and little five- and ten-acre groves in which there might still exist a ghost herd of deer. Ponds in which there might still lurk giant, sullen, doomed catfish, even with the city's advancing hulk blocking now partially the rising and setting of the sun.

Through such explorations we found the Goat Man as surely and directly as if he had been standing on the roof of his shed, calling to us with some foxhunter's horn, leading us straight to the hand-painted rotting plywood sign tilted in the mire outside his hovel.

BABY CLAVES, $15, read the sign, each letter painted a different color, as if by a child. We parked in his muddy driveway, the low-slung station wagon dragging its belly over the corrugated troughs of countless such turnings-around, wallowing and slithering and splashing up to the front porch of a collapsing clapboard shed-house that seemed to be held up by nothing more than the thick braids and vines of dead ivy.

Attached to the outside of the hovel was a jerry-built assemblage of corrals and stables, ramshackle slats of mixed-dimension scrap lumber, from behind which came an anguished cacophony of bleats and bawls and whinnies and outright bloodcurdling screams, as we got out of the car and sought to make our way dry-footed from one mud hummock to the next, up toward the sagging porch, to inquire about the baby claves, hoping very much that they were indeed calves, and not some odd bivalve oyster we'd never heard of.

We peered through dusty windows (some of the panes were cracked, held together with fraying duct tape) and saw that many of the rooms were filled with tilted mounds of newspapers so ancient and yellowing that they had begun to turn into mulch.

An old man answered the door when we knocked, the man blinking not so much as if having been just awakened but as if instead rousing himself from some other communion or reverie, some lost-world voyage. He appeared to be in his sixties, with a long wild silver beard and equally wild silver hair, in the filaments of which fluttered a few moths, as if he were an old bear that had just been roused from his work of snuffling through a rotting log in search of grubs.

His teeth were no better than the slats that framed the walls of his ragged corrals, and, barefoot, he was dressed in only a pair of hole-sprung, oil-stained forest-green work pants, on which we recognized the dried-brown flecks of manure splatter, and an equally stained sleeveless ribbed underwear T-shirt that had once been white but was now the color of his skin, and appeared to have been on his body so long as to become a second kind of skin—one that, if it were ever removed, might peel off with it large patches of his original birth skin.

The odor coming from the house was quite different from the general barnyard stench of feces, and somehow even more offensive.

Despite the general air of filth and torpor radiating from the house and its host, however, his carriage and bearing were erect, almost military—as if our presence had electrified him with hungry possibility; as if we were the first customers, or potential customers, he might have encountered in so long a time that he had forgotten his old patterns of defeat.

When he first spoke, however, to announce his name, the crispness of his posture was undercut somewhat by the shining trickle of tobacco drool that escaped through some of the gaps in his lower teeth, like a slow release of gleaming venom.

"Sloat," he said, and at first I thought it was some language of his own making: that he was attempting to fix us, tentatively, with a curse. "Heironymus Sloat," he said, reaching out a gnarly spittle- and mucus-stained hand. We exchanged looks of daring and double-daring, and finally Moxley offered his own pale and unscarred hand.

"Come in," Sloat said, making a sweeping gesture that was both grand and familial—as if, horrifically, he recognized in us some kindred spirit—and despite our horror, after another pause, we followed him in.

Since all the other rooms were filled with newspapers and tin cans, Sloat's bed had been dragged into the center room. The kitchen was nearly filled with unwashed pots and dishes, in which phalanxes of roaches stirred themselves into scuttling escape as we entered. The rug in that middle room was wet underfoot—the water-stained, sagging ceiling was still dripping from the previous night's rain, and on the headboard of the bed there was a small fishbowl, filled with cloudy water, in which a goldfish hung suspended, slowly finning in place, with nothing else in the bowl but a single short decaying sprig of seaweed.

The fish's water was so cloudy with its own befoulment as to seem almost viscous, and for some reason the fish so caught my attention that I felt hypnotized, suspended in the strange house—as if I had become the fish. I had no desire to move, and neither could I look anywhere else. All of my focus was on that one little scrap of color, once bright but now muted, though still living.

I glanced over at Moxley and was disturbed to see that he seemed somehow invigorated, even stimulated, by the rampant disorder.

So severe was my hypnosis, and so disoriented were both of us, that neither of us had noticed there was someone sleeping in the rumpled, unmade bed beside which we stood; and when the person stirred, we stepped back, alarmed.

The sleeper was a young woman, not much older than we were, sleeping in a nightgown only slightly less dingy than the shirt of the older man—and though it was midafternoon, and bright outside, her face was puffy with sleep, and she stirred with such languor I felt certain she had been sleeping all day.

She sat up and stared at us as if trying to make sense of us, and brushed her hair from her shoulders. Her hair was orange, very nearly the same color as the fish's dull scales, and Sloat stared at her in a way that was both dismissive and yet slightly curious—as if wondering why, on this day, she had awakened so early.

She swung her feet off the bed and stood unsteadily, and watched us with unblinking raptness.

"Let's go look at the stock," Sloat said, and we could tell that it gave him pleasure to say the word *stock*.

The three of us went through the cluttered kitchen and out to the backyard—it surprised me there were no dogs or cats in the house—and the girl followed us to the door but no farther, and stood there on the other side of the screen. Her bare feet were dirty, as if she had made the journey out to the stables before, but on this occasion lingered behind, perhaps made shy.

Sloat was wearing old sharp-toed cowboy boots, his thin shanks shoved into them in such a way that I knew he wasn't wearing socks, and he walked in a brisk, almost fierce line straight through the puddles and troughs toward the stables, as if he enjoyed splashing through the muck and grime, while Moxley and I pussyfooted from hummock to hummock, sometimes slipping and dipping a foot in one water-filled rut or another. Whitish foam floated on the top of the puddles, as if someone, or something, had been urinating in them.

Sloat pushed through a rickety one-hinge gate, and goats, chickens, and other fleeting, unidentified animals scattered before his explosive entrance. Sloat began cursing and shouting at them, then picked up a stick and rat-tat-tatted it along the pickets to excite them further, like a small boy, and as if to demonstrate their vigor to their potential buyers.

A pig, a pony, a rooster. A calf, or something that looked like a calf, except for its huge head, which was so out of proportion for the tiny body that it seemed more like the head of an elephant.

"I buy them from the Feist brothers," he said. "The ones that don't get sold at auction. They give me a special deal," he said.

The animals continued to bleat and caterwaul, flowing away, flinging themselves against the fences. Some of them ran in demented circles, and others tried to burrow in the mud, while the goats, the most nimble of them, leapt to the tops of the crude-hammered, straw-lined doghouses and peered down with their wildly disconcerting vertical-slit lantern green eyes as if welcoming Moxley and me into some new and alien fraternity of half man, half animal: and as if, now that Moxley and I were inside the corral, the goats had us exactly where they wanted us.

Moxley had eyes only for the calves, thin-ribbed though they were, dehydrated and listless, almost sleepwalkerish compared to the frenzy and exodus of the other animals. Six of them were huddled over in one corner of the makeshift corral, quivering collectively, their stringy tails and flanks crusted green.

"Which are the fifteen-dollar ones?" he asked, and, sensing weakness, Sloat replied, "Those are all gone now. The only ones I have left are thirty-five."

Moxley paused. "What about that little Brahma?" he asked, pointing to the one animal that was clearly superior, perhaps even still healthy.

"Oh, that's my little prize bull," Sloat said. "I couldn't let you have him for less than seventy-five."

Between us, we had only sixty-five, which in the end turned out to be precisely enough. We had no trailer attached to the back of the station wagon, but Sloat showed us how we could pull out the back seat, lash the seat to the roof for the drive home, and line the floor and walls of the station wagon with squares of cardboard, in case the calf soiled it, and drive home with him in that manner. "I've done it many a time myself," Sloat said.

The girl had come out to watch us, had waded barefoot through the same puddles in which her father, or whatever his relation was to her, had waded. She stood on the other side of the gate, still wearing her nightgown, and watched us as Sloat and Moxley and I, our financial transaction completed, chased the bull calf around the corral, slipping in the muck, Sloat swatting the calf hard with a splintered baseball bat, whacking it whenever he could, and Moxley and me trying to tackle the calf and wrestle it to the ground.

The calf was three times as strong as any one of us, however, and time and again no sooner had one of us gotten a headlock on it than it would run into the side of the corral, smashing the would-be tackler hard against the wall; and soon both Moxley and I were bleeding from our shins, noses, and foreheads, and I had a split lip—and still Sloat kept circling the corral, following the terrified calf, smacking him hard with the baseball bat.

Somehow, all the other creatures had disappeared—had vanished into other, adjacent corrals, or perhaps through a maze of secret passageways—and leaning against one of the wobbly slat walls, blood dripping from my nose, I saw now what Sloat had been doing with his antics. Each time the calf rounded a corner, Sloat had pushed open another gap or gate and ushered two or three more nontarget animals into one of the outlying pens, until finally the calf was isolated.

Sloat was winded, and he stood there gasping and sucking air, the bat held loosely in his hands. The calf stood facing the three of us, panting likewise, and suddenly Sloat rushed him, having waited to gauge when the animal would be midbreath, too startled or tired to bolt, and he struck the calf as hard as he could with the baseball bat, striking it on the bony plate of its forehead.

The calf neither buckled nor wobbled, but seemed only to sag a little, as if for a long time he had been tense or worried about something but could now finally relax.

Sloat laid his bat down almost tenderly—as if it were some valuable instrument to be accorded great respect—and then gestured to the Goat Girl, held out an open hand to her.

From her pocket, she pulled a short length of heavy rope. She climbed over the fence and carried it to him. Quickly, before the calf could rise, Sloat twisted the rope around the calf's bulging neck, gripping it with one fist, and then almost delicately at the same time pressed a thumb into the stricken animal's throat, probing a bit, searching for just the right cleft.

The calf's eyes fluttered, then closed with what seemed almost serenity. It shuddered once, then loosened, and Sloat stood up straight, pleased with the cleanliness, the precision, of his act. He paused only to catch his breath and then called to us to help him heft the calf before it came back to consciousness, though we could not imagine such a thing, and I was thinking at first that he had just stolen our money: had taken our sixty-five dollars, killed our calf, and was now demanding our assistance in burying it.

The Goat Girl roused herself finally from her strange reverie, and splashed through the puddles of foam and slime, out toward the car in advance of us, as if intending to lay palm fronds before our approach. She opened our car door and placed the scraps of cardboard in the car's interior, for when the calf resurrected.

"How long will he be out?" Moxley asked.

"Where are you taking him?" Sloat asked, and I told him, *West Houston*—about an hour and a half away.

"An hour and a half," said Sloat, whom I had now begun to think of as the Goat Man. He shook our proffered hands—cattlemen!— and told us, as we were driving off, to come back soon, that he had a lot of volume coming through, and that he would keep an eye out for good stock, for buyers as discerning as we were, and that he would probably be able to give us a better break next time.

Moxley slithered the station wagon out to the end of the drive— the Goat Man and Goat Girl followed—and Moxley stopped and rolled his window down and thanked them both again and asked the girl what her name was.

But she had fallen into a reverie and was staring at us in much the same manner as the calf had after receiving his first blow; and as we drove away she did not raise her hand to return our waves, and neither did she give any other sign of having seen or heard us, or that she was aware of our existence in the world.

Driving away, I was troubled deeply by the ragtag, slovenly, almost calculated half-assedness of the operation; and on the drive home, though Moxley and I for the most part were pleased and excited about having gotten another calf, and so cheaply, I was discomforted, could feel a rumbling confusion, the protest that sometimes precedes revolution though other times leads to nothing, only acquiescence, then senescence. I could see that Moxley did not feel it—and, sensing this, I felt weaker, and slightly alone.

The calf woke up when we were still an hour from Ben's ranch. The calf did not awaken gradually, as a human might, stirring and blinking and looking around to ascertain his new surroundings, but awoke instead explosively, denting a crumple in the roof with his bony head. He squealed and then began crashing against the sides of the car's interior with such a clacking of hoofs we were afraid he would break the glass and escape; and his frenzied thrashings (he was unable to stand to his full height in the back of the car, and instead began crawling) reminded me of how, hours earlier, the calf had been rounding the makeshift corral.

We attempted to shoo the calf to stay in the back, swatting at him with our hands, but these gestures held no more meaning for the bull than if we had been waving flyswatters at him, and his squeals transformed to full roars, amplified to terrifying proportions within the confines of the car. At one point he was in the front seat with us, having lunged over it, and in his flailings managed to head-butt me. He cut Moxley's shins with swift kicks of his sharp little hoofs so that they were bruised and bleeding, and Moxley nearly ran off the road, but then the calf decided he preferred the space and freedom of the back seat and vaulted over the seat again and into his cardboard lair, where he continued to hurl himself against the walls.

As the Goat Man had foreseen, and as a symptom of the ailment that had caused the calf to not be bid upon in the first place at the regular auction—the auction that had preceded the mysterious Feist brothers' obtaining him—the calf in his fright began emitting fountains of greenish diarrhea, spraying it midwhirl as if from a hose, so that we were yelling and ducking, and soon the interior of the car was nearly coated with dripping green slime. And though panicked, we were fierce in our determination to see this thing through, and we knew if we stopped and turned the calf out into the open, we would never capture him again.

Somehow we made it home, and in the darkness of the new evening, with fireflies blinking in the fields, we drove straight out into Old Ben's pasture, gray weeds scraping and scratching against the sides of the wagon with an eerie, clawing keen that further terrified the calf: and when we rolled down the tailgate's window he leapt out into that clean sweet fresh night air; and this calf, too, we never saw again, though the residue of his passage remained with us for weeks afterward, in cracks and crevices of the old station wagon, despite our best scrubbing.

Old Ben fell further into the rot. Moxley and I could both see it, in his increasingly erratic behavior; and though I had perceived Moxley to be somehow more mature than I—more confident in the world— I was surprised by how vulnerable Moxley seemed to be made by Ben's fading.

Ben was ancient, a papery husk of a man—dusty, tottering history, having already far exceeded the odds by having lived as long as he had—and was going downhill fast. Such descent could not be pleasant for Old Ben, who, after all, had once been a young man much like ourselves. His quality of life was plummeting even as ours, fueled by the strength of our youth, was ascending. Did Moxley really expect, or even want, for the old man to hang on forever, an eternal hostage to his failed and failing body, just so Moxley would have the luxury of having an older surviving family member?

We couldn't keep him locked up all the time. Moxley had taken over control of the car completely, took it to school each day, and hid the keys whenever he was home, but Old Ben's will was every bit as fierce as Moxley's, and Ben continued to escape. We often found him floating in the stock tank, using an inner tube for a life vest, fishing, with no hook tied to his line.

He disappeared for a week once after rummaging through the drawers and finding the key to the tractor, which he drove away, blowing a hole through the back wall of the barn. We didn't notice the hole, or that the tractor was missing, and it was not until a sheriff called from Raton County, New Mexico, asking if Moxley knew an elderly gentleman named Ben, that we had any clue of where he was. We skipped school and drove out there to get him, pulling a rented flatbed on which to strap the tractor, and he was as glad to see us as a child would have been; and Moxley, in his relief, was like a child himself, his eyes tearing with joy.

All through that winter we continued to buy more stock from the Goat Man, knowing better but unable to help ourselves, and lured, also, by the low prices. Even if one in ten of his scour-ridden wastrels survived to market, we would come out ahead, we told ourselves, but none of them did: they all escaped through our failed fence, usually in the first afternoon of their freedom, and we never saw any of them again.

We imagined their various fates. We envisioned certain of them being carried away by the panthers that were rumored to still slink through the Brazos river bottoms, and the black jaguars that were reported to have come up from Mexico, following those same creeks and rivers as if summoned, to snack on our cheap and ill-begotten calves, or *claves,* as we called them. We imagined immense gargoyles and winged harpies that swooped down to snatch up our renegade runaway crops. We envisioned modern-day cattle rustlers congregating around the perimeter of our ranch like fishermen. It was easy to imagine that even the Goat Man himself followed us home and scooped up each runaway calf in a net and returned with it then to his lair, where he would sell it a second time to another customer.

Or perhaps there was some hole in the earth, some cavern into which all the calves disappeared, as if sucked there by a monstrous and irresistible force. Any or all of these paranoias might as well have been true, given the completeness of the calves' vanishings.

With each purchase we made I felt more certain that we were traveling down a wrong path, and yet we found ourselves returning to the Goat Man's hovel again and again, and giving him more and more money.

We ferried our stock in U-Haul trailers, and across the months, as we purchased more cowflesh from the Goat Man—meat vanishing into the ether again and again, as if into some quarkish void—we became familiar enough with Sloat and his daughter to learn that her name was Flozelle, and to visit with them about matters other than stock.

We would linger in that center room—bedroom, dining room, living room, all—and talk, first about the weather and then about the Houston Oilers, before venturing out into what Moxley and I had taken to calling the Pissyard. We learned that Flozelle's mother had died when she was born, that Flozelle had no brothers or sisters, and that Sloat loathed schools.

"I homeschool her," he said. "Go ahead, ask her anything."

We could have been wiseasses. We could have flaunted our ridiculously limited knowledge—the names of signatories to obscure historical documents, the critical dates of various armistices—but in the presence of such abject filth, and before her shell-shocked quietude, we were uncharacteristically humbled. Instead, Moxley asked, almost gently, "How long have you had that fish?" and before Flozelle could answer, Sloat bullshitted us by telling us that the fish had been given to his grandmother on her wedding day, almost a hundred years ago.

"What's its name?" I asked, and this time, before Sloat could reply, Flozelle answered.

"Goldy," she said proudly, and a shiver ran down my back. If I had known what sadness or loneliness really felt like, I think I might have recognized it as such; but as it was, I felt only a shiver, and then felt it again as she climbed up onto the unmade bed (the bottoms of her bare feet unwashed and bearing little crumb fragments) and unscrewed the lid to a jar of uncooked oatmeal she kept beside the bowl, and sprinkled a few flakes into the viscous water.

Moxley was watching her with what seemed to me to be a troubled look, and after she had finished feeding the bloated fish, she turned and climbed back down off the lumpen bed.

With no further preamble, she asked, "Do you want to see my fur collection?" and when Moxley, with no hesitation, nodded, she took each of us by the hand, led us into the mud-splattered utility room—empty Popsicle wrappers and ice cream cartons cluttered the floor—and, releasing our hands (her own was remarkably tender and smooth, sensual), opened the freezer to reveal a menagerie of what was surely every dead animal she had ever found: not just gutted skunks, foxes, raccoons, squirrels, and opossums, but birds stacked like firewood, their feathers hoarfrosted as if made of silver: great horned owls, blue jays, cardinals, titmice, red-headed woodpeckers. Mockingbirds.

She stared at them without speaking, as if these creatures were her beloveds: stared down into them, forgetting we were there, I think, until frost-fog from the deep freeze began to boil up and around us; and then, just as gently, she closed the lid. And saying nothing, we all filed out through the kitchen and on into the Pissyard to go look at, and purchase, more stock.

Back before Ben had begun falling to pieces, Moxley and I had sometimes gone by my house after school to do homework and hang out. My mother would make cookies, and if Moxley was still there when my father got home from work, Moxley would occasionally have supper with us. But those days had gone by long ago, Ben now requiring almost all of his waking care. I helped as I could, doing little things like cleaning up the house. Whenever Ben discovered that he was trapped he would ransack the house, pulling books down off shelves and hurling his clothes out of his drawer. Once, he rolled up the carpet and tried to set the end of it on fire, as if lighting a cigar; when we arrived at the farmhouse, we could see the gray smoke seeping from the windows, and, rushing inside, we found Ben passed out next to the rug, which had smoldered and burned a hole in the plywood flooring, revealing the gaping maw of dark basement below, with the perimeter of that burned-out crater circular, like a caldera, having burned so close to Ben that his left arm hung down into the pit. All the next day we sawed and hammered new sheets of plywood to patch that abyss. For a few days afterward, Ben seemed contrite and neither misbehaved nor otherwise suffered any departures from sentience, as if such lapses had been, after all, at least partially willful.

I helped cook dinners, and some nights I stayed over at their farmhouse and made breakfast, and helped Moxley batten down the doors and windows before leaving for school. Knives, scissors, matches, guns, fishhooks, lighter fluid, gasoline, household cleaners—it all had to be put away. Moxley had tied a 150-foot length of rope around Ben's waist each night so if Ben awoke and went sleepwalking, wandering the dewy hills, he could be tracked and reeled in like a marlin.

The farmhouse was a pleasant place to awaken in the morning— the coppery sun rising just above the tops of the trees, and the ungrazed fields lush and tall and green, with mourning doves cooing and pecking red grit and gravel from the driveway—and the interior of the house would be spangled with the prisms of light from all the little pieces of glass arrayed on the windowsill, Ben's shrapnel collection. The spectral casts of rainbow splashed across the walls like the light that passes through stained-glass windows, and there would be no sound but the ticking of the grandfather clock in the front hallway, and the cooing of those doves, and the lowing of distant cows not ours. Moxley and I would fix breakfast, gather our homework, then lock up the house and leave, hurrying toward school.

I had some money from mowing lawns, and Moxley was pretty flush, or so it seemed to us, from Ben's pension checks. As much from habit now as from desire, we made further pilgrimages to Sloat's corrals that winter and spring.

And following each purchase, upon our return to Ben's ranch, sometimes our new crop of sickly calves would remain in the pasture for a few days, though never longer than a week, after which, always, they disappeared, carrying with them their daunting and damnable genes, the strange double-crossed combination of recessive alleles that had caused the strangeness to blossom in them in the first place—the abnormality, the weakness, that had led to the unfortunate chain of circumstances that resulted in their passing from a real auction to the Feist brothers, who would sell them for dog meat if they could, and then to Sloat and a short life of squalor, and then to us, and then to whatever freedom or destiny awaited them.

Ben caught pneumonia after one of his escapes. (He had broken out a window and crawled through, leaving a trail of blood as well as new glass scattered amid his sparkling windowsill shards of glass from fifty years earlier; we trailed him down to the pond, his favorite resting spot, where he stood shivering, waist deep, as if awaiting a baptism.) Moxley had to check him into the hospital, and after Ben was gone the silence in the farmhouse was profound.

Moxley was edgy, waiting for the day when Old Ben would be coming home, but that day never came; he would die in the hospital. And although it had long been clear that Ben's days at home were numbered, the abyss of his final absence still came as a surprise, as did Moxley's new anger.

We continued with our old rituals, as if Ben was still with us— cooking steaks on the back porch grill, and buying cattle—but the ground beneath our feet seemed less firm.

With Old Ben's last pension check Moxley and I went to a real auction and bought a real calf—not one of Sloat's misfits, but a reg- istered Brahma—a stout little bull calf. And rather than risk losing this one, we kept it tethered, like a dog on a leash, in the barn. It was not as wild as Sloat's terrified refugees, and soon we were able to feed and water it by hand: and it grew fatter, week by week. We fed it a diet rich in protein, purchasing sweet alfalfa and pellet cubes. We brushed it and curried it and estimated its weight daily as we fatted it for market. And it seemed to me that with some success having finally been achieved, Moxley's anger and loneliness had stabilized, and I was glad that this calf, at least, had not es- caped. It was a strange thought to both of us, to consider that we were raising the animal so someone else could eat him, but that was what cattlemen did.

As this calf, finally, grew fatter, Moxley seemed to grow angry at the Goat Man, and barely spoke to him now when we traveled out there; and though we still went out there with the same, if not greater, frequency, we had stopped purchasing stock from the Goat Man and instead merely went out into the Pissyard to look. After we had purchased the calf from the regular auction, Sloat's offerings were revealed to us in their full haplessness and we could not bring ourselves to take them at any price; still, we went to look, morbidly curious about what misfits might have passed through his gates that week.

Moxley asked Flozelle out on what I suppose could be called a date, even though I was with them. I wanted to believe the best of him, but it seemed to me that there was a meanness, a bedevilment. Moxley still had the same aspirations—he was intent on going to school and becoming a vet—but the moments of harshness seemed to emerge from him at odd and unpredictable times, like fragments of bone or glass emerging from beneath the thinnest of skin.

The three of us began to ride places together once or twice a week, and, for a while, she fascinated us. She knew how to fix things—how to rebuild a carburetor, how to peel a tire from its rim and plug it with gum and canvas and seat it back onto its rim again—and some-times, out in the country, we stopped beside the fields of strangers and got out and climbed over the barbed-wire fence and went out to where other people's horses were grazing.

We would slip up onto those horses bareback and ride them around strangers' fields for hours at a time. Flozelle knew how to gentle even the most unruly or skittish horse by biting its ears with her teeth and hanging on like a pit bull until Moxley or I had climbed up, and then she'd release her bite hold and we'd rocket across the pasture, the barrel ribs of the horse beneath us heaving; the expen-sive thoroughbreds of oilmen, the sleek and fatted horses farting wildly from their too-rich diets of grain.

She had never been to a movie before, and when we took her she stared rapt, ate three buckets of popcorn, chewing ceaselessly through *Star Wars*. She began spending some afternoons with Mox-ley out at his farm, and helping him with chores—mowing with the tractor the unkempt grass, bush-hogging brush and cutting bales of hay for our young bull. She showed us how to castrate him, to make him put on even more weight even faster, and she set about repairing the shabby, sorry fence we had never gotten around to fixing prop-erly.

The calf, the steer, was getting immense, or so it seemed to us, and though he still was friendly and manageable, his strength concerned us. We worried that he might strangle himself on his harness, his leash, should he ever attempt to break out of the barn, and so not long after Flozelle had completed her repairs on the fence we turned him out into the field, unfastening his rope and opening the barn doors, whereupon he emerged slowly, blinking, and then descended to the fresh green fields below and began grazing there confidently, as if he had known all his life that those fields were waiting for him, and that he would reach them in due time.

I had the strange thought that if only Old Ben could have still been alive to see it, the sight might somehow have helped heal him, even though I knew that to be an impossibility. He had been an old man, war torn and at the end of his line; no amount of care, or even miracles, could have kept him from going downhill.

To the best of my knowledge, Flozelle did not shower, as if such a practice went against her or her father's religious beliefs. In my parents' car I drove up to the farm one warm day in the spring, unannounced, and surprised Moxley and Flozelle, who were out in the backyard. Moxley was dressed but Flozelle was not, and Moxley was spraying her down with the hose—not in fun, as I might have suspected, but in a manner strangely more workmanlike, as one might wash a car, or even a horse; and when they saw me Moxley was embarrassed and shut the hose off, though Flozelle was not discomfited at all, and merely took an old towel, little larger than a washcloth, and began drying off.

And later, after he had taken her back home—after we had both driven out to Sloat's and dropped her off, without going inside, and without going back into the Pissyard to look around, I asked him, "Are you sleeping with her?"—and he looked at me with true surprise and then said, "I am," and when I asked him if she ever spent the night over at the farmhouse, he looked less surprised, less proud, and said yes.

What did it matter to me? It was nothing but an act, almost lavatory-like in nature, I supposed—almost mechanical and without emotion, if not insensate. I imagined it to be for Moxley like the filling of a hole, the shoveling-in of something, and the tamping-down.

It was not anything. He was doing what he had to do, almost as if taking care of her; and she, with all the things the Goat Man had taught her, had fixed his fences, had repaired the old tractor, the barn.

She had not led him down any errant path, and neither was his life, or mine, going to change or deviate from our destinies as a result of any choices made or not made. She was like fodder, was all. We were just filling the days. We were still fattening up. We were still strong in the world, and moving forward. I had no call to feel lonely or worried. We still had all the time in the world, the world was still ours, there was no rot anywhere, the day was still fresh and new, we could do no wrong. We would grow, just not now.

Her First Elk

She had killed an elk once. She had been a young woman, just out of college—her beloved father already three years in the grave—and had set out early on opening morning, hiking uphill through a forest of huge ponderosa pines, with the stars shining like sparks through their boughs, and owls calling all around her, and her breath rising strong in puffs and clouds as she climbed, and a shimmering at the edge of her vision like the electricity in the night sky that sometimes precedes the arrival of the northern lights, or heat lightning.

The hunt was over astonishingly quickly; years later, she would realize that the best hunts stretch out four or five weeks, and sometimes never result in a taking. But this one had ended in the first hour, on the first day.

Even before daylight, she had caught the scent of the herd bedded down just ahead of her, a scent sweeter and ranker than that of any number of stabled horses; and creeping closer, she had been able to hear their herd sounds, their little mewings and grunts.

She crouched behind one of the giant trees, shivering from both the cold and her excitement—sharply, she had the thought that she wished her father were there with her, to see this, to participate—and then she was shivering again, and there was nothing in her mind but elk.

Slowly the day became light, and she sank lower into the tall grass beneath the big pines, the scent of the grass sweet upon her skin; and the lighter the day became, the farther she flattened herself down into that yellow grass.

The elk rose to their feet just ahead of her, and at first she thought they had somehow scented her, even though the day's warming currents had not yet begun to ascend the hill; the last of the night's heavier, cooling currents were still sliding in waves down the mountain, the faint breeze in her face carrying the ripe scent of the herd downhill, straight to her.

But they were only grazing, still mewing and clucking and barking and coughing, and feeding on the same sweet-scented grass that she was hiding in. She could hear their teeth grinding as they chewed, could hear the clicking of their hoofs as they brushed against rocks.

These creatures seemed a long way from the dinners that her father had fixed out on the barbecue grill, bringing in the sizzling red meat and carving it quickly before putting it on her child's plate and saying, "Elk"; but it was the same animal—they were all the same animal, nearly a dozen years later. Now the herd was drifting like water, or slow-flickering flames, out of the pines and into a stand of aspen, the gold leaves underfoot the color of their hides, and the stark white trunks of the aspen grove making it look as if the herd were trapped behind bars; though still they kept drifting, flowing in and out of and between those bars, and when Jyl saw the biggest one, the giant among them, she picked him, not knowing any better—unaware that the meat would be tougher than that of a younger animal.

Raising up on one knee, she found the shot no more difficult for her than sinking a pool ball in a corner pocket: tracking, with the end of her rifle and the crosshairs of the scope, the cleft formed just behind his right shoulder as he quartered away from her. She did not allow herself to be distracted by the magnificent crown of antlers atop his head, and when he stopped in his last moment and swung his head to face her, having sensed her presence, she squeezed the trigger as she had been taught to do back when she was a girl.

The elk leapt hump-shouldered like a bull in a rodeo, then took a few running steps before stumbling, as if the bullet had not shredded his heart and half his lungs but had instead merely confused him.

He crashed to the ground as if attached to an invisible tether; got up, ran once more, and fell again.

The cows and calves in his herd, as well as the younger bulls, stared at him, trying to discern his meaning, and disoriented, too, by the sudden explosive sound. They stared at the source of the sound—Jyl had risen to her feet and was watching the great bull's thrashings, wondering whether to shoot again—and still the rest of the herd stared at her with what she could recognize only as disbelief.

The bull got up and ran again. This time he did not fall, having figured out, in his grounded thrashings, how to accommodate his strange new dysfunction so as to not impede his desire, which was to escape—and with one leg and shoulder tucked high against his chest, like a man carrying a satchel, and his hind legs spread wider for stability, he galloped off, running now like a horse in hobbles, and with his immense mahogany-colored rack tipped back for balance. What was once his pride and power was now a liability.

The rest of the herd turned and followed him into the timber, disappearing into the forest almost reluctantly, still possessing somehow that air of disbelief; though once they went into the timber, they vanished completely, and for a long while she could hear the crashing of limbs and branches, and then the sounds grew fainter and farther, and there was only silence.

Not knowing any better, back then, she set out after the herd rather than waiting to let the bull settle down and lie down and bleed to death. She didn't know that if pushed a bull could run for miles with his heart in tatters, running as if on magic or spirit rather than the conventional pump-house mechanics of ventricles and aortas; that if pushed, a bull could run for months with his lungs exploded or full of blood.

As if in his dying the bull were able to metamorphose into some entirely other creature, taking its air, its oxygen, straight into its blood, through its gaping, flopping mouth, as a fish does; and as if it were able still to disseminate and retrieve its blood, pressing and pulsing it to the farthest reaches of its body and back again without the use of a heart, relying instead on some kind of mysterious currents and desire—the will to cohere—far larger than its own, the blood sloshing back and forth, willing the elk forward, willing the elk to keep being an elk.

Jyl had had it in her mind to go to the spot where the elk had first fallen—even from where she was, fifty or sixty yards distant, she could see the patch of torn-up earth—and to find the trail of blood from that point, and to follow it.

She was already thinking ahead, and looking beyond that first spot, when she walked into the barbed-wire fence that separated the national forest from the adjoining private property, posted against hunting, on which the big herd had been sequestered.

The fence was strung so tight she bounced backwards, falling much as the elk had fallen; and in her inexperience, she had been holding the trigger on her rifle, with a shell chambered in case she should see the bull again, and as she fell she gripped the trigger, discharging the rifle a second time, with a sound even more cavernous, in its unexpectedness, than the first shot.

A branch high above her intercepted the bullet, and the limb came floating down, drifting like a kite. From her back, she watched it land quietly, and she continued to lie there, bleeding a little, and trembling, before finally rising and climbing over the fence, with its "Posted" signs, and continuing on after the elk.

She was surprised by how hard it was to follow his blood trail: only a still-wet splatter here and there, sometimes red and other times drying brown already against the yellow aspen leaves that looked like spilled coins—as if some thief had been wounded while ferrying away a strongbox and had spilled his blood upon that treasure.

She tried to focus on the task at hand but was aware also of feeling exceedingly lonely—remembering, seemingly from nowhere, that her father had been red-green colorblind, and realizing how difficult it might have been for him to see those drops of blood. Wishing again that he were here with her, though, to help her with the tracking of this animal.

It was amazing to her how little blood there was. The entry wound, she knew, was not much larger than a straw, and the exit wound would be only the size of a quarter, and even that small wound would be partially closed up with the shredded flesh, so that almost all of the blood would still be inside the animal, sloshing around, hot and poisoned now, no longer of use but unable to come out.

A drop here, a drop there. She couldn't stop marveling at how few clues there were. It was easier to follow the tracks in the soft earth, and the swath of broken branches, than it was the blood trail—though whether she was following the herd's path or the bull's separate path, she couldn't be sure.

She came to the edge of the timber and looked out across a small plowed field, the earth dark from having just been turned over to autumn stubble. Her elk was collapsed dead in the middle of it—the rest of the herd was long gone, nowhere to be seen—and there was a truck parked next to the elk already, and standing next to the elk were two older men in cowboy hats. Jyl was surprised, then, at how tall the antlers were—taller than either man, even with the elk lying stretched out on the bare ground; taller than the cab of the truck.

The men did not appear happy to see her coming. It seemed to take her a long time to reach them. It was hard walking over the furrows and clods of stubble, and from the looks on the men's faces, she was afraid the elk might have been one of their pets, that they might even have given it a name.

It wasn't that bad, as it turned out, but it still wasn't good. Their features softened a little as she closed the final distance and they saw how young she was, and how frightened—she could have been either man's daughter—and as she approached there seemed to be some force of energy about her that disposed them to think the best of her; and they found it hard to believe, too, that had she killed the elk illegally she would be marching right up to claim it.

There were no handshakes, no introductions. There was still frost on the windshield of the men's truck, and Jyl realized they must have jumped into their truck and cold-started it, racing straight up to where they knew the herd hung out. Used to hang out.

Plumes of fog-breath leapt from the first man's mouth as he spoke, even though they were all three standing in the sunlight.

"You shot it over on the other side of the fence, right, over on the national forest, and it leapt the fence and came over here to die?" he asked, and he was not being sarcastic: as if, now that he could see Jyl's features, and her fear and youth, he could not bear to think of her as a poacher.

The other man, who appeared to be a few years the elder—
they looked like brothers, with the older one somewhere in his sixties, and fiercer-looking—interrupted before she could answer and
said, "Those elk knew never to cross that fence during hunting season. That bull wouldn't let them. I've been watching him for five
years, and any time a cow or calf even *looks* at that fence, he tips—
tipped—his antlers at them and herded them away from it."

Jyl saw that such an outburst was as close to a declaration of love
for the animal as the old man would be capable of uttering, and the
three of them looked down at the massive animal, whose body heat
they could still feel radiating from it—the twin antlers larger than
any swords of myth, and the elk's eyes closed, and still only what
seemed like a little blood dribbling down the left shoulder, from the
exit wound—the post-rut musk odor of the bull was intense—and
all Jyl could say was "I'm sorry."

The younger brother seemed almost alarmed by this admission.

"You didn't shoot him on our side, did you?" he asked again. "For
whatever reason—maybe a cow or calf had hopped the fence, and
he was over there trying to get it back into the herd—he was over on
the public land, and you shot him, and he ran back this way, jumped
over the fence, and ran back over here, right?"

Jyl looked down at her feet, and then again at the bull. She might
as well have shot an elephant, she thought. She felt trembly, nause-
ated. She glanced at her rifle to be sure the chamber was open.

"No," she said quietly.

"Oh, Christ," the younger man said—the older one just glared at
her, hawkish, but also slightly surprised now—and again the younger
one said, "Are you sure? Maybe you didn't see it leap the fence?"

Jyl showed him the scratch marks on her arms, and on her face. "I
didn't know the fence was there," she said. "The sun was coming up
and I didn't see it. After I shot, I walked into the fence."

Both men stared at her as if she were some kind of foreigner, or
as if she were making some fabulous claim and challenging them to
believe it.

"What was the second shot?" the older man asked, looking back
toward the woods. "Why did it come so much later?" As if suspecting

that she might have a second animal down somewhere, back in the forest. As if this frail girl, this *child,* might have a vendetta against the herd.

"The gun went off by accident when I walked into the fence," she said, and both men frowned in a way that told her that gun carelessness was even worse in their book than elk poaching.

"Is it unloaded now?" the younger brother asked, almost gently.

"No," she said, "I don't guess it is."

"Why don't you unload it now?" he asked, and she complied, bolting and unbolting the magazine three times, with a gold cartridge cartwheeling to the black dirt each time, and then a fourth time, different-sounding, less full sounding, snicking the magazine empty. She felt a bit of tension release from both men, and in some strange way of the hunt that she had not yet learned, the elk seemed somehow different, too: less vital, in her letting-down. As if, despite its considerable power and vitality, her pursuit of and hunger for it had somehow helped to imbue it with even more of those characteristics, sharpening their edges, if only just a little.

The older brother crouched down and picked up the three cartridges and handed them to her. "Well, goddamn," he said, after she had put them in her pocket and stood waiting for him to speak— would she go to jail? would she be arrested, or fined?—"That's a big animal. I don't suppose you have much experience cleaning them, do you?"

She shook her head.

The brothers looked back down the hill—in the direction of their farmhouse, Jyl supposed. The fire unstoked, the breakfast unmade. Autumn chores still undone, with snow coming any day and a whole year's worth of battening down, or so it seemed, to do in that narrow wedge of time.

"Well, let's do it right," the elder said. "Come with us back down to the house and we'll get some warm water and towels, a saw and ax and a come-along." He squinted at her, more curious than unkind. "What did you intend to do, after shooting this animal?" he asked.

Jyl patted her hip. "I've got a pocketknife," she said. Both brothers

looked at each other and then broke into incredulous laughter, with
tears coming to the eyes of the younger one.

"Might I see it?" the younger one asked when he could catch
his breath, but the querulous civility of his question set his brother
off to laughing again—they both broke into guffaws—and when Jyl
showed them her little folding pocket-knife, it was too much for
them and they nearly dissolved. The younger brother had to lean
against the truck and daub at his rheumy eyes with a bandana, and
the morning was still so cold that some of the tears were freezing in
his eyelashes, which had the effect, in that morning sunlight, of making him look delicate.

Both men wore gloves, and they each took the right one off to
shake hands with her and to introduce himself: Bruce, the younger,
Ralph, the elder.

"Well, congratulations," Ralph said, grudgingly. "He is a big damn
animal."

"Your first, I reckon," said Bruce as he shook her hand—she was
surprised by the softness of it, almost a tenderness—Ralph's had
been more like a hardened flipper, arthritic and knotted with muscle—and he smiled. "You won't ever shoot one bigger than this," he
said.

They rode down to their cabin in the truck, Jyl sitting between
them—it seemed odd to her to just go off and leave the animal lying
there in the field—and on the way there, they inquired about her
life: whether she had a brother who hunted, or a father, or even a
boyfriend. They asked if her mother was a hunter and it was her turn
to laugh.

"My father used to hunt," she said, and they softened a bit further.

They made a big breakfast for her—bacon cut from hogs they had
raised and slaughtered, and fried eggs from chickens they likewise
kept, and cathead biscuits, and a plate of delicate pork chops (both
men were as lean as matchsticks, and Jyl marveled at the amount of
work the two old boys must have performed daily, to pour through
such fuel and yet have none of it cling to them)—and after a couple of cups of black coffee, they gathered the equipment required for
disassembling the elk and drove back up on the hill.

The frost was burning off the grass and the day was warming so they were able to work without their jackets. Jyl was struck by how different the brothers seemed, once they settled into their work: not quite aggressive, but forceful with their efficiency. And though they were working more slowly than usual, in order to explain to her the why and what of their movements, things still seemed to unfold quickly.

In a way, it seemed to her the elk was coming back to life and expanding, even in its diminishment and unloosening, the two old men leaning into it like longshoremen, with Jyl helping them, laboring to roll the beast over on its back, and inverting the great head with the long daggered antlers, which now, upended, sank into the freshly furrowed earth like some mythic harrow fashioned by gods, and one that only certain and select mortals were allowed to use, or capable of using.

And once they had the elk overturned, Ralph emasculated it with his skinning knife, cutting off the ponderous genitals and tossing them farther into the field with no self-consciousness; it was merely the work that needed doing. And with that same large knife (the handle of which was made of elk antler) he ran the blade up beneath the taut skin from crotch to breastbone while Bruce kept the four legs splayed wide, to give Ralph room to work.

They peeled the hide back to the ribs as if opening the elk for an operation, or a resuscitation—*How can I ever eat all of this animal?* Jyl wondered—and again like a surgeon Bruce placed twin spreader bars between the elk's hocks, bracing wide the front legs as well as the back. Ralph slit open the thick gray-skin drum of fascia that held beneath it the stomach and intestines, heart and lungs and spleen and liver, kidneys and bladder; and then, looking like nothing so much as a grizzly bear grubbing on a hillside, or burrowing, Ralph reached up into the enormous cavity and wrapped both arms around the stomach mass—partially disappearing into the carcass, as if somehow being consumed by it rather than the other way around: and with great effort he was able finally to tug the stomach and all the other internal parts free.

As they pulled loose they made a tearing, ripping, sucking sound, and once it was all out, Ralph and Bruce cut out with that same sharp knife the oversize heart, big as a football, and the liver, and laid them out on clean bright butcher paper on the tailgate of their truck.

Then Ralph rolled the rest of the guts, twice as large as any medicine ball, away from the carcass, pushing it as if shoving some boulder away from a cave's entrance. Jyl was surprised by the sudden focusing of color in her mind, and in the scene. Surely all the colors had been present all along, but for her it was suddenly as if some gears had clicked or aligned, allowing her to notice them now, some subtle rearrangement blossoming into her mind's palette: the gold of the wheat stubble and the elk's hide, the dark chocolate of the antlers, the dripping crimson blood midway up both of Ralph's arms, the blue sky, the yellow aspen leaves, the black earth of the field, the purple liver, the maroon heart, Bruce's black and red plaid work shirt, Ralph's faded old denim.

The richness of those colors was illuminated so starkly in that October sunlight that it seemed to stir chemicals of deep pleasure in Jyl's own blood, elevating her to a happiness and a fullness she had not known earlier in the day, if ever; and she smiled at Bruce and Ralph, and understood in that moment that she, too, was a hunter, might always have been.

She was astounded by how much blood there was: the upended ark of the carcass awash in it, blood sloshing around, several inches deep. Bruce fashioned a come-along around the base of the elk's antlers and hitched the other end to the iron pipe frame on the back of their truck—the frame constructed like a miniature corral, so that they could haul a cow or two to town in the back when they needed to without having to hook up the more cumbersome trailer—and carefully he began to ratchet the elk into a vertical position, an ascension. To Jyl it looked like nothing less than a deification; and again, as a hunter now, she found this fitting, and watched with interest.

Blood roared out from the elk's open carcass, gushing out from between its huge legs, a brilliant fountain in that soft light. The blood splashed and splattered as it hit the new-turned earth—Ralph and Bruce stood by watching the elk drain as if nothing phenomenal at all were happening, as if they had seen it thousands of times before—

and the porous black earth drank thirstily this outpouring, this torrent. Bruce looked over at Jyl and said, "Basically, it's easy: you just carve away everything you don't want to eat."

Jyl couldn't take her eyes off how fast the soil was drinking in the blood. Against the dark earth, the stain of it was barely even noticeable.

When the blood had finally stopped draining, Ralph filled a plastic washbasin with warm soapy water from a jug and scrubbed his hands carefully, pausing to clean the soap from beneath his fingernails with a smaller pocketknife—and when he was done, Bruce poured a gallon jug of clean water over Ralph's hands and wrists to rinse the soap away, and Ralph dried his hands and arms with a clean towel and emptied out the old bloody wash water, then filled it anew, and it was time for Bruce to do the same. Jyl marveled at, and was troubled by, this privileged glimpse at a life, or two lives, beyond her own—a life, two lives, of cautious competence, fitted to the world; and she was grateful to the elk, and its gone-away life, beyond the sheer bounty of the meat it was providing her, grateful to it for having led her into this place, the small and obscure if not hidden window of these two men's lives.

She was surprised by how mythic the act, and the animal, seemed. She understood there were only two acts more ancient—sex and flight—but here was this third one, hunting, suddenly before her. She watched as each man worked with his own knife to peel back the hide, working on each side of the elk simultaneously. Then, with the hide eventually off, they handed it to Jyl and told her it would make a wonderful shirt or robe. She was astonished at the weight of it.

Next they began sawing the forelegs and stout shins of the hind legs; and only now, with those removed, did the creature begin to look reduced or compromised.

Still it rose to an improbable height, the antlers seven feet beyond the eight-foot crossbar of the truck's pole rack—fifteen feet of animal stretched vertically, climbing into the heavens, and the humans working below, so tiny—but as they continued to carve away at it, it slowly came to seem less mythic and more steerlike; and the two old men working steadily upon it began to seem closer to its equal.

They swung the huge shoulders aside, like the wings of an immense flying dinosaur, and pulled them free, each man wrapping both arms around the slab of shoulder to hold it above the ground. They stacked the shoulders in the truck, next to the rolled-up fur of the hide.

Next the hindquarters, one at a time, severed with a bone saw: both men working together to heft that weight into the truck, and the remaining length of bone and antler and gleaming socket and rib cage looking reptilian, like some reverse evolutionary process, some metamorphic errancy or setback. The pile of beautiful red meat in the back of the truck, though, as it continued to mount, seemed like an embarrassment of riches, and again it seemed to Jyl that perhaps she had taken too much.

She thought how she would have liked to watch her father render an elk. All gone into the past now, however, like blood drawing back into the soil. How much else had she missed?

The noonday sun was mild, almost warm now. The scavenger birds—magpies, ravens, Steller's jays and gray jays—danced and hopped nearby, swarming and fluttering, and from time to time as Ralph or Bruce took a rest, one of the men would toss a scrap of gristle or fascia into the field for the birds to fight over, and the sound of their squabbles filled the lonely silence of the otherwise quiet and empty hills beneath the thin blue of the Indian summer sky.

They let Jyl work with the skinning knife, showed her how to separate the muscles lengthwise with her fingers before cutting them free of the skeleton, and the quartered ham and shoulder—the backstrap unscrolling beneath the urging of her knife, the meat as dense as stone, it seemed, yet as fluid as a river, and so beautiful in that sunlight, maroon to nearly purple, nearly iridescent in its richness, and in the absence of any intramuscular fat. And now the skeleton, with its whitened bones beginning to show, seemed less an elk, less an animal, than ever, and the two brothers set to work on the neck, and the tenderloins, and butt steaks, and neck loins. While they separated and then trimmed and butchered those, Jyl worked with her own knife at carving strips of meat from between each slat of rib cage.

From time to time their lower backs would cramp and they would have to lie down on the ground, all three of them, looking up at the sky and spreading their arms out wide as if on a crucifix, and would listen to, and feel with pleasure, the popping and realigning of their vertebrae, and would stare up at that blue sky and listen to the cries of the feeding birds, and feel intensely their richness at possessing now so much meat, clean meat, and at simply being alive, with the blood from their labor drying to a light crust on their hands and arms. They were like children, in those moments, and they might easily have napped.

They finished late that afternoon, and sawed the antlers off for Jyl to take home with her. Being old-school, the brothers dragged what was left of the carcass back into the woods, returning it to the forest, returning the skeleton to the very place where the elk had been bedded down when Jyl had first crept up on it—as if she had only borrowed it from the forest for a little while—and then they drove back down to their ranch house and hung the ham and shoulder quarters on meat hooks to age in the barn, and draped the backstraps likewise from hooks, where they would leave them for at least a week.

They ran the loose scraps, nearly a hundred pounds' worth, through a hand-cranked grinder, mixed in with a little beef fat to make hamburger, and while Ralph and Jyl processed and wrapped that in two-pound packages, Bruce cooked some of the butt steak in an iron skillet, seasoned with garlic and onions and butter and salt and pepper, mixed with a few of the previous spring's dried morels, reconstituted—and he brought out small plates of that meal, thinly sliced, to eat as they continued working, the three of them grinding and wrapping, and the mountain of meat growing on the table beside them. They each had a tumbler of whiskey to sip as they worked, and when they finally finished it was nearly midnight.

The brothers offered their couch to Jyl and she accepted; they let her shower first, and built a fire for her in the wood stove next to the couch. After Bruce and then Ralph had showered, they sat up visiting, each with another small glass of whiskey, Ralph and Bruce telling her their ancient histories until none of them could stay awake—their eyes kept closing, and their heads kept drooping—and with the fire burning down, Ralph and Bruce roused from their chairs and made their way each to his bedroom, and Jyl pulled the old elk hides over her for warmth and fell asleep immediately, falling as if through some layering of time, and with her hunting season already over, that year. That elk would not be coming back, and her father would not be coming back. She was the only one remaining with those things safe and secure in her now. For a while.

She killed more elk, and deer, too, in seasons after that, learning more about them, year by year, in the killing, than she could ever learn otherwise. Ralph died of a heart attack several years later and was buried in the yard outside the ranch house, and Bruce died of pneumonia the next year, overwhelmed by the rigors of twice the amount of work, and he, too, was buried in the yard, next to Ralph, in an aspen grove, through which passed on some nights wandering herds of deer and elk, the elk direct descendants of the big bull Jyl had shot, and which the brothers had dismembered and shared with her, the three of them eating on it for well over a year. The elk sometimes pausing to gnaw at the back of those aspen with roots that reached now for the chests of the buried old men.

Remembering these things, a grown woman now woven of losses and gains, Jyl sometimes looks down at her body and considers the mix of things: the elk becoming her, as she ate it, and becoming Ralph and Bruce, as they ate it (did this make them somehow, distantly, like brothers and sister, or uncles and niece, if not fathers and daughter?)—and the two old men becoming the soil then, in their burial, as had her father, becoming as still and silent as stone, except for the worms that writhed now in their chests, and her own tenuous memories of them. And her own gone-away father, worm food, elk food: but how he had loved it.

Mountains in her heart now, and antlers, and mountain lions and sunrises and huge forests of pine and spruce and tamarack, and elk, all uncontrollable. She likes to think now that each day she moves farther away from him, she is also moving closer to him.

As if within her, beneath the span of her own days, there are other hunts going on continuously, giant elk in flight from the pursuit of hunters other than herself, and the birth of other mountains being plotted and planned—other mountains rising, then, and still more mountains vanishing into distant seas—and that even more improbable than her encountering that one giant elk, on her first hunt, was the path, the wandering line, that brought her to her father in the first place, delivered her to him and made him hers and she his—the improbability and yet the certainty that would place the two of them in each other's lives, tiny against the backdrop of the world, and tinier still against the mountains of time.

But belonging to each other, as much in death as in life. Inescapably, and forever. The hunt showing her that.

Titan

The summer that I witnessed, breathed, lived the jubilee, I was twelve years old. My brother, Otto, who is four years older, was already on what he was calling the "fast track" to success, which he defined, and still does, as becoming rich. He is an investment banker, and I suppose it is fair to say that he has never known a moment's hardship. Even he refers to himself as *blessed*. I myself was never quite as comfortable in the presence of excessive bounty as he was.

Our parents were born in the heart of the Depression, grew up under its shadow, cowed and spooked I think by the fear and memory of it. Otto reacted by turning away from the cautious austerity of our parents, away from such fiscal and, some would say, emotional timidity, and struck out as soon as possible in the opposite direction, swimming hard and strong and eager for the profligate.

Our parents had worked hard establishing their own business as geologists—but it must have rankled Otto, as soon as he was old enough to notice such things: the way our parents held on to, and conserved, and reinvested their savings, setting aside safe and prudent amounts of it, as if against the coming storms of the world— storms that never came.

There was wealth almost everywhere in Texas in those days, and the fact that I have not participated in it since then, or rather, have chosen other kinds of wealth, does not mean the moneyed type was unavailable to me. I simply was pulled in another direction. Even then, I had my own hungers, and still do.

They say that traits in a family, or even in a nation, are prone to sometimes skip generations, rising and falling in crests and troughs like waves far out beyond the Gulf. And although Otto was only four years older, I often felt as if I were an only child, that he was from the generation before me, and that my parents were from the generation before that generation, so that I was able to witness, and live between, the two ways of being in the world. And I do not mean to judge Otto—but whenever my parents would attempt to have a cautionary discussion with him about his hungry, consumptive ways, he would brush them off.

There was nothing that he did not see as a commodity, able to be bought or sold or traded, and leveraged or even stolen from the future. He was then and still is simply a taker, and it is the only way he is comfortable in the world: and though one day I suppose the world will run out of things to take and to trade—or rather, will run out of worthwhile things to take and trade—that is not quite yet the case, and I'd have to say that all in all he's continuing to live a fairly comfortable and satisfied life, and that he's more or less content, even in the continued savagery of his hunger. I think that he has found his own balance.

Though it did not occur to me when I was twelve, I came to realize later that our elderly parents—they would have been in their midfifties then—might have been a little awed by Otto; by the unquestioning force of his desire, the crisp efficiency of his gluttony, and by the power of his steadfast commitment, almost as if to a religious philosophy, to seek out anything rare and valuable, and purchase it, and count it, and market it: to acquire and consume.

Listening to him talk about such things—stocks and bonds, gold and silver, treasury notes and soybeans, cattle and poultry, coal and oil—was like watching a great predator gaze unblinkingly, its jaws parted, at a herd of unknowing grazing creatures. My parents weren't frightened of their oldest son, but they were awed. And who were they, besides his elders, to speak to him, to tell him he was wrong, when they themselves had known a similar hunger but had simply grown up in a time when it seemed there was nothing available to acquire, and no means for the acquisition?

✳   ✳   ✳

My own hunger was for a closeness and a connection—a reduction in the vast and irreducible space I perceived to exist between all people, even within a family. It would have been fine with me if every morning the four of us had taken our breakfast together, and if the four of us had then gone out into the day to labor in the bright fields together, in some wholesome and ancient way, plowing and tilling, or harvesting and gathering, and to eat all our meals together, and to end the day with a family reading, an hour or more of dramatic monologue, or a chautauqua.

Instead, we all sort of went our own ways, day after day. The closest we came to conventional or traditional or mythical unity was every summer when we went on vacation to a place in south Alabama, on the coast, called Point Clear. The hotel and resort where we stayed— the Grand Hotel—was elegant, even if the coast itself was hot and windy and muggy. In the evenings we would eat delicious seafood in the formal candlelit dining room, surrounded by diners possessing far greater wealth than my parents': men and women who were no less than corporate titans. And each night, while I would sit there quietly, reflectively, dreaming a child's dreams, Otto would be looking all around, paying far more attention to the titans—to their mannerisms and overheard conversations—than he did to the meal itself. And, even then, I would sometimes be aware of the manner in which my parents beheld both of us, and of their unspoken thoughts, as they wondered, *How can two brothers, or two of anything, turn out so different?* And I could see also that they were perturbed by this difference, this distance. As if we were all moving away from one another: as if our desire for space was the greatest gluttony.

At the hotel, each night was attended by endless opulence. We would all dress up, titans and nontitans, and enter that grand formal dining hall and be waited on, hand and foot, with one delicacy after another being brought to us, treats and treasures to be had merely for the asking, while a band played music at the other end of the hall. And the next day, after a breakfast of bright fruit and fresh juice, Otto and my parents would go off to play tennis or golf, while I would be on my own, free to wander the well-kept grounds, free to inhabit the reckless lands of my imagination. There was so much space.

I prowled the cattails in the water hazards along the golf courses, catching fish and minnows and snakes and turtles and frogs—particularly the sleek and elegant spotted leopard frogs, which are already nearly extinct. They were everywhere back then, and no one could ever have imagined they would simply, or not so simply, vanish. What other bright phenomena will vanish in our lifetimes, becoming one day merely memory and story, tale and legacy, and then fragments of story and legacy, and then nothing, only wind?

I spent the middle of the afternoons sitting in the air-conditioned lobby, playing chess with and against myself, bare-chested in my damp swimsuit, sitting on a leather sofa with sand grains crumbling from between my toes onto the cool tile floor. I ordered root beer and grilled cheese sandwiches from the pool, charging them to our room, and in my concentration on the game I would spill potato chips into the folds of the leather furniture. I failed to notice the icy looks that must have been coming from the desk clerks.

There are so many different types of gluttony. Even now, just as when I was a child and without responsibility, I can lie on my back in the tall grass in autumn and stare at the clouds, an adult with not a thought in my head; and when I stand up, hours later, I will still be ravenous for the sight of those clouds, and for the whispering of that grass, and when I go to bed that night I will still be hungry for the memory of the warmth of that late-season sun, even as, in the moment, I am enjoying the scent and embrace of the darkness, and the cooling night.

At Point Clear, we'd meet up again for dinner—Otto and my parents tanned from the extravagances of their own day, and relaxed, appearing not quite sated—never that—but almost. Even then I felt acutely that I was between two lands. I wanted to take but I also wanted to give: though what, I wasn't sure.

Were there others like me? I had no idea. It was entirely possible I was alone in this regard: that even amid bounty, too much space surrounded me.

The jubilee was a phenomenon that usually happened only once every few summers in south Alabama, following afternoon thunderstorms in the upland part of the state. The storms would drop several inches of rain into all the creeks and streams and rivers in a short period of time. That surge of fresh cold rainwater would then come rushing down toward the Gulf, gaining speed and potency, doubling at every confluence, until finally, a few hours later—almost always in the middle of the night—the wall of fresh water would come rolling into the Gulf.

The moon was involved with the jubilee, too, though I don't know exactly how. Perhaps the moon had to be full, and pulling out a big rip tide just when all the extra fresh water came gushing out—or maybe it was the other way around, and the moon had to be bringing a high tide of seawater upriver—but anyway, the bottom line, or so said the brochure I had read at the front desk, was that when the jubilee hit, the flush of fresh water would stun or kill all the saltwater fish in the vicinity, and the fresh water would also carry out on its plume a swirling mix of freshwater creatures—catfish, gar, crawdads, bullfrogs—that would also be salt-stunned.

It was a rare thing, almost a once-in-a-lifetime thing, to see it. I made sure our family's name was on the list for the wake-up call. The first year I signed us up, I was seven years old. I'd lie there in our cottage every night, watching the moon through the window, waiting for the phone to ring. The woman at the front desk told me that whenever you answered the phone and heard the one word—"Jubilee!"—it meant the thing was on.

I would lie awake wondering if it had rained in the uplands that day. I would strain my ears to see if I could hear the shouts of "Jubilee!" drifting across the golf course, and up and down the beach.

Summer after summer passed in this manner, with me wandering solitary along the edges of the bright and well-kept lawns and gardens of wealth in the daytime, and lying there in the cottage each night, trying to stay awake for as long as I could, awaiting the call.

I imagined the jubilee was an event of such significance the hotel staff kept someone down at the beach each night on permanent lookout, like a lifeguard perched high in a chair, waiting to report its arrival.

In the summer when I was eleven, finally, the call did come, but

I was asleep, and didn't find out about it until weeks later, when we were back home. The phone had rung at two a.m., and when my father leaned over and picked up the phone, a woman's voice cried "Jubilee!" and then hung up. Neither my father nor my mother had a clue what a jubilee was, much less that I had signed us up for one.

The year that I was twelve—the year I finally saw the jubilee— I slept by the phone. It was very rare to have two jubilees in two years—and this time I got to the phone, and got to hear the woman say it.

She uttered just that one word and then hung up. I hurried outside, and could see people moving down toward the beach in the moonlight—some in bathrobes, others in shorts and sandals. Some had flashlights, though the moon was so bright you didn't really need one.

I went back inside and got my family up. At first they didn't want to go, but I kept haranguing them, and finally they awakened.

By the time we made it down to the water, people were already wading out into the ocean. The first thing that hit me—beyond the beauty of the moonlight on the water—was the scent of fresh fish.

It wasn't quite as I had pictured it would be. I had imagined there might be a thousand people, or even ten thousand; but instead there were only about forty of us, moving slowly through the waves, our heads down, searching for the stunned fish floating belly-up. I had thought people would hear about it on the radio stations, and through word of mouth, and that there would be cars parked all up and down the beach—that people would have come all the way from Mobile and Pensacola, and even farther: Biloxi, Hattiesburg, and the uplands—Selma, Columbus, and Tallahassee. But instead it was just us: the resort-goers.

I had thought you would be able to see the jubilee, too—that the plume of fresh water would be darker, like spilled ink, and you would be able to discern precisely where it entered and mixed with the bay, being diluted and spread laterally by the longshore currents. But it wasn't that way at all. I couldn't tell any difference between salt water and fresh. The waters looked just as they always had. Every now and then I could catch the faintest whiff of something fresh and dark—organic, like black dirt, forest, nutmeat, rotting bark—but always, just as soon as I became aware of that dark little thread of scent, it would disappear, absorbed by the mass of the ocean.

I had thought there would be more fish, too. I had thought there would be millions. Instead, there were only thousands. Some of the smaller ones appeared dead, but the larger ones were just stunned, swimming sideways or upside down, gasping and confused. They were out there for as far as I could see—white bellies shining in the moonlight—and other fish were careening as if drunk against my legs—fish panicked, fish drowning, is what it looked and felt like—and people carried pillowcases and plastic bags over their shoulders, filling them as if they were gathering squash or potatoes from a garden.

Everyone participated. Class distinctions fell away, and Otto and my mother and father and I loaded our pillowcases right alongside the rich and the superrich, as well as alongside the hotel workers, filling our sacks with our catches: crabs, catfish, red snapper, flounder, shrimp, bullfrogs, sheepshead, angelfish.... We didn't have to worry about sharks, because they wouldn't come in to where the fresh water was mixing. It was all ours. For that one night—or those few hours—it was all ours. Father and Mother were very happy, as were all of the people out on the beach, and it felt to me as if I had been drawn already into some other, older world—the land of adults—without having quite yet petitioned for or even desired such entrance, still pleased as I was by childhood.

In remembering the jubilee, I recall how different the quality of sound was. It wasn't extraordinarily loud; it was just different, a combination of sounds I had never heard before. The waves were shushing and the confused fish were slapping the water as they thrashed and fought the poison of the fresh water. There were a lot of birds overhead, gulls mostly, squalling and squealing, and the ten-piece band from the restaurant had come down and set up along the water's edge, and they were playing.

The hotel staff had set up dining tables with linen tablecloths out on the beach, and had lit torches and candles all along the shore, and around the dining tables. The chefs had come down to the jubilee also, and were chopping off fish heads and gutting the entrails, slicing off fillets and frying and boiling and grilling a dozen different recipes at once, luminous in their bright white aprons, knives flashing in the candlelight. There were cats everywhere, cats coming from out of the sea oats to take those fish heads and run back off into the bushes with them.

There was a boy walking up and down the beach, staying almost always just at the farthest edge of the light from the candles and lanterns and bonfires. He was barefoot, like all of us, and shirtless, and was wearing blue jeans that had been cut off at the knees; and as he paced back and forth, observing us, I could tell he was agitated. His agitation stood out even more, surrounded as he was by the almost somnolent contentedness of everyone else. The rest of us sloshed around in the waves, our heads tipped slightly downward like wading birds', with all the fish in the world available to us, it seemed, just for the taking.

The boy was roughly my age, and because he was hanging back at the edge of firelight, back in the blue-silver light of the moon, that is how I thought of him, as the blue boy. I hadn't seen him around earlier in the week, and I had the feeling that rather than a hotel guest he was some feral wayfarer who had wandered down our way from a distant, ragged shack back in the palmetto bushes.

He looked hungry, too—like those cats that kept dragging away the fish heads—and though I couldn't hear any voices over the little lapping sounds of the surf, I got the impression he would sometimes call out to us, asking for something, and I avoided observing him too closely, out of concern that he might somehow seek me out.

Once the chefs had most of the fish prepared, they began ringing a series of large copper bells mounted on heavy wrought-iron stands and tripods, and as that gonging carillon rolled out across the waves, most of us turned and waded back to shore, to seat ourselves at the long dining tables set up in the sand; though still a few people remained out in the water. Some of them had borrowed tools from the gardener's shed and were raking in the fish, or shoveling them into

baskets—unwilling to stop, even when the feast was ready and waiting, and set before them.

We ate and ate. The chefs mixed champagne and orange juice in
pitchers for us at sunrise and blew out the torches. We could see the
fish out in the ocean starting to recover when the sun came up. The
surface of the water was thrashing again as fish spun and flopped and
rolled back over, right side up.

The blue boy had disappeared when the thirty or so of us had
turned and come marching back in from out of the waves; but now he
reappeared, came out into the soft gray light of dawn, and I could see
my initial impression had been correct, that he was scraggly and feral,
rough as a cob; and that indeed he was agitated, for now he waded
out into the waves and began scolding the dozen or so guests who
were still out there with pitchforks and shovels and bushel-baskets
and trash cans, still raking in those stressed and wounded and compromised fish. He was hollering at them also to leave the biggest,
healthiest fish, and was shouting at them to come on in, that they had
taken enough, had taken more than enough.

With the boy's attention focused elsewhere, I was free to observe
him without being noticed, and there was something about him that
made me think he was not from this country—though what other
country he might have been from, I could not have said. A country, I
supposed, where they had run out of fish.

The pitchforkers ignored the blue boy, however, and kept on reaching for more and more fish, stabbing and spearing them, scooping and
netting them into their baskets, until finally all the fish were gone and
the sun was bright in the sky: and the blue boy just stood there, staring
at them, nearly chest deep in the waves, and then he turned and made
his way back to shore, and disappeared into the dunes.

The sun rose orange over the water, and the ocean turned foggy
gray, the same color as the sky. The band stopped playing, the waiters
and waitresses cleared the tables, and we all went back to our rooms
to sleep.

For two days afterward we would see all these rich people who'd
come to this place for a vacation working on their fish instead. They

kept them cool in garbage cans filled with ice, and would be scaling and filleting fish all day long: these bankers and lawyers and doctors and titans. Some of them used electric knives, and we'd hear that buzzing, humming sound, a sawing, going on all day.

They were slipping with the knives and chopping up their hands, so that at dinner the next couple of nights we would see people trying to eat with their hands wrapped in gauze bandages, with blood splotches soaking through them.

The rich people would have fish scales all over them, also—not a lot, just one or two, stuck to a thumbnail or sometimes a cheekbone, or in their hair—and they wouldn't realize it, so the scales would be glittering as they ate. It made them look special, as if they were wearing some new kind of jewelry, or as if they were on their way to a party or had just come from one.

We ate fish for breakfast, lunch, and dinner. They were far and away the best fish I've ever eaten. The clerk in the lobby said she'd actually been disappointed by the yield—that it was one of the briefest and smallest jubilees she'd witnessed yet—and when I asked about the blue boy who'd been so upset, she said he lived just a mile or so up the beach and was always there during a jubilee, and that in years past his father and grandfather had been there also, shouting the same things.

She said his was a fishing family, and that his warnings were not to be taken seriously, that they probably just wanted all the fish for themselves. Still, she admitted, the jubilees *were* getting smaller by the year, and less and less frequent. She said the blue boy came from a large family; she guessed he had at least a dozen brothers and sisters, and they were all churchgoers, fundamentalists, and very close, like some kind of old-fashioned feudal clan. She said if you crossed one of them, you brought down the wrath of all of them, and that it was best to steer clear of them. She said they were all alike, that there wasn't a hairsbreadth of difference between any of them.

For the next couple of days Otto and I got up early and went back down to the beach just before daylight, to see if by some freak chance the jubilee might be happening again, if even on a lesser scale—like a shadow of the jubilee. We went down to the beach and waded out into the ocean. The water was dark, and the sky was dark—once or twice a mullet skipped across the surface—but that was it. Things were back to the way they had been before, big and empty.

It was almost kind of restful, standing there in the ocean without all the noise and excitement. Or it was for me, anyway. How was I to know then that Otto, standing right next to me, was looking at the same ocean in an entirely different way? That he wanted another jubilee right away, and then another, and another.

"That fucking boy," he said, speaking of the blue boy. "We weren't hurting anything. The ocean is filled with fish, *overflowing* with fish," Otto said. "The whole world could eat that many fish every day, and the new fish being born into the ocean would be filling their places faster than we could eat them. We could drag one giant net from here to China, and by the time we crossed the ocean the waters behind us would have filled back in with fish, so we could turn around and go back in the other direction, filling our nets again and again."

I saw that it was important for him to believe this, so I said nothing. But there was nothing in the ocean that day, and neither, I am told, was there ever another jubilee at Point Clear. We were witnesses to the last one. We were participants in the last one. I do not think we were to blame for its being the last one, and neither do I think that if people had listened to the blue boy things would have turned out differently. I think there are too many other factors, but I also think there was too much gluttony, and not enough humility.

I can understand the nature of gluttony. I think it is the nature of the terrible truth these days—that there is not quite enough of almost everything, or anything. Or maybe one thing—one gentle, unconnected thing—though what that thing might be, or rather, the specificity of it, I could not say.

We left for home on the third day following the jubilee. We wrapped all our leftover fish in plastic bags and newspapers and put them in boxes with ice in the trunk and drove through the night to stay out of the day's heat. The ice kept melting, so fish-water was trickling out the back the whole way home. Every time we stopped for gas, we'd buy new bags of ice. But we got the fish home, and into the deep freeze. They lasted for about a year.

Otto has been living in New York City for more than thirty years now. I still live in Texas, along the Gulf Coast, and miss him, and it has been a long time now since we've been out in the woods, or the ocean, together. Our parents eventually died, without seeing another jubilee, though we went back to that same vacation spot again and again for many years afterward. All that remains of the jubilee is my own and a few others' dimming memories of it.

When I remember the jubilee, and those days of childhood, what I think about now is not so much the fish made so easily available to us, or the music of the big band, or the candlelight feast, but rather the way all of us converged on one place, one time, with one goal, even if that goal was to serve ourselves, rather than others.

Even if we were ferocious in our consumption, we were connected, that night, and those next few days. We were like a larger family, and there was bounty in the world, and the security of bounty, and no divisiveness or hierarchies, only the gift of bounty, all the bounty that the land and the sea could deliver to us, and with us never even having to ask or work for it.

It was like childhood. Nothing, and no one, had yet been separated from anything else—not for any reason. I am glad that I saw it, and though this in itself might seem a childlike wish, I find myself imagining some days that we might all yet see it again.

The Lives of Rocks

Things improved, as the doctors had promised they would. She still got winded easily, and her strength wasn't returning (her digestion would never be the same, they warned her; her intestines had been scalded, cauterized as if by volcanic flow); but she was alive, and between spells of fear and crying she was able to take short walks, stopping to rest often, making her walks not on the craggy mountain where she had once hiked, but on the gentle slope behind her house that led through mature forest to a promontory above a rushing creek.

There was a picnic table up there, and a fire ring, and sometimes she would take her blanket and a book, and build a fire for warmth, and nestle into a slight depression in the ground, and read, and sleep. On the way up to the picnic table she would have to stop several times to catch her breath—when she stopped and lay down in the pine needles she felt the world was still carrying her along, although once she reached that promontory and built her little fire and settled into her one spot, she felt fixed in the world again, as if she were a boulder in midstream, around which the current parted. It was a spot she strove to reach every day, though some days it took her several hours just to travel that short distance, and there were other days when she could not get there at all.

She slept at least as much as she had when she was a baby. Some days it was all she could do to get to the hospital for her daily treatment, so that the days were broken into but two segments, the twenty hours of sleep and the four hours of treatment, including the commute to the hospital.

Her nearest neighbors were a fundamentalist Christian family named Workman, a name that had always made her laugh, for she had rarely seen them *not* working; the mother, the father, and the five children—three boys and two girls, ranging in age from fourteen to two.

The Workmans lived only a few miles away as a raven flew, though it was many miles by rutted road to the head of their valley, and even then a long walk in was required. They lived without electricity or running water or indoor plumbing or refrigeration or telephone, and they often were without a car that ran. They owned five acres downstream along the creek, the same creek that Jyl lived by, and they had a fluctuating menagerie of chickens, milk cows, pigs, goats, horses, ponies, and turkeys.

When they traveled to town, which was not often, as it was difficult for them to get out of their valley, they were as likely to ride single file on a procession of odd-sized, multicolored horses and ponies as they were to travel in one of their decrepit vehicles, smoke rings issuing from both the front and back ends as it chugged down the ragged road.

No family ever worked harder, and it seemed to Jyl sometimes that their God was a god of labor rather than mercy or forgiveness. When she saw them on the road, they were usually working—often pulled over in the shade of cottonwoods, dipping water from a puddle to pour into their steaming radiator, or stopped with their small remuda haltered in a grove while they examined some injury to one of the horses' or ponies' hoofs—and even when all was well and the horses, or truck, were in motion, they seemed to be ceaselessly working: the girls riding in the back of the truck, knitting or sewing small deer hide knickknacks to sell at the People's Market, the boys husking corn or shelling peas or cracking nuts, their fingers always moving, in a way that reminded Jyl of the way she herself had addressed the mountain before her illness, with her long strides just as relentless.

From the Workmans' cabin came the sounds of industry at all hours: the buzz of chain saws, the crashing of timber, the splitting of wood, the jingling and rattling of mules in chains pulling stumps and stoneboats to carve ever more garden space in the side of the rocky hillside of the mountain beneath which they lived. They were forever adding on this or that strange-shaped loft or closet or cubicle to accommodate their expanding brood, as well as the developing needs for space and privacy among their older children, so that the steady sounds of those renovations filled their little valley, and the smoke from burning stumps and piles of slash and smoldering stubble fields, as well as from their various wood-stove chimneys, rose from the cove day and night and in all seasons, as if just over the mountain there were some long and inconclusive war being waged, or as if such a battle had just finished and only the ruins remained now, still smoking—though always, the next day, the sounds resumed: the clangings and bangings, the buzzing, grinding, hammering and sawing, backfires and outbursts.

On her hikes to the top of the mountain and back, particularly late in the autumn when the leaves had fallen from the deciduous trees, opening up greater views, there had been a space where Jyl had been able to look down from one of the deer-trail paths that ran along the high cliffs and see into the Workmans' little valley, and it had seemed to her that the dominant activity in that landscape, and in that isolated little family, had been the gathering of firewood—always, there were children trundling from out of the woods, their arms filled with ricks of limbs and branches—and, if not that, the gathering of water: the children traveling back and forth to the river, ferrying double bucketloads with each trip, trudging slowly and carefully to avoid sloshing too much but spilling some nonetheless—the younger children having to set the buckets down frequently to stop and rest, and to massage their stretched-out arms.

And in berry-picking season, the entire slope of the mountainside seemed covered with Workmans, wearing faded sun-soft overalls and straw hats against the bright sun, dropping their berries one by one into straw baskets; and down at their home there would be smoke rising from the chimneys on even the hottest summer days, as the mother, Sarah, boiled water for sterilizing the canning jars and for boiling the berries down to make preserves and jam. Jyl would watch for them as she hiked up the mountain, observing them sometimes in little glimpses through the trees, in all seasons, and she would pass on by.

She remembered a game she had played as a child, often while waiting for her father to come back from the Far North, from the Andes, from China and Mongolia—from all the wildernesses of the world, all the treasured storehouses of elemental wealth.

She had constructed paper boats and then launched them downstream in the little mountain creeks, running along beside them, following them as long as she could, hurdling logs and boulders, pretending the toy boats were ships bound for sea, ships on which she should have been a passenger—voyages for which she had a ticket, but with the ship having embarked without her. And though she knew it was only her skewed and selective memory of childhood, it seemed that that was how she had spent most of her time then, chasing after those bobbing, pitching little boats.

Seeking partly to provide entertainment and even a touch of magic for the hardened lives of the Workman children living downstream from her—and seeking also some contact with the outside world—she began to craft little boats once again, while waiting at the hospital, or at home, at night, in the last few minutes before sleep, seeking to integrate something new into her life other than sleep and pain.

As if these little boats would bring her father back, where nothing else had before.

She whittled the boats out of willow and pine—catamarans, canoes, battleships, destroyers, yachts, and pleasure boats—and scrolled up notes inside dollhouse milk bottles, dated and signed, "Your neighbor on the other side of the mountain," and sealed them with candle wax before launching them; and as she had so long ago, she hurried alongside them through the snow and ice, as best as she could, though she had to stop quickly now, due to the breathlessness.

On the notes inside the bottles, she penned impressionistic entries, commenting on the beauty of the season, the wonder of the landscape, and the goodness of life in general. She crafted increasingly intricate vessels, and took pleasure in doing so—though as the weeks passed and the children did not come to visit her, she had pretty much given up hope that her tiny ships and their messages would ever be found, and she figured that even if they were, it would be by someone so much farther downstream that the identification "Your neighbor on the other side of the mountain" would have no meaning.

And that was all right, she supposed. It was enough for her to be speaking out to the rest of the world, to the wider world—enough to be striving for some other contact, to be reaching out from within the darkness that threatened to envelop her, and to be testifying, even if to a perhaps unseeing future, about the beauties she was still witnessing, even in her fear. Perhaps someone—perhaps the Workman children themselves—would find the ships far into the future, as adults. It didn't matter. It was enough for Jyl to be making beautiful little carvings—no matter that only the rivers and forests themselves might be all who ever saw them, like prayers not so much to a god who did not exist, as to one who simply chose not to respond.

So she was surprised when the fourteen-year-old boy and his seven-year-old sister knocked at her door one afternoon, waking her from a deep sleep.

There were still a couple of hours of daylight left, and it was snowing lightly. Snow was mantled on the backs and shoulders of the children. "Come in," she said. "I would have thought you'd be out hunting, in this good snow."

The boy, Stephan, looked surprised. "We've already got our animals," he said, though the season had only been open a couple of weeks. He paused. "Have you?"

Jyl shook her head. "I haven't been out yet."

A look of concern crossed the boy's face and, to a lesser degree, the girl's. "You're going, aren't you?"

Jyl smiled. "Maybe," she said.

Stephan just stared at her, as if unable to conceive of a life in which meat, free meat, could be turned down, or not even pursued.

The girl, Shayna, took off her pack. Jyl had assumed both of their packs were loaded with extra coats and scarves and mittens—a flashlight, perhaps, and a loaf of bread—but instead there were her ships, every one of them.

"We were thinking if we brought them back you can maybe send them to us again," Shayna said.

Stephan rattled the glass bottles in his pocket, fished them out and held them before her, a double handful. "We liked the notes," he said. "We're pasting them into a scrapbook. They look real nice. I'm not sure we got the ships and messages in the right order, but they kind of tell a story anyway." He handed her back the bottles. "Some of the smaller boats might get caught under the ice, but the middle of the creek will probably stay open all winter, and the larger ships will probably be able to still make it."

He paused, having thought it all out. "You could put the important messages in the big boats, the ones that you really wanted to get out, and the other, little, prettier messages, in the little boats, so if they got through in winter, well, all right, but if we didn't find them till spring, then that'd be all right, too—they'd fit in anywhere, being so pretty and all."

Jyl laughed. "All right," she said. "It sounds like a good plan." She invited them in, watched them stomp the snow from their boots and dust it from their arms and shoulders, helped them hang their coats and hats on the door hooks as if they were proper adults rather than children bearing adults' ways.

The pantry was almost empty—she'd been able to drink some fruit juice, and sometimes to gnaw on an orange for strength, or, strangely, raisins—she had developed an affinity, if not a craving, for them—and the children wanted none of these, but she was able to find a couple of old envelopes of instant oatmeal, as well as some equally ancient packages of hot chocolate mix.

They sat at the table, where Jyl had not had company in several months. She tried to remember the last company she'd had, and could not. The memory of it, the fact of it, seemed to get tangled in the snow falling outside the window, which they sat watching.

"Mama said to ask you how you're doing," Stephan said. "If you need anything. If there's anything we can do." He peered sidelong at Jyl, evaluating, she could tell, her girth, or gauntness, to take back home to tell his mother—glancing at her and making a reading or judgment as he would in a similar glance the health of a cow or horse, or even some wild creature in the woods, one he was perhaps considering taking. "She said to ask if you're eating yet." He gave another glance, as if he'd been warned that the interviewee might not be trusted to give direct or even truthful answers. "She said to ask if you needed any propane. If you needed any firewood. If you needed any firewood split. If you needed any water hauled."

He said this last task so flatly, so casually and indifferently, that his practiced childish nonchalance illuminated rather than hid his distaste for the job, and again Jyl smiled, almost laughed, and said, "No, I don't need any water hauled, thank you, I've got a well and a pump"—and a look of pure desire crossed both children's faces.

"But you need some wood," Stephan said, glancing at the nearly empty wood box by the stove. "Everybody always needs wood, and especially split wood." He studied her physique further—the wasted arms, the pallor. The steady fright.

"Yes," Jyl admitted, "I could use some wood. And I've been wondering, too, what I'll do if I go out hunting, and do get an animal down. Before my illness—my cancer—I could just gut it and drag it home from wherever I'd shot it. But now it would take me so many trips that the ravens and eagles and coyotes would finish it off long before I ever got it all packed out."

Stephan nodded, as if the concern were music to his ears. "We can help with that," he said, and she saw that already his indoctrination was complete, that work had become his religion, that it transcended escape and was instead merely its own pure thing; that from early on, he and his brothers and sisters had been poured into the vessel of it, and it would be forever after how they were comfortable in the world. "We can take care of that," he said. "If you get an animal, you just let us know."

"Send us a note," Shayna said, again quiet and shy. Magic sparking in both of them like the tapping of flint against steel.

Stephan finished the rest of his hot chocolate in two gulps, then was up and headed for the door, with Shayna behind him like a shadow; and Jyl was surprised by the wrenching she felt in their sudden leave-taking.

She followed them out to the porch—they had already put on

their coats and hats and were pulling on their gloves—and, slipping on her own snow gear, hurrying to keep them from waiting, she went out into the falling snow with them and down to her toolshed, where she showed them the saw, the cans of gas, the jug of bar oil. The battered wheelbarrow, unused since last summer.

"That rifle, back there on your porch," Stephan said. "It looked like an old one. Did it belong to your father, or your grandfather?"

"Yes," said Jyl. "My father's. I don't know where it came from before that—if it was his father's, or not."

Stephan was already sniffing the gas-and-oil mixture to see how old it was, and he looked up at Jyl as if this were the first thing she had said that had surprised him—as if he found such an admission unimaginable—and he said, "Are you a Christian?"

His expression was so earnest, his face so framed with concern, that again Jyl's first impulse was to laugh; but then her legs felt weak and the blood rushed from her head, so that she looked around quickly for a stump, and she took a seat and braced herself against the waves of dizziness, and the nausea. The snow was coming down harder: curtains and curtains of it.

"No, I don't guess I am," Jyl said. "I mean, I don't know. There's parts I believe, and parts that touch my heart"—she raised a gloved fist to her chest—"but the whole package...I don't know." She looked up in the direction of the craggy mountain, invisible now in the falling snow. "I guess I find God more in the out-of-doors, and in the way we treat one another, than in any church. I've never cared to sit inside for anything unless I absolutely had to."

Stephan glanced over at Shayna with a look that Jyl could not identify, then hefted the chain saw and started up the hill toward a lichen-shrouded lodgepole. "You mind if we cut that one?" he asked, and Jyl smiled, shook her head, and said, "That was the one I was going to pick myself."

The saw had been idle for almost a year, and it took Stephan nearly ten minutes of cranking before it would even cough. During that time, Shayna and Jyl sat hunkered on their heels in the hard-falling snow, watching Stephan wrestle with the starter cord, panting and pausing to catch his wind—and from time to time he would look over at Jyl with the realization that not in a thousand years would she ever have been able to start the saw, in her weakened condition— and what would she have done then, with no wood? Driven into town and lived like a homeless person until the spring? Spent eight hours a day scrounging the snowy hills for damp twigs and branches? At-tempted, in her weakness, to gather her firewood with an ax?

The saw finally caught—went miraculously, suddenly, from a weak and faint sputter to full-throated burbling roar, complete with belch of blue smoke—and Stephan stood up straight, relief and pleasure on his face.

He moved to the tree and eased the spinning blade into the dead flesh—white chips flew like rice at a wedding—and he cut a notch, which he slid out of the tree expertly, and then went around to the other side and made the back cut. And as if following the bidding of some master anti-architect, in which there was as much grace in the laying down as in the building up, the tree eased itself gracefully down the hill, falling slowly through the swirling snow in such a man-ner as to disorient all three of them.

The tree bounced when it hit, and the dry branches snapped and popped and went flying in all directions; and even before the sift-ing clouds of snow stirred up by its impact had drifted away, Shayna had risen and was moving alongside the fallen tree, gathering small branches in her arms, gathering a double armful, as many as she could carry, and taking them to the porch, some fifty yards distant, trudging through snow that was over her knees.

Jyl watched and tried to recall bits of her own childhood, and won-dered if childhood felt to Shayna as it once had to her, when she had been so small—as if sometimes the world was filling with snow and trying to bury her.

Stephan was moving quickly along the fallen tree, bucking it up, severing more limbs, and Jyl went out to help him, began gathering her own armfuls of limbs and branches, and started carrying them back to her porch, following the initial trail Shayna had plowed in the snow.

They smiled at each other in passing, Shayna returning with arms empty for another load, and Jyl struggling with hers full; and now Stephan had the log delimbed and was cutting it into fire-wood, spacing his quick and neat cuts in metronomic sixteen-inch spacings that seemed as precise as the bobbings of a water ouzel perched on a streamside boulder, crouching and dipping cease-lessly: always the same distance, always the same motion, like a wind-up toy.

It was not a very big tree, and they had it dismembered, split and hauled and stacked within a half hour: a porch full of bright, gleam-ing new-cut firewood, and a fresh-lumber scent dense upon them, like the odor of new beginnings, and possibility.

They went inside to dust off for a moment, to wash the scent of oil smoke from their faces and to pour a glass of water. The darkness was coming quickly.

"We'll be back tomorrow to get some more," Stephan said. "Or as soon as we can. And to do other things."

"Listen," said Jyl, "I know how busy you all are. I know how much you have to do at home. This is more than enough. I'll be fine, really. It's so kind of you to do even this. I'll be fine. Thank you. Tell your mother thank you."

"We can't keep a regular schedule," Stephan said. "There's too much to do at home. We can just come when we get our chores done."

"I'm here in the evenings," Jyl said. "Mornings, I'm almost always sleeping. After lunch, I go get my treatment. But I'm here at night."

"When do you sail the boats?" Shayna asked, her voice little more than a whisper, like the stirring of a bird back in the brush. More of a fluttering than a voice.

"Afternoons," Jyl said, "when I get back from the hospital, and just before I go in to nap."

"We usually get them right before suppertime," she said.

"I'll send one tomorrow," Jyl said. "I'll send two, a big boat and a little boat, each with the same message, so that if one gets hung up the other one might still make it through."

"Oh, no," Shayna said quickly, surprising Jyl with her assertiveness. "If you send two you can write different messages, because we'll find them both. We'll go upstream looking for them. We'll find them."

"Is that what you've been doing?" Jyl asked. "If one doesn't come by your house, you go upstream, searching for it?"

Shayna nodded. "He takes one side and I take the other. It's fun. We go after chores, and after supper. Sometimes we go at night, and use lanterns."

"Do you ever worry that one gets past you—that you never see it?"

The children looked at each other. "We all keep a pretty good eye out for them, most of the day," Stephan said. He paused. "Some of the kids wanted to put a fishnet across the creek, and check it regular, but Shayna and I didn't want to do it that way."

"It's okay if there's days you can't send one," Shayna said. "We know you're busy, and that there's days you have to rest."

Jyl smiled. "I'm getting better," she said. "I can't make any promises, but it's good to know the ships are getting through."

The snow was still falling hard, and although such a heavy snowfall so early in the year assured them of a long winter, it also meant a reduced fire season, next summer; and knowing this, they accepted both the hardship and the blessing of it with neither praise nor complaint, and instead only watched it, as animals might.

"Do you need another flashlight?" Jyl asked. "Or do you want to stay here for the night?"

The children looked horrified at the latter suggestion. "We've got to be up early," Stephan explained.

"How early?"

"Four," he said.

It was almost dusk. Jyl could smell the chain saw odor on them and wondered if they would bathe when they got home or simply crawl into their sleeping bags in the warm loft, surrounded by the breathing sounds of their sleeping siblings and the occasional stove creak of one of their parents adding wood to the fire downstairs, and the compressed hush of the snow falling on the roof, just inches away from their faces as they slept warm in that loft.

"Thank you," she told them as they set off into the gloom, with Stephan breaking trail for his sister.

After their light had disappeared, she put on her heavy coat and gloves and got her father's rifle and went into the woods a short distance and sat down beneath the embrace of a big spruce tree. She waited a few moments to settle in—to adjust her heart, pounding from even that small exertion, to the space and silence around her. She took off her gloves and blew through cupped hands.

She put her gloves back on, lifted her rifle, and waited, listening to the falling snow. It was right at the edge of being too dark to shoot. She could hear the creek riffling behind her, and she listened to that for a while, lulled. Her cabin, not a hundred yards distant, beckoned, as did her bed—for a moment her mind strayed ahead to the relief, the dull harbor, she found in sleep each night—and she began to feel ridiculous, tucked in so invisible against the world, as if in a burrow, as if she were hiding in the one place where no one could ever find her, the one place where she was least likely to find her quarry.

She was settling into a reverie, had already given up the notion of hunting and was instead merely dreaming, when there came into her consciousness a sound that was unlike the other sounds and silences that had been surrounding her: a jarring, clumsy sound of eagerness, hoofs slipping on wet rocks, a clattering and splashing, and silence again.

She sat up and peered through her lattice of branches. She heard the sound of quiet steps approaching, but then the steps ceased. She waited for five minutes, ears and eyes straining—she tried to catch the scent of the animal but could smell nothing, only wet falling snow—and then she heard the animal crossing back over the creek, going away; and when she rose stiffly from her crouch, her warren beneath the tree, and went to examine the tracks, they were already filled in with new snow, and it was as if the thing had never existed.

When she got back to her cabin and its warmth and yellow light, she was surprised by how late it was—she had been confused by the luminous blue light cast by the snow in the fading dusk. It was nearly seven o'clock, and she was cold, wet, and shivering.

She was still stimulated by the hunt, and by the children's visit, and would have liked to have stayed up late, or even until a normal hour, taking a hot bath and curling in bed afterward, reading until midnight, as she had once done in the freedom of her health.

But she had extended herself too far, that day, and in the end she simply sat by the wood stove, shivering, and feeding it more wood. One of the propane lanterns in that corner of the cabin sputtered and coughed into darkness, leaving only one remaining lamp hissing over on the far side of the cabin; and though the silence was still lonelier, in the subdued lighting she took a short fragment of firewood from the wood box and got out her pocketknife and tried to begin carving a new toy ship.

She had not carved more than three minutes, however, before fatigue overtook her—not so much physical exhaustion or the brutishness of fear, but instead the cumulative fatigue of loneliness combining with all those other exhaustions —*five percent chance of survival,* the doctors had told her, *five percent, five percent*—and yet somehow, frugal and efficient to her core, she managed to rouse and walk the ten paces over to the other side of the cabin and turn off the lone remaining lamp.

She was chilled immediately, however, away from the stove, and so she pulled a quilt off her bed and went back over to the fire, stoked it up again, and, too tired to even change out of her damp clothes, curled up against the stove's base, wrapped herself in the quilt, and fell asleep there on the floor, with no padding, no comfort, no thoughts, no anything, only falling; and with the pocketknife still open beside her, and the block of wood with less than a handful of shavings carved off beside it.

Despite the depth of her fatigue, she dreamed: as if the mind or spirit requires no energy, or, rather, feeds from some source other than the body, flowing almost continuously.

She dreamed of traveling her mountain again: of traversing it that night, at times following the same trail the children had made going home, and other times making her own. In the dream it was still snowing, and the snow was over her knees, as it was in the real life just outside her door; and there was something about the dream, some synchronized in-the-moment aspect to it, that made it seem extraordinarily vibrant and refreshing. It was almost as if her spirit was trying to heal or repair itself, even where her body could not or had not yet; almost as if so severe was the damage to one, the vessel of her, that the other current was also becoming abraded. And as if it would do whatever was necessary, for the healing.

She moved with strength and steadiness up the trail. It was not easy going, but the labor felt good. The snow was falling on her face, and though she was wearing a heavy coat and gloves and gaiters, her head was bare, and at times she would stop and shake the snow from her hair.

She ascended steadily. Even though she was only walking, time seemed to pass more quickly than it ever had—as if an hour were now only a second—and in no time she was back on the ledge that ran along the high cliff of the mountain's west face.

Looking down through the slanting snow, and down through the snow-shrouded canopy of the dense forest so far below, she could see lights moving, a handful of lanterns scattered through the trees and along the river, some coming and others going.

The lights looked like the flares from torches, or drifting sparks from a campfire, or scattered wildfires seen on distant mountains at night in the autumn; but the slow carriage of them was distinctly that of humans, on foot.

At first Jyl thought the lantern carriers were searching for something; but, pausing to watch the course and pacing of their lights, she understood they were engaged in some sort of labor, and, as she stood there a while longer, with the snow piling up on her back and shoulders, the picture became even clearer for her, and she understood that it was the children, passing back and forth through the woods, carrying buckets of water for the family's baths, the family's cooking, and the family's drinking.

The loaded-bucket travelers moved slowly, on their way back from the river to the cabin, the lights of which were not visible—perhaps extinguished for economy at that hour. The empty-bucket travelers, going from the cabin back down to the river, moved faster while passing through those same woods, and when one of the going-away lanterns passed one of the coming-up lanterns, there was no pause— each kept traveling in his or her own direction—and though Jyl had no real way of knowing, it seemed to her that in such weather and amid such weariness, and at so late an hour, no words were passed between the travelers.

Jyl remained standing, watching, as if turned to a statue. The snow kept piling up on and around her, and after a while—long hours, perhaps, though in the dream it seemed like only moments—the procession ceased; the water tanks had all been filled.

The lanterns assembled in one place on the front porch, and then one by one they blinked out, until only two were remaining.

These two did not blink out, but instead turned and moved back into the forest, again barely visible through the falling snow—disappearing, at times, beneath its burden, as if having been submerged before reappearing a little farther into the forest.

The river, though not visible, was identifiable as a wandering line between darkness and light, an imaginary border in the forest, at which all the lanterns had previously paused at the end of their bucket-filling marches.

Jyl watched as one of the lanterns went slightly farther than any of the others had—the traveler, either Shayna or Stephan, crossing snow-covered mossy stones to stay dry.

And it was a helpless feeling for Jyl, being up there on the mountain, on the cliff, knowing she had not sent out a vessel that day, or a message, a missive, no little painting or inscription.

She tried her best to call down to the searchers, but the words seemed lost even before she uttered them; as if all the world was snow and as if speech were a phenomenon that could not exist in this dream-world—and so she tried to will the children to turn around and give up, not to waste their time, though still they came on, moving slowly, one on either side of the river, stopping and starting, and searching: lifting up fallen logs, she supposed, and peering carefully into riffles and eddies, hoping and searching.

And in the dream, it was too sad to watch, and Jyl was eager to be moving again, eager to be on her mountain again, having had her strength and energy restored to her, even if only for the evening; and so reluctantly, the statue of her melted, turned from its frozen position, shedding that thick mantle of snow, and hurried on farther up the mountain to the top, pushing on through the knee-deep and then thigh-deep snow like a plow horse, on past the faint and lost-looking smatterings of light so far below, and on up to the mountaintop where she had been so many times before—a place she had previously taken for granted, but which she did not that evening, in the dream.

Instead, she lay spread-eagled on its top, face upturned to the whirling, sifting snow, and, in its embrace, she slept—just for a little while, just long enough to grow warm, and long enough to remember, and savor, what it had been like to be healthy.

And in the dream she did not have to descend, did not have to pass back by the searchers, but instead woke at daylight by her cold extinguished wood stove, her breath frosty in her cabin.

She poured a glass of water for breakfast. She ate two crackers, which was two more than she had the stomach for. She built the fire back up and sat beside it and resumed whittling, falling asleep sometimes with the knife still in her hand and her head leaning against the cabin wall, only to jerk awake again, having returned in her nap to the mountaintop, and with too much snow atop her now—having slept too long.

What story to tell them, in the little bottles? Was her own childhood of any importance to them, or was it better to help them create their own?

Should she tell them, for instance, that her father, a bush pilot, had invented a system for retrieving rock samples from the sides of mountains by using a dangling claw hook, like a backhoe's digging bucket, which trailed below the plane like a kite tail and snatched at the side of the mountain, gouging and clawing at it, as he flew past—jarring the plane terribly, but managing to grab, in that manner, a bucketful of stone, in country that might otherwise have taken weeks to get to on foot?

Should she tell them that he helped pioneer a methodology of analyzing the tops of trees—isolating and identifying by chemical analysis the minerals present in the green needles and leaves—and from those assays he would fashion a map of the mineral content of the subsurface formations below, as if the spires of the trees were but extensions of those rocks, those minerals—still fixed in place, but born now into towering life?

He would fly over vast stretches of forest, lowering his claw-bucket sample-chopper, and would snatch up one treetop after another, reeling it up like a fishing line, flying the plane with one hand and running the crank with his other; and in this manner he covered thousands of square miles more effectively than entire squadrons of geologists could have done, achieving in a single field season that which might have taken less daring or driven geologists a lifetime to accomplish.

Should she tell them that many days she considered being—desired to be—a mother?

Or should she tell them fairy tales—stories of princes and princesses of extraordinary power and purity, beings unhindered by flaw or imperfection—durable, enduring, even immortal? Myths and tales toward which the children could move, as if sighting a lantern lit in the night, not too far ahead of them?

Still frightened of the past, she chose the latter. She kept her father's stories within her illness-racked body, and even her own stories, and instead worked on a story about a prince and princess.

In the story, the ruler of the boy and girl's country, a kind and wise king, is washed over a waterfall while trying to save a small girl in distress, a girl caught out in the rapids; though the child is saved, the great king is swept over the falls and broken into pieces below, with his parts carried downstream for miles.

Over the years, the great king's parts—head, arms, legs, feet, hands, back, chest—wash up on shore from time to time and become hardened into stone, or driftwood; and walking along the river, the prince and princess occasionally come across his remnants, and gather them up to take back home.

Slowly, over the years, they collect enough pieces to begin reassembling the great king, and one day they come to understand or believe that if they can fully reassemble him he will come back to life, in all his previous goodness and fullness and glory and power.

But the boy and girl are growing up now, and soon it will be time for them to assume the responsibility of becoming the leaders of their country; and as they find more and more body parts of the old king—a finger, a foot, a nose, an ear—they are hesitant to finish putting him back together, hesitant to bring him back to life.

Still, they cannot stop searching. Each day they walk along the river, looking, and they search at night, too, with lanterns: for sometimes there are parts of the old king that emerge from the depths, from beneath the gravel and silt, under the pull of the moon.

Sometimes a muscled driftwood arm will float in the dark waters in the night, glinting beneath that moonlight, only to sink again at dawn; and the children, nearly grown now, continue searching, but cannot decide whether to complete their search or to finally turn away from it and travel on into the future, leaving the broken parts behind.

The tedium of her days, the tedium of her new life: for a long time it had been getting harder and harder for her to summon the strength to get in the truck and haul herself to town for the treatments. She thought she might be getting better, though, when the fatigue began to give way to boredom. It wasn't a regular boredom, but was instead so overbearing as to masquerade at first as continued fatigue. Slowly, however, she came to realize the subtle difference—the subtle improvement. The cancer was gone, and her normal cells, with their normal mandates, were returning slowly, whirling and dancing and executing their ancient motions of electrolysis, glycogen transfer, oxygenation, and tissue repair—and even as the darkness of winter fell over the land, she could feel faintly the dynamics of light returning to the fragile, fire-bombed husk of her body.

She continued to carve her ships in the waiting room, where the doctors, nurses, and other patients were amazed by them. She sanded and polished their bows and hulls of willow and pinewood until they were smooth as eggs. She wrote each day's sentence in a careful script of calligraphy, watercolored each illustration, and launched the ship each afternoon upon returning home from the treatment.

There was no way for her to visit the Workmans. They had no mail service, no phone. The ships were the only way in.

Upon returning home from her treatments she would nap, and then rouse herself at dusk and go out into the woods with her rifle. The deer were more active now, with the rut ongoing, and with the deepening snow forcing them to travel almost constantly, searching for food, using the trails they had cut through the snow, used over and over again, becoming almost pedestrian in their regularity—but still she was not seeing any.

Sometimes she would hear their feet crunching through the snow and ice, and she would even catch a glimpse of a dull silhouette of a deer as it was already turning away, having sighted or scented her just before she noticed it. She would see a glint of antler; and in the leap of adrenaline that rushed upward in her like fire at such a sight, she knew more than ever that she was getting better: but still, the deer would not let her have it.

Her father had been gone twenty years now. Her father had never known her diminished. Were she and he like two different mountains, she wondered, slightly different kinds of stone through which the same river of time ran, or were they like two braids or forks of a river separating—running across, and cutting down into, the same one mountain, the same one face and body of stone?

And what if we had it all backwards, she wondered. What if it is the mountain and the past that are living, while the river and the present are the unliving: merely a physical force, like wind, or electricity, but not really alive, not in the sense that blood or memory is alive?

It was nonsense, she knew. Of course rivers were alive. Of course mountains and stones were alive. And of course the world possessed an invisible topography of spirit, with ridges, valleys, glaciers, volcanoes, tides and creeks and bays and oceans of spirit, and with as many different carriers of spirit, in that invisible world, the world of the past, as there were carriers of life in the visible, physical world: elk, bison, man, woman, child, antelope, deer, bear, tree, bird...

Her father had collected fossils and gemstones—tourmaline, topaz, opal, jade, malachite, amethyst—and upon his death, she had carted all the various shoeboxes of minerals back to her home, where she kept them stored in the basement.

And, believing now that her stories and illustrations were no longer sufficient to summon the children, she began putting little gems and crystals in the ships, as if laying treasures before young kings and queens.

Whom should she serve—the future, or the past? How much time did she have left to serve? What value was any mineral, any fossil, compared to the spark of life? She felt guilty, releasing some of her father's finer treasures, but each day she filled the boats higher and higher with glittering bounty.

It was nearly a week before Stephan and Shayna returned. They came on the weekend before Thanksgiving.

She was out hunting again, or if not actually hunting, sitting with her back propped against a spruce tree, beneath the protection of its branches, watching the snow, mesmerized by the snow, and waiting for a deer to perhaps walk past.

When she heard the children's voices coming over the mountain, she did not understand at first that they were coming her way, coming to visit her, but thought instead she was dreaming again, and was traveling to go see them, to meet them in their little valley, and that as she drew closer she was now able to hear them more clearly. When she saw them appear from out of the woods, barely visible at first in the falling snow, her first thought was that they were wolves, or even bears. There was something about their movements that did not make her think of people.

Even as they crossed the creek, stepping carefully from stone to stone, trying to stay dry, they did not appear through that screen of falling snow to be fully human; and when she saw they each carried in their arms burlap sacks filled with something, still they did not remind her of her own kind; and while the drift of their voices, more audible now, was the sound of children, their conversation did not seem to be connected to the figures she saw tiptoeing across the river.

She unchambered her rifle and rose to greet them—they were already knocking on her door, calling her name, and, not hearing a response, going into the cabin—and as she moved toward them through the snow and darkness, there seemed to be little difference between how she felt now and how she had felt in her earlier dream of ascending the mountain and looking down upon their wandering lights; though she was aware, tripping and stumbling, of a palpitation of her heart, and an overarching eagerness that had not been present in the dream.

She had been leaving one lantern burning low each night, in case they should come after dark—in the hopes that they would come, so that they, too, would be able to look down from the mountain through the falling snow and see her own light, visible in the storm, and home in on it, not so much as if lost but instead sighting the thing they had been searching for.

As she approached her cabin, she saw the lantern flare more brightly—illuminating the thousands of individual snowflakes floating past the windows—and she felt safe, and as if life had not yet even called out to her, as if her life had not yet even begun.

She saw them moving around inside the yellowing dome of light, talking to one another and looking up at the books on her shelves; and when she stomped the snow from her boots and went inside, still wet and snowy from her vigil beneath the spruce, she was warmed by the relief on the boy's face, and by the joy on the girl's.

"Did you see any deer?" Stephan asked, straightaway.

She shook her head, hugged them—they seemed glad to receive the hugs—and shook her head again. "I think they can smell my illness," she said. "I can hear and sometimes see them coming closer, but at the last minute they turn away."

Stephan sniffed the air. "I can't smell it," he said, "and usually I can smell anything."

Jyl shrugged. "It's there," she said. "Even I can smell it."

"What does it smell like?" Shayna asked.

"Metal," Jyl said, pouring water into the cast-iron kettle and setting it on the stove, then opening the stove and stoking in some more kindling, which the dull coals accepted and ignited quickly. "I don't know. Steel, platinum, copper, gold, silver. Some kind of cold metal," she said. She waggled her jaws as if to rid herself of the taste of it.

"Is it on your breath?" Shayna asked. "Do you think we could try to smell it?"

Jyl covered her mouth and turned away. "No," she said. "I don't want you to smell it."

They were quiet for a while, after that. Finally Stephan said, "We really can't smell anything like that. But if you think the deer can, maybe you should try and mask it. Maybe you should have a piece of peppermint or licorice before you go out next time. Maybe they'll be curious and come a little closer. Maybe they'll think it's another animal."

She had restocked her pantry, hoping that the children would come again. She'd bought far too much food, beyond her budget, and, not knowing what they liked and did not like, had guessed— some sugary cereals, a kind of frozen Popsicle treat, some TV dinners of mashed potatoes and cod, apples, oranges, bananas, some frozen salmon fillets, Canadian bacon, a frozen pizza, and a frozen strawberry cheesecake—and when she asked what they wanted for supper they told her they usually had rice and pineapple, and that was about all they liked. Rice and pineapple, and venison and elk.

She felt a despair, a failure that she had not known since the hardest days of her treatment. She was surprised by the tears that leapt to her eyes, and she turned to where they could not see them. When she had composed herself, she asked, "Would you eat a cheesecake?"

They nodded solemnly, as if it were a trick question, and Stephan said, "We'll eat anything—it's just that we only like rice and pineapple and elk and venison." They were surprised, then, she could tell— almost spooked—when she burst into wild laughter.

She set about preparing some salmon, thawing it out in warm water. She cut the cheesecake into little wedges and served it to them first, and put a couple of the TV dinners in the stove as well, in the hopes they might find something to pick at. She needn't have worried, for soon they were asking for more of the cheesecake, and she even had a piece, and then had to put the rest out on the porch, or they might have eaten it all.

"It'll refreeze," she said. "You can have the rest of it the next time you come."

She put the salmon in the oven with the TV dinners, braised it with butter and garlic and lemon and orange, then sat by the stove and took the bolt from her rifle and began cleaning and oiling it while they sat at the table next to her and ate the cheesecake and drank hot chocolate. When she was done she put the rifle back together and hung it up in the snow room, and changed into dry clothes.

She could tell that although the children were still cold and weary, they were uncomfortable relaxing, and were anxious to be leaving. She sought to detain them with stories and knowledge. She walked over to a bookshelf and pulled down an old textbook, *Ancient Sedimentary Environments*, published in 1940. Dust motes rose from it as she opened its covers, and from across the room, still eating the cheesecake, both Stephan and Shayna sniffed the air, and Stephan said, "I can smell that."

"It was my father's. It's got pictures," Jyl said, bringing it over to the table. She thumbed through the pages, and her eyes blurred as she read for the first time some of the markings he had underlined in pencil a lifetime ago.

"The consensus of geological opinion is that there are a finite number of sedimentary facies that occur repeatedly in rocks of different ages all over the world. But no two similar sedimentary facies are ever identical, and gradational transitions are common.

"One of the main problems of determining the origin of ancient sediments is that, though essentially reflecting depositional environments, they also inherit features of earlier environment. The infilled sediment reflects the nature of the source rocks and the hydraulic of the current, while the rolled bones and wood and other fossiliferous inclusions are derived from non-depositional environments that lie for the most part beyond the stream's usual reach. No rock is ever finished, all stones are continually being remade, until they vanish from the face of the earth. And yet, even then, once reduced to windblown dust, they are reforming."

The children had stopped eating, their forks in midair, and were listening, though Stephan was slowly raising his hand in what was unmistakably mild protest. Jyl could tell also that they were suspicious, as if they understood somehow that their fundamentalist faith might be challenged by such language. Still, she read on:

"A classic example of this fallacy can be found in a profile of the Bu Hasa Rudist boundstones, with fragments of large benthonic Orbitoline forams. The rudist boundstone passes south toward the Arabian shield into faccal pellet muds, with miliolid foraminifera. Locally, however, the basinward crest of the boundstone is replaced by a detrital grainstone."

There was a look very close to despair on Stephan's face—Shayna showed no such distress and was instead only staring at Jyl with utter wonder—but Jyl could see that Stephan wasn't going to give up or back away. With his brows furrowed, he reached for a pencil and paper on the table and asked carefully, slowly, "What's rudist?"

Jyl couldn't hold back her laughter—it spilled from her again, clean and clear, with a feeling of release that she could not remember experiencing before, and she said, "I don't know."

Stephan took the book from her and looked through it, at the many such passages underlined in long-ago pencil. "But he knew all this stuff, right?" he asked. "Your father knew all this?"

Jyl nodded, her eyes stinging with pride.

"I'd like to read this book," Stephan said. "I know it means a lot to you, and I wouldn't ask to take it with me—I wouldn't want to get it banged up—but I'd like to read it, and make notes from it, while I'm over here."

Jyl smiled. "All right. But let's start over. Let's start at the beginning." She took down a roll of butcher paper, spread it across the table, and began with the basics, explaining the different ways rocks can be formed from the ash and guts of the earth: the igneous rocks arising straight from the cooling subterranean fire; the sedimentary rocks the cumulative residue of dust and grit and silt being deposited with the earnestness of a mason, the sediments not settling by fiery will, but obedient instead only to the inescapable mandates of gravity; and the metamorphic rocks, her favorites: stones so substantially altered from their original form by the world's and time's pressures, smoothed now into graceful curves and folded into fantastic swirls and reversals, so that the geologist examining them could sometimes not tell at first in which direction the past ran and in which, the future.

As she talked, she illustrated her lecture with watercolors, sketching mountains and oceans, rivers and storms, showing how the simple forces of weather—morning sunrise, wind, frost, snow and rain—in conjunction with the earth's own subtle movements, its faint stretches and belches and yawns, conspire across the arc of time to wear even the largest and most jagged mountains down to desert plains. She showed them how even the oceans fall back to reveal their gleaming, glittering mud, which is then lifted miles into the sky, creeping upward a thousandth of an inch per year, but leaping nonetheless, and carrying in that hardened crypt many of the fossils that had once lived far beneath the sea, and which would now be spending eons so much closer to the sun, suspended atop mountains, exposed to wind and rain and snow, the hoofs of mountain goats, and the curious eyes of man, with all the glittering green world shining below.

With her sketches, she detailed the creation of alluvial fans, tectonic plates, unconformities. The world-beneath-the-world, the stone world on which rested the living world, was born for the children that night, and they began to understand that it, too, was living, though at a different pace, and that although such knowledge might trouble their parents' beliefs, they were riding on the earth's back, and beneath the stone world there was even another, third world, on the back of which the stone world rode, and that that third and even lower world was the river and current of time.

Jyl had started painting the cross sections of geological time for them, starting at the surface and intending to work all the way down, through the dinosauric creations and into the world-flooded Devonian and Silurian, into the stone-cold Cambrian, and then farther, into the colder, utterly lifeless time of Precambrian; but Shayna reminded her of the salmon and the TV dinners in the oven, and Jyl looked up in surprise, having been so immersed in the teaching, and so unaccustomed to cooking, that she only vaguely remembered having put the food in the oven. Setting her paintbrush down and hurrying over to the stove, she found that the salmon was perfect, though the TV dinners were a little crispy.

They suspended their geology lesson for the evening and sat around the fireplace and ate their dinners. Jyl told them about her time in Alaska, and about a pilot she had known there, a young man who had flown her around in a floatplane to much of the same backcountry where her father had worked—visiting the same lakes and walking along the same beaches, looking at the same mountains. It was this same pilot who had sent her the salmon they were eating, and she told them that when she got better she had it in her mind to go back up there and visit him.

"Will you marry him?" Shayna asked. A fairy tale.

Jyl laughed. "No," she said, "he's just a friend. Just a bush pilot. But I like his company."

"We were in Alaska," Stephan said. "Just before she was born."

"Where?" Jyl said. "Doing what?"

"Missionary stuff. We were in Seward, but Pa would fly in to the villages a lot. I'm pretty sure it was missionary stuff."

"How long were you there?"

Stephan shrugged. "Just a couple of years. Mama didn't like it. Nobody liked it. It was beautiful, but nobody liked it."

They were all quiet for a while, before Shayna finally said, quietly—as if in Jyl's defense, or defense of Jyl's father—"I would have liked it."

Jyl smiled. "So y'all like it here?"

Stephan shrugged. "I think so," he said. "Sometimes it's a little hard—the work—but I think so."

"I do," said Shayna. "I love it."

It was past nine o'clock—the latest Jyl had stayed up since before the illness. She took down some old elk hides from her closet and prepared twin pallets for the children next to the wood stove, and then, feeling her weariness returning like the break of a towering wave, she barely had time and energy to clean the dishes before collapsing into her own bed. She was asleep even before the children were, even as the children were still visiting with her, talking between themselves and asking her occasional questions; and when they realized she was asleep, Stephan got up and wrote his questions down on the butcher paper with its illustrations so that he would not forget them. Questions about different minerals, and different kinds of salmon; about the floatplane, and about her father.

Then he turned out the lantern, and he and Shayna, though restless in the new surroundings, tried to get to sleep as quickly as possible, knowing that they would need to conserve their strength for the trip home and the coming day. The unfamiliar stove burned its wood differently, made different sounds, and through the glass plate in its door they could see the sparks and embers swirling and glowing, and they stared at it as if viewing the maw of a tiny volcano.

The children slept until two, when they awakened to a fire that was nearly out—Stephan built it back up—and they dressed and went out into the night to fell another tree for Jyl before leaving.

The storm had passed, leaving a crystalline glaze over the world as the temperatures fell, and the snowflakes, quick-frozen now, tinkled like glass scales as they passed through them. Their breath rose in jets of fog when they spoke, and when they came to the next dead pine, Stephan started the saw, felled the tree and bucked it as fast as possible, not wanting to awaken Jyl, and then shut the saw off, and let the huge silence of the stars sweep back in over them.

Because the snow was deep, it took them more than an hour to split and carry that wood to the porch, stacking it with as little sound as possible; and by the time they had the saw and maul and gas and oil cans stored, and the bark and snow swept from the porch, they were later getting away than they had intended, so that they had to run, galloping through the snow like draft horses, and steaming from their effort.

They made it back to their cabin—exhausted—and set about their labors in preparation for the day.

Jyl dreamed again she was running, though with difficulty this time rather than the effortless glide of the previous dream. And there was a pain in her gut as her glycogen-depleted organs cramped and sought to metabolize her muscle and bone—metabolizing anything for just a bit more available energy, in order to keep going, to keep struggling up the hill.

It was a sensation she recognized from her earlier days of strength, when she had been able to run without ceasing; and in the dream, though it was painful, she welcomed it, glad as she was to be back on the mountain.

Finally, though, the pain awakened her, and she sat up, trying to be as quiet as possible to avoid waking the children. When she went to get a glass of water, she saw they were gone; lighting a lantern to see if they had left a note, she found none, though she did see the questions Stephan had written down on the butcher paper in the middle of the night. And the sense of loss she knew was sharper than any stitch in her side, far deeper than any absence of glycogen.

Unable to get back to sleep, she built the fire up again and fixed a cup of tea, and set about answering their questions, writing the answers in the tiniest of script so she could scroll them up into some of the larger message bottles and place them in one of the larger crafts, to set sail later that afternoon.

Her answers would be a departure, a break, from the saga of the broken king, but one she welcomed; and as she worked on her notes—feeling as she had in college, laboring over an exam in which the correct answers were of utmost importance—she had the feeling also of being lured up from out of the depths and the darkness, and out into the bright light of some open and verdant spring meadow: as if she, and not her father, was the broken king, but that she was daring now, or at least desiring, to be reassembled.

It was almost dawn when she finished her answers. Though she knew she should go back to sleep, she was surprisingly restless, and the idea of going out to hunt a deer came to her so strongly it was like a summons. She rose and began putting on more sweaters and her big coat. She took her rifle down from its rack and loaded it, and went out into the darkness, past the scent of all the newly stacked firewood; and then, following the children's tracks, she went into the woods, to the new stump.

It was almost daylight. The tops of her ears were cold, and she snuggled in tight against another big spruce, hid herself close among its lower branches, digging a little snow hollow in which to sit, and waited.

When it was light enough to see the shapes of things, the outlines of the trees coming into focus, she squinted and listened even more intently.

From across the river there came a crashing of sticks and branches so close and severe she did not believe the sound could be made by any animal as graceful and stealthy as a deer but instead that it was Stephan and Shayna—that they were still in the forest, searching for more firewood—and she was tempted to call out to them.

She remained silent, however, and the crashing came once more, followed by a silence, and then a splashing.

She leaned forward, trying to see through the gray and barely penetrable light; and, as if sensing the acuity of her attention, the deer stopped midstream, just beyond her sight, and waited, weighing the danger, a hunger the deer could feel thick and living.

And as he stood there, water riffling around his ankles (Jyl could hear the different sound in it, the variance in splashing river rhythm as it braided around and past his four planted legs), the gray light grew more diffuse, and she was able finally to see the shape of him: his bulk and the rack of his antlers so startling it seemed he must be carrying in the nest of them a tangled mass of branches from farther back in the forest.

Before the excitement hit her, and the trembling, she had the thought, for half a second, that he, too, like the children, was bringing her firewood; that he was delivering it to her in his antlers.

As the light grew stronger and more detail was revealed, she saw that the cluster of his antlers was all his, all hardened bone. He stood there as motionless as a garden statue. Only his eyes showed life, and though it seemed he was looking straight at her, had spied her hiding back in the branches, he finally moved again, emerging from whatever stony reverie he'd been in, and began walking toward her.

He reached her side of the river and stepped out, dripping.

He paused again, as if he had forgotten where he was. He seemed to enter another reverie, and as she watched him at this closer range she could see the scars around his face from ancient battles, could see the clouds of breath coming from his nostrils, the old buck breathing hard from even so mild an exertion as the river crossing.

He appeared to be in some slightly other universe, some different level or plane, suffused with grace and confidence even in his senescence. She imagined she could see doubt or anxiety entering the buck's gaze, his suspicion that something was wrong—and for a moment Jyl was overwhelmed with a feeling of unworthiness at being so close to such a wild creature, much less to be on the verge of taking his life.

The buck stepped out of his trance once more and reentered the world. He turned away from Jyl now and began walking along the trough made in the snow where Stephan and Shayna had felled their second tree. He stepped carefully over and among the tangle of branches Stephan had limbed from the tree, then lowered his head to browse on the lichen that clung to those branches; and each time he did so, Jyl felt a moment of disorientation when the crown of antlers lowered—as if a large bush was attached to the deer's head and was beginning to move in animal fashion.

She was so amazed by the elegance of the old deer's movements— his careful steps through and over the latticework of torn and sawn limbs—that she forgot she was hunting him. She watched as he lifted his head occasionally to glance around and then lowered it to the snow and sniffed like a hound at the children's tracks.

Several times the deer stared off in the direction of her cabin, and Jyl had the feeling the deer believed he was safe, that he was secure in the faith that Jyl was still in her cabin, asleep. She could easily raise her rifle and drop him where he stood, while he stared as if transfixed at the yellow squares of her cabin—and yet something within her, some place of warmth, dissuaded her from making the shot. Instead she watched him watch her cabin.

After a while, he lowered his head to browse again, and drifted on farther into the woods, and though she wanted a deer, she was glad she had not taken this one, even though she knew she might not get another chance.

She had only one more week left of treatment. Millions of patients had been through it before—they would all call it the most physically grueling and spiritual thing they'd ever done, and spoke of the hidden blessing of the cancer, of the way it awakened in them incredible awareness of even the simplest pleasures. But such testimonials irked Jyl, for she did not feel she had taken those little moments for granted in the first place. On the contrary, she had always been acutely aware of them, even worshipful of them. It wasn't fair.

The treatment had been calibrated to reach its toxic peak during its last week, but she felt in every way she had already turned the corner, that the worst week was just behind her, and that despite the increasing radioactive and chemical bombardment, her body was growing stronger again. And when she told the doctors this, they shrugged and said that it was possible, that different patients responded in different ways.

She sent forth another boat, relating her saga of having seen the big deer, and inviting the children to return when they could. She told them she looked forward to it, and that she would bake a cake, that she had gotten rice and pineapple at the store. She told them she wished the current would flow both ways, like a tide, so they could send her messages.

Now the treatment hit her like a dump truck. The previous exhaustion had been nothing compared to this final wave. She was more chilled than ever, and wore her ski cap over her bald head continuously, and kept the fire roaring. She had already nearly depleted the second load of firewood and was beginning to look out the window at the forest, searching for the tree she would cut next. Her body felt as if her blood had been filled with lead. She was certain the doctors had made some mistake, had doubled or tripled her dose, or prescribed her a treatment for a three-hundred-pound football player, but she finished the treatment later that week and was free to return home to do nothing but shit and puke and sleep and cry.

She avoided her mirror—the blackened eyes, the astonishing weight loss, and the otherworldly fatigue—and settled in to wait. There were days when she did not get out of bed except to use the bathroom and empty her bedpan, and she felt certain she was dying, felt each day as if she had only one more day left. The doctors had gone too far, she was certain: had overcompensated for the challenge of the enemy.

She dreamed often that Shayna and Stephan came looking for her, that they could not find her and were disappointed. She dreamed they were sending her notes in the river, or attempting to, but the ships were all being carried away farther downstream, and ending up beached beside other people's cabins, or never found.

She dreamed they came wandering through the woods, searching for her—that they found her cabin, but, unable to rouse her, left notes tacked to her door, and to the outside of the cabin walls—and then she dreamed they no longer cared for her, were no longer interested in her.

She fell further into her dreams. The feeling she was going to die soon left her. She began to imagine she might survive for weeks, then months, and then even years.

They came over the mountain as they had said they would, with their arms and packs filled with sacks of food: loaves of bread, and servings of deer, elk, moose, and grouse, as well as a remnant of turkey carcass, and even some antelope, left over from a hunt their family had made to the eastern side of the state earlier in the fall.

They stepped up onto the porch, calling her name, arms too burdened with bounty to knock on the door, and when Jyl opened the door to greet them she saw they were covered with snow, and they handed Jyl their bags one by one, and then knelt and unbuckled their snowshoes and slid off their heavy packs.

They had brought two jugs of apple cider, two gallons of their own honey, jars of jam made from wild huckleberries, plums and strawberries they'd gathered from the valley, and jars of smoked trout and whitefish taken from the same creek on which she sailed her ships to them daily.

They had bags of dried mushrooms as well, morels and chanterelles, which represented but one of the hundreds of ways they made a living, and Jyl was touched not just by the dollar value of such gathered goods withdrawn from their hand-to-mouth seasonal income, but by the amount of labor that had gone into the gathering and then preparation of those foods.

The degree of their devotion to Jyl was evident on their faces—as if it were one of the great pleasures of their lives to be able to bring her these gifts.

The children stepped inside and put some food in the stove to warm—though the children had eaten a big midday meal with their family, they were famished again from their afternoon chores as well as the long hike over the mountain—and as the odors of warming food began to fill the cabin, the children sat at Jyl's feet on either side of her and helped her sketch the next ship, the design of which was the grandest yet, with their ambitions and imaginations having grown larger in the long absence of ships.

As Jyl drew, the children pointed to her sketch and suggested additions and alterations: intricate carvings along the gunwales, a howling wolf on the bow. A keel made of a deer's rib, and the ivory from cow elk teeth and the incisors of deer decorating the deck like a mosaic of bright tile. Dollhouse furniture—a chest of drawers—fastened to the bow, so the sketches and notes and stories could be stored in the tiny drawers.

"Write a story with three chapters," Shayna urged her. "The first chapter can go in the top drawer, and the second chapter in the middle drawer, and the last chapter in the bottom drawer."

The food was warm again—they could detect its odors stirring—and they brought it to the table, and, after Stephan and Shayna said a prayer, the three of them ate with wordless focus, the children moving through their meal with startling intensity. They ate for an hour, attacking the meal in the manner with which they attacked any of their labors—working hard, yet deriving great pleasure from it, as well—and when they were too full to eat any more (and yet, bounty still remained), they cleared their plates and dishes, and they and Jyl began carving that evening's ship, whittling it from one of the same lengths of pine the children had cut for her firewood on their last visit.

The flakes of wood fell from her knife like petals of light or slivers of flame, and over the course of only about an hour the boat began to emerge, like a living thing working its way free of an egg or even a womb; and in the hour after that, they took turns sanding and polishing it. And though there were differences between the way they had sketched it on paper and the way it was turning out in real life, it was still a beautiful craft, and reflected well the care and attention they were giving it. And more than ever, as she watched the children work, Jyl had the thought that it was as if the children were hers—and not because she had made them hers with her love and attention, but vice versa: they had claimed her. And she dreaded already the day when she would be released.

Soon enough—too soon, Jyl thought—the little boat was ready to go, and, delighted, the children put it up on the mantel, proud of their work but excited, also, at the messages it would bring, over and over again.

The evening was still young, and everyone was relaxed from the big meal. The children were lying on the floor next to each other at right angles, their heads on pillows, absently fingering and twirling each other's hair rather than their own—as if despite the differences across the years they were somehow twins, or so like each other as to be the same, one self indistinguishable from the other.

Jyl took down from her windowsills several of the more alluring minerals she had found on her field trips, in the retracing and back-tracking of her father's steps. Elbaite, also known as tourmaline; azurite, with malachite embedded. Hemimorphite, from Leadville, Colorado. A diamond from Canada. Obsidian, from the Yellowstone country.

She let the children sort through them and handle them as she began another geology lecture. She told the children there are only about four thousand known minerals on the planet: that of all the elements trapped on the earth, there were only a finite number of arrangements or possibilities of composition available.

"Almost any mineral will form crystals," she told them. "A crystal is nothing more than an orderly, repeating atomic structure." She looked at Shayna and backed up for a moment, and told her about atoms—how they were the tiniest bricks in the world; that atoms in a rock were like atoms in a human being, or any other living creature.

She took her time lecturing, and watched the children examining the crystals before them. They did not want to set the minerals down but kept holding them, handling them.

"They start forming underground," she said, "when a few similar atoms cluster together, usually in water or lava, to form crystal seeds," she said. "As more and more atoms lock on to the seeds, they keep repeating that initial atomic arrangement, so the little seed crystal just keeps getting bigger and bigger, like a kind of blossoming."

Shayna raised her hand, and for the strangest moment Jyl had the feeling she was going to ask her some question about God, or about her own beliefs, her chances of salvation. Instead Shayna asked, "Can an entire mountain be made of a crystal?" She was holding a piece of amethyst, peering through it at the lantern, and Jyl smiled, imagining what she was seeing, and said, "Absolutely. Most of those kinds of mountains are way underground. It's when they get exposed to the surface that they start getting broken apart and crumbling, and being washed away." She nodded toward the amethyst. "The atomic structures of different minerals are what determine the mineral's shape, and its hardness—the way it responds to the world, and the way it reacts to the world's light, giving each mineral its own unique color, its brilliance, its fire."

Stephan raised his free hand. In his other hand he held a lumpen, uncut ruby, as dark as a deer's heart.

"How long did it take to make this one?" he asked. Imagining some organic gestation involving perhaps months, or maybe even years.

Jyl smiled. "Probably a million years," she said.

She had thought they would be pleased by such a revelation, treasuring their crystals even more, and was surprised at first by the dismay that crossed their faces, until she remembered that theirs was still a world in which miracles unfolded literally like the leaves on trees in the passing seasons, or as the blossoms of flowers emerged, or as ice melted, or snow fell, or as one simple match ignited one large fire.

She laughed, wanting to remind them that even a million years was not so long, but then said nothing, and instead let them simply hold the rocks, let the weight of their mass, and their beautiful, inescapable density, speak the rocks' own truths to the children's hands.

They carved another ship later that night, a much smaller, simpler one requiring only about thirty minutes of work, and then, with Jyl fading quickly, suddenly—she lay down on the couch for a quick nap—the children went out into the snow to find another tree, to bring her more wood.

Again they felled and limbed it, then sawed and split it and hauled it to the porch, wearing a new path through the snow.

This time Jyl heard them thumping around on the porch—it was almost midnight—and she sat up and went out to praise them as they finished stacking enough wood for her to stay warm for another week.

They came inside to gather their bags and packs and empty dishes, and she loaded them down with several of the larger and more attractive gemstones, including a small diamond and an emerald. And though they protested at first, she could tell they were overjoyed with the gifts, and they promised to take good care of them forever; and it pleased her, watching them set off into the night, their one flashlight beam cutting a lane through the swirling flakes, to see that their packs were heavier, leaving, than they had been upon their arrival.

Another dream: the children's labors were hardening them, threatening to turn them to statues, even as Jyl's loneliness—the fiery rawness of it—was keeping her alive. Consuming her, but in that burning giving life. The children were on a ship, they were leaving, being drawn away, years were passing in a single blink, a single thought, the children being pulled away by some current that hardened them and consumed her, until in the end none of them would remain as he or she had been, or even remain at all—only memory and stone, and yearning, like wind.

She sat up with a shout, then got out of bed and accidentally kicked several of the rocks they had left on the floor, sending them skittering and clattering across the room.

With shaking hands she found her matches and lit a lantern, and began gathering the rocks. They were still holy to her, talismans, not only in that her father had discovered and claimed them, had deemed them worthy of preservation, but also because she determined now to give all of them to the children, whichever ones they desired; and after building a fire in her stove, using more of her precious supply of firewood, she began carving new ships.

And because she was still chilled at first, her hands slipped once so that she cut her finger, causing the boat's bow to be smeared with her blood; and rather than sand it clean, she applied a symmetrical smear on the other side, so that it seemed like a painted pattern.

When she was finished, she put a note, a story, and a crystal into the ship, walked down in the darkness to the even darker river, and turned the boat loose.

It was a yellow boat, and for a moment it looked like a spark, a live coal, in the river. Had her father ever dreamed or imagined, she wondered, that of the gems he brought back from the mountains any might ever undertake such paths and journeys? Such *motion,* and bringing such joy: almost as if they had had the breath of life breathed into them, and had become inspirited.

She continued to carve and send boats all during the next week, and then into December. Deer season had ended and a new silence fell upon the mountains, one that was welcome. Jyl did not mind that she had not gotten a deer. She had seen the giant king once, and that had been enough.

She continued to send messages, stories, and drawings, as well as gems and crystals and fossils—sending several out in the same day, staggered over different departure times—and in some of her drawings, as her loneliness grew, she would make little watercolor sketches of the three of them sitting around a table loaded with food, as they had at Thanksgiving, with gleaming candelabra casting a shining light upon a roast turkey, a wild goose, and all other manner of game upon their plates; and in the tiny rolled-up paintings there would be wreaths hanging on the walls, images indicating the future, Christmas, rather than the past, Thanksgiving.

She never came right out and said, *I am lonely, please come back,* but as December moved forward and still her visitors, her friends, her little children, had not returned, she went even further with her pleadings and sketched a picture of her diminished woodpile.

She had been unable to get the saw to start once more, and though she still had some wood left on her porch, she had taken to wandering the forest around her house, pulling down dead limbs and branches and carrying them back to the house.

She was beginning to consider for the first time that the children might not be coming back.

They have grown up already, she feared. *They no longer care for me.*

The days grew ever shorter, plunging toward the solstice.

She tried not to panic. After all she had been through, this was still the worst.

She found herself standing at the window some days, watching for them, and staring at her woodpile—trying to conserve what she had, even though it made no sense, as this was the coldest time of year, and the children had not cut the wood for her to hoard, but rather to spend. But it disappeared so fast.

This newer, deeper, down-cutting loneliness was worse than the fears she had known before her diagnosis—those strange weeks when each traverse of the mountain had been more and more difficult— and worse than the first weeks after the diagnosis. This deeper loneliness was worse than the physical agony of the treatments, and worse than the captivity of the hospital room.

She moved around in her cabin, pacing, the walls lit with the wavering light cast by one of her lanterns as it sputtered low on propane. She was crying, pacing, crying, and when the lantern finally blinked out she was too upset to connect it to a new bottle of propane but instead kept pacing, from darkness to light, light to darkness.

Soon the limitations of her frailty overtook her, so that she was exhausted and could pace no more. She collapsed onto her bed as if accepting her grave, and yet the loneliness continued—though finally she sank into a state of merciful catatonia, staring at the ceiling until daylight, and then beyond.

The fire in her wood stove went out and still she did not move, but lay feeling the glaze of ice settle over her heart, feeling the salt residue of her tears dried to a taut mask across her face. And whereas most of her adult life she had felt as if she were always only a step or two or three behind her father, it seemed to her now that as she drew nearer to entering the place where he might be resting, he was paradoxically moving away from her again; an irony, now that she was so close.

She lay there, stunned, while the temperature in her cabin grew colder and her fingertips grew numb and her face blue, and then she was shivering, her body having no fat to burn, no anything to burn, only spirit and bone; and then she was warm again, and her breathing was steadier, and, slowly, she felt the deep loneliness draining away, though still she was frightened.

She blinked and found herself focusing on one faint sound: as if she had traveled all that way, descending so far, to come into the presence of that one sound.

It was a tiny groaning sound, all around her: a sound of contraction, of pulling in. Every now and again it would make a single tick, as if living, or striving to live—sometimes two or three quick ticks in a row—before subsuming again into a slow, dull groan.

She listened to the sound, so near to her, for more than an hour before her chilled mind could make sense and clarity of it; and even then, the knowledge came to her like a kind of intuition, or memory.

It was the sound of her pipes freezing. She was aware of the great cold outside her cabin, the weight of it pressing down like a blanket, or like shovelfuls of loose dirt being tossed over the cabin—but in the final comfort of her numbness, she was surprised by the water's protest.

She lay there longer, listening and thinking. She could hear music—was this the sound her father heard now? Perhaps it was coming from her father's blood, the part of him that remained in her.

Surely he could hear what she was hearing now.

The pipes groaned louder and she blinked, then gasped, as another moment's clarity intruded: the duty and habit of living. She lay there for another half hour, determining to get up and build a fire, if not to save the shred of her life, then to keep the pipes from freezing.

And in that time, she thought of nothing else but the goal of rising one more time. She lay there, trying to find the strength somewhere, like a pauper digging through empty pockets, searching again and again for the possibility of one more overlooked coin caught between linty seams.

She imagined Stephan and Shayna finding her bed-bound and blue, should they ever return, and the useless guilt they would shoulder, and she forced herself to find and feel a second surge of warmth.

Despite her numbed hands and legs, she slid out of bed, and with the smoothness of habit, she walked as if gliding, as if drawn, over to the cold stove, and crouched before it as if in prayer, then opened the door—a breath of cold air blew out, a breath like ice—and she crumpled some newspaper into it, and stacked a few toy sticks of kindling atop it—there was so little left now—and then lit a match.

The roar of the paper and kindling was deafening, and she stared at the dancing fire, amazed at how something so silent a moment ago could make so much noise only an instant later.

Slowly she added more sticks to the fire and leaned in against the stove while it warmed, as one might rest against a sturdy horse; and when it grew too warm for comfort, she backed away and listened to the caterwauling of her pipes as the metal, and slushy ice within, creaked and groaned and stretched and contracted but did not break. Beginning again, and yet different this time.

She wouldn't do any more lost king stories in her boats to the children. She had found him. She had gone into his icebound room, and he had been sleeping. It had been dark in there, so she had never seen him, but she had been close, had heard him breathing.

He had sounded at peace. And she had left a part of herself in there with him. Or perhaps a part of her had always been with him, had remained with him forever: a part he had held all his life, and beyond, like a pebble, or a gem.

She waited until there was but a week left before Christmas, and then one more day—inside of a week—before determining she had to humble herself and go over the mountain to find them, if they would not come to her. She could not imagine traveling so far, through such deep snow, even on snowshoes, but there was no choice; she had to see them. She worried an ice jam might have breached the river, so that none of her ships were getting through, and lamented yet again that the family had no mailing address, and that once winter came, there was no way of getting in and out of their little valley save on foot or horseback, or by snowmobile.

It still astounded her to realize that as recently as a year ago she had been capable of running up and over the mountain, and then back, in a single day, a single afternoon.

She packed a lunch and sleeping bag, in case she had to stop and rest, and left before daylight, in a light falling snow. She had carved and painted presents for the children, little miniature toy rocking horses, but other than that, her pack was light.

The first hour was the hardest, as it contained the steepest ascent, and in the bulky snowshoes she could travel only ten or twenty paces before having to stop and pant, not just to catch her breath but to still the quivering, the revolt of weakness, in her once-powerful legs, her thighs burning now as if aflame.

Gradually, however, she gained the elevation to the mountain pass and was able to walk along the level contour that led from her valley into theirs; and thrilled by the knowledge that soon she would be seeing them, she took no notice of the time, and instead only leaned into the slanting snow, with the canyon below—carved long ago by the river's erosion—completely obscured by cloud and snow.

She knew the trail well, even in the darkest of conditions—she knew it almost by touch and the pull of gravity—and she knew without being able to see it when she had crossed the pass and come into their valley. She knew to descend, knew where the path was that led to the valley floor. It was the path of her life as well as of her dreams. She could have gotten there blindfolded.

With her hair and eyebrows caked with snow and her face numb, Jyl reached the plowed and level field of their garden—the autumn-turned furrows resting already beneath two feet of snow—and made her way into their yard, listening for any signs of activity, and then, as the shadowy shapes of the outbuildings and the cabin itself came into view, looking for a glow of light through the curtain of snow.

She was surprised by the absence of sound, and the absence of animals—the corral was open, and no barking dogs greeted her arrival, no chickens clucked or called from the henhouse. Their truck was gone, with no tracks in the snow to indicate it had been driven out recently, and when she came closer to the cabin, she saw with an emotion very close to panic and despair that no smoke was rising from the chimney.

They are asleep, she thought wildly, even though it was at least noon. *They worked so hard the day before that they are still asleep.*

When she drew even closer, she saw that the doors and windows were boarded up, and again, the drifts of snow against the door- and window-jambs indicated they had been that way possibly for weeks; perhaps since the day after Thanksgiving.

She sat down on the steps in a daze, her mental and physical reserves equally devastated now.

Had they known they were leaving? she wondered. Surely not. And yet she could not help but feel wounded: as if the children had somehow become frightened of her increasing need, her upwelling of loneliness, and had fled from that weight, that extra burden in their already burdened lives.

She knew it was not that way, that surely their itinerant parents had insisted they leave, for some unknown reason, perhaps economic, perhaps evangelical—leaving, summoned, in the midst of an evening meal, perhaps—but it was how she felt, that they had somehow become frightened of her.

Only the little boats remained, stacked up beneath one window. Out in the garden, gaunt deer pawed through the snow. The cabin was shut down yet preserved, protected, as if one day the travelers might return, though not for a long time—years, doubtless—and with the children by that time all grown up.

She sat down on the steps and began to cry. She cried for a long time, and when she had finished, she looked up—as if in her despair she might somehow have summoned them—and then wandered around and around the cabin, and out to the various barns and sheds. They had taken nearly every tool but had left an old short-handled shovel and a rusty hammer with one of its twin claws broken; and with these discards, she was able to pry away the boards over one of the windows and crawl into the cabin.

It was dark inside, with a strange bluish light, as if she had entered a cave that had been closed off for centuries. They could not have been gone for more than two or three weeks, yet there was no residue whatsoever of their existence. The floor was swept and the walls were scrubbed, and all the furniture was gone, as was every other item— every spoon and fork, every dish and towel and article of clothing, every stick of firewood, every piece of kindling. Only a few more of the little ships remained, stacked neatly on the windowsills.

The gemstones that had been within the ships were gone, as were the drawings and stories. The boats sharpened her despair, for when, she asked herself, could she possibly ever use them again?

She ransacked the tiny drawers, all empty. *Write to me, think of me, speak to me,* she implored them, calling out to wherever they were.

Again and again, she searched through the cabin—examining every shelf, every cabinet, every drawer. She was a child. Had her father ever called out this way to her, after he had gone? If so, she had never heard him, and she feared the children could not hear her.

She crawled back out of the frigid, lonely cabin, and into the great snowy silent whiteness of late December. She boarded the window back up tightly. She sat down on the steps and cried again, and it began to snow, as if her tears were somehow a catalyst for those flakes to form. As if the shapes and processes of all things followed from but an initial act, an initial law or pattern, like crystals repeating themselves. She sat very still, almost completely motionless, as the snow continued to cover everything, even the silent cabin. She concentrated on the tiny seed of fire housed in her chest. She sat very still, as if believing that, were she to move, even the slightest breeze would blow it out.

NEW STORIES

Falco told me, "I don't know exactly what has happened. I am the same person, yet I am no longer the same.... Under the sea, everything is moral."

—Jacques-Yves Cousteau

How She Remembers It

T hey left Missoula with a good bit of sun still left—what would be dusk any other time of year. The light was at their backs, and the rivers, rather than charging straight down out of the mountains, now meandered through broader valleys, which were suspended in that summer light, a sun that seemed to show no inclination of moving. Lilly's father had only begun to lose his memory, seemed more distracted than forgetful then. He had been a drinker, too, once upon a time, though Lilly did not know that then; it had been long ago, before she was even born. A hard drinker, one who had gone all the way to rock bottom—good years wasted, her mother would later tell her—but he was better now. Though some of his memories—the already reduced or compromised roster of them, due to his years of drinking—were now leaving. Sometimes what left was the smallest thing, from the day or a week before, other times more distant memories, but nothing serious yet.

The pastures were soft and lush, the grass made emerald by May's alternations of thunderstorms and sunlight, and the farmers had not yet begun their first cutting of hay. The rivers had cleared up and were running blue, scouring the year's silt from the bottoms, cleaning every stone. From time to time she and her father would see a bald eagle sitting in a cottonwood snag overlooking the river. There were more deer in the fields than cattle—occasionally they'd see a few black Angus, like smudges of new charcoal amid the rainwashed green, but mostly just deer, some of them swollen-bellied with fawns that would be born any day, while others were round with lactation, their fawns already having been dropped, but not yet visible, in those tall grasses. The velvet antlers of the bucks glowed when they passed through shafts and slants of that slowly flattening light. Lilly was twelve, and her father was only fifty-two.

They rode with the windows down. The air was still warm but not superheated now, and in the brief curves of canyons they could detect a cooling that felt exquisite on their bare arms, with so much sun elsewhere, all around. It was only another four hours to the Paradise Valley, south of Livingston, where her father had friends, though he said if she wanted to stop and get a room or camp before that, they could. Lilly said she didn't care, and she didn't. It was enough to just be driving with the windows down, with her father, looking around and thinking about things.

Now the tinge of valley light was shifting, the gold and green becoming infused with purple and blue, and the touch of the air on their arms was more delicious yet. Mayflies were hatching out along the river, drifting columns of them rising dense as fog or smoke and bouncing off their arms like little needles. Farther on, the larger stone flies began to emerge and were soon thudding off the windshield and smearing it with a bright pastel of green and yellow and orange, which the windshield wipers turned to slurry before wiping the glass clear again.

Nearing Deer Lodge at the beginning of true dusk, just before ten, they saw the colorful lights of a tiny carnival, one of the portable setups that's able to fit all of its equipment onto a single long flatbed tractor-trailer, with the various parts for five or six ancient rides so cloaked with grease and blackened with oil, and the hydraulic hoses so leaky and patched together with pipe clamps, that no self-respecting parent would let a child ride; and yet in the summer, when a carnival suddenly appeared on a once-vacant lot in the middle of such a small town, and knowing that in only a few days the carnival will be gone, what self-respecting parent could say no?

Passing through Deer Lodge, the highway was slightly elevated above the town, so that from their vantage they were looking slightly down on the carnival. Viewed through the canopy of summer green cottonwoods, the lights of the fair—and, in particular, the lights of the Ferris wheel, which seemed to rise up into, and then somehow rotate through, the foliage—gave the impression of slow-budding continuous fireworks going off, at their peak barely rising above the canopy. It looked like a secret, private festivity. They exited as though it had been their planned destination all along.

The carnival was so tiny that once they were on the downtown streets of Deer Lodge they couldn't even find it at first. The streets were wide and dusty, and they could smell the waxy buds of the cottonwoods, which were just opening. Both sides of the street were lined with the white fluff of cottonwood seeds, piled like drifts of snow. Up ahead, they could hear the grinding machinery of the fair, the squeak and rattle of ancient gears, though there was no loudspeaker music, so the atmosphere was not so much one of frivolity as instead a more dutiful, even morose, labor.

Still, it was a fair, and when they rounded the last corner they could see the lights again: a weak yellow 40-watt glow coming from the popcorn stand, as well as a few lights still burning on various whirligig rides. A portable yellow iron fence surrounded the vacant lot on which the carnival had set up shop.

The Ferris wheel, along with the other rides, had stopped since they turned off the highway, and there were no other children around, despite darkness only just now descending. They parked beneath one of the big cottonwoods and got out. The sweet-scentedness of the buds and new leaves was almost overwhelming, and a strong dry wind was blowing from the west, sending cottonwood fluff sailing past them. There was no one at the well-worn turnstile, so they walked right through. They wandered around, looking at the rickety equipment, marveling at the decrepitude of the infrastructure—rides that had been manufactured in the 1940s and '50s, with puddles of oil already staining the dust of the gravel lot and scraps and flanges of steel welded into patches atop the oil-darkened machinery, so fatigued now by time and the friction of innumerable revolutions that it seemed the wind itself might be sufficient to snap some of the rides off at the base.

The carnival laborers, nearly as oil-stained as the machinery, were smoking their cigarettes and beginning to disassemble the rides. The tractor-trailer on which it would all be folded and stacked and strapped down was already being revved up, rumbling and smoking—in no better shape than the rides—and as Lilly and her father went from one ride to the next, asking if any might still be open, might be cranked back up one last time, the men who were busy with wrenches and sockets shook their heads and spoke to them in Spanish, not unkindly but in a way that let them know the momentum of their world was different from the leisurely pace of Lilly and her father's. In a perfect summer evening in the country, she and her father would have ridden in the Ferris wheel up above the canopy of the green cottonwoods, high enough to look out at the last rim of purple and orange sunlight going down behind the Pintler Mountains, their crests still snowcapped; but in the real world they were just able to buy a cotton-candy cone before walking back out to their truck and continuing on their journey.

And it was enough, was more than enough, to have the pink cotton candy, and to be driving on, and to simply imagine, rather than really remember, what it would have been like, riding the Ferris wheel around and around, with the whole carnival to themselves. It's been so long now that in Lilly's mind she almost remembers it that way—they were only a few minutes removed from having it happen like that—and yet in a way she can't explain or know, it was almost better to not; better to miss, now and again, than to get everything you want, all the time, every time.

They stopped for gas at a Cenex convenience store. Her father still wouldn't shop at an Exxon, for what they had done at Prince William Sound—not the spill so much as the cover-up—and while he went inside to get a cup of coffee, having decided they would drive on through the night, all the way to the Paradise Valley, Lilly looked out her window at the woman in the car parked next to them.

She was sitting behind the wheel of an old red Cadillac, the paint so faded it was more of a salmon color, and the fender wells rusted out from decades of plowing through salty winter slush. It was a soft-top, with a once-crisp white vinyl roof crackled and stained a sickly greenish yellow by years of parking outdoors and under trees.

Lilly noticed that the Caddy's tires were not only balding but mismatched in size and style. Though the woman had not asked Lilly's counsel, Lilly found herself recalling one of her father's many strongly held opinions—always invest in the best tires possible—and she found herself wanting to tell the lady to replace them. The car was an eyesore, but the tires themselves, fraying steel wires sprung from the thin rubber, were an actual affront, and a hazard, her father would have said.

The woman was perhaps in her early fifties, though possibly simply hard used and much younger—or, just as possible, much older and simply preserved, pickled somehow, by toxins. She had brittle orange hair, a sleeveless red T-shirt—what Lilly's father called a wifebeater—and a weight lifter's shoulders, though with pale, flabby arms. She wasn't so much fat, Lilly recalls now—not really fat at all—as loose; as if once she had been hard but no longer and never again, and she was just sitting in her car smoking a cigarette, smoking it down to a nub. She labored at it a short while longer, then flicked it out the window in Lilly's direction without even looking, or noticing that Lilly was looking, and then turned away from Lilly to murmur some endearment to her traveling companion, a nasty rat-colored Chihuahua.

The woman lifted a pink ice cream cone—which must have been her reason for stopping—and held it up for the little dog to eat. He scampered into her lap and began licking at it, fastidiously at first, but then really gnawing at it, wolfing it down, and she continued to hold it for him, fascinated and charmed by his appetite, as the ice cream—bubblegum? strawberry?—began to froth around his muzzle. She was still murmuring her adoration to him, enchanted by what she clearly perceived to be his singular skill, when Lilly's father came back out and got in the car.

He barely glanced at the woman, and as they backed out and then pulled away, the Chihuahua was still attacking the ice cream cone, both sticky paws up on the woman's chest now, laboring to get down into the cone, and still the woman beheld the little dog as if he were an amazement; and for all Lilly knew, when he had finished that cone, she was going to go in and get him another one. She appeared to have completely lost track of time and easily could have remained there all night, slumping a little lower in her seat, settling, seemingly intent upon going nowhere. It was terrifying in a fascinating way, and as they continued on through the night— satisfied for having simply gotten off the road briefly and having at least seen the fair, if not actually ridden any of the rides—Lilly ate her cotton candy leisurely, slumping down in her seat and pretending, for a moment, with a delicious thrill, that she was the woman in the Cadillac: that her life would or might end up there—lonely and lost, and needing to feed a nasty little dog ice cream to have even that friendship.

As they drove, the stars blinked brightly above them—her father had cleaned the windshield again—and Lilly pulled little stray tendrils of her cotton candy and released them out the window, into the wind, where she imagined birds up from South America finding them and, not knowing they were edible, weaving them into their nests.

She thought up stories about the woman with the dog: She had just gotten out of jail after serving twenty years and didn't have a friend in the world, or her husband had just that day been sent to prison for life, or maybe her whole family. Or maybe she had found out that her little dog was going to have to be put down—maybe he had a tumor the size of a grapefruit, or at least a ping-pong ball, hidden in his stomach. Maybe the woman had been a great beauty once, in another life, another town, another state, thirty or more years ago— back when her car had been new—and maybe, at times, she still believed herself to be. Maybe...

"What are you thinking?" her father asked.

"Nothing," she said.

They rode, putting safe distance between themselves and the woman with the dog, with music playing from a cassette mix Lilly's father had made. Lilly tries to remember, now, but can't recall every song— Emmylou Harris and Neil Young, she knows—though if she were to hear one of the other songs it would come back to her in an instant.

Driving on, peering forward into the night, and thinking about Yellowstone.

When she woke up, they had crossed over the Divide. It was the middle of the night and they were in the Paradise Valley. They were driving slowly down a rain-slicked winding road, and hail was bouncing off their roof and windshield like marbles. Her first image, and the reason she had awakened, was of her father slowing to a stop, with the hail coming down so hard he couldn't see far enough ahead to continue. The roar on the roof was so loud that even by shouting they could not hear each other.

They sat there for a few minutes with the engine running, the hail streaming all around them, and then the storm began to ease off, loosening back into drumming rain, and the road ahead reappeared, steaming and hissing in their headlights, paved with hail three inches deep.

They proceeded, the mist clearing in tatters like smoke from a battlefield, and with the road untraveled before them. They crossed the Yellowstone River, which was still running muddy and was frothy already with the quick runoff from the storm. Green boughs of cottonwoods drifted past crazily, bobbing and pitching, so that Lilly knew the storm must have originated farther upstream, earlier in the evening—the high snowy mountains attracting lightning as soon as the evening began to cool—and as they cracked their windows in order to clear the fog from the windshield, the summery scent of hail-crushed mint from along the riverbanks was intense, as was that of the shredded cottonwood leaves and black riverside earth, loam-ripped by the rushing waters.

The grass was tall on either side of the narrow road, taller than the roof of their car. Bright white fences lined both sides, and more cottonwoods grew close along the road, forming a canopy above. The road was covered with a mix of hail and leaves, some of the leaves with their bright green sides up and others with the pale silvery undersides showing.

Several times her father had to stop and get out and clear the road of limbs downed by the storm. He dragged them to the side as if pulling a canoe, his breath leaping in clouds, his tracks crisp and precise in the fresh hail.

For a while it rained lightly, with a south wind sending the fallen green leaves skittering across the top of the hail. They turned up a gravel side road and drove past a series of old red barns. Her father seemed surprised to see them, stopped and looked for a minute, then gestured toward one and said he and Lilly's mother had slept in it once when they first visited this part of the state, but there had been an owl living in there, and it had kept them awake most of the night.

Farther on, the road came to its end at a trailhead, where there was barely room in the tall summer grass for the car to turn around; and when they did—the neatness and solitude of their tracks revealing them to be the only travelers out in such a storm, and in such a world—the effect was profound: as if all of the mountains, and all of the valley through which they had driven, were theirs and theirs alone. As though they were not exploring lands that had already been traversed many times over but instead territories not yet dreamed of or discovered.

The rain had picked up and was drumming and blowing past them now in curtains and sheets, and Lilly stayed in the car while her father set up the tent in the steaming blaze cast by their headlights. The rain appeared to be drifting in a curtain only along the foothills because she could see now in the valley below them a few faint and scattered lights, farmhouses and ranches spaced far apart but with their infrequent lights defining the shape of the valley and the course of the river. When her father finished putting the tent up, he unrolled their sleeping bags, and Lilly raced from the car to the tent, crawled into her bag, as warm and dry as she could remember feeling, and slept without dreams or recollections of the day.

The valley was gilded with light when they awoke in the morning. The air was cool and scrubbed clean from the storm, and the hail had already melted. Other than the downed limbs and branches and leaves, there was no evidence the hail had been there in the first place. The sound sleepers in the valley would awaken and look out and think they had slept through a thunderstorm, and would know nothing of the winter scene they had missed completely.

There was a rainbow over the valley and steam rising from the river far below. Lilly turned and looked behind them and was stunned to see the Beartooths right at their feet. She could feel the cold emanating from their glaciers, as when one opens a freezer or refrigerator door. It made her laugh out loud to see such immense and jagged mountains rising right before them and for her to have been standing there with her back to them, unknowing, as she stared out at the green valley.

She and her father were at the front gate of the mountains, next to the trailhead leading up into the crags and ice fields. Lilly kept looking back out at the valley, then turning and looking up at the Beartooths. How could any traveler decide? She chose both, and stared out at the Paradise Valley for a while, and then at the Beartooths, as her father stowed the sleeping bags and shook the water from the tent fly before spreading it in the back windshield of the car to dry in the morning sun as they drove.

They got in the car and traveled down the winding road, away from the mountains and down into the lush summer valley, puddles splashing beneath them.

They drove down to a diner with some little guest cabins along one of the side creeks that fed into the fast and broad Yellowstone River. A series of tiny log cottages, painted dark brown, lined the edges of the rushing, noisy creek—Lilly's father and mother had stayed there a few nights when they were young, exploring and wandering around.

A garish 1950s-style faux-neon sign above the diner—hugely oversize and illuminated by bright rows of painted lightbulbs—was welded to an immense steel post to hold its weight: the kind of sign one might see outside a lounge advertising itself as the Thunderbird or the Wagon Wheel, but would generally not expect to encounter back in a quiet grove of trees far off the beaten track in southern Montana. *Pine Creek Lodge.*

It pleased her father to see that the sign was still there, by the rushing creek, and he got out and took a picture of it to show her mother, though he said that to appreciate it fully one needed to see it at night.

A cardboard sign hung on the door said that the restaurant was closed for the day. As they left, they saw that the other side of the marquee, visible only to northbound traffic, advertised an upcoming outdoor concert the very next night—Martha Scanlan and the Revelators—and it was strange to see how quiet and isolated the hidden little grove was in contrast to the garish ambition of the sign. Lilly felt bad for Martha Scanlan, whoever she was, and her Revelators. No one would ever find this place, and no one would ever see the spectacular illumination of her name in the colorful lights. Perhaps a few cows from the pasture across the road, and the horses on the other side of the creek. At least Martha would maybe get to eat breakfast in the diner. Lilly found herself loving the name Martha, loving the musician herself.

Lilly could imagine the cigarette smoke, and the dusty display case of Certs breath mints by the ancient cash register. She imagined Martha Scanlan tuning her guitar, beginning to prepare already, days ahead of time, for this bad idea of a concert. A barbecue was advertised to go along with it. Perhaps Martha was in one of the Dakotas at this very moment, hurrying on toward Pine Creek Lodge in an old Volkswagen bus, imagining a throng awaiting her, and a buzzing building, rather than this quiet, secret little grove of seven cabins. Perhaps the same storm that had washed over Lilly and her father the night before was now lashing Martha, out on the prairie somewhere, out in the Badlands.

They stopped instead at a KOA along the river, where an elderly couple was just opening their store, still a few minutes before seven. Lilly and her father saw them walking over together, holding hands, to unlock the building. There were pink and yellow rosebushes blooming by the log-cabin storefront—back home, the roses would not bloom for another week or two—and the storm had torn loose numerous petals, which were cast onto the damp pavement like alms. The bushes had surely been planted and tended by the old lady or perhaps both her and the old man, but they appeared not to notice the spoilage, or, if they noticed, not to mind. Their breath rose in clouds as they spoke quietly to each other, and perhaps they simply thought the storm's residue was pretty.

There were no other residents up and about. Perhaps a dozen or more behemoths—Winnebangos, her father called them—rested back among the old cottonwoods, their silver sides as shiny as salmon, but not even a generator was stirring. Lilly imagined it must have been a pretty rough night for all the old folks, no more able to sleep through the storm than had they been in a giant popcorn popper. After the storm had passed through, they must have wandered outside to inspect the damage, hoping for the best: that if the hail had caused any blemishes to their beloved, shiny homes, the damage would not be visible to the larger world, but would be confined to the roofs, unseen by anyone or anything but the birds passing overhead.

Lilly and her father gave the old couple a minute or two to get the lights turned on and the cash register opened up, and then they went inside and bought a breakfast bar each, some dry and unsatisfactory crumbly little thing. Her father got a coffee and added cream to it, which surprised her—she'd never seen him do that before—while she got an orange juice, and then they were on the road again, driving early, through the greenest part of the summer.

They were just riding, she and her father. She didn't know then that something was wrong with him, and that he wasn't going to get better—though she did know that there was something wonderfully right with her, something gloriously good. She didn't know then, though she suspects now, that he had a clue what was up. That he must have.

They had not traveled five miles before they saw the faded red Cadillac broken down on the side of the road, its hood elevated like the maw of a shark. Despite the chill of the morning, smoke and steam boiled out from the engine's interior. It was not the simple white steam of a boiling radiator, but instead a writhing column of black smoke from burning oil. One of her father's many great gifts to Lilly was to make sure she understood how engines worked, and, looking at the car, Lilly saw the smoke of an expensive repair bill, or maybe no repair bill at all.

The woman with the dog was sitting on the side of the road next to the car. The dog, clutched in her arms like a teddy bear, appeared to be concerned by the situation, occasionally writhing and struggling, but the woman herself was the picture of reflective calm, save for the half-empty bottle of vodka sitting in the gravel beside her. She seemed resigned, so accustomed to this type of situation that her relaxed demeanor could almost be viewed, Lilly supposed, as a form of confidence.

Lilly's father hesitated—Lilly thought she detected a quick burst of annoyance, and she understood: there was now a complication to their perfect day, this unwelcome challenge or summons to Good Samaritanhood—but she was surprised by the flare of something almost like anger in him.

He looked straight ahead then and drove on past the woman, not so much deliberating—she and her father both knew he was going to stop and turn around and go back—as allowing himself, she thinks now, the brief luxury of believing he could keep going. Of believing he was free to keep on going.

The woman watched him pass but made no gesture, no outreach or call for help other than to make a sour face briefly as she confirmed once again that she understood how the world was—that there was no mercy in it for her, and that people could not be expected to do the right things and could in fact be counted upon to do the wrong things—but then she quickly settled back into her I-don't-give-a-fuck serenity, just sitting there and watching the western skies and holding tightly to the dog.

She was surprised, Lilly could tell, when her father pulled over and, checking for traffic, made a wide loop of a turnaround and headed back. The woman was already drunk and a little unsteady as she labored to rise from her cross-legged position, still gripping the dog, and whether her inebriation was the result of new efforts in that direction already begun that morning or left over from the previous night, Lilly had no way of knowing.

Where had she spent the night during the storm, Lilly wondered, and what had she thought of it? Had she even noticed?

Lilly stayed in the car but with her window rolled down while her father got out and walked over to assess the woman's smoking car. Even over the scent of the burning oil, she could smell the woman now—old sweat and salt and above all else stale alcohol—and Lilly heard her ask her father in a raspy growl if he would like a sip, holding the bottle up to him as if it were a particularly fine vintage.

"I was going to Yellowstone," the woman said, staggering a bit. The dog in her arms like a sailor in a crow's nest was ready to leap free should she topple, but with the practiced familiarity also of a veteran who had weathered many such tempests. "I wanted to go see the buffalo," she said. She made a small flapping motion with one hand. "*Wooves,* and all that shit." Danger. Excitement. Now she looked at the dying car, her pride and freedom, her other self. Her better self. "I don't reckon you can fix it," she said to Lilly's father.

There was a pay phone back at the KOA. The woman and her dog got in the back seat. Lilly turned and smiled at both of them, hoping not to betray her revulsion at the stench.

The day was warming and not in their favor. Her father drove fast, and he and Lilly each experimented with the windows. It was hard to tell which was more unbearable: to have them rolled down and the foul aromas swirling around their heads, or rolled up, with the noxious odors heavy and still. They finally settled on a combination that left each window cracked several inches.

Their passenger was becoming more talkative, even in that short distance, telling them about—surprise—an unhappy relationship, a disappointing man, and now Lilly's father was pressing the accelerator so hard that the woman, none too steady to begin with, was pinned against the back seat, though still she kept talking, an occasional curse spilling from her lips followed by a surprised look in Lilly's direction—how did this child get here?—and an overwrought apology.

They skidded into the gravel parking lot of the KOA—a plume of white dust announcing their arrival—and the old couple, who were out watering their roses, looked up with mild curiosity, prepared for some level of disapproval. Lilly's father got out and opened the door for the woman, who was having difficulty with the task.

Lilly heard her father offer the woman twenty-five cents for the phone, but the woman declined, insisting with great protest that she had more than enough money for a phone call.

"Do you need anything else?" Lilly's father asked. "Are you sure you'll be all right?"

The woman held the Chihuahua under one arm like a purse and the vodka bottle in her other hand. Unobserved by the woman, the icy breath of the Beartooths mingled with the rising lovely warmth of the day. The sound of the Yellowstone River, full runoff, in the distance.

"I'll be fine," she slurred. "Right as rain."

Hostility now rushed into her, and she all but snarled at Lilly's father, with a scornful glance in Lilly's direction, and said, "Y'all go on with your little vacation, don't you worry about me at all. I'll be just hunky-dory." The last two words took stupendous effort to pronounce, and she turned and weaved her way toward the pay phone, stopping now and again as if to ascertain whether it was retreating from her and seeming surprised that she had not already reached it.

The old man and woman turned their hoses off and came walking over to see what the problem was.

"She's in a bad relationship," Lilly's father said—the truth, certainly, though also the closest Lilly would ever hear him come to telling a lie. He opened his billfold and handed the old man six twenty-dollar bills—enough for four nights' lodging in one of the cabins, and some modest amount of groceries, assuming she didn't spend it all on booze. Lilly was surprised—flabbergasted—for they were not in the least bit rich, and it was a huge outlay for them.

"I don't know her," Lilly's father said to the old man and woman, and nothing more. They saw that the woman was not making a phone call—who really would she call and what was there to say?—but was instead just resting, leaning against the inside of the Plexiglas shell framing the phone, seemingly satisfied, momentarily, for having achieved some destination; and Lilly and her father left before she emerged from her reverie, fearing she might hail them, might seek to lay claim with some nebulous moral obligation, or fearing, perhaps, that they might simply have to witness more humiliation, more desperation.

Lilly for one didn't feel at all bad about leaving her behind. The woman could stay and hear Martha Scanlan, could go to the barbecue. She might not get to see Yellowstone but she would be close; one never knew, it might work out somehow. And Lilly remained astounded by her father's generosity.

They started back in the direction they had already traveled. They didn't say anything about what had happened, and it amazes Lilly now to consider that her father had the restraint and discipline not to try to put too fine a point on what they had seen. She knew—and knows—it would have been well within his rights to look over at Lilly and say, *Don't drink, ever.*

They drove with the windows down, the clean valley winds scouring the green fields and washing through the car, blasting away the scent of their previous occupant. They drove past the woman's car, which was still smoldering, and then, not much farther on, her father got excited and pulled off the road.

At first Lilly had no idea why, thinking—fearing—he had spied another stranded motorist, another pilgrim. But instead he grabbed the binoculars from the back seat and pointed out a yellow-headed blackbird in a clump of cattails not far from the road—a sunken little wetland in which a few dairy cattle stood and beside which old metal barrels and an abandoned tractor rusted back down into squalor, while just upslope, a dingy mobile home perched crookedly on an irregular stacking of cinder blocks, the trailer tilting toward the black-water pond below.

Two white PVC pipes jutted from the earthen bank above the pond—overflow, no doubt, for various effluents—but it was the shocking beauty of the bird, its boisterous, exuberant singing, incredible yellow head thrown back and trilling to the blue sky, having survived the storm, that fixed their attention.

"Would you look at that," her father kept exclaiming, handing her the binoculars so she could see the bird's beauty close up, and then, moments later, asking for them back, wanting to see it again, then growing more excited and passing them back to her, while the bird sang on and on.

A grizzled middle-aged man, probably no older than her father but much worse for the wear, came out onto the porch, unnerved by their scrutiny, and Lilly began to imagine all the days that might have been that led him to this place—this downward slide, this rendezvous with failure.

What would it be like to be him, Lilly wondered—the man in the stained T-shirt, staggering onto the porch and blinking at the bright sunlight? Only her own victory of being loved deeply allowed her the luxury of such indulgent imaginings.

They waved to the man—he did not wave back—and drove on. They began to see other travelers streaming toward Yellowstone: a landscape all the travelers had surely heard described as mythical, beautiful, otherworldly. She could sense her father's excitement as well as mild confusion. He told her they were going into an old and vast caldera that long ago had been a fountain of gurgling, uncontrollable fire but had since cooled to stone, and where—across the many millions of years—every kind of beauty had crept in, reborn and flourishing.

He told her he couldn't wait for her to see it. That it was a fantastic land of geysers and bears, ocher cliffs and cascading waterfalls, burbling mud pots and hot springs: a fantastic land, he said, something she would remember always.

There was only one main road leading into Yellowstone, but her father seemed tentative, kept looking at side roads as if lost, as though unsure whether memories attached to those branching little roads or not. He was wondering, she thinks now, if there were important or interesting stories at the end of some of those side roads, and that he had been trying—bluffing—to remember them, there on the main road.

The blackbird had been good. She leaned her head out the open window and breathed in deeply.

There was no way for him to tell her then in words the truth that he must have been discovering each day: that to be increasingly isolate is better than being numb, if it comes down to a choice. That even forgetting might be all right, eventually, after a long enough time, if the first-burning is hot enough.

She remembers stopping at the stone archway outside the park so they could take a picture, her father setting the camera up on the hood, pressing the timer, then running quickly to join her. Huffing, when he got there, having sprinted into the wind, as if into the past. His arm tight around her. How vast our brains must be, she thinks now, to remember even such tiny and essentially useless and fleeting things. How dare anyone sleep through even a moment of it?

The Blue Tree

W ilson, a logger, lives in the forest with his wife, Belinda, and their two daughters. He's old to be felling trees—forty-five—but he's always been able to recover from his mistakes, as if he carries within him a sphere of grace. A dozen broken ribs, three broken vertebrae, and innumerable sprains and fractures. Bones snapping like branches. But anything that breaks has always mended.

Wilson saws six days a week; the seventh he spends in the forest with his family. In the summer he, Belinda, and the girls—Lucy now nine, Stephanie twelve—carry a picnic hamper down the trail to the lake in the woods below their cabin, where they eat and swim. Fried grouse and black-pepper biscuits with cream gravy is their favorite. They lie on towels and look up at the clouds and at the canopy of towering trees—larch, fir, spruce, hemlock—while Wilson reads them stories, all of which they've heard before and never grow tired of.

As the day warms, he and Belinda watch the girls wade back into the gleaming lake. They plunge forward, their bodies glinting like fish, like mercury. They're good swimmers: fluid, easy in the world, adept at navigating its currents, its seasons. They're comfortable with change, Wilson thinks, because they have such a base of constancy.

"You can't keep them here forever," Belinda has said more than once. Lately, it seems to Wilson, she has become more irritable and, perhaps, a bit restless. She's been driving Lucy to dance lessons over an hour away once a week, and has also been talking about hiring a math tutor for the girls—not that they can easily afford either tutors or dance lessons. "They have potential," Belinda says, "they should have opportunities."

Stephanie's the scientist—little glass-jar terrariums line the shelves in her room, everything neat and in its place—and Lucy is the dreamer, and rescuer of things. Crooked-winged butterflies, frogs, salamanders, fledglings. One year, an injured baby flying squirrel. What does Belinda mean, potential and opportunity? Isn't heaven here and now enough?

She's been teasing him—or is she serious?—that he shouldn't expect the girls to become lumberjacks. Wilson has never really thought they would. Making a living by hard physical work can be a wonderful thing, he's told them, but it's a dead-end road. Better to do something involving their minds. And yet he wants them to know everything about logging, and the forest, and living off the land. Both girls can start a fire with a bow drill, can distill drinking water from the dew. They know the names and calls of birds, and understand what is meant with each song. There are different kinds of learning, he tells Belinda.

On windy days on their picnics, all of them lying on their backs, Wilson points out the skyborne etchings of the tips of each of the trees surrounding them. He shows them how the healthiest trees act in a high wind, their tops waving in a graceful circle, while the trees with weaker roots pitch back and forth like metronomes, the bulge of earth at their trunks lifting, ever so slightly, from the movement above.

Wilson and his family live off the grid, and for this, their blue tree is all the more miraculous. It's a giant outdoor Christmas tree, an immense spruce, wreathed top to bottom in blue hand-painted bulbs, which are powered by solar panels on the back of their cabin. Wilson dug a trench and laid an electrical line out to the tree, which stands a hundred feet from their house. The girls, who share the loft, can look out their window and see the tree, glowing, at any hour of the night, in the holiday season.

The night Wilson strung the tree, five years ago, was the first time he'd climbed that far up in many years. His balance isn't quite what it used to be—his hearing damaged by years of sawing—and since the girls were born he's tried to stay out of the tops of trees. Still, climbing it was the only way to get the lights up there.

He enjoyed being up high again, looking down on things, and he stayed for a while, aware of the sheaves of colder and warmer air resting in the boughs and of how his movements caused them to spill and slide around him, as if he were in the embrace of the tree, as if it had the pulse and breath of an animal.

Given his compromised hearing, he was surprised how much he noticed—the sounds of almost everything. The pop of a log in his fireplace, the crunch of a deer's hoof in the snow. It seemed he could even hear conversations among the stars, between the electronic tracings of the constellations. He felt like a pine marten or a bear cub up there, and he remained a long while, a child again. But then it was time to get to sleep so he could rise in a few hours, in darkness, and go back to work.

He starts work early each day, is out in the woods before first light so he can be done in time to pick the girls up from school, a one-room log cabin with but a single teacher, grades kindergarten through eighth. Enrollment rises and falls: four students one year, eight or ten the next.

Some days Wilson arrives before school's out. In winter he beholds the scene as one might a snow globe. A curl of gray twists from the chimney. A glow in the squares of the windows, even in midafternoon. Each day, each hour, is so much like the one before it, compressed as if to ice beneath the blue weight of winter. When it is not snowing, it is about to snow.

The door pushes open then and Lucy runs out, flying to his truck like a prisoner released, while Stephanie stays inside to socialize with the few older students, the cool kids. Lately Stephanie has been asking her parents—"elk hippies," she's taken to calling them—why they live in the middle of nowhere, hiding in the woods. It's a fair question, Wilson supposes, though he knows they love their life in the forest.

Sometimes Stephanie will meander out on her own; other times

Wilson will send Lucy in for her. There's no rush; his work is done for the day. There are always chores around the house, never-ending. It's a lot of effort to keep the dream aloft. Snow has to be shoveled and machinery cared for. Water pipes freeze and must be thawed with great caution; as they swell and bulge in their subtle readjustment, they are at risk of bursting. But his work in the woods is finished until the next day. The felled trees lie sleeping on their sides, with the sweet-scented boughs and limbs piled in tent-shaped mounds waiting to be burned.

No one gets as tired physically as Wilson does, but each night, overnight, a phenomenon occurs: he curls up against Belinda, wraps his arms around her, and wakes up strong again. Never mind that she is growing crosser with him. Who is to say, when he's lying entwined with her, who is the twist, and who is the core? He doesn't take Belinda's irritability personally. He is not religious but knows well how perfection requires the inspiriting breath from a few strands of imperfection to give it strength and durability.

Way before daylight, Wilson eases downstairs, fixes his coffee, makes his oatmeal. He washes his dishes, careful not to clank. Lucy's various art projects lie scattered across the big dining-room table. Stephanie's books are stacked neatly beside her reading chair, next to the wood stove; like Belinda, she gets cold easily. He builds the fire up, surveys the scene of his sleeping household. He loves being the first one up.

In good weather he parks his logging truck away from the house, up the driveway, so its rumble doesn't wake Belinda and the girls. He likes the ritual of walking up the dark lane. He likes protecting their sleep, the faraway sound of the truck's idle perhaps entering their subconscious, their dreams, as a distant gurgle of assurance.

In the sweet dream of Wilson's life, Christmas is the best time of year, each day melting into the next in the quickening dusk. Riding their toboggans down the driveway, in the last seam of light, after school and before dinnertime. The howl of wolves, down by the river.

The four of them settling in afterward, cooking. The delicious odors of the holiday: ginger, cardamom, peppermint. Hanging the stockings and raising the fragrant Christmas tree in their living room, decorating it with familiar and beloved ornaments, each one with a different provenance, recalling a certain story.

The family feast, a candlelit dinner in their warm home, just the four of them, with snow coming down outside—the elegant dessert, a chocolate chess pie or flaky rhubarb—and then the reading aloud of "The Night Before Christmas" (never mind that Stephanie no longer believes, and that Lucy is hovering on the edge; this may be her last year for even partial belief: and all the sweeter, Wilson thinks, for that going-away-ness), until at last the opening of one gift each from beneath the tree.

Stoking the wood stove before going upstairs to their beds. Leaving on the table by the hearth the half cup of milk in the ancient Santa mug, the plate heaped with cookies, the carrots and celery stalks for the reindeer.

Wilson's work is seasonal, and most years he is laid off by late fall. But with more housing starts this year, he has worked right up until the week before Christmas, and time has gotten away from him; it's already the day before Christmas Eve. He wants them to decorate their tree first thing tomorrow morning, Christmas Eve Day, as is their tradition, so they need to get it tonight.

"Just wait," Belinda says, "you can get the tree tomorrow. What's the difference?"

"We won't be too late," he promises. "I know where some good ones are." He's already prepared their old beater Subaru for the journey—thermos of hot chocolate, ax and matches, flashlight. "Come on, girls," he says. "Dress warm."

"You'll get stuck," she says. "At least take the truck."

He laughs. "I'll be careful," he says.

She gives him a look.

"The truck's too loud," he says, "and I don't want us to smell like exhaust. This is fun, not work. We're not going far."

The girls run upstairs, grab their coats, fly back down, and hug

Belinda goodbye. Wilson tries to remember how many years it's been since Belinda went with them to get the tree: two, maybe three now?

When he kisses her, a complicated look of war-and-peace flickers on her face. He whispers, "Don't forget to turn the tree on, please, after we're gone."

This will be the first time the girls have gotten a tree at night—*adventure!*—and they rush outside to the Subaru. Wilson joins them, and as the car pushes up the long driveway into the darkness, its crooked headlamps light random patches of snow-clad forest. So many trees.

"I love this time of year," Stephanie announces, and Wilson feels almost faint, he's so happy.

After Thanksgiving, the county stops plowing the road at the turnoff to where Wilson is taking them. Cat hunters cruise it in their big trucks, their lion hounds kenneled in back. The ruts they leave are a little wider than the wheel track of the Subaru, and the car pitches around and planes unevenly, like a sleigh, its undercarriage brushing the fresh powder between the ruts. They travel about five miles, ascending a long ridge, the road lined with white-caped evergreens, to a grove of balsam firs Wilson has been thinning.

It's a cloudy night but not snowing. Wilson parks and the girls get out and run ahead of him, sharing the flashlight. Wilson has brought their favorite, a self-generating wind-up light he's had for years. Watching them point it this way and that makes him smile—it's almost a toy, but projects a decent beam. Wilson himself would rather just let his eyes adjust. It's surprising, really, what you can see in the darkness, once you get used to it.

The girls zig and zag, patches of bouncing light in the forest ahead of him, stopping at different trees they proclaim perfect until Wilson points out various deficiencies.

Maybe he wants the girls to become loggers after all, he thinks. He loves showing them the cross sections of trees he cuts—how to read the growth rings of each tree like a book, each year a page, mysteries revealed: where a tree grew more slowly beneath the shade of other trees; the way slow growth makes the wood stronger.

Scars, too, show up in the hidden texts. Here, a bolt of lightning or a fire, a great wound encased; the tree wrapping around the scar as if to embrace the wound. The tree survived, the scar becoming little more than a hard, glassy knot within—invisible, after long years.

They walk on, farther into the dark forest. On a hillside, the girls make snow angels. Despite telling Belinda they wouldn't be long, Wilson stops to build a fire. They nestle beneath the boughs of a big spruce and drink the hot chocolate he's brought, watching the fire and the glazing scallop of snow around it.

Then they resume their search. Wilson knows where the tree is. He's leading them in circles around it, incorporating just the right amount of difficulty into the hunt. When they come to the tree, he pauses as if for breath. Glances around.

Lucy, with the light, sees it then and, too incredulous to call out, walks around it, illuminating the crown, hoping it stays perfect.

"This is it!" Stephanie cries. "We found it!"

Wilson steps back, looks up. "It's amazing, and you girls are amazing," he says. "I've never seen anything like it."

He approaches the tree as if it's a shrine, takes his hatchet from its holster on his belt, says "Thank you," and eases in under the dense branches. He estimates the place to cut so that the tree will be the proper height for their living room, and begins to chop, while Lucy holds the flashlight.

The tree shakes and sways as he cuts. Scented chips skitter onto his ski cap like confetti tossed at a celebration seen only by the three of them. Snow sprinkles down from the branches like sifted sugar.

For a while it seems that his efforts are having no effect. But then a hinge point is crossed and the treetop begins to lean, until at last the tree lurches and falls with a buoyancy, the faint swishing harpsichord of its needles combing the cold air. It descends like a parachute onto the snow below, and there is just as suddenly a new spaciousness where the tree had stood, and a brush of colder air, invigorating, against his face.

They take turns hauling the tree. The wandering trail of it behind them sweeps the snow like the quills of a porcupine's dragging tail, the needles erasing their tracks. With the cloud cover, there are no stars; it's darker than twenty thousand leagues beneath the sea, and colder, for that darkness.

They reach the road knowing they're a little late, but delighted with their bounty. The girls help lift the tree onto the roof of the Subaru, tie it down with rope, and get in the car, which, when Wilson turns the key, doesn't start. Won't even click.

The one thing he neglected, in this year's abbreviated holiday rush: to trickle-charge the battery in the old car. Damn the cost of perfection. He breathes out powerfully, as if to expunge the stress of too-high expectation. In the grand scheme of things, it's no big deal, nothing's ruined—it's simply a long walk home. The mood is what matters, keeping things festive and light.

He knows it won't help, but he unlatches the hood and gets out of the car. He examines the battery terminals and jiggles the cables, hoping for a loose connection but really just buying a minute to compose himself. A million non-Christmas thoughts are going through his head—mostly one in particular: Belinda was right. Somehow, she knew, even without knowing, that something would go wrong. That he was pushing too hard and a rivet would pop loose somehow, somewhere. Damn it, she knew.

He stands there, staring at the raggedy old engine.

"Dad, what's wrong?" Lucy asks.

"Nothing," he says, his voice light as helium. "I'm just looking at some things."

But they can read his voice like a map.

Stephanie, from the back seat—bless her twelve-year-old-ness, her going-on-thirteen-ness—says, "Should have listened to Mom." He imagines Stephanie shaking her head.

Just as quickly, Lucy—protector of the broken and damaged—defends him: "Right, like it's Dad's fault the *battery* died."

Stephanie snorts. "The car's a piece of crap. I'm just saying..."

Wilson blows out another long breath of steam, closes the hood with extraordinary gentleness, gets back in the car, turns the key again. Nothing, of course.

"Girls," he says, "my mistake, okay?" He tries the key once more. "Well, damn," he says, "shit"—a quick anger, or frustration, hot enough to melt ice—but then recovers and forces himself to think of this as something they'll remember fondly someday, one of the little fissures that make a thing stronger. "It'll be a good Christmas story," he says.

"I guess we don't need to lock it," Stephanie says. Wilson just laughs.

Even stalwart Lucy doesn't look too happy about this new twist, but she gathers her coat, takes the wind-up light from Wilson, and the three of them set off down the road, into the darkness; united, Wilson thinks, in their adventure.

His dream of Christmastime togetherness lasts for mere seconds. Wilson learns only now that Lucy is wearing her old black vinyl cowboy boots and did not even take the time to put on socks, believing her father when he said they would be back home soon.

"What were you thinking?" Stephanie asks her. *"Lame,"* she adds, just loud enough for them all to hear.

Please, Wilson thinks, *calm, please.*

Not only are the vinyl boots brittle against the snow, offering little more protection than a pair of plastic bags, but they have slick-bottomed soles, so each of Lucy's steps forward yields half a sliding step backward.

"Come *on,*" Stephanie urges. "We don't have all night."

Wilson watches Lucy struggle, but doesn't fuss at her. On the contrary, a sweetness floods him, that she should still be so trusting of the world, unaware of the way it rebels against almost all of mankind's planning. A cowgirl, a ballerina, a fairy princess: soon she will have to grow up—as Stephanie is doing rapidly—but there's still time.

Lucy is shivering even as she walks, and she allows Wilson to give her his jacket, leaving him in just a T-shirt. They travel a little farther, and Stephanie, lacking mittens, permits Wilson to stop and take off his socks, which she turns inside out and slides down over her hands for mittens. He pulls his boots back on over his now-bare feet, and they continue.

From time to time Stephanie stops and tries to see behind them, which causes Lucy to turn also and look back. Whenever Lucy winds the flashlight, it flickers, flares, like a candle guttering.

They descend a long hill to a switchback that looks down on the dark forest below, and Stephanie, a few paces ahead, stops and holds a hand up, then steps backward. "What's that?" she says.

At first Wilson thinks she's trying to scare Lucy—that she's still being snarky—but he takes Lucy by the hand and moves up so the three of them are closer together than they've been all night. Now Wilson hears it too, something moving quietly across the snow on the hill below; not a deer, the sound of which he knows well, but something different. The hair on his neck prickles.

He takes the light from Lucy and shines it ahead but sees nothing in its beam, only sparkling snow glint. He speaks firmly into the darkness, saying, "Go on now, we're coming through here."

He does not say, *Go on, lion,* as he does not want to validate the girls' fright. "It was probably just a deer," he tells them, but they can hear the lie in his voice, and they draw closer to him. Lucy's grip on his hand is that of a blacksmith's upon the hammer, and she has begun crying quietly. She never cries.

"Don't worry," Stephanie says, "I won't let anything happen to you."

They hear the soft soundprints upon the snow again, closer, and Wilson tucks the girls in tight. He's prepared to receive any charge. He speaks again to the darkness—"It's just us, go on now"—and when there is no response, he's emboldened and shouts into the night, and the girls shriek.

He thinks he can hear the lion breathing. Wilson tells the girls, "Okay, let's get going." He has no idea if they are moving toward the lion or away from it, no idea what will come next. Though he's careful not to show it, his terror swells.

From the darkness, beyond the modest throw of their light, there is the jolt of a shadow; Wilson thinks he sees the lion rush toward them from out of the blackness. He yells again, and the dark shape flares against the snow—did he really see it, or was it a tunnel-vision specter? The girls shriek once more, sounding like prey, and Wilson roars yet again, to let the lion know they are not prey, but formidable.

After that, there is quiet. There is nothing.

"It's gone away," Wilson says. "It's more frightened of us than we are of it."

The necessity of little lies.

In many ways, this is the worst: hoping, wanting to believe, that the lion is behind them now, and that they are moving away from it.

No lion can resist something that's moving away from it. Wilson does not tell the girls this.

Their eyes have adjusted to the darkness, and Wilson is pleased to see that Lucy has stopped winding the light, is secure enough to just follow the trail of the snowy road through the blue-black forest.

After a while, Stephanie begins talking about how the school play went, believing they are out of harm's way, and he wonders how much to tell them. He wants them to learn everything, but he wants them to be protected, and assured. It also occurs to him that Stephanie may still be on edge but telling the story to help Lucy believe they are safe. And maybe to convince herself as well.

Wilson can feel the lion still following them. He can feel it in the sweat on his back, and in the way his blood will not get warm.

He reaches for their hands as if in affection. They swing their arms as they walk three abreast.

He imagines the lion remaining a calculated short distance behind them. It is possible, he knows, the lion will follow them all the way home, to the top of their driveway; but if they can make it that far, they'll be safe. The lion won't come down the drive, knowing that people live at the end of it and sensing it could be a trap.

It's just a couple of miles more to their cabin now. How often has he walked those two miles in pleasure, with the time passing in but a blink? Plenty. Not this dark evening. He finds himself making prayers, and promises, to the world and to himself.

There's a long flat stretch, and then the road pitches down toward the top of their driveway. Wilson is amazed to discover that his legs want to buckle. He feels as though his entire inner chemistry has been converted to the purity of adrenaline.

But it's downhill all the way now. The girls walk more quickly, with Lucy still slipping in her vinyl boots. She holds on to Wilson's arm.

She stopped crying a while back, though some of the tears are still frozen in her lashes.

Wilson pulls her close, squeezes her. "I *love* the cold air, the frost-blushed cheeks!" he cries, parodying his usual enthusiasm. "It reminds me I am *alive!*" Neither girl reacts, both clearly still rattled by the unexpected turn of their evening.

They reach the top of their long driveway, and it's all the girls can do to keep from breaking into a run.

"I'm sure the lion is gone," he tells them. "But let's don't run."

They're coming down the homestretch. Soon the windows of their cabin will come into view, the yellow light tattered at first through the trees, but then reassembling into buttery squares. They'll see the rope of smoke rising from the chimney.

Wilson wonders what the girls will remember. Is it possible they'll recall only the good—the adventure—as if he had never made a mistake, had never been in any way imperfect? Or better yet: that they saw the mistakes—of course they did—but loved him anyway?

The run-in with the lion is not yet an hour behind them, and already Wilson is adapting, attempting to get back out ahead of the flow of time. After the girls are warmed up and settled, he and Belinda will go back out and jump the dead battery. Maybe she'll be so happy to see them she won't be cross. It could be another adventure.

They'll have to tuck the girls in, so it'll be just him and Belinda. They can take a couple of beers. After admiring the tree and getting the car started, they'll kiss, there in the cold black night, and she'll lean her head in against his shoulder. He won't tell her everything about the lion—how close it was.

It will be late by the time they get back, but then the tree will be there on the porch the next day, ready and waiting for them. They'll bring it inside, fragrant and perfect, and begin decorating it Christmas Eve morning, right on schedule.

He's got time. Hell, he thinks, he's got all the time in the world.

The girls hurry even faster, with Lucy, despite scrambling in her slippery boots, drawing alongside her sister.

The first thing that comes into view is not their cabin, but the blue tree, astounding and otherworldly in its brilliance, singular, alone in the deep darkness.

She still loves me, Wilson thinks, *everything is going to be fine.*

The tree is even more amazing for the fact that it is wreathed in snow, the blue lights encased in ice. The lights do not burn with individual twinklings, but instead emit a great blue glow, like a light-house: something they would never have imagined seeing in their own yard. The heat from each bulb has melted the snow, which has then refrozen, so that the tree is ice-clad, and shimmers and pulses with that blue glow.

The girls stop and stare at it without speaking, their hearts, like Wilson's, beating hard. He stands there with them—three breaths rising in one cloud—and he looks at the tree.

Its blueness is perfect. Only black night surrounds it. It's perfect.

This is all he wants. This is enough. Five seconds, six seconds, seven seconds, eight.

They stand there, catching their breath, and then Stephanie hurries on down the hill and past the tree to the cabin, and Lucy, still sliding a bit, runs along behind her.

And though Wilson knows he cannot make his memory be their memory, he lingers, staring at the glowing blue tree. But already the moment is beginning to dissolve, and in nothing else but the darkness after the long walk, with his daughters no longer beside him, the sight diminishes like a fire dying out, until it is nothing more than a pretty blue tree in the dark forest, and Wilson, too, hurries down to the cabin, and to what remains of the moment, hoping it has not already moved on. Hoping they themselves—all four of them—are still invisible to the unseen depredations of time.

Lease Hound

In the beginning, most of our work was speculative. We chipped away with six acres here, ten acres there. We picked up a lot of twos and threes the way a child might scoop up a penny from the sidewalk. Back in those days, you could get ten-year leases for only a one-eighth royalty. The up-front money was almost nothing. Nobody in those Alabama hills thought there was oil beneath them; they hardly knew what oil was. The hill people were ancient, barely hanging on, and almost always took what we offered without argument. Their children had long ago moved to Birmingham to work in the steel mills. It was 1980, and the country was on fire with hunger.

Even as a kid, just out of Utah Mormon white-bread college, I knew there were two worlds. My time spent in Utah had been like years bathing in a vat of milk and honey. I knew my world was small and clean, but now it was time to move out into the larger, mysterious world.

My degree was in church history, but the jobs were in oil. The shah had been overthrown and we were driving big muscle cars fast. Some grads were going to Saudi Arabia, being paid two hundred dollars an hour to stuff envelopes, sweep floors, teach English to the sons and daughters of sultans. There was a fever that pulled you in.

I worked the uranium play in southern Utah for a few months, learning to do courthouse work, mostly title searches. I learned all I needed, then took a job in Mississippi, where I was assigned to map an unknown province three hours to the north, in Alabama, called the Black Warrior Basin: shallow Paleozoic sands, only half a mile down, beneath the dense forests and rumpled foothills of the Appalachians.

Underground, the Black Warrior was the bowl of an old ocean, but up above, it was red-clay woodland, stippled with hilltop farms where clodhoppers scratched at fields of stunted corn. Gaunt cattle stood clay-gripped to their hocks in ruts sun-hardened as if to bronze. When it rained it did so for days at a time, transforming the clay hills into slaughterous sheets of red, as though they were the flayed carcasses of animals.

Beneath those hills and hollows was the true basin, where the Gulf of Mexico had once come inland. White-sand beaches, and great toothy dinosaur-fish roiling just offshore. In this place, mankind was still several hundred million years distant, as if the table had been set, but then someone had stepped away and forgotten us.

In Utah, Brother Janssen had told us hell was nothing but an estrangement from God, an acknowledgment of what some, he said, thought of as a curse—the innate, inescapable, and beautiful loneliness of man—but his sermons were often puzzling to the point of apostasy.

The man I worked for, Homer Young, lived in a mansion. He had personal chefs, a private jet, multiple homes, a limousine. Money poured through him like water through a weir. Some men are hungry for power or experience, but his ravening was solely for money; and for that, I pitied him his captivity.

For a long time, we were the only ones working the Black Warrior. It was all ours, and we fell upon it with a hunger. Rigs were cheap back then, and it took only a week to reach total depth.

The wells were rarely big producers, but if you drilled enough of them, you could make a living. In this regard it was impossible to go backward: there was only accumulation, and the shining example of our old silver-haired boss, who spoke to us only of oil, never anything else.

Sometimes we found natural gas instead, which back then was useless. When this happened, we flared it, burning off the gas cap to get to the meniscus of oil that rested below. All throughout the

Alabama backwoods, the flames from such wells danced, ascending thirty, forty feet, hissing and roaring, as if our shafts had been sunk to the center of the earth, and the center of the earth was fire.

The oil was what we were after. But it is a mistake of the ages, thinking some things are sweet, while others are waste. Brother Janssen had said everything in the God-made world has value, that there is no waste or loss other than that which we choose not to celebrate. That the only real ruin lies in our inability to fully engage, in every incandescent moment, in the brief longshot of having been chosen for the human experience.

In our ward, Brother Janssen had been largely ignored; he was viewed as well-meaning, but a little off the tracks—though by the time I got down in Alabama, I found myself strangely recalling much of what he'd said, things I'd thought I wasn't paying attention to at the time, but which, due to the intensity of his storytelling, had remained with me. He abhorred the slave owner Philemon, but was a big fan of the angel Moroni, and shuddered when recounting the days of the prophet Jeremiah. He said it was life's greatest journey to encounter doubt; that to truly know God, one had to become lost, had to find oneself crying in the wilderness. Only then could we begin to approach the beauty of the same divine loneliness that had made us. A loneliness so profound it no longer was even loneliness, he said.

My fieldwork was in the Alabama hills and in the sleepy courthouse there in Fayette, but my office job was down in Mississippi, in the hot glittering city of Jackson. I spent two or three days a week in Alabama, and the rest at the office in Jackson.

In Mississippi, I had a girlfriend, Genevieve, I'd met coming out of a gun and knife show. I had no business being there, but was curious about the phenomenon, as she was. She was fascinated by almost everything. Her piece-of-crap car had broken down, and I caught her admiring the wire wheel spokes of my company car—kind of a pimpmobile, really, but it was what Homer wanted me to drive—and she asked for a ride back to her grandparents' farm. They had died several years earlier and the farm was pretty run down. I stayed the night, and that was that.

Genevieve never accompanied me on my trips to Alabama. It wasn't that she would have been bored by the hills and farms; she just didn't want to drive three hours then wait around while I did the courthouse work. She lived an hour outside of Jackson, in the opposite direction from Alabama, near Vicksburg, along the river, not far from the great battlefield. My life then was a long triangle, and I spent my time traversing it; driving, never stopping.

Genevieve stayed in Mississippi: painted, rode her bicycle along the river, read in the hammock she had strung on her back porch, gardened. She was tall, with long black hair, and often wore a headband, which made her look like an Indian. Sometimes she went into Vicksburg and played cards with the old drunkards who in good weather sat on benches on the high bluff and looked across the impossibly wide river, mesmerized by the volume of sediment flowing past—old mountains to the north dissolving and being carried to the sea; stumps, logs, branches, and giant foaming whirlpools—and by the barges, always straining.

This was back in the days when there was money everywhere. Genevieve said material wealth was overrated; that what mattered was the quality of life lived. Almost every day she made a new discovery or had a new adventure.

If there was any pain in her past, she never acknowledged it, seemed even to willfully ignore it with her steadfast pursuit of happiness and the more elusive thing, *peace*. It made almost no sense, why we were together—she with her bohemian mores and lifestyle and me with my allegiance to the Man—but we were. Perhaps we were both drawn to the vast middle ground between us.

Back and forth I went; ceaseless, indefatigable.

The lights from our rigs glowed in the forest like the brilliance cast by distant cities. It was a strange and powerful thing to be driving in the darkness and come around a bend and see the illuminated tower of a drilling rig lit like a temple.

Other times the rig would already have been moved off, and the flare ignited. At night the flares pulsed and wavered in a mesmerizing, soothing way, like deep-sea fronds at the bottom of the ocean.

The wellheads were always in the middle of a clearing; even in their roaring, they could burn only themselves, powerful but solitary, and, in that isolation, were no danger to anyone or anything else. Sometimes it took days or weeks for the flares to burn themselves out; other times, years. The geologists never knew how much they'd found until it was all gone.

When each well neared its end, its burning was preceded by an even greater roar as the gas molecules spread ever farther apart, becoming more dilute with each passing second. The death roar could be heard for miles, across the folds and blue ridges, and lasted for several hours. After that came a great rasping as the earth burped the last of its gas; and then the geologists discovered whether the treasure of oil lay beneath that cap of gas, or only salt water.

My apartment in Jackson was at the south end of town, in a cheap complex. Rabbits lived in the vacant lot next door. Genevieve never came to visit me there—the place had no soul, and I did not need it to possess any soul. I arrived there tired, late at night, slept without dreaming, left again without even fixing coffee. Not a single picture adorned the bare walls. My work was taking leases in Alabama and my play was with Genevieve in the bottomlands outside of Vicksburg.

The girl who clerked in the courthouse, Penny, had been in and out of my mind for some months. She wasn't movie-star beautiful like Genevieve but there was something about the way she greeted the day, and her smile—her happiness—that got me every time. Some people can annoy you with their irrepressible good cheer. They are living unquestioned lives, you might think. But Penny wasn't that way. Her happiness seemed to come from some deeper core. She reminded me of where I had come from.

She was there at eight o'clock every morning to open the courthouse doors, where I would often be waiting on the foot-smoothed marble steps with a carton of milk and a doughnut, having risen predawn in Mississippi to make the drive. Sometimes I thought about bringing her a doughnut too, but I was happy with Genevieve and didn't want Penny to misconstrue it as flirting.

It was usually already warm by the time Penny opened the doors, but inside the high-ceilinged courthouse, the air was cool, still and quiet. She always dressed up for work, light cotton dresses with bright floral prints, and smelled as if she had just gotten out of the shower. She lived next door to the courthouse, and would let herself in through the back door that connected to her yard. The courthouse was one of the oldest in Alabama, one of the few that had not been burned in the Civil War. The records in Fayette County had not been transferred to microfilm, and computers were nonexistent. Everything was still written down by hand—every wedding and divorce, every birth and death, every property deed and transfer of title.

In transferring land, rarely was there any reservation of mineral rights. People could not envision anything of value residing beneath them. There was only the surface, back then. It was an easy place to work.

Of the secret world below, the old sandy beaches, the hill people had no concept. They had a clearer vision of heaven and its gold-lined streets than they did of the sea that had once lapped and rolled below them.

Homer's geologists were good at what they did, and they were relentless. They could find the oil wherever it was hiding: beneath a preacher's barn, or the town square; beneath cemeteries; beneath the mighty Alabama River, farther east, in which giant whiskered sturgeon cruised the bottommost mud.

They sometimes drilled dry holes, finding impermeable clay beds where they had prophesied there would be oil-bearing sand—and when this happened, a pall settled over the office that lasted the rest of the week. But they always found more oil, more gas: flaring the gas until the sweet oil came rising up.

The geologists placed huge pressure on me as well. Once they believed they had the oil corralled, they would instruct me to go out and get the leases, and not to take no for an answer; while in the meantime, Homer had provided me with a budget line I was not to cross. It was a lot of pressure.

There was one lease Homer wanted above all others in the Black Warrior, near the center of an area we called the Antioch prospect. The property belonged to an old woman named Velma Carter. Homer instructed me to go after it, and after her, and I did.

The ancient beach buried deep beneath the old woman's farm was the same shape as the hills above, with the surface resting over the old dunes like a blanket draped over a pillow. Half a mile below her house, said the geologists, was an anticline, and the beach below that anticline was full of oil. Up above, Velma's property was encircled by a halo of dry holes where other attempts had just missed. They were so close to what they wanted.

Other suitors had approached Velma—courtroom drifters, unattached to any team of geologists, fly-by-night title searchers known as lease hounds: shiftless geezers who held a worldview that the only way to get rich was by feasting on the mistakes of others, buying leases for a pittance.

They straggled into the basin like starving wolves looking for lambs. They would shadow me, and when they discerned the regions I was interested in, they began taking speculative leases in that area.

In this, I relied upon Penny to help keep our company's intentions hidden from the other lease hounds. Surprisingly, it was her idea, not mine. She kept my leases in a special drawer, waiting for me to say when to file them, which she would then do all at once. This wasn't illegal; there was no law that a lease had to be filed within a certain number of days for the transfer to be valid. A backdated or earlier signature meant nothing. All that mattered was the date the lease was entered into the courthouse records. Whoever filed first owned it.

By this point I had secured most of the leases for the Antioch prospect. But in order to keep them secret, I couldn't file them until I got Velma's critical lease. In this, I was vulnerable.

If Penny had liked another lessee better than me, and that lease hound had top-leased me—taking a lease on the same property I'd already leased, so that the landowner got paid twice—Penny could have recorded that second lease before my original one, and I would have been in trouble with Homer. There would've been a legal kerfuffle. But she liked me best. She had her cap set for me, I think now—well, I know it now, and I knew it then. It was an old story. I had come in from the outside, brought drama and novelty.

I realize now that it was Penny, not me, who held all the power, as she let those leases stack up, accumulating like the days themselves. We were all waiting on Velma. It was Penny who dispensed those records of desire, the great double-winged books she slid squeaking and squealing from their castered drawers at my behest. The sharp odor of the heavy books as they first emerged back into the light; the flex of Penny's slender arms as she retrieved them for me. She loved me those mornings, there in the cool silence of her courthouse.

I would thank her, take the great registry books, as if receiving Joseph Smith's golden tablets from outside the hills of Cumorah, and carry them into the adjacent workroom, which I usually had to myself.

From those books—ordered by section, township, and range, their every economic gesture ledgered within—I made meticulous notes about ownership interests, and then went out into the field. I left Penny behind and walked out into the sunlight of the town square, past the statues of Confederate dead, and got in my company car: an outsider's car, a two-tone Chevrolet Caprice with those wire-spoke rims. I would spread my maps on the velour seat beside me and drive up into the hills, searching for the hidden people, the hidden prospects.

After the gas cap burned off a well, if there was only old salt water, brined by the ages, utterly useless, it would come gushing out in a glurping fountain, splattering everywhere, ocean-scented, and the geologists would curse. Engineers would be called in to pump concrete down the hole, to set a bridge plug across the perforations that had allowed the gas to rush out in the first place, as if from a genie's bottle.

Welders were summoned, wearing their astronaut hoods and tall boots, mucking through the mud, and with the blue spark of their hissing torches would weld a steel plate over the top of the casing as if sealing off the territory of the never-born.

For a year or two, nothing would grow in the vicinity of the failed well, the vegetation having been poisoned by the salt. But after a couple more years, the dead gray ghosts of trees would tip over in a storm, and the dazzling salt pan, as white as the scuffed hardpan beneath a schoolyard swing set, would be refreshed following a few seasons of rain and rot. Green would spread back in over the scar, returning with such vigor that it buried even the warped clay road that had led to the failure, and no one would know there had once been a great fire.

Other times—and these were the times we lived for—the sweet green-black oil came leaping up from the well once the last of the gas was gone. The oil pulsed onto the ground in ropes and rivers, and the engineers scrambled to shut off the wellhead.

The oil smelled delicious, with just the faintest whiff of sulfur—in the way that while driving at night in the summer you can catch a whiff of faraway skunk, and find the odor pleasing—and the bouquet was enhanced by the heat of the midday sun.

Glittering dragonflies were drawn to it immediately, dabbing their abdomens into it as if for a taste. They bumped and clattered into one another, crashing into the oil and coating their wings with it, struggling upon its syrupy dark surface.

They decorated the oil with their futility, and the more nimble butterflies—azures, monarchs, zebra swallowtails—were summoned also, seeking any moisture they could find in the heat and falling into the soup, where they continued to flap, not as in the misery of leave-taking but as though unconcerned by their predicament.

Velma Carter had gone senile, was the thing. A haunted husk of the woman who had borne her clan, she lived at the end of a long winding red-clay road. Her relations said she had been in decline for years. Her house, the highest point in the county, was perched so far above the lowlands that you could stand in her front yard and peer down upon hawks soaring on the warm currents that rose in puffs from the green fields below.

The house was crumbling, but carried, still, the ghost of grandeur. It had once been a mansion, and even in its awful senescence there was something magnificent about the exuberance of its rot. The roof and walls sagged, but the porch columns were still intact, and immense. Virginia creeper vines shrouded it, as though holding it together.

Velma lived there not with her prosperous children and grandchildren, but instead with the more wastrel of her kin. I was never sure, on my visits, how many of her relatives resided there. On some occasions there would be eight or ten, and yet when I made a return trip, there could be twice that many. They came and went, seemed to use the house as a way station in their desperate lives.

Despite this, there were always unused rooms. It was hard to imagine why the house had been built so large in the first place; hard to imagine what lives had passed through it: though there seemed to be no ghosts but the living inside.

People in the hills said Velma used to be a pistol, in the old days. A dancer and a churchgoer both: a woman with a spine of steel. Folks still recounted how she drove her purple roadster through the hills at night, dragging a heavy logging chain behind it just to watch the sparks.

All intensity had fled her eyes now. She seemed to see almost nothing, and what she did behold was with a gaze so soft as to no longer even belong to her. She was a stranger to herself, and to all who had known her; gutted by the gone-away fire.

Each time I went up to her house in that sled of a muscle car—a V-8 with a bad muffler, so that my approach sounded like the rumbling of artillery—the impression I got from the Carter clan holed up with her was that they were outlaws, even within the realm of their kin. At least four and most likely five generations resided there, but what was most striking to me, and unsettling, was the spirit of lethargy and barely contained despair that pervaded all the inhabitants.

Even the toddlers—grimy, snot-nosed sausage eaters clad only in ill-fitting diapers—played somberly with their dump trucks, ramming them listlessly into each other, as if such gestures, performed enough times, might yet result in the realignment of some intricate system of fate that would change their lives.

The adults sat mutely, watching the toddlers engage in such clashing play. Sometimes I could feel an anger building in them, but it seemed to have no source or reason, and instead simply burned in them, rising and falling.

I had come to the house seeking the lease many times, courting Velma for over a year, traveling up the hill two, sometimes three times a month. I would not say the Carters looked forward to my visits, but I got the impression they listened to me. There was something in the stillness of their torpor, and the monologue of my entreaties about why Velma should lease, that came to remind me of sermons. They would have leased to me for the right price — an exorbitant amount — but the decision wasn't theirs to make.

In the beginning, I had addressed Velma with great earnestness, believing she was able to perceive more than they gave her credit for. Who was the prisoner, I wondered: she, with her dependence upon them for her every daily need now — her food and water, the warmth in her stove, the quilt they drew over her at night, the changing of her nightgown — or were the rest of them prisoners to her descent? It seemed to me they were all prisoners.

One thing was certain, according to her grandson Dexter: back in the time of her cognizance, Velma had not wanted to lease, not under any conditions. Dexter had a long greasy black mullet and was wearing, each time I saw him, the same dirty white wifebeater, which showed off a prison tattoo of barbed wire encircling his biceps, a tattoo that seemed a paradox of the sag and flab into which he was sinking, having been out of the pen and away from its weight room for a good two years.

He told me Velma had long ago said she didn't want to put up with all the noise, and that she thought drilling for oil was an abomination; that it would ruin their water well and make all the food in their garden taste like oil. He laughed his prison laugh, a hoarse know-it-all laugh, when he told me this, as if such an idea were absurd. I did not correct him.

Velma could no longer walk, and there was not money for a wheel-chair. Her family had relegated her to a small pallet on the ground floor next to the windowsill, where she had reclined for years, think-ing who knows what thoughts. A visitor to their ramshackle house would likely not have even noticed her shrunken body, there in a tan-gle of sheets. Her skin was so dry and papery as to appear almost translucent, so that sunlight piercing through the dingy south-facing window seemed to pass over and through her in such a way as to cre-ate brief prisms of color that shifted whenever she stirred.

It was not a brilliant light, but I saw it, now and again, and I won-dered if she did, too, and what it felt like to her.

I had assumed I might be able to buy Dexter out for a few coins and was surprised by his noncommittal attitude. I couldn't charm him, couldn't persuade him, and he never picked up on the intima-tions I made about how I might be able to line his and his clan's pockets with some bonus money, in exchange for their assistance in securing his grandmother's signature.

I came to understand that they were all using Velma to live there, but this only puzzled me further. Why wouldn't they try to talk her into accepting the lease money, if only so they could then take it from her?

I wondered if they were afraid of her—if they knew her to be a witch.

For all of our tranquility together, from time to time Genevieve and I had flare-ups and disagreements. She smoked a lot of pot—ev-ery day, sometimes twice a day—and rather than becoming mellow, she could sometimes be cranky. Her amplitudes were bright zest fol-lowed often by a distant, moody funk. There were times she wanted me to be close, and times she wanted me further away than I already was. She could be ice-cold, for no reason I understood. The sepa-rations seldom lasted more than a day or two, though, and she was always glad to see me again.

Of my drives out of the hills of north Alabama back down into the bayou country of Mississippi, I don't remember much, just a shutter-ing of vignettes flashing across the windshield, as if I were viewing a

movie rather than inhabiting those places. I passed through the dappled light but never stopped.

A roadside bait shop, its hand-painted sign advertising crickets,
worms, minnows. A barbecue shack, the blue haze of the hickory
smoke billowing from the outdoor grill, and the scent of it as I hurried past. An old white woman wearing gardening gloves, pruning
roses in a front yard enclosed by a wrought-iron fence rusted to
the color of old copper coins. The road was so familiar to me that I
traveled it by rote, and dreamed instead of a land millions of years
gone.

Then, the crunch of gravel in Genevieve's driveway as I pulled up
under the full moon. The scent of marijuana smoke coming from her
open window. The lone yellow glow of her bedroom as she lay awake,
reading. The scent of bayou, the freshly turned fields. The lowing of
cattle, the drift of fireflies. What heaven was this I had fallen into?

I would leave my clothes on the porch and walk in naked, stiff and
ready, pale as marble, the screen door closing behind me. She would
have heard the car on the gravel and would welcome me. So much of
it was sex, but there was more.

In the mornings we lay in the hammock on the porch and would
read in that sweet wedge of the day before it vanished into heat:
waves and shimmers rising from the rich black soil, as if it covered
still-burning coals. That cotton, or anything else, could grow in such
heat amazed me. But it grew well.

We lay coiled like great cats lounging, having feasted, or considering the next feast. She had a huge garden, lettuce and tomatoes and
snow peas. They grew in that soil as I had never seen any other veg-
etables grow. She would go out into the garden midmorning and eat
a late breakfast of peas and strawberries.

I don't know where the afternoons went. It is as though they never
existed. We must have napped on the antique bed in her darkened
bedroom, the shades drawn and the lone air-conditioner window unit
rattling and humming. Or perhaps those were the days I drove to the
office in Jackson, ascended to the eleventh floor, and went through
my paces like a trained tiger, assembling manila folders of titles and
division orders.

I do remember the dusks, in her kitchen, boiling shrimp for gumbo and shelling peas. A bottle of wine. Crickets, as the first shade of night fell.

I remember the evenings, when the heat of the day fell away.

Some nights we rode our bicycles. The road leading to her house was rarely traveled: farm country, forgotten or never known other than by the few who leased and worked it in various seasons. I remember the animal feel of the wind over our bodies—down her road, across the Big Black River, and out onto the black-ribbon lane of the Natchez Trace, with no cars out that time of night. Flying.

We'd get back around one or two in the morning, perspiring from the humidity and the leafy green moisture of the growing things around us. We'd go into the darkened bedroom, where we might sleep until nine or ten in the morning, then walk into the kitchen, with its streaming sunlight. The scent of drip coffee from Hawaii, her one indulgence. The clatter of her old Monte Carlo starting up, before we drove the fifteen miles into town to get a thin newspaper, or a single Coke.

The fields scrolling by, endless.

Each time I left, she fixed a cup of coffee for me, packed a sandwich, then watched me drive off as if regretful but also relieved to have the day to herself; though some rare days, I got the sense she might have wanted to take another step closer.

My days were divided into fractions: ten-year leases, paying out only an eighth royalty, or, when I was less successful, five-year terms, with the more ponderous three-sixteenths obligation. Time was slowly splitting me into wedges and slivers, but it did not feel like diminishment. I could live two lives, even three, with the same ease as one. I loved matching the vigor of my youth against the eighty-hour workweek, spending forty or more hours each week in Homer's office, down in Mississippi, in the metropolis of Jackson, returning to the sterile cave of my apartment only to shower and nap, and just as many hours on the road, back up to the hills of north Alabama, to attend to the wells and to pursue the leases.

In Alabama, I'd stay at the Brown Motel, a little place just off the town square. Brown bedsheets, brown curtains, brown lampshade. It was a room for sleeping, nothing more. I wasn't just burning the candle at both ends—I had tossed the whole candle in the fire.

And there were the dark woods at the edge of the rich plowed fields, with their velvet earthen furrows, where Genevieve lived. I went there as often as I could. I simply did not sleep. Or perhaps it was all sleep. Perhaps it was all a drifting dream, a dream of burning.

I saw Penny coming out of church one day. She was radiant, squinting in the sunlight, and was helping an old woman down the steps. She noticed me driving past, and lifted her hand to wave at me, as if to gesture, *Come here, come on over, the water's fine, come on in.*

It continued to surprise me, how so many of Brother Janssen's teachings stayed with me. The church elders had never allowed Brother Janssen a pulpit, but he did teach small classes and seminars in basements and windowless rooms. He did so with the energy of a man who had been rescued from a deep well and given a second chance. He told stories of the old days, when everyone was smiting or being smitten. Tales of hair-trigger accountability, of great hardship and paucity. Tales of reckoning, in which choices mattered. He loved parables: David and Goliath; Samson and Delilah; Jason and the Golden Fleece. Not all were from the Bible or the Book of Mormon; some felt made-up: a man who was gone a long time at war—like a precursor to Odysseus—or a woman in the desert, a weaver, who worked without pause in order to keep the earth turning.

When he spoke, his eyes burned like ingots—though, in a cruel irony for one so pure, he resembled, in his whippet-thin visage, a weasel, an unfortunate and unfair likeness. As if the fires within him consumed all fat.

Brother Janssen was a bachelor, and didn't socialize much. The assumption was that he was solitary because he was too obsessive and intense, too off-kilter for a partner. He spent his days studying ancient scripture. Candles filled his windowsills, the curtains scorched from countless windy mishaps. He could be inattentive to the most obvious things—traffic, the mood of a conversation, social niceties—and yet he also seemed to know, with just a glance, exactly what you were thinking.

For that reason, Brother Janssen might have had a better shot at getting Velma Carter's lease than I did. The two of them might not have been so dissimilar, once upon a time. Perhaps he would have told her strange and even fantastic parables until he earned her trust with his luminous passion. He might have shared with her one of his favorite beliefs: that for every mysterious curve of the land, there is a similar shape in the human heart; and because of this, no one ever needed to feel he was alone.

"What's Mississippi like?" Penny asked me, once. She could as easily have said *Mars*.

I didn't answer right away. *She wants to ride back there with me*, I thought.

There was no way I could tell her what it was like. No way I could tell her about Genevieve's garden, and that life of lust. "Hot," I said.

What I also didn't tell her was how far away it always seemed when I was in north Alabama; how the three hours felt half a lifetime away. How the land changed quickly, coming down out of the hills: flat hardwood swamp bottoms, and then out into the dazzle of red-clay Delta, cotton. Narrow roads, workers' sunstruck hoes flashing in semaphore. A kettle of vultures. A shack up on cinder blocks. And then, back into the swellings of Jackson's little hills, and my apartment, where I rarely even stopped, but continued on, another hour westward, toward the bayou that conjoined with the Mississippi itself. A land of Spanish moss, antebellum plantations, black soil, and Genevieve.

For a few months, outside of Tupelo, there had been a young black bear, little more than a cub, in a rough-welded cage of steel bars right by the side of the road, meant to draw onlookers who would then become customers, but the bear looked instead much more like a penitent being shamed; and there, too, I never stopped, only rushed past, and one day the cage and bear were gone.

There was a phrase in my profession describing circumstances where material wealth could be taken from an individual: non compos mentis. Unable to compose one's mind. Back then it was an easy process to have someone declared such. A doctor's signature could seal the deal, and often did. There was no standardized test to declare whether one's mind was still functionally intact. It took only a triumvirate of family members to make the decision. Or at least that's all it took in north Alabama.

It was not a much-utilized procedure. Even the least ethical of land men viewed the application of such a process as an admission of failure: a statement that indicted forever not only the sanity of the person designated non compos mentis, but likewise the ability of the land man to secure the lease by traditional means. To use it was the hallmark of bumblers and losers. *If we can't get the old man or old lady to sign, we'll just find a crooked doctor, or three pissed-off family members, and we'll wrap this thing up.* Move the rig in and begin drilling. Bring forth the tongues of fire.

Velma Carter sat on top of the Antioch structure—We could not go forward without Velma Carter—but in the meantime, we continued securing the flanks, and for those other leases, I had the luxury of dealing hard—not negotiating, but making simple take-it-or-leave-it offers. The hill folk had little choice; it was free money and they took it. And as we drilled more wells in the basin, they came to learn enough about the process to gather around the rigs whenever total depth was neared so they might be present for the testing, in the manner in which they might seek to be near the birthing of a foal or calf.

They were hungry for anything but salt water. The old Paleozoic ocean—the gurgle of it charging back up the pipe, and the salty smell of waves and surf no human had ever scented—was the one thing no one wanted to come rushing up the borehole. They wanted oil, but were happy even with the waste gas, for the spectacle of the flares, and for the hope of oil that might lie below.

Every time I walked into the courthouse with a new sheaf of signed leases, Penny was made happy by the sight of me. Had she been watching for me, hoping, even believing, that in some way her waiting might summon me?

We never so much as shared a meal. The closest we ever came to doing anything together was one day when I came into the court-house at noon. The bell in the town square was ringing and she was locking up for lunch. She was about to walk over to her house and water her flowers, she said, but asked if I wanted her to open the courthouse back up. I told her it was fine, I could wait.

I surprised myself by asking if I could see her garden. I was in love with another, or if not quite fully in love, at least *involved;* but it made me feel good to see how happy Penny was made by my presence. It was such a simple thing.

We walked around the side of the courthouse and through the gate that went into her backyard. I understood why she liked me. I was a clean-cut young man. No blemishes were visible. I knew that she herself was a churchgoer. There was joy in her heart. All I wanted to do was look at the flowers in her garden. If that made her happy, so what?

She picked up her gardening clippers and a straw hat. The flow-ers—azaleas, camellias, strong-scented gardenias—were in partial sun. Her gloves and rubber boots sat on a table. She slid her sandals off but then paused and decided, in that little hitch, not to put the boots on.

She walked into the garden barefoot on the gravel trail leading through it. No pets, no boyfriend, nothing: just the courthouse, ledgering those transfers of title.

Did my heart catch, watching her walk down that bright trail, nipping the withered blossoms and casting them out of the gar-den as if hurling favors at a wedding? Of course it did. I was human, I was young. But it wasn't a dangerous catch; it wasn't a *must-have, must-take* moment. It was merely an observation of beauty.

After she had trimmed and plucked the blossoms, she watered the plants, careful to run all the sun-warmed water out of the hose first before diverting the cold trickle onto each thirsty plant. I walked be-hind her, lulled. At one point she turned toward me and laughed, told me to take my shoes and socks off, and I did.

As if conditioned by her appearance, sparrows swerved to her garden around the water, sipping at puddles. A pollen-dusted bumblebee nestled in one of the camellia blossoms, stirring vigorously. The flowers, wet now, gleamed.

I turned away. The sun was already drying the water on the tops of my feet and I felt I had to decide whether to follow her one step farther into the garden, or back out.

I chose the latter.

Why I turned back from following Penny farther in, I don't know. I don't know. It wasn't because of Genevieve. We hadn't laid claim to each other in that way. It seems silly now. What might have been different, if I had continued on? Everything?

You can't know the paths not taken. You can only look back at the ones you've chosen and say *Here,* this was good, and *here,* this was a mistake. You can't even prune. The Garden of Eden was not pastoral, but a seething wilderness of possibility, of bounty, given to us. A test, I think now, to see how we would handle it.

I sat down in one of the chairs in the sun and wiggled my toes and watched her finish watering the plants. She looked back with surprise and understood what had happened. Something held me back, and whether it was the last of a purity that was in me then, seeking to protect her, or the first of a corruption, becoming more comfortable with squander, I still cannot say. Not all things turn on or off as if with a switch. Some things echo before dying.

Each day that I went into the courthouse—its marble floors worn smooth as the interior of a nautilus—the beating of my heart slowed, and I felt that the roar of the world above could not find me, and I was free to operate entirely without judgment.

With Penny's help, I was able to penetrate lands no one else even knew existed, and to rearrange property interests, manufacturing wealth. Only I knew of the world to come, and Penny kept the evidence of that world hidden away for me. In that, then, I had the knowledge of a prophet.

I don't know what Penny thought each time I drove away, headed back home. It's possible some hope remained in her, glimmering. It's possible she wished I would change my mind, come to my senses.

But I know what I believed, which was that I existed without accounting, and that the road was free and open before me.

Genevieve had a life beyond mine. She welcomed me whenever I returned but did not come looking for me. She didn't even ask me about work. Our time together was always about the moment, and the body, and the resting afterward.

I remember the first few months, when our senses were still aflame with the newness of each other, that time when, scientists tell us, the addicting chemical of dopamine pulses from our mind furnaces, a great outwelling from the pleasure dome of the brain running in ribbons through the blood, with nothing else in the world but that sweet chemistry. Even hippie Genevieve, in all her coolness, was burning with it.

"Do you want me?" she asked late one night. We were in her big bed, had loved again sometime earlier. The lamp was still on, appearing sulfur-tinted, as if from a century ago.

"I don't know," I said carefully. What I meant was *Maybe*. What I meant was *Yes*.

"I want a lot of things," I said.

I felt more than heard an exhalation leave her, and though she was not that kind of person, it seemed she might be counting to ten. Finally, she said, "Like what?"

"That's not right," I said. "What I meant was, I want everything to stay like it is forever. Don't you?"

She started to cry, an event as unfamiliar and startling to me as it must have been to her; she stopped, then composed herself with a speed that could come only from anger, and I think that she had cried not at my answers, but that she had asked the question at all.

"Come on," she said, reaching for my hand as if for a child's.

Where had the anger gone? Would I see it again? She was forgiving me.

We dressed and went out into the darkness, and in the way that time always swirled and eddied whenever I was at her house, I saw it was not the middle of the night as I'd imagined, but nearing dawn.

We walked out across the furrowed field behind her house, past her large garden, stepping over each loam-scented soft row, crushing little cotyledons of cotton and soybean with each step.

It was half a mile to the big trees along the bayou, where the silt turned to swamp. Wild magnolias, tupelo, cypress, black gum, and, on hummocks, live oaks, with curtains of Spanish moss hanging to the ground. We were still holding hands, and she hurried now, as if purging the sadness of that short time ago.

We left the field then and went into the woods, and the steaming fog. The wild turkeys on their roosts were beginning to gobble. Genevieve found a hummock to sit on, and we edged in shoulder to shoulder, and then she called to the turkeys, luring them to us.

We could hear in the silence following her call their suspicion, but after that, when they began to call back, we could hear their hunger. The woods changed to the color of pale milk, and the turkeys marched toward us, their gobbling coming from all directions.

We sat motionless. The fog was like smoke, a land before time, and when the gobbling grew so loud that we could hear nothing else, at last we began to see them, first one gobbler, his tail spread wide, chestnut red and gold, head bright blue like a beacon, strutting and spinning in the clearing before us, and then another, and another.

A single file of hens followed behind them, clucking and yelping, moving like a military procession, past our hiding area: a fourth, a fifth, then a nation of them, serenading, and still we didn't move, not even when the mosquitoes found us. The sun came up orange through the swamp and ignited the tendrils of hanging moss, each strand a burning filament, and it did the same to the turkeys' tails, which were now fans of flame.

While such beauty presented itself to us, the rest of the world slept.

The mosquitoes grew larger, swollen. We had to shoo the ones around our eyes. *The blemish in the garden.* A tiny smudge of blood, and only the slowest gesture, but the turkeys saw it, and, refocusing, saw us, and dropped their heads and fans and ran clucking back into the forest, then flew, their wings flapping like carpets being whacked.

Genevieve and I stood on stiff legs and walked back across the field in the warming day, in the broad sun, and I fixed a big breakfast of eggs and Parmesan cheese, grilled some toast in the skillet. After breakfast she went out to the hammock and lit up, and I kissed her goodbye and drove on to work in Jackson as if it were just another day.

I could look at a quitclaim deed and know in a glance what had happened; could tell, almost as if by divination, why it had been filed, however complicated the assignment of rights. But the amplitudes of the human heart, no matter whether hidden or exposed, I was less adept at reading. The heart seemed always in motion, like something lost and wandering, searching always for a home.

The more time that passed without my getting Velma Carter's lease, the more certain the geologists became that there was a vast dome of oil beneath her old leaning house on the hill. Late that September, Homer and I went for a walk downtown at lunch, an event so un-precedented I worried I was about to be fired.

He was too smart for that. He needed me, and it was fair to say I needed him. I had a comfortable life, despite working those long hours in the field while also holding down my office hours in Jackson. It wasn't a pace I could sustain forever, but I had gotten pretty used to claiming, hour by hour, my unofficial comp time on those morn-ings when I stayed over at Genevieve's after getting in late from the road, sleeping in a bit, and then lounging in the hammock a while longer.

"We've got to have the Carter lease," he said. "I have to drill now." A company from Arkansas had just signed a joint venture to begin exploring the basin, he said, and he couldn't risk them finding out where we were leasing. We had to have the Carter prospect now, be-fore it was too late.

I had not told him about Penny. I couldn't tell him not to worry, that the leases he had paid for had not been filed and were instead hidden away in a drawer, though he might have appreciated the sub-terfuge.

"You've been living a life of balance," he said. We weren't out on a true walk, I realized, but were instead making a lap around the block. "It's good that you have a girlfriend and get to spend time with her," he said. "The days go by fast. But I am going to ask that you get the Carter lease before taking off any more time from work."

The day was warm and we walked in the bright light; our black shoes clacked on the sidewalk, our socks shimmered almost iridescent. We walked a few steps in silence as I did the math—could I quit and still maintain my life of leisure?—an equation Homer himself had no doubt already calculated.

"All right," I said. "What's the most I can offer her?"

He gave me a number five times what we had ever paid. We would essentially be giving her the oil as well as the cash. It made no sense, unless we could make it up from other wells on the perimeter. I had never known him to be so addicted before, and it unsettled me. It was his money; what did I care? But it bothered me nonetheless.

"I'm not sure it's about the money," I said.

We had completed our first lap and he paused, not having anticipated the need for a second. A sheen of perspiration limned his big balding forehead; his wire-rimmed silver glasses looked hot on his face. I knew enough about him to understand he could turn savage quickly. Yet I saw him also for the first time as the old man he was fast becoming. It was as if he were sliding down a steep slope into a pit, until one day he would reach the bottom and curl up and close his eyes to the bright wonders of a world he had never noticed. The first few shovelfuls of earth would drum onto his velvet-lined box while his associates stood around in their suits thinking about their upcoming tee times, or about market futures, or about more prospects, or about their fractured families, and the confusing architecture of numbness that was their lives.

I missed Genevieve, on that second lap. I felt, with an emotion close to panic, that I would do almost anything in order to have a little more time in the hammock with her.

"All right," I said again, my voice thick. Homer was sweating like a horse now. We were halfway around our second lap, and it was strange to realize that although he held power over me, I would bury him. "But she might not want to lease for any price," I said. "Or her family might not. I could try for non compos mentis."

We rounded the final corner back to the office. Homer stopped and stared down at the sidewalk as if he could divine some movement beneath the surface. "You're not hearing what I'm saying," he said. He looked up, and I saw that although he was old, he was not yet weak. "Do what you have to do," he said.

Several days later I went back to Velma's. I arrived in the afternoon, and there was a different energy outside the house. Young people were coming and going—two boys, one scrawny and spindly, the other obese, trudged alongside the house half clad in football uniforms, plastic gear flapping—and Dexter was out in the yard, raking mounds of damp leaves into a burn pile.

Billows of purple smoke seeped from the pile, and the scent, while not entirely pleasing, plumbed in me the depths of nostalgia. When I asked if I could go in and visit with Velma again, Dexter scowled at me so darkly I thought she might have died.

His face was smeared with ash and charcoal and his eyes were watering from the smoke.

I saw now that the burn pile appeared to be a kind of house cleaning. A plastic purse, a bowling bag, and other man-made items. As the vinyl of the bowling bag melted, revealing the glowing ball, it looked like a skull, and, horrifically, a pair of women's shoes protruded from the bottom of the pile.

She had died and Dexter was cremating her, I realized, and then I had the thought that she hadn't died of natural causes, and that they were disposing of her.

He continued to look at me with hostility, and I had the do-gooder's impulse to rush over and grab Velma by the ankles and pull her from beneath the leaves. She might recover. I wanted to believe it was possible.

Dexter turned from me and poked at the base of the burn pile with his rake, stirring the old lady's white shoes, and I was further sickened to see that they were no longer attached to her. *Too late.*

It was clear he had been planning a conflagration—buckets of water stood at the ready—but the fire was barely smoldering, just a slow gnawing at the base, a few bright coals gleaming like jewels. A hiss emanated from the pile, and a sound like moaning.

And yet in that moment I felt hope. Perhaps the pile was only rubbish after all, and I had let my imagination fly away.

Dexter gestured to me to go into the house, as if I might find what it was I was looking for there. And in the way the world sometimes mystically announces its truths, I understood I would finally get the lease. That my long-suffering endurance would be rewarded.

I went inside, where Velma was absent from her perch, the pallet nowhere in sight. Household members were arranged in their usual states of numbness bordering on narcolepsy. I greeted them like a member of the family and, without asking, went up the rickety stairs to find her. I did not want her to be gone, did not want this family of miscreants to have terminated her, yet I knew also I would have been sickened for the lease to have slipped through my fingers, and so I resolved to accept whatever lay in store.

And yet as I ascended those raggedy stairs, I was certain what I was doing was wrong, and it wounded my spirit. Something was seeping out of me, and I did not know how to stop it.

Upstairs, I went from room to room. Some had crusty food bowls in them, dirty utensils, half-empty bottles; there were broken windowpanes, bird feathers, cobwebs. Drop cloths and sheets had been draped over some of the furniture. Cat feces peppered the hallway, and the stench of the bathroom was that of heated ammonia. I passed by an open window and looked down at the burn pile again, its plumes of resolute smoke, the glimmerings at its base. Those small flames would never consume all of the wet leaves, and I knew the burn pile would be there forever, one more landmark to sloth and rot.

The farther view outside was another matter: it was beautiful from the second floor, up above the canopy. Some of the leaves were off the trees, though enough remained to yield a mosaic of red and gold, a beauty that could soothe a soul in turmoil.

I found Velma, alive, in one of the unused rooms on the front side of the house. She was still on the pallet. They had placed her by another of the south-facing windows, presumably so she might live out her last days milking the weak warmth of the autumn sun, like a basking cat.

The window was dusty, which made the light softer, and in the instant I opened the door and saw Velma there, all my worry went away, and the stain on my heart fled. I was being given another chance at purity. I could yet turn away from my quarry.

There was love, there in the room, and I stepped in and closed the door behind me, wanting to hoard it, fearful it might leak out. It was coming from her in pulses like solar flares, a mother's love: sweet, calm, steadying. That room was a safe place to be. I pulled the sheet off a wingback chair and sat down.

Then, as quickly as the feeling had appeared, it ebbed. There could be no mistaking that Velma was dying.

She turned her head to behold me, and I studied her, trying to discern what she knew. What she could still comprehend, what she could remember of the past, and even perhaps glimpse of the future.

For a moment it felt as if we were communicating, as if a few neural pathways of electricity still coursed through her. I believed she knew I wanted the lease, and she was willing to discuss it; willing, perhaps, to negotiate.

I started to speak but lost my nerve. I just sat there, watching and waiting. Her family needed to be present for such a discussion.

I stood and took a Kleenex from my pocket and scrubbed one of the windowpanes, again admiring the view. In the distance a few of the gas flares burned, visible even in the daylight. They were our wells, our fields, and they were not so far away.

I don't know why, because I had more pressing matters at hand, but in that moment I found myself thinking of Penny. I knew her crush would subside, that she would not wait forever for me to show interest, and that I was using Penny just as surely as Velma's family was using her.

That awareness made me homesick again for Genevieve, and for the elemental quality, of our leisure; but staring at Velma, I felt for the first time that these days of leisure might recede. They would burn brightly until one day, perhaps soon, they would be gone.

I patted Velma on the arm. With great effort, she turned her head toward me again. She smiled weakly this time. I like to think that in that moment she had changed her mind, close as she was now to the veil, and had decided to give me the lease.

In any case, I took that smile as a sign and went downstairs to find Dexter and tell him we wouldn't need the non compos mentis, that Velma had decided to lease. That we would be paying good money, more than we had previously discussed, and that I needed witnesses. The Fayette County courthouse held a small handful of scattered old deeds and titles marked *non compos mentis*. I was glad not to have my name attached to such a document.

I handed Dexter the bank draft—forty thousand dollars to pierce a little hole in the top of the hill—and his first question to me after he had taken it and stared at it was "Is she dead?"

"No," I said, but thought that we had better hurry.

We trooped back up the stairs. I have no idea what Velma thought when she heard the heavy boots. Dexter smelled so strongly of the smoldering-leaf smoke that she might have feared the house itself was on fire, if she still had any thoughts.

I sat down beside her and reiterated the terms: three years and a three-sixteenths royalty, in addition to the forty grand.

The light outside was fading fast. I felt as if I were reading her the last rites and that a candle should be wavering. The other denizens of the household had gathered to view the momentous occasion that would slide into family lore, and whether they perceived the momentousness to be the changing of Velma's mind after a long lifetime of resistance, or simply a grand bilking, I did not know.

I placed the lease on a clipboard before her ghostly arm, then handed her a pen, which she took and held with the deep familiarity of a lifelong writer of letters. I imagined she might have boxes of them up in the attic, the one- and two-cent stamps mouse-nibbled— correspondences with her mother and grandmother, whose mother in turn would surely have been a slave owner.

I wasn't doing anything wrong, I told myself.

I did it, I thought, as I watched Dexter guide his grandmother's nearly limp hand into a spidery signature—had she fallen asleep midsignature?—but I did not feel the victory I had imagined. Instead, I felt the sickness of shame, and even fear, as if with her signature we were setting in motion some indictment of all our days to come—an assignation that would be impossible to overturn.

The others clumped back down the steps, the old house shaking with their descent—its shell so flimsy that it seemed a single storm might level it to kindling. I sat up there with Velma a while longer, believing that as long as the husk of her still had a heartbeat, and as long as there was respiration, there had to be trickles of memory, and consciousness, creeping through the hills and ravines and blue ridges of her wizened brain, and that it would be that way until the light went all the way out.

It was indulgent of me—seeking absolution so immediately—but I told her things were going to be better. I told her she had made the right choice, taking care of her family—her loving family!—and there would be oil, maybe vast stores of it, beneath her hilltop house. That they would all be cared for after this, forever and ever, and times would get better, not worse.

I told her good night and said that I would see her again sometime, and then I went down the stairs myself and out into the cooling night, and the stench of the burn pile. For some reason—malice against the universe?—Dexter had tossed an old tire at the base of the little flames.

"Keeps mosquitoes away," he said. My friend now, after all these many months of courtship. And did he think, since we had become pals, I might bring him more checks?

I got in my car and rattled down off the mountain.

In the morning, I was waiting on the steps long before the courthouse opened. Penny's smile—her radiance—was as bright as ever when she unlocked the giant double doors and let me in. Yankee troops, under Grant's command, had been turned back from this venerable building, but here I was, sailing in whenever I wanted, with the free pass of trust and the religion of commerce. It threw me every time, why she was still made so happy by the sight of me after I had failed to pursue her.

I handed Velma's lease to her, neither with a flourish nor with shame but with an understated gesture that suggested, perhaps,

Sometimes you just get lucky. Her eyes watered with pleasure, and I could tell she wanted to give me a hug.

She examined the document as if it were a religious artifact.

"I knew you could do it," she said. "May I record it?" she asked. "May I record them all now?"

She was so good, so pure! All this time, she had been waiting for me. She believed in what I did: took it as an article of faith that because I wasn't a bad man, my work was good.

There was no one back in those hills, and in those times, in fact, who viewed our solitary flares as anything other than good, as proof that we were getting close to the thing we were after—the thing we desired with so blind an instinct that no understanding was necessary.

What is the worst sin? Brother Janssen said it was the sin of inattentiveness. Of taking God's glories and gifts for granted. Of assuming they are our due. When we do so, he said, although we are forgiven with each rising of the sun, we are nevertheless thieves in a beautiful garden.

There was oil under the Carter property, as the geologists had insisted there would be. I worked the Black Warrior for several more years before moving to North Dakota during the deep shale play, and after that coal-bed methane in the Powder River, in Wyoming and Montana. My success with the Antioch prospect, it turned out, had not gone unnoticed, and as word had gotten out, I had become a sought-after lease hound.

All this started over thirty years ago and more. By the time I left Mississippi, Genevieve and I had grown gradually apart, and Penny's interest in me had cooled to disappointment, masked by the mild affection of easy friendship. Her garden was as bright as ever but it seemed that something inside her was beginning to dim, and I did not try to light it again.

I saw Dexter only once more, and barely recognized him. It was a little over a year after we'd obtained the lease. He came out to witness the testing of his grandmother's well. I had almost forgotten him, having gained from him all I needed. While he would never be mistaken for anything other than a renegade, he had attempted to dress up for the occasion—clean new blue jeans, and a brilliant white starched shirt—as if believing that might somehow influence the yield from the old ocean below.

It was a raw night in November and we were all standing around the wellhead: Dexter, myself, the geologist, the engineer, the well techs, and a few neighbors.

The well tech opened the valve—there was a great gust—and then he lit it.

The contained explosion thrilled us every time, even those of us who had been seeing it all our lives. It singed our eyebrows, scalded our faces, and we scrabbled backward, laughing, as the fire went straight up, harmlessly scorching the star-dark sky. We stood there, happy, hoping the gas would burn away quickly and we might then be the recipients of what we really wanted, the oil: the elixir.

One of the spectators went to his truck and returned with a large glass jug of what looked like gasoline, but turned out to be moonshine. Everyone proceeded to pass it around, drinking it at first with all the ceremony and formality of communion. Dexter surprised me by acting like a connoisseur; he took but one swallow, then another sip, which he swished before spitting it onto the fire, where it burned as if from a dragon's breath. For the rest of the night he declined any more, instead only watching the flare, waiting; waiting.

The rest of the visitors passed the jug with increasing intimacy, until soon they were all rolling around like monkeys—and, later, going off into the bushes to heave and puke. I did not miss any of that fun, no sir. I was proud of my religion that night, and as they continued to behave like fools, I abstained, remained sober and vigilant, and, along with Dexter, watched the well burn, waiting for daylight.

It was a big flare, higher than most. More people showed up, drawn by the height of the burning. Many of them sipped from the great glass jug. They kept coming, and stood there gawking at the flame, a dim awe glimmering in them as they observed the spectacle, as if nothing more than their attendance and dull hunger were causing the fire to burn, in some self-sustaining fashion—and I understood: that despite it appearing thus, we do not burn the essence of the earth, but instead are ourselves somehow the burning, though ours cannot be seen.

That night, while so many of the heathens around me howled and vomited into the bushes, with the towering flare illuminating their movements for all to see, I stared at the world turned brilliant.

Had Brother Janssen known where I was going—into the outside world—and divined, like a prophet, the difficulties I would meet? He had told me all I needed to know, but I find now, so many years later, that I want more from him—though too late, I fear.

What were my missteps? I still have no idea, but I could have been better. I wish I could have been given another opportunity. Such desire I suppose is the fuel of any religion—the realization that we squander our mortal days, but that maybe, one day, we will indeed be given another chance.

I had created all this, and was responsible for the world I now beheld. The thought made me dizzy. I retreated from the scrutiny of that scorching, roaring light, and went up a nearby hill, back at the edge of the forest. In the darkness I felt better. I lay with my back against the slope of the hill and watched the fire, the way it washed out the stars, erasing everything but itself. I could feel the earth trembling, and the fire roaring not just above, but below, rushing up to meet us all.

The River in Winter

A boy in the valley, Brandon, fifteen years old, stared down into the Whitefish, the river in which his father had drowned a year earlier. Some weeks back, in the dead of winter, a truck had plunged through the ice, which had then sealed back over. Now Brandon, full of rage and heroism, had volunteered to everyone in the bar to retrieve the truck by diving down and fastening a chain to it, whereupon the rest of them could pull it out. It had been a long winter, and if there was anything better to do that night, no one could think of it.

The truck was old, of little real worth, but as the evening wore on, wagers had been made, and the proposed act's value rose to exceed that of the truck itself. Brandon had no interest in the bets, only in the doing, and shortly before midnight he found himself standing on the ice, as if on the smoothness of a marble ballroom floor, in front of a hole above the dark moving water, his way made ready.

Men and women stood with lanterns on the narrow stone beach at river's edge. A few ventured onto the ice, where their lamps cast blurry, flickering reflections. Beside the lanterns and the small fires they had built along the shore, the villagers were but dim silhouettes, not a one of them recognizable in the wavering light. It reminded Brandon of the funeral service: all candles, all darkness, so far north.

His mother, unaware, was not present at the river. He knew she worried since his father's death about what kind of man he might become.

He closed his eyes, fastened the chain around his waist, and dropped through the hole.

Brandon gripped the heavy chain like an umbilical cord as it took him straight to the bottom, even faster than he had expected. As he sank, the river seemed at first to contract at his touch, as if recoiling from his heat, but then came back in and pressed against him. He couldn't see anything; beneath the ice, it was blacker than night. He could feel his fear echo around him.

He landed on the roof of the truck, was swept across it almost before he realized what it was. He lunged for something, anything, and caught the brace of the side-view mirror, and was tempted to fasten the chain to the mirror bar and be done with it.

In the current, he felt as if he were being sucked down the gullet of a writhing animal. It swept his hair back and tried to peel open his lips. He worked his way upstream, toward the rear of the truck, trying to imagine how the driver had made it out. His air was already leaving him, but he knew he would see this through to whatever end. He thought about all the townspeople waiting for him up above, their fires and lanterns along the shore. Eyes open, eyes closed, it did not matter; down below, the darkness was complete.

The chain tangled around him as he struggled upstream, and he panicked, sucked in a little water but then clamped his mouth shut tighter. He ducked and twisted, untangling himself from the chain — an expensive use of air, something he had always taken for granted.

Grabbing at the truck, hand over hand, he arrived at the back bumper. He was nearly out of air, but he crawled under the truck and groped for the frame, barely able to make his hands work, the great cold already shutting him down.

The current wanted to drag him away, but he found the frame and worked the chain through it, looped it twice, then kicked out from under the truck and scissored toward the surface, his lungs burning. As he rose, he felt as if something or someone beyond him was hoisting him up, though in his confusion he had let go of the chain and was swimming free; he had not thought how it could lead him back up to the hole.

Nor had he considered how hard it would be to find the hole. No one had told him how to do any of this; he had just jumped in. He realized he must be downstream of the opening. He kicked harder, and bumped his head against the ice, solid as concrete. He reached around, but there was no hole. Something greater than terror seized him.

Some distance away, he saw through the ice the ghostly traces of lanterns moving back and forth, villagers searching for him. Smears of yellow crisscrossed what had to be the vicinity of the hole. He had no air left.

He followed the lights above him in a clumsy breaststroke against the current, rapping at the underside of the ice. Someone heard him and thumped back, tapping a lantern-lit path toward the opening. The glow grew brighter, nearer. A dozen hands reached down and grabbed him, yanked him up and out. In his first breath, he took in a mountain of air.

They dragged him onto the ice like a fish and he lay there coughing and gasping, his blue face turned to the villagers along the shore.

The men helped him to his feet and led him over to one of the fires, where they gave him his own lantern, seated him on a stump, and wrapped and covered him. He sat thawing before the flames and spitting up river water, which steamed as it splashed against the lantern.

"Did you get it hooked up?" someone asked, and Brandon, still numb with cold and unable to speak, nodded.

"Good job," he heard someone else say. "Good damn job." He turned to see who had spoken, but in the darkness beyond the lantern's glow he couldn't tell.

He could not get warm; the blanket wrapped around him had frozen like a shell. But the townspeople were no longer concerned he might be in danger. He was back up on the surface, and that was all they needed to know.

They had turned their attention to the truck. Now that it was fastened to the chain, the villagers were ready to grab hold and pull. They had brought horses to harness to the chain as well.

Brandon did not want to remain alone by the fire, which wasn't warming him anyway. He stood and took a place in line along the chain, and people clapped him on the back as he passed.

Some of the men had axes, and if the villagers could lift the truck off the river bottom to just beneath the ice, the axmen could chop a lane for it, and in that manner they would reel it in. The small fires, untended as everyone gathered along the chain, burned lower, more coals than flames. The villagers placed their lanterns like streetlamps at ragged intervals along the length of the chain, beginning at the frozen shoreline and traveling into the woods.

Thirty men and women, sixty hands, four horses: when they began to pull, the truck started to move. The force required was beyond anything they could comprehend. The line, taut now, quivered like a muscle itself, as though given life. They pulled hand over hand and felt the truck leave the bottom, its tremendous weight twisting in the current.

Behind and in front of Brandon there were murmurings that the task was harder than people had thought it would be.

From the back of the line, farther into the woods, the order was given to halt. The horses had gone as far as they could—the forest became too dense for them—and needed to be unhitched and reharnessed closer to the shore. The pullers held the line, which trembled again as if the entire river, and all it contained, was alive and pulling back. It was all they could do, without the horses, not to lose ground.

After the horses had been reharnessed, the order was given to pull again, and progress resumed. The heat of the animals in their effort radiated as if from ovens. The muscles of the horses shone and steamed, and once more the chain began to move. The pullers leaned in with the horses and marched toward the forest again, a quarter step at a time, pigeon-toed.

The men on the ice shouted and struck at the ice as they worked to widen a channel. Looking back, the pullers watched cold blue sparks from the ax blows skitter and blaze out. Now the chain cut into the ice as if it might saw the whole river in half and swallow them all. The axmen labored to keep pace with the chain. The pullers were sweating as much as the horses now, and steam rose from their backs, too, so that a fog enveloped them. They felt the truck resisting, yet they found it within themselves to pull harder still.

Once more the order was given to halt, and the horses were unhitched. This time, as each horse was unfastened, the chain slipped back several links and a shout went up from everyone, believing the truck would haul them all into the river.

They slid backward, a number of them falling and being dragged along the ground near the shoreline. As some rose, others fell, and they lost further ground. Brandon, still clumsy with river-cold, fell twice, tumbling down toward the river. He was certain he was being claimed, summoned.

They scrabbled and dug in any way they could to stop the slide. Just in time, the horses were rehitched, and they too leaned in, lunging. A white horse slipped to its knees, showering the pullers with divots of snow, a lantern catching the glint of its hooves just before it was kicked over. Instantly, the woods along that section of chain grew dark.

The pullers managed to slow their backward momentum only when they reached the light of the next lantern, where, with the white horse and the pullers having scrambled to their feet, they were able to stop the truck's descent.

All of their prior work seemed for nothing, or almost nothing; it was time to begin again. But their way was a little easier now. They had worn a path in the snow. They understood better what was required. They found their rhythm and pulled as if they had been doing it all their lives, and plowed forward, steady and strong, soon passing where they had been before.

Just as the horses neared the point where they would have to be unhitched and reharnessed again, the truck, like some great whale amid chunks of jagged ice, breached the river's surface. Its back end rose above the ice, with the tailgate sprung open and belching water. The pullers leaned so far in the opposite direction to hold their position that they were now lying almost facedown, bent forward like tall grass flattened by a strong wind. The horses were marching in place, and then galloping in place, tossing up more divots of snow, which pelted the pullers' faces, but the truck and chain would go no farther. The pullers could do no more than keep the truck where it was, and only with all of their effort could they prevent the river from taking it back.

The men on the ice threw down their axes and hurried to fasten new chains to the frame. They tied the chains to a giant larch so that, their progress secured, the pullers could at last rest for a moment. Their relief was an ecstasy, but then the order was given to resume pulling; and the truck, now more like a monstrous crustacean climbing onto the ice, cleared first one rear wheel and then the other. Water rushed from every window, and then the front wheels were up and out of the frozen river as well.

In the darkness, the pullers felt the chain go slack, then heard the axmen bellow, and for a terrible moment they did not know if the truck had been lost—the chain having broken loose somehow—or if they had gained it, clear and clean, up onto the ice; and they went running out onto the ice to see.

And beholding the truck, which was still gushing water, they took off their shredded gloves and ran their hands over its frigid curves. The water poured from the truck like a long breath exhaled, one that chilled them as they considered the world beneath the ice, and yet they felt victorious, and congratulated themselves with loud whoops for having brought it back from the frozen deep.

To give the horses a rest, the pullers tied a tow rope to the truck and drew it behind them on the ice along the riverbank, which was like a frictionless highway—a single person might have been able to pull the truck in this fashion—and the procession of villagers accompanied the truck, with the horses limping behind like lame circus animals. Once they were out to the road, they did not leave the truck behind to be collected the next day, but hauled it all the way to the cabin of the man who had driven it into the river, whom Brandon did not know.

In the days to come, the man would disassemble the truck and dry the parts in front of the stove at night and on his porch in the daytime, in the dry south winds of the coming spring; and later into the spring, the truck, cleaned and oiled, would be running once again. And for many years, the story of how the truck had been reclaimed would be told; it belonged to all of them now, not just Brandon, and it drifted through the village like dust blowing off the mountains, though over time it began to seem that the words would endure as long as the stones in the mountains themselves.

After his father's death, the villagers had referred to Brandon as the boy whose father drowned in the river, though never again. Now, instead, he would forever be the boy who rescued the truck from the river. While it wasn't an even trade, his father for the truck, it was a start, and Brandon felt that he had moved some distance forward—though he could not explain the anger and confusion he felt whenever he saw the truck drive through town, newly polished and running fine.

Coach

I t's late in his career and Coach's mother is ill. They have left their home in the eastern plains. There was another controversy this season, nothing too outrageous—Coach just got a little too carried away with a ref's call, had a bit of a tantrum, hurled a chair, not in anyone's direction, but the chair slid across the court, knocked the legs out from under an opposing assistant coach, or so he claimed; Coach thinks he took a dive. And so Coach was forced to seek a job in the mountains, where, for whatever reasons, the players are less talented, and less committed to the holy sport of basketball.

The job in Placerville for which he has been hired is ostensibly teaching—he is a good teacher, but he's a coach first. Forty-three years old and with his own flesh beginning to mortify, ravaged by hypertension, the survivor of thirty-five overtimes, fifteen double overtimes, four triple overtimes, and—it nearly killed him—a quadruple overtime, as well as numerous twenty- and even a couple of thirty-point comebacks, plus the run-of-the-mill heart-stopping one- and two-point victories at the buzzer, Coach has spent most of his adult life wondering if he is a genius or just someone who works really, really hard.

When the genius is in him, he knows it for what it is, and is scoured, burnished by it—but when it leaves him, he feels ridiculously ordinary, vulnerable, exposed, undeserving of the responsibility he has dared to assume and pursue.

This is the beauty of small-town high school girls' basketball: there is almost never any game that cannot be won, almost never any game that cannot be lost.

Basketball on the eastern side of the state—the windy prairie, where he has most often coached—is an entirely different sport: a steady-burning, year-round religion, Indian ball, dominated by hot-shooting, trick-passing, full-court-press teams from the reservations, teams filled with players who possess intimidating names like Mankiller and Bearpaw, girls who play every second of every game as if basketball is the only thing in life and yet also as if they have nothing to lose. Up in the mountains, however, the same sport can be a precise and careful game, one in which the focus is on the sustained avoidance of mistakes rather than daring flights of brilliance.

And that's okay; Coach knows how to win anywhere, with any kind of team. He would like to have stayed out on the prairie but got no offers there and had to take this job to keep his mother on his insurance. He was born when she was forty, which was when she first got sick. The doctors had told her not to have the child but she did anyway. She got better, but now she's sick again, and has been for the last decade, battling the illness year after year, one day at a time, confined to a wheelchair. It's too bad about his last job, not twenty miles from the family farm where he grew up; that was one he'd hoped would last, especially given his mother's condition.

But few coaches stay put forever. Their nights are haunted by memories of the shots that didn't drop—shots that bounced two, three, four times before falling off the rim, or that swirled around before spinning out as if repulsed by a negative polarity. Memories of the girl who traveled in the backcourt with four seconds left; the girl who went glassy-eyed while inbounding and passed it straight to the defender, who then took one step forward for the easy, victorious layup; and the win, or loss, that extended one coach's career but finished another's—because no matter what the school board and principal and fans and parents say about building character, you have to win.

In the poorer communities, winning *is* character—there is nothing else left, or so it seems to them. It's a desperate lifestyle Coach has gotten boxed into, here in his forty-fourth year. Win or go home;

win forever, or leave, banished from one's community, one's home-
land.

The first and foremost talent, Coach knows, is nothing less than
being able to look into the souls of these girls and know what they are
capable of, and then to tease it out over the four years you have with
them—which is to say, you have to fall in love with them.

You proceed with the secret knowledge that such love is temporal,
and, in this sense, corrupted, susceptible to being diluted, or even
dissolved, by one too many losses. It can be diminished even by
something less final than a loss. A failed quarter, a failed inbounds
play, a failed free throw—failure lurks everywhere, always seeking
to destroy that condition of love. His own love is abiding, but the
world's, less so.

Every gesture matters in those four years. One day that intensity,
that attachment between him and the girls, will fade, and either they
will graduate or he will be fired, spurned and abandoned by those
whom he once loved, and sent to search for new love.

Coach has been to the state championships only once. He lost, but
it was the single most transformative event in his life. The season
itself, intoxicating and transcendent, had been marked by scrap-and-
claw jockeying for an upper-tier berth in his division—in his girls' division—with setbacks and reversals, last-second blocked shots, long-
range heaves at the buzzer, and titanic battles in the paint. His Lady
Bearkats (how he hates the differentiating "Lady" moniker—why
were the boys not called the Gentlemen Bearkats?) barely squeaked
into the district playoffs, but then caught fire, clamping down on superior teams and winning one low-scoring game after another, with
Coach making genius substitutions, creating matchups based sometimes on long nights' scrutiny of game films for each opponent, and
other times on intuition alone. More exhilarating than any drug was
adrenaline, the sweetest chemical, chased second by heart-pounding
second with boilermakers of desire, desperation, and pure and elemental hope.

He had never known, and has never known since, anything more
wonderful, has never felt more fully the incredible power of being
alive, and of being able, through dint of will, to shape one's world into

the precise outcome one yearns for—all the more thrilling because everything is at risk, the deep and lightless abyss of failure attends one's every choice, and consequence is compressed into every melting second on the game clock.

To say that basketball for him is a matter of life and death is not to put too fine a point on it. Every day he can feel how big and yet how damaged his heart is. The cage that holds it is immense, though the heart inside grows less strong with each passing year. Sometimes it makes him think of a bird caught in an attic, fluttering against a dusty window, unable to find an exit. The only way out is to win—always and forever—and so again and again the bird hurls itself toward that window, scrabbling toward the light.

At that long-ago state championship, having defeated teams thought to be their betters in both the district and divisional play-offs, the Lady Bearkats were finally—what sweet and temporary alchemy!—considered superior themselves. The entire town of Tiber, all five thousand people, chartered buses and traveled to the final in Bozeman, where, in the university arena, they stood together with the players' relatives from all over the state roaring their passion for the courageous hearts and cunning of their team and coach. Pride radiated like a thermonuclear expansion. So much so that standing there in the elegant field house while the national anthem was being played, in that shining and suspended moment, Coach had the brief and blasphemous thought, lasting just half a breath, as he took his eyes off the flag to look up into the stands, that right then was as good as it would ever get. This was the pinnacle. Everything could and perhaps should end right here, he thought, before there was a winner and loser—for who needed more euphoria than this? Upon whom would one wish such heartbreak, following such ecstasy?

The adoration of the entire town, for one long, focused, unified moment, and the pride of being your best self, beyond your best self—transcending your flaws and limitations, so that you're in communion with some force you didn't even know existed: Coach has known this feeling once, and would give anything to know it again. He wants it desperately for every girl he ever coaches, and for every town he ever moves to, in his wandering drift, in the repetitions of passionate and sustained failure, year after year.

The interview in Placerville went well. The school board said all of the things boards always said, no matter where he interviewed— that a quality education was the key goal of the school district, and that there were singular challenges these days, particularly in underserved rural areas, to be competitive in the ever-changing global marketplace. And that with regard to sports, the board was more interested in building character than in winning per se. Their team had won only three games in the last two years while losing thirty-four, and in the abbreviated part of the interview that covered basketball, the school board stressed how their main concern was that the girls have fun and continue to learn good sportsmanship.

It was what every school board said when they were losing, and it rankled Coach to hear it. Just once he longed to sit down in an interview in which his teaching credentials—Montana history and Native American studies—were given a cursory examination and then have the board tell him, *Listen, we're tired of losing. It's bad for our school, bad for our girls' spirit and self-esteem, and we want you to come in and do something about it.*

The truth was that losing all the time was no fun at all, while winning would be as much fun as anything these girls had known up to that point in their lives. But he never told school boards this. Instead he laid out his boilerplate twofold path to turning around a losing program. *Number one: Family first. The parents must love their kids. I need to know, and the girls need to know, that someone besides me will always have their backs. Number two: I'll stress academic excellence. Only when we establish those two things will athletic excellence return.*

Always, in these small schools, athletic excellence had been there at some point before; always the remnants of it hung in the hallway above the entrance to the dimly lit gymnasium, in the dusty, sun-faded photos of long-forgotten teams from thirty, forty, even fifty years ago, those past fleeting glories so distant as to mock the same passion with which the players, parents, and fans now pursued the game.

In every interview, Coach mentioned his experience of the state championship, but only casually, for he knew that in their initial earnestness, the school board members believed what they were saying about wanting only for the girls to build character and have fun (as if there were anything fun about losing). Only after he began to win games for them would they yield to the temptation of putting winning first.

For now, he dialed it way down; but even so, he could not completely squelch the incandescent fury he felt for the game and all its virtues. And in Placerville, as in all the other towns he had coached, the school board was at first amused—not yet captivated—by his passions, though they offered him the job immediately, after assuring him that his mother would be able to continue her health coverage under his state teacher's policy.

The interview had taken place over a Memorial Day weekend during which a snowstorm passed through, an unusual but not unheard-of occurrence for that time of year in the mountains. The first thing they took him to see, the very next day, after he had accepted the job, was the volcano, or what they called a volcano. Up in the mountains south of town was an old copper mine that, over time, had had so much ore gouged out of it that, following the big snows of 1963, the overburden of stone had collapsed like a fallen cake, and was still collapsing, the crater widening every year like some great beast gagging on the earth.

In subsequent years wildfires burned across the rubble of the ever-deepening pit, igniting newly exposed strata of high-sulfur coal, which themselves burned down deeper into the mountain's heart, issuing at almost all hours an acrid yellow-brown smoke with the scent of rotting eggs. The mist from those vapors was so acidic that the downwind drift of it stung the eyes and lungs of Placerville residents, and turned the lawns and maple leaves in town a speckled, mottled yellow, and dulled the luster and finish on the paint of Placerville's cars and trucks so that, in time, all of the vehicles had the same appearance—as if they were a fleet owned by a single company.

The school board members and town boosters rode up to the mountaintop with Coach in a caravan of four-wheel-drive vehicles, their tires spinning against the slurry of springtime runoff, the trucks slipping and fishtailing in snow that would be gone within the day. Already the late-morning sun was routing the storm's residue. Slender branches heavy with snow catapulted skyward with the suddenness of traps being sprung as they shed their melting loads. All around them the woods danced and leapt in this fashion, and steam rose from the forest as if it were afire. Churning gravel thunked against the undercarriages, and the trucks bogged down, roared, then lunged forward again: an armylike procession.

As they labored up the mountain, encountering the first burned-out scablands of lukewarm coal water and rivulets of toxic runoff from the old days of cyanide and arsenic heap leaching, past charred and broken mineshaft timbers protruding from the ground, Coach came to understand that his new employers were proud of rather than repulsed by the smoldering volcano.

"The kids come up here to drink on weekends," one of the boosters said. "We need to put a gate on it but haven't gotten around to it."

They were still driving, close enough to the crater that no snow remained—even in deepest winter, they told him, the area around the crater stayed snow-free because of the slow-burning seams of coal. The creep of the smoldering coal occasionally encountered the roots of one of the sulfur-strangled trees killed in previous years. Then the fire would find the one thing it needed most, oxygen, within the tree's hollowed husk, and the entire tree would burst into crackling flame. It could happen at any time, the boosters said.

They stopped at the edge of the pit and got out. It was windy, and the acid stung Coach's eyes and made him squint. Little flames and embers hissed underground, vapors rose from the dried-out soil, and did he imagine this, or was the ground on which they stood trembling? He detected a hollowness just below him, as though it might collapse.

The rotten-egg smell was overwhelming, as was the burning in his eyes—tears streamed down his face. He wiped them clean with the crook of his arm, leaving a smudge on his shirtsleeve. He hadn't noticed it at first, but there was another odor, too, intermingled with the sulfur and charred wood. Peering down into the gullet of the crater, where a few live coals flared like winking teeth in a jack-o'-lantern, he saw that it was being used as a town dump; that it was stippled with the carcasses of old televisions, recliners, blistered and smoldering car batteries and tires, couches, refrigerators, card tables, broken-down treadmills, and, poking through semi-melted plastic garbage bags, deer bones, watermelon rinds, banana peels, cereal boxes, corncobs, and seemingly all the other detritus of the century.

Though there was a local no-dumping ordinance, the boosters admitted that people had been doing it for so long that there was really no way to stop them—it had become a tradition. They seemed almost to embrace its toxicity.

Coach asked whether they'd tried to do anything with it. He'd read about various ways to turn this kind of mess to an advantage, he explained: methane gas capture, or even piping warm water down the mountain and beneath the streets and sidewalks in town to keep them free of snow in the winter.

No, they said, nothing like that; and they glanced at one another, smiling, delighted with the deal they appeared to have gotten—all that useless extra firepower in Coach, all that spitting passion, the constant need for forward motion. He would wear himself out here in the mountains, where nothing ever changed.

The stench permeated not just Coach's clothes and his short-cropped, thinning hair, but also his skin. He could not wait to get back to his motel room to take a shower. He turned away from the pit, saying he was chilled, and went and got back in the truck, while the boosters lingered a while longer, admiring their abyss and listening to the faint subterranean cracklings.

When they finally joined him back in the truck, the sulfur and garbage odors seeped from their woolen sweaters. Coach asked if they could go see the gym now and said he was eager, also, to meet the girls.

The boosters smiled at one another again. What energy—what a bargain!

Before coaching, he was in the army, where he loved the orderliness. Before that, there was only the windy prairie, in the farmhouse where he lived alone with his mother after his father abandoned them both, leaving his mother, still sick, to raise the then-six-year-old boy by herself. He has not seen his father since.

Coach and his mother hired out when they had to, but in good years, when his mother was strong enough, they ran parts of the falling-down farm by themselves. It was his mother who instilled in him a love of all sports. They would listen to the radio in the evenings, following the nightly fates of whatever acoustic drift came their way, picking up occasional marquee events—heavyweight title bouts, World Series games, even the Davis Cup each September, when the cottonwoods were beginning to turn yellow and the summer's terrible heat was finally leaving—but more regularly listening to the scratchy windstream of Pioneer League baseball, local high school basketball and football, hockey from Missoula, girls' volleyball from as far away as Lewiston and Miles City.

A hero is a hero in any age, under any setting; the fact that almost none of the local athletes whose exploits they listened to would ever play in college, much less professionally, meant nothing to Coach and his mother. The athletes had names and specific characteristics, valor and passion, strengths and weaknesses, and as long as the radio was working, they were always there, separating Coach and his mother from the darkness that surrounded them. The broadcasts were shimmering electrical threads tracing the night air, extending the players' every gesture from Great Falls, or Choteau, or Havre, or wherever they had originated, out past their farmhouse and all the way south to the wall of blue mountains, the immense and snowy Front Range.

In the years when his mother was up to farming, Coach helped her clear the fields of the wind-varnished glacial moraine deposited there ten thousand years earlier. The stones and boulders, remnant and residue from the great ice shield that had once overlain the prairie, seemed infinite in number, most about the size of a basketball, and no matter how many times they dug them up out of the loose, rich soil each spring, there were always more the next year, ice-polished boulders rising through each season's frost heaves, expelled like ancient eggs waiting to incubate in the mild sun.

In addition to listening to the games at the kitchen table with his mother every evening, those are Coach's other deepest memories: trudging on stolid ankles across the farm, arms wrapped around one boulder at a time, re-clearing the field each spring and summer while his mother, often lacking a tractor, followed behind with a plow and a single mule, after which the two of them planted whatever section of field they had been able to clear, with long spells of daydreaming by Coach as he walked in a trance, and labored, it seemed to him, in a sea of light, as if at the bottom of the shallow old sea that had been there so long ago.

He was betranced, also, by his own physical exhaustion: for as long as there were stones—or, rather, for as long as there was daylight, for there were always stones—he would march back and forth across the fields, belly-gripping each boulder as if he were fused to it. In the absence of any tractor clatter, the only sound was the ever-present wind, and his own huffing as he struggled onward, the muscles in his neck and back and upper legs burning, his calves sometimes so aflame that it seemed he could light a cigarette just by touching it to them. He was not a tall boy, but his arms stretched longer over the years.

Occasionally in his work he spied something glinting in the loosened dirt—an arrowhead, the tip of buffalo skull—and stopped to pry it out, the regularity of his days leavened by such small discoveries.

A pocketful of arrowheads, and then a box of them, then several boxes, to sell to the museum in Great Falls for spending money. (Later, when he got older, he returned all his unsold arrowheads to the tribe that had last occupied that land, the Blackfeet.) It was said that farther down were the bones of dinosaurs from millions of years ago. But his and his mother's work never plowed deeper than the last few hundred years. He was never bored, for even then he knew he was waiting, that something big would happen, and when it did, he would be in charge, for once, of the change.

In junior high school, still a boy, he pined for his father, but then hardened up, welded shut that lockbox. He played high school ball, and with his long arms was a leading rebounder and a pretty fair shooter but a rogue defender, always fouling out in the fourth quarter when his team needed him most. The welds on the lockbox were not yet firmly set, and seeps of loneliness and desire still trickled into it at inopportune times. Confusing his coach with his father, raging and rebelling and acting out, frustrated by his inability to be perfect, he quit midway through his junior year, thinking the coach would come pleading for him to return.

No such drama ensued. He was replaced with a lesser player who, as if by mere mechanical tooling, soon developed into the same caliber of player Coach had been, and the team neither anguished nor prospered in his absence but instead continued on as if he had never been there—a realization that sent him reeling into yet more rebellion and trouble, including numerous fistfights, early in his senior year. A little juvenile detention. But then his old coach intervened, and took him back under certain conditions: community service, a curfew, extra time in the gym. Nothing revolutionary, just attention and faith or, if not that, hope.

Coach had been mere days—perhaps hours—away from the abyss. And yet one of the attributes of a small town, for better or worse, seemed to be that you could never really get all the way lost. So many paths and choices and dead-end trails were available to him in small-town high school; before his coach got hold of him, the only two plays he knew were quit or fight. But that old coach— long gone now—essentially adopted him; mentored him in the art of pick-and-rolls, give-and-gos, diamond-plus-ones; blew heavy, iron-forging bellows into the last fissures remaining in the hidden lockbox. He set Coach afire, transformed him into a crackling pyre of unrestrained hunger, and made the confines of the basketball court the new boundaries of the world. He taught him where the cracks and secret crevices of the game were, so that giants might be toppled. Showed him, in other words, how to coach.

School ended. With no money for college and no scholarship offers, he went into the army. Stationed in Germany, he played basketball at various overseas bases, and served long enough to qualify for college on the GI Bill. He came back home and, in addition to studying Montana and Native American history, got a degree in psychology. There was little new he learned in the psych classes other than the names for the things he already understood.

His father, who had never even coached, survived a major stroke when he was thirty-nine. Coach is a ticking bomb, has always been one, but how glorious has been the pulse of each victory, and how excruciating and torturous each loss, whether large or small, expected or not.

His early years of coaching were easily the best of his life. He was back on the eastern plains, his mother was in remission, his heart was not yet bothering him, and he had a couple of flashy sophomores with whom he could envision standing beneath the bright lights of the state championship in a couple of years. Of course, there was no guarantee he could hold his team together for that long. The pressures of small-town, rural communities on adolescents were intense, on or off the reservation, and he was forever losing his most promising players to scholastic probation, bulimia and anorexia, teen pregnancy, drug and alcohol abuse, divorce and family dramas and relocations.

Still, he loved it. He loved it all. He involved himself in every possible hour of his girls' lives, riding herd on their friends, keeping track of whom they hung out with and what they did, and scheduling as many team dinners and bowling nights and movie nights as he could. It was high energy, high maintenance, but necessary to weave a fabric, a culture, of success.

Then the army called him up—he'd stayed in the Reserves. He was stationed in Lebanon, was shot at and dodged bombs for two full years before there were any studies confirming what everyone already knew: that two years of bombings were not good for the psyche; that one single blast event could take a lifetime to recover from. When that conflict ended he was still alive, and still loved basketball, still had the blind spots of a genius, and now, courtesy of his patriotism, a new impatience and irritability that he chose to confuse, though he knew better, with his old drive.

He relaunched himself into his true heart, his one self, with such momentum and focus that for the most part he was able to stay out ahead of the trauma, as if he'd slapped the ball away from an opponent and was sprinting down the court with no one between him and the orange rim of the basket. Even in the off-season, when he couldn't rely on being consumed by coaching, he managed to ward off those memories of war: the shock of the first attacks in Lebanon, the shock of being hated indiscriminately and collectively—unfairly, it seemed, rather than specifically—when the first bombing victims, some Lebanese civilians and some American soldiers, were carried into his barracks.

How had he made it back to something as safe as girls' high school basketball, and with his soul intact? A good upbringing, he guessed. Through the game, he could put the horrors aside and keep them blocked out the way he taught his smaller players to lock down larger opponents with hinge-and-flange maneuvers. (He remembered a game from the reservation, before he went overseas, when his five-two guard and five-five small forward had manhandled a six-three girl, the district's leading scorer—held her to zero points and reduced her to a sobbing hulk on the bench midway through the third quarter, her confidence wrecked for the rest of the season and, to some extent, much of the rest of her career.)

Indeed, the mix of high passion and deep irrelevance wrought by basketball was therapy. He could use it to heal from a lifetime of setbacks and pain, as he urged his girls to do. He'd convinced himself that by making basketball his existence, there would be nothing left of his own disappointments to bleed over into the game. He knew it was a brave and foolish stratagem, simple and reckless.

Obsession can carry the obsessed a long way, but has its costs. He had trouble making friends anywhere. So much in this regard conspired against him, from the peripatetic nature of journeyman coaching to the social discomfort of being a military veteran in a politicized era. But it would be even harder here in the mountains. At least on the eastern plains, whenever he had taken a new job, he was swarmed with dinner invitations, neighborliness, potlucks; here, in Placerville, he hasn't received a single such invitation in his first two full days in town. Placerville strikes him as a place of brooding, of self-absorbed doubt and paranoia, as he has been told is the nature of most of the mountain folk, particularly during the basketball months—the dreary lock of winter followed by late-season slush and soggy gray. But no matter, the girls will be everything; he has staked his life on them, wants to save their lives just as his mother saved his.

It's true there's been a little dizziness and shortness of breath in the middle of some games. A few clustered strobes of eerie green light in the swimming darkness. Pain, sure, high in his chest, but what coach doesn't feel that sometimes? And if he is to be taken, is it not better to be taken quickly? What greater cruelty is there for an athlete than the slow diminishment of age?

All loss is abhorrent. In such matters, grace is nonexistent. Only passion matters.

On his third day in town, a Monday, the boosters invite him to a team dinner to meet the girls. He has already received his five-hundred-dollar signing bonus, courtesy of the state of Montana, and has taken his mother to meet her new doctor, who seems to know what he's doing. He's transferred his insurance policy to the new school, filled out the necessary paperwork for the twice-monthly trickle of a contribution into his teacher's retirement fund. He has met with the utility company and had the power turned on, and spent the weekend hammering and sawing, installing a wheelchair-access ramp for his mother. He's had the phone connected and the satellite dish installed, so they can watch all the world's various sporting events together, and so she can watch them by herself when he's at practice or traveling to away games. There are so few schools in their division in all of western Montana that the bus trips will be long, with the team often not arriving home from these distant points until around midnight.

Late on the afternoon of the team dinner, he finishes photocopying and hole-punching the playbooks he has prepared for the girls, and organizes the folders containing inspirational proverbs, exhortations, and mottoes as well as a list of training rules, philosophies, and regulations. He showers and shaves, kisses his mother good night—she naps every evening from five to eight, then reawakens to watch the delayed telecasts from Europe, or the late-start games from the West Coast.

The new doctor, who is more honest than the previous one as well as closer to her age, said, when asked his assessment of her future, that at this stage every day is a blessing, and that surely she must be aware of how fortunate she is to have lived so long and seen so much, and how proud she must be to have a son who loves her. And then, although the doctor is not really a basketball fan, he talked about the team, and their hopes for the coming year.

Coach leaves a note for his mother, just as he used to do as a boy when he went somewhere and she wasn't home. And then, feeling twenty years younger—every time he leaves one job and starts anew, it is this way, both terrifying and invigorating—he lugs the cardboard box, bulging with folders and playbooks, out to his truck, a 1982 Datsun, 360,000 miles, two-wheel drive, rust-gutted from road salt and the howling winds of the prairie.

Every bit as eager as a bridegroom preparing to lay eyes on his bride for the first time, he hurries, as though the church bells are beginning to ring, the short distance to the school, wanting to arrive before the girls do. He doesn't think he's seen any of them yet, though he's kept an eye out. The girls he's glimpsed, here and there, traveling through town or in the café or the grocery store or at the bowling alley, did not look like any basketball girls he's ever seen— though you never can tell. He's willing to be surprised.

He's the first one there. He puts a playbook on each of the nine desks at the front of the classroom. He makes sure there's chalk for the chalkboard. After a while, the boosters arrive, smiling and nervous and eager themselves, carrying grocery sacks and armloads of unidentifiable casseroles, salads, brownies. A crock pot of moose chili. Bread, cake, spaghetti: the meals of a thousand nightmares, but never has he been so glad to see them.

And then, at last, the girls themselves, trickling in, laughing and loose, graceful yet also wary, like wild animals stepping to a spring for a drink, knowing to be observant, perhaps even cautious, despite their thirst. But laughing, secure in one another's company.

Look at them! My God, they are beautiful—so young—loving each moment, not thinking about winning, or even basketball.

Coach smiles at them, more nervous than he can remember ever being before. He cannot help but read them with computer speed, and in his mind is already diagramming plays on the chalkboard and then erasing those plays and starting over.

He watches them slide into their seats. He had worried they might not be wonderful, might not be happy, might not be perfect.

Now the athletic director is introducing him, though Coach barely hears the words. He looks out at the girls, and still is not sure what he will tell them. This is the best part—the beginning—even better than the addiction of the game itself. He can tell by the athletic director's cadence and by the accruing stillness in the room—as when concentric ripples in a pond begin to vanish—that the introduction is winding down.

As if through a muffled tube, Coach hears the athletic director recite the ancient bromide about building character being more important than winning. No saying infuriates him more, but Coach tries to remain cool, and keeps smiling, almost stupidly, as if in agreement. He wills the throbbing vessels at his temple to stay submerged. He tries to think of something calming, something far away. Then he considers instead the joy of these girls gathered before him. The speed with which they are leaving childhood.

It's intoxicating to behold: this evanescent, yet enduring, moment of youth. And once more he stands at the edge of it. Hiding his secret heart—*I must win*—he smiles at them. It's really only an instant, melting already, but he steps up to the podium, into a place and a time where, and during which, no one will ever grow older or in any way diminish, but instead will burn brightly, purely, cleanly, and where each of them, even Coach himself, will, if only they can win, always be loved.

An Alcoholic's Guide
to Peru and Chile

It was late March in Montana, which meant fall in South America. At the bottom of the world, things were upside down. The leaves of the trees along the rivers were gold, orange, yellow.

Wilson had been out of work, out of logging, for over a year. A snag had broken off when he was sawing and had fallen and shattered his ribs, punctured his lungs. Belinda had been gone almost a year by then. He hadn't seen that coming either.

He had been drinking hard over the winter—well, longer than that; maybe a few years, depending on what *hard* meant—but planned to stop for this trip, spring break with the girls. Or to slow down, anyway. It was almost the same thing. It felt like stopping. The girls lived with him, in Montana, but soon enough, they would be gone altogether: grown up, departed also.

He didn't need to drink. He liked it, but he didn't need it. He knew that was the stance of someone who did need to drink, but he was different. Well, actually, he needed it, but he could go a little bit without it. Beer was safe. He was drinking too much but he could stop. He *would* stop, he promised himself, for the trip.

In North America Belinda had told him he was a bum, but in South America he could be...well, whatever the opposite of that was. He was pretty sure he could stay off the sauce. Chile was said to be good wine country.

His older daughter, Stephanie, had just turned eighteen, and asked most of the questions in the family. Lucy, fifteen, answered them. In a few months, Stephanie would be off at college: gone forever, he believed. Though he didn't have the money to pay for her college—there was that small detail—nor for their journey to South America, nor for much of anything else, really. Even their cabin in the woods—built by Wilson—was no longer secure. Workers' comp hadn't been enough, and then had run out anyway. Soon enough he wouldn't be able to pay the mortgage. He felt life draining away and, panicked, topped out his last credit card. He needed this trip with the girls, one grand last hurrah before everything changed.

He'd asked Belinda to go with them. She was living in Oregon. He asked not with any hope for reconciliation—there remained only the final legal and financial disentanglements—but wanting to believe she might, for old times' sake, come on the trip, that they might re-create some semblance of a family, if only for a short while. But she'd refused. "It's a farce," she said. "There's no money."

Nothing Wilson didn't already know. "I'll make it back," he told her, though his ribs, a year later, still hadn't fully healed and he didn't know when he'd be able to work again. "I know it's been a little rough, but I can get us out of this."

She refused to have anything to do with it. "Go ahead," she told him, "burn it all. I don't care anymore."

He supposed he understood how she could think he was becoming a bum.

It didn't used to be that way. The bars: Trixi's in Ovando. The Murray in Livingston, and Gil's. The Home Bar in Troy, site of an alarming number of shootings. Charlie B's in Missoula. Wherever there were big trees and chain saws to cut them down with, there were good bars, where the real business was drinking, to numb sore muscles and still the vibrations of the big saws. Anyone who ran a saw knew where they were.

He was not an alcoholic back then. Each night he had walked home to his hotel from such places, weaving a bit, but possessed of an athleticism that allowed him to correct any imbalance. A tightrope walker of fallen logs. Stopping to look up at the stars and watch his breath leap in exultant clouds, like smoke billowing from a slash pile. *Not a drunk*. In a few hours he'd be booting up to go back into the woods and run the saw all day. Burning the days on the elixir of joy and adrenaline, living a life that had meaning. Under such rigor and focus, he had flourished.

The day he met Belinda he had not been drinking. He was hauling a load of pulp to the old paper mill in Frenchtown, coming up out of the Bitterroot with a trailer of burned logs. He'd been idling in Missoula traffic: Reserve Street, August, 104 degrees. He would have liked a beer, had six cans bright and shiny in the ice chest—back then, a six-pack might last him a couple of days—and her car was stalled in traffic right in front of him.

He pushed the gears into neutral, set the parking brake—five tons of burned lodgepole glinting and shimmering black in the haze of late summer. The hills beyond town were still burning from summer fires. He climbed down and walked over to her car. He could feel the soles of his boots softening against the heat of the pavement.

Her window was already down. "Who are you?" she asked. Her eyes were hidden behind the designer sunglasses she would always wear in the years to come, her smile warm and engaging.

"I was sent to rescue you," Wilson said.

"You goddamned took long enough," she said. She was wearing shorts, flip-flops, and a yellow T-shirt. She'd just applied lipstick; he thought it might have been the first thing she'd done when her car overheated. He thought she might be an actress.

The traffic parted around them. Anyone driving by would have thought they were passing an accident.

Belinda got her purse and gym bag, locked the doors, and handed the bag to Wilson. She walked with him back to his truck and climbed up into the cab from the passenger's side.

That night they went up to Rock Creek, drove way up the canyon to the swinging bridge, suspended far above the shimmering rapids. In the cold heart of the canyon they sat on the bridge's old planks— the bridge slung low in its center with their weight, like a belly, so high above the rapids. They drank beer and watched the stars, with the scent of forest fires farther back in the mountains sweet-smelling in the cool of the canyon. Then they lay on the bridge and slept with their heads tucked together, no need for a blanket, the river low and loud far beneath them.

They got married and he stopped going to bars. Soon enough the girls were born. Everything got magnificent, everything was perfect.

Why Peru, why Chile? Like so much in his life of late, it was almost all about instinct, with little if any calculation or reason. A kind of falling, a kind of leaping. It was true he was fascinated by the rock work of the Andes—stone walls and churches that had withstood the diminishments of the centuries—and wanted the girls to see that. He wanted to lay his hands upon something that had endured, and would go on enduring. He wanted to see two stones, three stones, four stones fit so tightly together a dollar bill could not be squeezed between their seams.

He'd checked out a few travel guides from the library, not quite the most current editions, and had printed out a map and made some reservations on the Internet.

In Peru, the first temple on their loose itinerary was in a small town with a long name that Wilson didn't even try to remember. They'd driven the rental car up a long unmarked road of crushed white limestone. They passed wicker stalls, thatched-roof huts where vendors sold leather goods: purses, bags, hats. Tiny burros stood in the shade, swishing their tails, their backs loaded with what seemed impossible burdens.

Wilson used to pay close attention to things—back when he'd gone into the woods every day—but now there were times when he seemed to see almost nothing. In these fugues, the world's sights and sounds came to him as if he were underwater.

At one point he noticed the girls clutching bags; they must have passed through a market. He couldn't recall. He looked at their bags—full of trinkets for their friends back home, he imagined. Such thoughtful young women, so fully engaged in everything. And they were definitely watching him. How badly he wanted a glass of wine at lunch, and a beer in the evening. A once-in-a-lifetime journey. He deserved it! But he would wait. At least until they were more settled into the trip.

Worse than their watching him to see if he was going to drink, his daughters appeared to want from him some kind of guidance—not where to go or what to do, but the deeper kind—and when he noticed this, all he could think to do was try to keep them from seeing quite how bad a spot he and they were in. He could think of nothing witty or charming or courageous or even intelligent to say.

For Stephanie, the questioner, he knew it was harder to ignore the various intimations of trouble; she tended to believe the worst of a situation—a defense mechanism, he understood, a way to prepare herself for when things went sour, as they had all too often in the past few years—while Lucy preferred to see the best in everything, whether it deserved it or not.

Their guide at the temple, a short elderly man with skin the color of a dried fig and large silver glasses—like a little owl—had been talking for some time. He was telling them about the Dominicans, who, Wilson gathered, had painted all the lurid murals after stripping the walls of the gold with which they were lined. They had razed much of the structure with halfhearted malice, a kind of bored destruction. But they had gotten tired before they finished the task and so built their church upon the ruins. And then one day they, too, vanished.

"This way," the little man was saying, and at first Wilson had the thought the man was trying to take care of him. But the guide turned his back on Wilson and was bending the herd down one hallway and then another. "Follow me," he said, leading several tourists by the elbow. He was beginning to work the softies—the old ladies, young professional couples—for tips, sizing up his marks.

"We are walking through the corridors of what was once the richest place on earth," the guide said. "The most beautiful place." In his fervor, the guide had developed the trace of a lisp, and whether it was affected or evidence of true emotion, Wilson could not be sure.

It was excruciating, watching the other tourists—German, British, Japanese—lean forward, made rapturous by these whispers of wealth. All Wilson wanted was a drink. A nice cold beer in a frosted glass with a lime perched on top of it. A pale golden lager with the South American sunlight strafing through it, a cyclone of bubbles rising through that light with their vortex of promise. His hand, reaching slowly for it.

The guide unclipped from his shoulder strap the case he'd been carrying and set it down on a nearby table, then flipped the locks open. Wilson had thought it was a camera bag, but the guide lifted the lid and stared down as if gazing at an artifact—a great treasure he had been saving for the point in the tour when the travelers became worthy of it.

The case held a series of wires, a small black box with red LED digits, and a tiny gray plastic cup, which the guide placed on the tip of his left index finger. He turned the machine on and watched as the digits melted, then reestablished: 96, 97, 98, 99, 100.

The guide smiled. "My blood oxygen," he said, "is good. I notice that some of you are looking pale. We are at a great elevation here. You are not used to it. I must take your oh-two counts. I am responsible for you." He took the cup and placed it on the tip of the finger of the eldest woman, slipping it on as he might a wedding ring.

"Ninety-four, ninety-five...Oh, lady, I think you had better sit down for a minute." He rested his hand on her back and led her to an ornate emperor's chair made of dark carved wood. The guide patted the old lady's hand and moved on to the rest of his marks.

Mostly ninety-eights. "No one ever has one hundred," the guide said. "I am the only one." He did not place the cup on the children's fingers because, he said, "Children are immune to the changes in elevation."

Wilson knew this to be untrue but did not protest. He looked over at Stephanie and Lucy and saw that they were all right, they did not appear weak or afflicted with malaise in any way. *Sturdy*. Then, without knowing what devilment seized him, he held out his own hand for the guide, who glowered—time was wasting—but came over and fitted him nonetheless. *No tip money here,* Wilson's eyes said, illumined with brief mirth, and he and the guide watched as the meter pegged 97, but no higher.

"Perhaps you should sit down," the guide said, not kindly, "and have a cup of coca tea." Wilson's eyes hardened. *He knows,* he thought, *how can he know?*

The guide was already turning away, packing up his apparatus.

"Come on," Wilson said to Stephanie and Lucy. "We need to go."

"Wait," Stephanie said, "I have a question." At first Wilson thought she too wanted to have her oxygen tested, and was surprised to hear her ask the guide, "Those Dominicans—did they ever bury their victims alive?"

The guide was taken aback. His mouth, as though instinctively, began to form itself into a *no,* but then—perhaps because Stephanie, with her straw-blond hair, freckles, small nose, and pale blue eyes like a saint, was so unthreatening—he admitted he didn't know.

Now everyone looked around as if seeing the temple anew, with empathy not only for the way the great temple had been reduced to rubble, but also for the way its inhabitants had been forced to swallow the dirt heaped upon them by their destroyers as their voices and very breath, shovelful by shovelful, had been taken from them, until finally they were gone.

Lucy—looking much like a younger version of her sister, but slighter, almost delicate—raised her hand.

"Of course they did," she said: as if she had been reading about it for months, years, beforehand.

Her voice has changed, Wilson thought. When did that happen?

Back at the hotel in Lima that night—the fourth night of their journey—Wilson tripped over one of their suitcases in the room and, as he was falling, hit his head against the wall. His shoulder was dinged, and his head scraped, but he was otherwise okay. Nevertheless he saw in the girls' eyes the fear that he had been drinking, which annoyed him, as he had assiduously avoided a drop since arriving in Peru.

He tried to think of a way to reassure them he was in control. But to say *I'm not drunk* would be to acknowledge that it was sometimes a problem. All he could do was dust himself off, and make a to-do about placing the suitcase in a corner, where it should have been in the first place, rather than where anyone could trip over it.

He didn't like seeing fear or even discomfort in the girls. He remembered, randomly, a line from a children's book he had read to them when they were little: *She was not raised in the jungle to be frightened of a lion.* If they wanted to be worried about something, he thought, the more understandable concern would be money. When he thought about their finances, he couldn't breathe—what use was there for a logger who could no longer run a saw? The thought was burying him, and he tried to avoid it.

And yet Stephanie, with her typical intuition and prescience—as though she were wired directly to his heart—asked later, while Lucy was in the bathroom, "How bad off are we?"

He flinched at her use of "we." He still wanted to believe it was all his burden.

But Stephanie had noticed he wasn't buying food for himself when they went out to eat. He'd been gathering fruit from hotel-lobby baskets and eating flat breads and grapes—whatever was free on restaurant tables.

"It's a tight spot," he admitted, "but it'll be okay. It's the eye of the needle, is all. We'll get through it, and then we'll be on the other side."

"How?" she persisted. "What are you going to do?"

"I'll cut more trees," he said. He looked around at their brown-carpeted room. It could have been a hotel room in Billings, or Havre, or Stevensville: anonymous, soul-sucking. The real life, the real world, was on the outside. Oh, how he wanted a drink. For his ribs, if nothing else.

"Dad," she said, "you can barely tie your boots some mornings."

He paused, wondering when she had seen that. "I'm healing up," he said. "I'm recovering."

She wanted to believe him, and yet wanted not to be fooled. He saw this in her—the way she existed perfectly, and with some effort, in the middle: sharp-eyed, vigilant—and he felt a flicker of guilt for it. He was the one who existed at the edges and extremes, he thought, forcing others to hold on to the middle.

Sometimes it seemed to him there was a chapter missing from his life. A part he had neglected to live, something he had left undone, and that all of this tension and unease was solely his burden and responsibility. That he possessed in his essence something unlovable that communicated itself to the world, making him then even more so.

Still, the idea lingered that he could always saw his way through the forest and into the light; that if only he had worked harder at controlling the journey, everything would have been better, and he would have been loved more. Somehow the world had gotten the upper hand on him when he looked away.

He remembered crossing the Missouri River once, on the old ferry near Virgelle, when he and Belinda and the girls had gone on a rare vacation. A two-day drive from northwest Montana out to the prairie, up and over the mountains and into the forever flatlands. Summertime. They'd followed country roads. Grasshoppers clicked up in front of them and gravel tinkled against the undercarriage of the car. Mourning doves, feeding on sunflowers, sprang up from both sides of the road before the car's approach, the doves' wings fanning as if spreading alms. The girls were nine and six.

Wilson had it in mind to go see the White Cliffs near Geraldine, and the sandstone rock where William Clark had carved his name, two hundred years earlier.

By the time they reached the crossing at Virgelle it was dusk, with the last of the day's light sinking into the chalky soil like an animal bedding down for a nap. In the tall grass at the edge of the broad river a tilting hand-lettered sign, its red paint sun-faded, directed them to push a buzzer mounted on a pole, as if ringing a doorbell. The ferryman would come over and pick them up.

The river, the color of chocolate milk, made deep gurgling sounds and ran with great force, carrying an occasional cottonwood trunk, but the girls trusted everything. Across the river a deer stepped out of the grass and lowered her head to drink from an eddy. She lifted her head and watched them.

Behind the deer, in that dimming light, stood a big white house within a grove of wind-bent cottonwoods, their leaves summer-thick. A deep porch encircled the house, and Wilson imagined the shade of the trees kept the house cool, as did the high ceilings. A tire swing hung from a branch of one of the largest trees. He wondered briefly about the family who lived there. He pictured their lives filled with an almost unbearable happiness.

Even as they were looking at the house it was vanishing, as the onrushing darkness rolled over it like a surf and the night covered the house. A light flared inside and moments later a figure emerged, accompanied by all manner and sizes of children, as if in a controlled evacuation. The silhouettes made their way to the river, where the barge lay canted on the shore like some wreck from a distant war.

A lone cable of frayed steel, anchored to concrete blocks, spanned the distance to the far shore. A motor started, and the barge began laboring toward them, low in the water, battling the current. Only now that the barge was broadside to the current could they see how truly strong the river was—quick, deep, relentless.

Midway across, the motor faltered, then stopped, and the ferryman lit a lantern and went into the engine room. A few moments later, the engine coughed back to a start and the journey resumed, and Wilson's heart flooded with the sweet sensation of being rescued, an emotion no less pleasurable for the fact that he and his family were in no actual danger.

The barge—still straining, but resolute—breached their shore, sending up wavelets of fish-smelling water, and they saw now that the ferryman was a woman. Wilson counted ten children with her. Some stayed on the barge, while others leapt off even as she was releasing the winch that lowered the gangplank.

The barge was not much wider than their narrow car, and Wilson realized it had been built back in a day when all cars were small: Model As, Model Ts. If it had lasted this long, surely it had one more run in it; and with the ferrywoman motioning them aboard, he and Belinda and the girls got back in the car and eased forward onto the ferry, which bobbed under their weight. As if running late, the ferrywoman pulled the gate up behind them quickly. Before they knew they had started, they looked down and saw that they had reversed direction and were plowing the Missouri.

Stars; a crescent moon. A heron flew downriver, its wing beats unheard over the throb of the motor. The silhouette of the slender cable above them—their tether—trembled like a fishing line.

The barge was tilted—one side sucked slightly down into the upstream current, and the opposite side pitched up—and was without a railing. Yet all around them, the woman's children rolled and tumbled like puppies. One of them, a boy, climbed up onto the hood and peered inside at them, made silly google eyes. *Nasty boys,* Wilson thought. *Damn, I was lucky.*

A warm breeze blew through their open windows. Beside them, the ferrywoman lit a cigarette, watched the ferry's progress, and leaned in Belinda's window. Like a winged harpy, another of her boys leapt from out of the darkness and onto her back, fastening himself to her. A few sparks from her cigarette jarred upward, but other than that, she seemed not to notice.

She told Belinda, "You can get out, if you want."

They stepped from their car. Wilson held each girl's hand too tightly—they wriggled in his grip, accustomed to it and resisting it at once. With the caution of horses going onto a frozen pond, the four of them walked to the bow of the barge to look out at the moon, and at the darker line of the shore toward which they strove. Wilson's head filled with images of how, if a sunken log, current-driven, jarred against the barge, the girls could be pulled from his grip and spill into the big river. He marveled again that there was no railing.

And yet: the air was delicious, a true wind now. Belinda's and the girls' hair swirled and clung to their faces. Wilson had never experienced a power like the current beneath them. He felt it, electric, through the iron boat. Still gripping the girls' hands ferociously, he turned to kiss Belinda. She smiled at him, but stepped back then, somehow nervous. Or was it more than that?

The engine struggled—missing but never quitting. Midriver, the sagging cable keeping them on track seemed more insubstantial than ever.

The ferrywoman joined them out on the bow.

"Are all those yours?" Belinda asked.

How do they know not to leap in? Wilson wondered.

The ferrywoman's cigarette glowed brighter. "Yep," she said. There was neither pride nor exhaustion in the statement.

"Does this thing ever break?" Wilson asked, pointing to the cable. Imagining the swirling ride downstream, spinning in teacup circles.

"It never has, for me, yet," she said. Wilson noticed that she spoke in commas, as if accustomed to a life of rowing. "It did, once, to the woman before me," she said.

That might have been the place, Wilson thinks, deep into his excavation, a continent away from the land of his heart. How tightly he'd held on to the girls' hands, and how fitting and proper it had been to do so. They had been little, back then, mountain girls who knew nothing of big rivers. It had been terrifying but exhilarating, and after they reached the far shore and paid the ferrywoman, they continued through the black night of the prairie with the windows rolled down, the air washing over their arms and the afterglow of the experience illuminating their blood, as if with an effervescence.

But they had continued on, deeper into the night, and he had not changed.

In a light rain, Wilson and the girls visited another ruination. It was an outdoor shrine, one of the largest in Peru—out in a broad and green valley, with hewn boulders so immense they radiated their own life force and gravity.

The Incas had believed the stones possessed their own wills. Their new guide, a clean-shaven Peruvian who had studied history at Purdue not so long ago, told them that the outline of the boulders, which wandered the meadow in sinuous fashion, was actually arranged to form the perfect shape of a mountain lion. The anatomy was precise, with each bone-to-body ratio exact. The stone puma was half a mile long.

"You can see it from outer space," the guide said, "but here on the ground, you can see none of it." He cast his hand toward the horizon. "There are no mountains high enough to give a clear view of this structure. How did they get it perfect? It is a mystery. You cannot see it. You cannot know it."

The guide seemed to descend then, to the bottom of a cool, deep well within himself, dwelling there for a moment or two before reemerging with a slightly different, more compassionate bearing— and Wilson thought, *I could have a drink with this fellow.* A man with two countries, two continents.

The guide, having kicked back upward from his brief introspection—like a conch diver rising to the shimmer of light above—looked at his clients now with tenderness. "Do you think this structure was built during a time of war," he asked, "or a time of peace?"

"War," said a middle-aged British man; his son, a round behemoth, nodded in agreement. There was no doubt about it, and like the cheepings of birds, the word *war, war,* rose now from the lips of many, a staggered, murmuring assent.

The guide, serene from the place he had visited moments ago, shook his head.

"I myself think it must have been a time of great peace," he said. "Such care and attention could not have been possible during the strife of war. *No.* I think the puma was built as an offering to the Inca god, and to say to all, *Look at how powerful we are, do not attack us.*

"It took fifty years to build," the guide said.

The rain was coming down harder, and the tour-goers pressed in closer against one of the puma's boulders, having no idea whether it was a haunch, paw, or neck, seeking only respite from the cold rain; but there was no protection.

Vendors appeared, selling plastic ponchos and plastic puma key chains. Stephanie bought a key chain and handed it to Wilson. "Not as fierce as our Montana lions," she said, and laughed. How much she looked like her mother when she laughed.

Another vendor, clad in a metallic sandwich board—an aluminum beer keg cut in half and wrapped around him—waddled toward them with a hissing propane stove attached to the improvised metal jacket, which possessed various nozzles for the dispensing of hot water, cocoa, or coffee.

The apparatus steamed in the mist. The vendor carried paper cups and a change pouch. The silver keg looked not unlike the armor conquistadores had worn in their malicious advance centuries earlier, and Wilson bought the girls hot cocoa, and a coffee for himself, and nearly wept at the injustice that there was no brandy, no rum, no anything, just lukewarm coffee and cold rain.

The guide was still talking. "Fifty years and twenty thousand workers," he said. "It would have taken one man a million years to build this. But working together, they did it in fifty. Each man wanted to build something that would last forever. Which they did. You are standing in it," the guide said. "You are in the remnants of greatness."

That afternoon, in Lima, they went to a large outdoor market. They stopped on the way to watch a military celebration on a great lawn, some kind of anniversary, rows of horses in military dress and men in heavy wool uniforms sweating in the bright equatorial sun, bedecked with guns and swords, their leather boots creaking. A general came out onto a third-story balcony and spoke to the throng, his words unintelligible and strident. The horses were sweating too, their legs and chests laced with thick veins. Wilson and the girls walked on, away from the megaphonic soundscape of the shouting general.

The market was crowded, tables jammed up against one another, overflowing—birdcages, woven shawls, wallets and purses, wooden carvings. The girls, rather than seeking curios for themselves, collaborated on a purchase for Wilson: a pair of handmade leather dress shoes, a fawn color, soft and delicate, only ten dollars, and a well-tailored blazer to match, the same amount. What does a logger need with these things? he wondered, and then had a chilling thought: *Maybe they think I won't recover. Maybe they're picturing a second part of my life, one where I'm no longer in the woods.*

Back home, such luxuries were unthinkable—he would never have purchased these things for himself—and he felt a catch in his throat and his eyes mist.

They like me the way I am, he thought, *but maybe they just want me to look a little better.* He examined the beautiful jacket and could not imagine ever wearing it, but touched the clean new fabric, beheld it as he might the raiment of a king.

The rush of traffic and jackhammer clatter of Lima agitated Wilson. But at the Hotel Ajo there was an extravagant garden in the lobby, an atrium of orchids, bromeliads, and birds of paradise, along with dining tables set next to splashing fountains—a great calmness, like that of a greenhouse. It was here that Wilson devised a plan. He would lie awake as the girls fell asleep, waiting until around one a.m., when he would go downstairs and out on the town to find a drink—just one, or maybe two—and then return to the room, brush his teeth, and change out of the clothes in which he had taken the drinks. Not that he would spill anything, he was not that kind of drinker, but the girls would be able to smell the sharp fumes of vodka clinging to the fibers of his shirt, or the oaty scent of beer. After changing out of his clothes, he would sleep until seven or eight, ready to begin the day.

It was workable, he decided. It would not take him away from his daughters. It would not take him away from anything. It was a simple solution and there were plenty of hours in the day.

Damn it, he thought, walking out the door barefooted, carrying his sandals in his hand. It had all gone by too fast. Now would come college, then jobs; boyfriends, husbands, children, grandchildren. He could feel the last of it falling away.

The hotel was at the edge of an upscale suburb, but, as seemed so often the case to him down here, the rich existed shoulder to shoulder with the less fortunate. By turning away from the glow of town and toward the darkness, he would be able to find what he was looking for soon enough.

He walked, alert, looking for a light, any light. The bars he passed were all closed; the streets were narrow and uneven. He felt extraordinarily sober but intended to change that. A cat dashed across the street in front of him, then stopped and looked back, as though believing, briefly, that Wilson might have something for it.

At last he came to a building where he could smell alcohol, could hear bar sounds: voices and the delicate clink of glasses and bottles. As if he had prayed the place into existence. But it didn't seem like a real bar; instead, it was simply a large room with a low-leaning adobe doorway where, inside, some people were drinking. Definitely not a tourist haunt, just a local drinking room. Was an invitation necessary? He hoped not.

He stepped inside: dark, with a dirt floor. Three haggard old men sat at the bar—more of a long, high table—drinking slowly, heroically, so drunk that it took great effort and willpower for them even to lift their mugs, which they did from time to time.

All manner of local characters were present. Wilson had barely gotten his first drink before a man sidled up and, with no explanation, took a deep breath and then sat there, quivering and turning blue, for long moments that melted, unbelievably, as if into years, until the man finally gasped, and sucked in a double lungful of what surely was the sweetest-tasting air imaginable.

Once he had regained his composure, the man explained that he was an ex–conch diver who, long ago, had been able to hold his breath for five minutes. Although he could no longer go quite that long, it was a tradition, he said, that any time he held his breath for three minutes the recipient of this demonstration had to buy him a beer. Wilson obliged.

There were others in the strange room: a man who said he used to be a sword swallower; an old gaucho with holes in his dusty boots, through which the tips of his battered toes protruded; and another fellow who claimed to be an ex-general. The house specialty was a dark rum drink served from a large clay urn with bright wedges of lime floating in the top of it.

No Americans, which made Wilson comfortable. How wonderful for this late-night stroll to have brought him an authentic, nontourist experience, and how very much his drinking had come in handy here, helping him to achieve it, and to be accepted—welcomed even!

A lady appeared, an American he thought at first, but no, Argentinean born and raised, it turned out, black eyes, smile as wide as an alligator's. She was luminous in the darkness, wearing a simple bright yellow sundress, and her skin was dark, though as she drew closer he saw how sun-damaged it was. She sat down on the stool next to him and held his arm, speaking to him in accented English. Her facial expressions were extravagant—the lift of her eyebrows, the pursing of her lips—and labored, as if in slow motion.

She had a blue-sequined box with a strap on it, like a case made to carry an accordion but with breathing holes punched into it, and she said the box was full of guinea pigs. Wilson had not yet mentioned his daughters, but she urged him to buy one, to buy more, one for each of his children. She too was drinking the dark rum from the urn, and offered to help name the guinea pigs, if he would buy them.

He guessed the woman to be in her midfifties. She still possessed a haggard allure, but the aura of shipwreck was strong upon her now.

Her silvering hair was lovely, and when she smiled, her lined face was festive, promising a great merriment to which she must once have been accustomed. Yet the instant she stopped smiling, it seemed that she was sinking, and no one cared any longer to hazard a rescue.

Wilson felt a compassion for her, a surprising bond of intimacy. And as they drank and talked, he came to understand that she could see inside his own fall. That she understood his love for his daughters, his distress at his family's ongoing dissolution, and the widening gyre of his daughters' growing-up lives. The dawn of his own physical diminishment—he who had once been nothing but physical. Maybe, he thought, they could hold each other up for a night, and he reached out and put his hand on her arm, just to see how she would take it; and she smiled at him.

This was how it had been in the rough bars and logging camps of his youth, he remembered. Long nights of great fun and nothingness, an unending scroll of meaningless encounters. Now he had nothing again. A loneliness greater than the sum of its empty parts.

He knew he was leaning on his girls like a drunken sailor, and they knew it too. He understood, briefly, during one of the drinks, that he needed to lighten up and let them go.

In an effort to stir more drink-buying, the bartender turned on a staticky radio. Wilson and the guinea-pig woman danced. He was having fun now, he thought, but with the terror of a greater loneliness yet. The small of the woman's back in his hand felt like an animal that might bolt, or charge him. He wanted to get home to his girls, but kept waltzing. Finally he leaned in and rested against the woman. It would take thirty, forty years to come to know her fully. The idea astounded him. He needed to get back to the girls before they were gone.

When the dance was done, Wilson had three more rum-and-lime drinks—drank them until after they had lost their limey, fizzy luster. The conch diver had long ago fallen asleep at his table, though in his sleep he had a troubling cough.

The guinea-pig woman had a million stories, as he'd known she would: as if she were composed of stories. Her fatigue seemed to elicit them. They came flowing from her now, as though they were the essence of her sleep, and her dreams. She loved animals. She had run a zoo, she said, where she lay down to sleep with the elephants. She stretched a long, languorous arm toward him, and he noticed a jagged scar on the inside of her elbow. She leaned closer against Wilson and laid her head on his shoulder. There were more stories. She had worked on a sailboat in the Galápagos, taking people out to swim with dolphins and even whale sharks, whose spots, she said, look like the lights of cities sunk to the bottom of the sea.

She looked down at her scar, massaged it as if with great affection. "But I have a dark side too," she said. "I have spent time in jail." She said this as if she had nothing to do with it, and was as puzzled by it as she would be by an unexpected turn in the weather.

Wilson did not betray his surprise. "Well, a lot of people have," he said, "at least for a day or two." He squeezed her hand. "I'm sorry." He started to ask why but sensed, even in his growing inebriation, that if she wanted him to know, she would have told him; and he imagined that if he was patient, he would find out soon enough.

"I must be a dangerous woman," she said, her head still on his shoulder.

He glanced down at her and smiled. She looked up then, and he touched her cheek. She was no longer young but it still felt good to Wilson for someone to care enough to make up such stories. He ordered yet another drink.

The woman looked over toward one of the room's dark corners, where a large man was watching them unhappily. "He does not like you," she said. "He does not like us talking."

Wilson asked if she wanted another drink but she said no, that she was done. She sat with him while he finished his and told him a convoluted tale of family—sisters and bad husbands, wronged and complicated women, harsh circumstances, strife. Wilson tuned out the second half of it as he had been doing with the tour guides— his endurance for almost everything was gone—and then the woman was saying that the story had made her sad, that she was going out-side to clear her mind of such things. She asked if Wilson wanted to join her.

He was surprised to realize that he did not want to go any further.

He was hammered, and ready to call it an evening, but walked out with her to say good night.

Outside, she lit a cigarette and drifted away from the weak light in front of the drinking room. She seemed lost, still troubled by the last story she had told. She stopped in front of a hedge with large pink blossoms that seemed to glow in the darkness. Their scent was sweet, like too much perfume, almost overpowering. The tip of her cigarette glowed, and she was visible only in dim silhouette.

After a minute she turned toward him and nodded, as though finally coming out of her funk. As he walked toward her, someone tapped him on the shoulder.

It was the big man from the bar, disturbingly close—he smelled like a dog in need of a bath, and was angry. Wilson understood he was about to be struck, but before the big man could hit him, the guinea-pig woman's face loomed in front of him, leering now.

He was confused and realized only then just how drunk he was. The woman's face was garish, streaked as if with war paint: as if she had applied it for this very occasion. She raised a brick—at first he thought it was a loaf of bread, that she wanted to feed him, and he felt a great hunger—and then, though without great force, she struck it against his head.

He felt his teeth and nose break, or so it seemed, and he was so stunned he did not even fall, though he wanted to. Now the big man hit him twice in the face hard and fast, so quick that Wilson understood he was a boxer—the man hitting him twice when once would have been enough, as he was already on the way down, but then checking his third swing—and Wilson's knees sought the pavement, and then his elbows, a mendicant.

The woman was reaching in his pocket, wrenching his billfold from him, while the man kicked his ribs, once on each side, as if to drive the air from Wilson's lungs so that he could not cry out for help; but Wilson had no intention of crying out for help. His ribs were not yet fully healed from his logging accident and yet here they were, being broken yet again.

The sensation of their breaking was so familiar—half a world away—that it staggered him. When the tree snag had broken, his first thought was *How can something I love hurt me?* And here it was again, muted but the same: he had been feeling affection, though certainly not love, and yet look, his ribs were now broken all over again.

Just a mugging! he thought, with the raw sorrow of loneliness, of foolishness. *I would have given them my wallet.* He felt her going away somehow, felt both of them leaving, and he thought, *I miss her.*

He crawled, slithering toward and then into the sweet-scented hedge, and heard them laughing as they walked away.

The wallet didn't matter. He'd spent most of his cash on the drinks, and the credit cards were useless. His luck continued. His passport was in the room along with most of their traveler's checks, which he had allowed Stephanie to look after on the trip. She enjoyed being the organizer, the indexer, of all things large and small, in this regard not unlike her mother. He felt warm, cared for—relaxed, even though in pain.

He lay there for a long while, napping, happy in a way that mystified him and yet for which he was grateful. As if he had somehow gotten what he had been wishing for.

When he awoke, roosters were crowing and the day was not quite light. He rose and weaved down the street, still a little drunk, trying to find his way back to the hotel but not sure where it was and unable to remember its name, or even what it looked like.

But, feeling that his great luck was continuing, he arrived, after walking a long time, at a wrought-iron gate he recognized, and saw a cat in the garden he remembered—a small black cat with a white tuxedo vest. Wilson pressed the buzzer and limped up the steep steps and went inside, back into the familiar garden, where the desk clerk looked at him with concern but said nothing. He passed an elderly couple seated already for breakfast—damn their normalcy, their sweet and enduring matrimony. He felt a desire to harangue them. Instead, he hobbled up to his room, tried to sneak in quietly and crawl into bed, but the click of the door awakened both girls, who sat up and looked at him as if without recognition.

His shirt was torn and bloodied, his bloody nose had dried to a crust, a tooth was chipped, and one of his eyes was purple-black already.

He smiled his new crooked-toothed smile at them and they both began to cry immediately, and hurried over to him. They hugged him far too hard—he could barely stand to have his ribs touched—and he yelped, which made them draw back.

They smelled the rum and cigarettes, and cried harder as some of the pieces came together, while he in turn could smell sharply, even through the dried blood in his nose, their clean nightclothes. They smelled of home, smelled faintly of the forest and of wood smoke, of their shampoos and soaps. He knew those scents, and he was loved. He saw the fear in both their faces, but another thing, too, like anger, and he wanted to explain, to defend himself: *This was not my fault; this was not my doing.*

Something dark—darker than a storm cloud—passed across his fevered mind and, as if paralyzed, he watched it sail from one side of his mind all the way to the other, with its chill and its pure silence. Then, in the electrical storm of his brain, he thought: *How amazing that despite all this I am still in charge. How amazing that I am still in control.*

There was a feeling that they all needed to say something, and yet there seemed to be no words that could suffice, for no one spoke. Some glances around at each other, but nothing else.

He blacked out then, after watching the black cloud, and slept.

When he awoke, the girls looked pale and exhausted. He hurt far worse than when he'd gone to sleep.

While he'd been passed out, Lucy—fifteen!—had gone to a pharmacy and in pidgin Spanish purchased gauze bandages and wraps, tape, antibiotic ointment, and a tear-open packet of two aspirin, while Stephanie had sat beside him, wakeful, to make sure he did not vomit while sleeping and choke. He woke once to hear Lucy asking "Is he going to be all right?" and saw Stephanie look at her sister as if across a gulf greater than three years.

They still seemed unable to speak of it, the three of them struck equally mute, and with no discussion, the girls helped him into the bathroom. Wilson coughed and nearly fainted from the pain—he gripped their shoulders or would have fallen—but he had been down this path before and knew not to panic, to take shallow breaths, little sips of air, like a man who after swimming a great distance—days and nights—finds he must rest and tread water for a while.

Could he get better without talking about this? he wondered. How close to the edge was he? Correction: How far past the edge? His first honest thought in perhaps years. He didn't like the weight or density of it and quickly shoved it away. *Beer,* he thought, *I need a beer.*

"I know you're probably a little worried," he told them. His swollen, abraded face throbbed. He felt the roughness of his chipped tooth with his tongue. His sheets were bloody. He knew he looked a fright.

"What happened?" Lucy asked. "Were you drinking?"

"I don't know," he told them. "Not really. It was just a mugging." He saw the look on both their faces and paused. "Well," he said, "yes. I was drinking a little. Not too much." He shook his head. "I guess someone might say I had a little too much. I won't let it happen again."

Lucy's eyes watered, but she didn't cry. She had already cried.

Stephanie wanted to take a break from seeing ruins, so that same day, because Wilson was so sore, they took a cab across the city to one of Lima's museums. In a moment of further humiliation in the hotel room, he had asked Stephanie to chip in the few hundred dollars she had on her debit card, from babysitting, to supplement what remained of their traveler's checks. He hated to ask, he said, but he needed the extra help to tide them over. They rode through the traffic-clotted streets, through the horns and heat and the meat smoke of curbside vendors, to one of Lima's museums, where the highlight for all three of them was the spectacular, even gothic, *retablos*: hammered-tin dioramas filled with doll saints and angels, some wreathed in barbed wire, all of them untouchable, anguished, beautiful. The figures were jammed into miniature houses that were too small, as if the saints and angels were poised to fly out of the boxes that housed them—and although each *retablo* was similar, each one was different, too. The girls lingered for some time, unable to look away from the tortured Madonnas.

After the museum, the day had cooled enough that Wilson decided they could walk back to the hotel, three miles distant. Walking like an old man, slow and steady, he found himself daydreaming, pondering how the girls had studied the *retablos* with the same intensity with which they had once considered their dollhouses and the sagas that attended each doll. Always, perfect families.

When he finished his reverie and looked around, the girls were gone—a sea of strangers swarmed around him, all flowing the same direction he was going: and whether the girls had gone ahead, or he had passed them by, he had no idea, no intuition, and knew instead only the ancient and agonizing panic of solitude.

He surged ahead, certain at first they were in front of him; but after a while, he reversed his thinking, imagined that the minute they saw he was not with them, they would have stopped, and that he had therefore passed them by already, so he went back. And in this manner he traveled back and forth, doubting and re-doubting, before finally steadying himself enough to recall where he had last seen them, and return to the nearest street corner, and wait, right on the edge of the street, hoping to make himself visible.

His return to the corner worked. They had indeed gone on without him, and now looped back and found him. "Where were you?" Stephanie asked, even as Wilson was asking the same of them.

"Please don't do that again," he said—almost a scolding. "I can't take it, not down here."

They both looked at him with an expression he recognized as one of his own: like parents frustrated with a child who'd repeated the same mistake once more, and it occurred to him that from their perspective, it was he who had gotten lost.

There were few injuries more painful than broken ribs—the jagged edges of the break irritating the surrounding tissue with the expansion and contraction of every breath, and the wound so slow to heal, always. He took Advil with the wine he was now openly drinking at meals. Lucy said she'd read that too many Advil were bad for one's liver, and Wilson assured her he'd be careful and not overdo it. It surprised him how quickly they had all become accustomed to the frightfulness of his black eye and the abrasions and lacerations scattered across his face, one of which might have benefited from stitches, though it had bandaged up pretty well. He wondered if they were accepting this new visage because it was the face that fit him now, or simply because they loved him.

He felt the girls eyeing him as he drank, but there was no mistaking that the Advil and alcohol together eased the pain in his ribs. He had started with several glasses of wine or beer, taken, like medicine, throughout the afternoon and evening, but by the day before Machu Picchu, he was having an entire bottle of wine with lunch. The girls eyed his fourth and fifth glasses, the rich plum color, with skepticism and disapproval, but they let it go, perhaps granting it to him as a necessity.

And they were eating in restaurants, which, Wilson told himself, had certain standards and clearly approved of his consumption and demeanor and did not consider him a drunk. Far from it: it was important for the waitstaff, as well as the girls, to see that he was a man of great capacity, one who could not easily be brought down by the weaker forces of the world, the mugging notwithstanding. In a big life, there were always exceptions.

In truth, the broken ribs were a blessing; Wilson didn't know what he'd do without that excuse. He imagined he'd have to find another, and was glad not to have to.

The girls were definitely rawer now, though. Even he could see that. Frightened, but also—could he be mistaken?—somehow more awake.

He felt good, beginning with that fourth glass of wine. The fifth was fine, more than fine, but it was the fourth glass that really took the edge off his pain and everything else. He needed to relax. It was important for the girls to see him happy. When he finished the bottle and the waiter asked if that would be all, he pretended not to want any more. He was proud that when he paid and rose to leave, he was in no way incapacitated, nor would it have been apparent to anyone else that he had been drinking. He just moved a little more slowly, but that was because of his recent injuries. The girls glanced back and forth at each other. He knew there was really nothing they could say, not right now, anyway. He was in control, for at least a while longer.

The day of their Machu Picchu excursion, Lucy woke them before the alarm went off. Wilson stirred slowly, and when he opened his eyes to the dim room—another soulless accommodation: no artwork, only two beds, thin carpet, ugly orange curtains, fully drawn—Lucy stood there looking at him, as though she'd been there for a while, watching him sleep. He felt a great distance from her, and that she had been regarding him, considering him, the way she had once studied the characters in her fairy-tale books.

They boarded the bus to Machu Picchu just before dawn. It had rained heavily in the night but was only misting now. They rode up a narrow winding river canyon, the diesel double-decker bus groaning and swaying, precipitous cliffs visible out one side of the bus and then the other. *Today,* Wilson thought, *I am going to drink only one beer, a good Incan beer, simply for the taste.* His aches and pains were slowly subsiding, and the mugging was far enough in the past for him to convince himself it had had nothing much to do with his being drunk.

He looked over at Lucy. In a heartbeat she would be Stephanie's age, and then gone, too. He studied the darker blue and green flecks in the blue of each girl's eyes. Chips of minerals, each chip a repository for the most amazing sights they'd seen together, both here and back home.

The tour-bus guide was speaking over a microphone. "No one knows why Machu Picchu was built," she said. "Some think it was a place for sacrifices. Another theory is that it was a retreat for the kings, a place to rest and relax."

No sooner had the bus at last circled into the empty muddy parking lot than the fog shredded to tatters before the rising sun. The mountains, earth brown and jagged as the fins of dinosaurs, stretched up through the wisps and shrouds.

They disembarked, stood in line to receive their passes, then edged through the already crowded turnstiles and entered the hallowed playground of royalty. Other travelers shuffled around them, but inside the park, there were any number of stone stairways and terraces that could be traveled; the clots and masses dispersed.

Wilson and the girls had received their own guide. *What great luck,* Wilson thought. *We can ask any questions we want.* He'd been fucking up the whole trip, he knew—paying attention only intermittently, and even then without true focus or resolve. His life was passing by with the speed of a plummet. *Try hard today,* he told himself. *Be present. Try.*

But already the guide was talking too fast, gesturing and animated, and though Wilson tried to listen and engage, to ask questions and learn, he couldn't. The concentration required was too overwhelming.

They went up, they went down. The steps had been worn smooth by the passage of feet across time, with their own adding to the smoothness. The guide's words simply would not attach to Wilson's mind—it seemed there were catacombs inside his head, spaces through which the words passed—and he tried to slow things down, but it was coming at him too fast: the verdant terraces, the teeth of the sunlit peaks opening all around as if to swallow them.

They were walking between those teeth now, and the rain clouds and fog wreaths kept peeling back and away as if funneling down a drain. Ivory torrents of waterfalls plunged down forested canyons on the other side of a great cleft. Far below, at the bottom of the cleft, surged the rushing river along which their bus had labored to get them here.

The guide was saying that the headwaters of the Amazon were on the back side of Machu Picchu. He was saying something about lookouts and sentries being posted, though against what danger was not clear—a threat so obvious it apparently did not need to be named. He said they would flash mirrors to one another across the great distances from one peak to the next and would blow conch shells to sound further warnings.

Much of the talk went past Wilson, but he became aware that what had started for the girls, earlier in the day, as a kind of determined happiness was giving way to something more natural. Their smiles were the most free and unguarded he had seen on the trip. They snapped photos of each other on promontories and in stone cottages. Everywhere they turned, they saw majesty, beauty, here at the top of the Incan world.

And there was farther to go—a special hike, through the last of the forest and up to the very highest peak, torturous and straight uphill. They passed through the next turnstile, narrow as a birth canal, and continued on, ascending now, with the help of ropes, over haphazard steps. The path felt like a secret passage and the girls charged up it with great spirit. Wilson followed, the stones slippery and mossy, the spray of sunlit waterfalls moist with rainbows.

The girls emerged at the top with even wider smiles. Nowhere higher to go.

Lucy posed swanlike for her sister, on one leg, arms outstretched atop the cone-shaped peak, all the world below her.

He was proud of them, and as if crawling up from some pit, he realized that part of the reason they were so capable was that he'd been screwing up these last couple of years. These last three or four years. They were tough and resilient, stronger than he'd known. He'd almost ruined the trip, and yet they were happy. The novelty of this idea—that their happiness was unmoored from his own and they could go on without him—struck him hard and deep; jarred something in him that, while good, still felt more like fear than pleasure.

If, even in his blindered state, he could see this, how much more was he missing? He gaped at the mountains around him with the sudden intensity of a man trying to burn away fog with the focus of his will alone; but the effort made his head hurt, and he found that still, or only, he wanted a drink.

Another memory. Who is chosen to stay; who is chosen to leave? As a child Wilson had been a poor swimmer, yet drawn, now and again, to the very thing that could destroy him. On numerous occasions, while other children splashed and plunged in waters where he could perceive no bottom, he would edge out, pale and tentative, toes gripping the bottom, stretching his child's frame upward until the water was up to his thin chest, then his neck, then his chin. A buoyancy, a toppling.

Still, he would push a bit farther: hopping, bobbing on his toes, trying to join the others. If he fell forward, he would be lost. How many times in his life had he approached this invisible but distinct barrier? Balancing on as little as one toe, sometimes. And yet, always, he had been lucky; always, he had been saved, as if by the hand of another. Fate went his way and he made it back into the shallows, when so easily he could have been lost.

He had not remembered this in ages. Maybe his mind was coming back to him. Maybe he was getting better.

In Santiago, they boarded a bus that was the cleanest Wilson had ever ridden: a double-decker that, for less than ten dollars, would drive them southward, down the coast toward Patagonia, ever farther down-country, down toward the narrows, where the once-robust continent thinned to bits and fragments, a chain of islands, each lovely and distinct but isolate, and requiring ferries to reach. Often, the bus came to the end of land and had to board a ferry. The bus seats reclined into beds, and with the bus uncrowded, they all had their own spaces, with pillows and light blankets. They rode through the night, lulled and sleeping well, and awoke on Easter morning to a brilliant sunrise, the road still rumbling beneath them. A smiling bus stewardess brought them hot coffee and tortillas. Shortly thereafter, on the big overhead screen at the front of the bus, a showing of *RoboCop* began.

They got off the bus in Chilicote. Somehow, with all of the cabs, rental cars, the bus, and other logistics, he had gone almost a day and a half without drinking. That evening, they ate in an open courtyard just off the town square overlooking the ocean, dining on fried whole fish, every fin intact, the crumbs of the delicate batter that crusted it glistening in the late sunlight, the hot flesh white and clean—fish that only hours earlier had been swimming in the blue water they beheld. He did not order a beer, despite noticing the price: twenty-five cents for a liter.

He drank a cold Coke in the bottle instead, along with his daughters, and they admired the way the sunlight, so different in the Southern Hemisphere, caught the gleaming batter crumbs as well as the rinds of freshly cut lemons that decorated the heavy white plates.

Afterward they walked around the square, where young parents were pushing toddlers in strollers or taking their small children to get ice cream cones, as Wilson and Belinda had once done.

They walked back to their hotel, a mile outside of town and up a hill: past the crab nets drying in the late-day sun, the nets glinting with an occasional ungleaned minnow; past the dock where one- and two-man boats, all freshly painted—red, green, yellow, orange— lay overturned, brilliant as Easter eggs. In the blue water beyond, a bright red boat puttered away from the bay, a single fisherman heading out again, and Wilson imagined he could live this life, could be that man.

The air smelled extraordinarily clean.

Back at their room, which had two small beds and a kitchen with a white table, lace curtains fluttered from the breeze through the open windows, and they went out on the balcony and watched the bay— never were there more than two or three boats on it—and, after that, the sunset. He badly wanted a glass of wine but gave himself over to not drinking, as if opening his heart with a blade hewn of obsidian, and gave the girls his sobriety, if only for the evening.

After dark, they found a deck of cards in a drawer and played games they hadn't in years—Speed, Battle, Paradise Lost, childhood games of chance. Then he read to them: the only book they had, which Lucy was reading for school.

Atticus sat looking at the floor for a long time. Finally he raised his head. "Scout," he said, "Mr. Ewell fell on his knife. Can you possibly understand?"

In the autumn light of southern South America that evening, here at the very bottom of the world, time seemed to be made of amber, as if they were all three only just now setting out on the great journey of their lives. He watched the comforting routine and leisure with which the girls prepared for bed—Stephanie brushing her teeth so carefully, and Lucy combing her hair almost carelessly, and yet at great length—as if time had lain down and stopped, while the curtains continued to stir.

When he went to sleep, Stephanie was at the small kitchen table, writing letters—one to Belinda, he was sure—like some Victorian traveler of yore. He thought about saying *Tell your mom I said hey,* but remained quiet, and slept well.

In the morning they pushed farther south, deeper into wonder. They boarded another ferry, bound for another, even smaller island—countless stony clumps of isolated landmass, surrounded by such sweet blue. They left the ferry's observation room and stood on the deck, leaning over a railing, smiling in the sun and warm wind. He reminded the girls to put on sunblock. He put some on as well. His scratches from the guinea-pig woman barely stung. He felt strong. He was starting to breathe more easily; he thought his oft-cracked ribs were beginning slowly to knit back together.

He was better when he didn't drink, he thought. So much better.

But oh, how good a cold beer would taste. It was only late morning but already the sun was warm.

Dolphins swam alongside the boat, and they seemed to Wilson to be smiling at him. He remembered the stories of how they would rescue sailors who had fallen overboard, and he leaned closer, studying the merriment in their eyes, imagining their hearts to be too large for the bird-size ribs that encased them. He admired the silvery way they knifed through the water, inhabiting it without resistance: liquid electricity, liquid joy.

Without a word, but with a euphoria so large in his heart it felt monstrous, Wilson climbed over the railing and leapt in.

The ripping splash that filled his ears did not at first seem to be in any way associated with him, but then he understood that it was. Underwater, everything felt immediately better than it already had.

The water was cold, and he gasped, swallowing some, then kicked for the surface and burst back to the top, cold, refreshed. Gasped louder, sputtering.

He was so thirsty he could drink the whole damn ocean, he

thought. This was no good. The sweet feeling he'd had for a moment was slipping away. He would wait until it returned.

A small wave caught him unawares, and he swallowed more water, then spit it back out again, choking and coughing. It was saltier than other ocean water he'd tasted, and it made him even thirstier. He treaded water, admiring the blue sky, the blue sea. The blue ferry, only a short distance from him now. Not too far away yet. *As long as I stay here*, he thought, *I'm safe. Maybe I'll just stay here all day.*

The girls appeared at the railing, at first panicked but then, when they saw he was all right, embarrassed and confused—had he fallen, or had he jumped? But when he smiled at them, they smiled back, and laughed. They studied him closely; and he, in turn, looked up at them. The ship's captain had joined them, his hand on the round orange lifesaver buoy, prepared to toss it. More passengers appeared at the railing—some curious, some amused, others alarmed.

Everyone stood by, ready to help.

It was the beginning of Wilson's spring, if no one else's. Pretty much the first day. Never mind that it was already fall, down in Chile. As if months, even years, had passed by uncounted.

He continued to tread water and look up at the ship. All he had to do was raise up a hand and ask.

Fish Story

In the early 1960s my parents ran a service station about sixty miles west of Fort Worth. It was in the middle of the country, along a reddish, gravelly, rutted road on the way to nowhere. You could see someone coming from a long way off.

When I was ten years old one of my father's customers caught a big catfish on a weekend trip to the Colorado River. It weighed eighty-six pounds, a swollen, gasping, grotesque netherworld creature pulled writhing and fighting up into the bright, hot, dusty world above.

The man had brought the fish, wrapped in wet burlap in the back of his car, all the way out to my father's gas station. We were to have a big barbecue that weekend, and I was given the job of keeping the fish watered and alive until the time came to kill and cook it.

All day long—it was late August, school had not yet started—I knelt beside the gasping fish and kept it hosed down with a trickle of cool water, giving the fish life one silver gasp at a time, keeping its gills and its slick gray skin wet; the steady trickling of that hose, and nothing else, helping it stay alive.

We had no tub large enough to hold the fish, so I squatted beside it in the dust, resting on my heels, and studied it as I moved the silver stream of water up and down its back.

The fish, in turn, studied me with its round, obsidian eyes, which had a gold lining to their perimeter, like pyrite. The fish panted and watched me while the heat built all around us, rising steadily through the day from the fields, giving birth in the summer-blue sky to towering white cumulus clouds. I grew dizzy in the heat, and from the strange combination of the unblinking monotony and utter fascination of my task, until the trickling from my hose seemed to be inflating those clouds—I seemed to be watering those clouds as one would water a garden.

The water pooled and spread across the gravel parking lot before running in wandering rivulets out into the field beyond, where bright butterflies swarmed and fluttered, dabbing at the mud I was making.

Throughout the afternoon, some of the adults who were showing up wandered over to examine the monstrosity. Among them was an older boy, Jack, a fifteen-year-old who had been kicked out of school the year before for fighting. Jack waited until no adults were around and then came by and said that he wanted the fish, that it was his father's—that his father had been the one who caught it—and that he would give me five dollars if I would let him have it.

"No," I said, "my father told me to take care of it."

Jack had me figured straightaway for a Goody Two-Shoes. "They're just going to kill it," he said. "It's mine. Give it to me and I'll let it go. I swear I will," he said. "Give it to me or I'll beat you up."

People at school said he and I looked the same, but we did not.

As if intuiting or otherwise discerning trouble, my father appeared from around the corner and asked us how everything was going. Jack, scowling but saying nothing, tipped his cap at the fish, and walked away.

"What did he want?" my father asked.

"Nothing," I said. "He was just looking at the fish." I knew that if I told on Jack and he got in trouble, I would get pummeled.

"Did he say it was his fish?" my father asked. "Was he trying to claim it?"

"I think he said his father caught it."

"His father owes us sixty-seven dollars," my father said. "He gave me the fish instead. Don't let Jack take that fish back."

"I won't," I said.

The dusty orange sky faded to the cool purple of dusk. Stars appeared and fireflies emerged from the grass. I watched them, and listened to the drum and groan of the bullfrogs in the stock tank in the field below, and to the bellowing of the cattle. I kept watering the fish, and the fish kept watching me, with its gasps coming harder. From time to time I saw Jack loitering, but he didn't come back over to where I was.

Later in the evening, before dark, but only barely, a woman I thought was probably Jack's mother—I had seen her talking to him—came walking over and crouched beside me. She was dressed as if for a party of far greater celebration than ours, with sequins on her dress, and flat leather sandals. Her toenails were painted bright red, but her pale feet were speckled with dust, as if she had been walking a long time. I could smell the whiskey on her breath and on her clothes, I thought, and I hoped she would not try to engage me in conversation, though such was not to be my fortune.

"Thass a big fish," she said.

"Yes, ma'am," I said, quietly. I dreaded that she was going to ask for the fish back.

"My boy and my old man caught that fish," she said. "You'll see. Gonna have their pictures in the newspaper." She paused, descending into some distant, nether reverie, and stared at the fish as if in labored communication with it. "That fish is prolly worth a lot of money, you know?" she said.

I didn't say anything. Her diction and odor were such that I would not take my first sip of alcohol until I was twenty-two.

Out in the field, my father was busy lighting the bonfire. A distant *whoosh*, a pyre of light, went up. The drunk woman turned her head, studied the sight with incomprehension, then said, slowly, "Wooo!" Then she turned her attention back to what she clearly thought was still her fish. She reached out an unsteady hand and touched the fish on its broad back, partly as if to reestablish ownership, and partly to keep from pitching over into the mud.

She had no guile about her; the liquor had opened her mind. I could see she was thinking about gripping the fish's toothy jaw and dragging it away, though to where, I could not imagine. As if, given a second chance at wealth and power, she would not squander it. As if this fish were the greatest luck that had happened to them in ages.

"You don't talk much, do you?" she asked. Wobbling even in her sandals, hunkered there.

"No, ma'am."

"You know my boy?"

"Yes, ma'am."

"Do you think your father was right to take this fish from us? Do you think this fish is worth any piddling sixty-seven dollars?"

I didn't say anything. I knew that anything I said would ignite her.

"I'm gonna go get my boy," she said, turning and staring in the direction of the fire. Dusk was gone, the fire was bright in the night. She rose, stumbled, fell in the mud, cursed, and labored to her feet, then wandered off into the dark, away from the fish, and away from the fire. As if she lived in the darkness, had some secret sanctuary there. She hummed "The Yellow Rose of Texas" as she went.

I kept watering the fish. The gasps were coming slower and I felt that perhaps a fire was going out in the fish's eyes. Lanterns were lit, and moths rose from the fields and swarmed those lanterns. Men came over and began to place the lanterns all around the fish, like candelabra at a dinner setting. I hoped that the fish would die before they began skinning it.

Moths cartwheeled off the lantern glass, wings singed, sometimes aflame—like poor, awkward imitations of fireflies—and landed fuzz-wrecked on the catfish's glistening back, where they stuck to its skin like feathers, their wings still trembling.

A man's voice came from behind me, saying, "Hey, you're wasting water," and he turned the hose off. Almost immediately, a fine wrinkling appeared on the previously taut gunmetal skin of the fish—a desiccation, like watching a time-lapse motion picture of a man's or woman's skin wrinkling as he or she ages, regardless of the man's or woman's wishes to the contrary.

The heat from the lanterns seemed to be sucking the moisture from the fish's skin. The fish's eyes seemed to search for mine.

The man who had turned off the water was Jack's father, and he was holding a bowie knife. I tried to tell him to take the fish, but found myself speechless. Jack's father's eyes were red-drunk, and he wavered in such a manner as to seem in danger of falling over onto the dagger he gripped.

He beheld the fish for long moments. "Clarabelle wants me to take the fish home," he said, and seemed to be studying the logistics of the command. "Shit," he said, "I ain't takin' no fish home. Fuck *her*," he said. "I pay my debts."

He crouched beside the fish and made his first cut lightly around the fish's wide neck with the long blade as if opening an envelope. He slid the knife in lengthwise beneath the skin and then ran an incision down the spine all the way to the tail, four feet distant. The fish stopped gasping for a moment, opened its giant mouth in shock and outrage, then began to gasp louder.

In watering the fish all day and into the evening, I had not noticed how many men and women had been gathering. Now when I straightened up to stretch, I saw that several of them had left the fire and come over to view the fish. Could the fish, like a small whale, feed them all? Most of them were drinking.

"Someone put that fish out of its misery," a woman said, and a man stepped from out of the crowd with a pistol, aimed it at the fish's broad head, and fired.

My father hurried over from the fire and shouted, "Stop shooting, damn it," and the man grumbled an apology and retreated into the crowd.

The bullet had made a dark hole in the fish's head. The wound didn't bleed, and the fish, like some mythic monster, did not seem affected by it. It kept on breathing, and I wanted very much to begin watering it again.

Jack's father had paused only slightly during the shooting, and now kept cutting.

When he had all the cuts made, two other men helped him lift the fish. They ran a rope through its mouth and out its gills and hoisted it into a tree, where roosting birds rustled in alarm, then flew into the night.

The fish writhed, sucked for air, and, finding none, was somehow from far within able to summon and deliver enough power to flap its tail once, slapping one of the men in the ribs with a *thwack!* The fish was making guttural sounds now—that deep croaking they make when they are in distress—and Clarabelle said, "Well, I guess we need to cook him."

Jack's father had a pair of pliers in his pocket, and he gripped the skin with the pliers up behind the fish's neck and then peeled the skin back, skinning the fish alive, as if pulling the husk or wrapper from a thing to reveal what had been hidden within.

The fish flapped and struggled and twisted, swinging wildly on the rope and croaking, but no relief was to be found. The croaking was loud and bothersome, and so the men lowered the fish, carried it over to the picnic table beside the fire, and began sawing the head off. When they had that done, the two pieces—head and torso— were still moving, but with less vigor. The fish's body turned slowly on the table, and the mouth of the fish's head opened and closed just as slowly; still the fish kept croaking, though more quietly, as if perhaps it had gotten something it had been asking for, and was now appeased.

The teeth of the saw were flecked with bone and fish muscle, gummed with cartilage and gray brain. "Here," Jack's father said, handing me the saw, "go down and wash that off." I looked at my father, who nodded. Jack's father pointed at the gasping head, with the rope still passed through the fish's mouth and gills, and said, "Take the head down there, too, and feed it to the turtles—make it stop that noise." He handed me the rope, the heavy croaking head still attached, and I took it down into the darkness toward the shining round pond.

The full moon was reflected in the pond, and as I approached, the bullfrogs stopped their drumming. Only a dull croaking—almost a purr, now—was coming from the package I carried at the end of the rope. I could hear the sounds of the party up on the hill, but down by the pond, with the moon's gold eye cold upon it, I heard only silence. I lowered the giant fish head into the warm water and watched as it sank quickly down below the moon. I was frightened—I had not seen Jack's mother, and I worried that, like a witch, she might be out there somewhere, intent upon getting me—and I was worried about Jack's whereabouts too.

Sixty-seven dollars was a lot of money back then, and I doubted that any fish, however large, was worth it. It seemed that my father had done Jack's family a good turn of sorts but that no good was coming of it; I guessed too that that depended upon how the party went. Still, I felt that my father should have held out for the sixty-seven dollars and then invested it in something other than festivity.

The fish's head was still croaking, and the dry gasping made a stream of bubbles that trailed up to the surface as the head sank. For a little while, even after it was gone, I could still hear the raspy croaking—duller now, and much fainter, coming from far beneath the surface of the water. Like the child I was, I had the thought that maybe the fish was relieved now; that maybe the water felt good on its gills, and on what was left of its body.

I set about washing the saw. Bits of flesh floated off the blade and across the top of the water, and pale minnows rose and nibbled at them. After I had the blade cleaned, I sat for a while and listened for the croaking, but could hear nothing, and was relieved—though sometimes, for many years afterward, I would dream that the great fish had survived; that it had regenerated a new body to match the giant head, and that it still lurked in that pond, savage, betrayed, wounded.

I sat there quietly, and soon the crickets became accustomed to my presence and began chirping again, and then the bullfrogs began to drum again, and a peace filled back in over the pond, like a scar healing, or like grass growing bright and green across a charred landscape.

Back in the woods, chuck-will's-widows began calling once more, and I sat there and listened to the sounds of the party up on the hill. Some of them had brought fiddles, which they were beginning to play, and the sound was sweet, in no way in accordance with the earlier events of the evening.

Fireflies floated through the woods and across the meadow. I could smell meat cooking and knew that the giant fish had been laid to rest above the coals. I sat there and rested.

The lanterns up on the hill were making a gold dome of light in the darkness—it looked like an umbrella—and after a while I turned and went back up to the light and to the noise of the party.

In gutting and cleaning the fish, before skewering it on an iron rod to roast, the partygoers had cut open its stomach to see what it had been eating, as catfish of that size were notorious for living at the bottom of the deepest lakes and rivers and eating anything that fell to those depths. And they had found interesting things in this one's stomach, including a small gold pocket watch, fairly well preserved though with the engraving worn away so that all they could see on the inside face was the year, 1898.

The partygoers decided that, in honor of having the barbecue, my father should receive the treasure from the fish's stomach (which produced, also, a can opener, a slimy tennis shoe, some baling wire, and a good-size soft-shelled turtle, still alive, which clambered out of its leathery entrapment and, with webbed feet, long claws, and outstretched neck, scuttled its way blindly down toward the stock tank—knowing instinctively where water and safety lay, and where, I supposed, it later found the catfish's bulky head and began feasting on it).

Jack's father scowled and lodged a protest, but the rest of the partygoers laughed and said no, the fish belonged to my father, and that unless the watch had belonged to Jack's father before the fish had swallowed it, he was shit out of luck. They laughed and congratulated my father, as if he had won a prize of some sort, or had even made some wise investment.

In subsequent days my father would take the watch apart and clean it piece by piece and then spend the better part of a month, in the hot middle of the day, reassembling it, after drying the individual pieces in the bright September light. He would get the watch working again, and would give it to my mother, who had not been at the party; and for long years, he did not tell her where it came from—this gift from the belly of some beast from far below.

That night, he merely smiled and thanked the men who'd given him the slimy watch, and slipped it into his pocket.

The party went on a long time. I slept for a while in the cab of our truck. When I awoke, Jack's mother had rejoined the party. She was no less drunk than before, and I watched as she went over to where the fish's skin was hanging on a dried mesquite branch meant for the fire. The skin was still shiny and damp. She turned her back to the bonfire and lifted that branch with the skin draped over it, and began dancing slowly with the branch, which, we saw now, had outstretched arms like a person, and which, with the fish skin wrapped around it, appeared to be a man wearing a black-silver jacket.

In that same detached and distanced state of drunkenness— drunk with sorrow, I imagined, that the big fish had slipped through her family's hands, and that their possible fortune had been lost— Jack's mother remained utterly absorbed in her dance.

Slowly, the fiddles stopped playing, one by one, so that I could hear only the crackling of the fire, and I could see her doing her fish dance, with one arm raised over her head and dust plumes rising from her shuffling feet, and then people were edging in front of me, a wall of people, so that I could see nothing.

I still have that watch today. I don't use it, but instead keep it locked away in my drawer, as the fish once kept it locked away in its belly, secret, hidden. It's just a talisman, just an idea, now. But for a little while, once and then again, resurrected, it was a vital thing, functioning in the world, with flecks of memory—not its own, but that of others—attendant to it, attaching to it like barnacles. I take it out and look at it once every few years, and sometimes wonder at the unseen and unknown and undeclared things that are always leaving us, constantly leaving us, little bit by little bit and breath by breath. Of how sometimes—not often—we wake up gasping, wondering at their going away.

Acknowledgments

An incomplete list of people—writers, editors, friends, agents, book-sellers, and organizations—who have directly helped with these stories over the last thirty years, and by whose individual and cumulative generosity I am humbled, includes Nicole Angeloro; Tom Jenks and Carol Edgarian; Carol Houck Smith; Camille Hykes; Harry Foster; Larry Cooper; James Linville; Leslie Wells; Will Vincent; Will Blythe; Rust Hills; Gordon Lish; Joy Williams; Elizabeth Gaffney; Brooke and Terry Tempest Williams; Jim and Hester Magnuson; Bill Ferris; Ivan Doig; Jerry Scoville; Annie Dillard; Tom McGuane; Jim Harrison; Craig Nova; Howard Frank Mosher; Lynn and Page Stegner; Janisse Ray; Mark Richard; Amy Hempel; John Rybicki; Ron Ellis; Laura Pritchett; Lois Rosenthal; Evelyn Rogers; Bill Kittredge and Annick Smith; Shannon Ravenel; Peter Matthiessen; Larry Brown; Michael Ray; Wallace Stegner; Russell Chatham; Barry Hannah; Richard and Lisa Howorth; George Plimpton; John and Jane Graves; Barry Lopez; Debra Gwartney; Erin Halcomb and Pat Uhtoff; Michael Griffith; Cristina Perachio; Wynne Hungerford; Molly Antopol; Skip Horack; Lorrie Moore; Mary Gordon; Joyce Carol Oates; Daniel Halpern; Robert Penn Warren; Gary Snyder; Doug and Andrea Peacock; Dick and Tracy Stone-Manning; David James Duncan; Carl Hiaasen; Ron Carlson; Pam Houston; Bob Shacochis and Barbara Peterson; Helen Graves and Malcolm Sturchio; Dan O'Brien; Dan Brayton; Bill McKibben; Denis Johnson; Brian and Lyndsay Schott and the *Whitefish Review;* Eudora Welty; the Lannan Foundation; the Mesa Refuge; the

National Endowment for the Arts; the Guggenheim Foundation; the Lyndhurst Foundation; the Mississippi Institute of Arts and Letters; the Texas Institute of Letters; the Montana Arts Council; Bob Dattila; Timothy Schaffner; Scott Slovic; Corby Skinner; Bob Compton; Stellarondo; Caroline Keys; Gibson Hartwell; Bethany Joyce; Jeff Turman; Travis Yost; Nate and Angie Biehl; Amy Martin; Martha Scanlan; Barbara Theroux; Garth Whitson; Ginny Merriam; Ralph and Bruce Thisted; Betty Gouaux; John Evans; Malcolm White; Doug and Lyn Roberts; John and Yves Berger; Dominique and Christian Bourgois; Marc Trivier; David Sedaris; Karl Kilian; Rick Simonson; Pat and Angi Young; Tom and Jan Lyon; Moyle Rice; Nancy Williams; Deborah Purcell; Clyde Edgerton; Pete Fromm; Amanda, Stephanie, Mary, and Molly Woodruff; and Kirby Simmons and family. I'm grateful to Jessie Grossman for her assistance, friendship, and support in the seemingly interminable editing of these stories.

At Little, Brown, I'm grateful to Karen Landry for production editing, to Sean Ford for book design, and to Allison Warner for the lovely jacket art; to Tracy Roe for incredible copyediting and to Leslie Keros and Katie Blatt for proofreading—and to Daniel Jackson for editorial assistance. This book was the idea of my Little, Brown editor, Ben George. Throughout the editing process, he has been opinionated, passionate, stubborn, relentless, always thoughtful and considered, and I am grateful for all of that, and the book is in his debt.

I'm grateful also to my extraordinary agent, David Evans, who, like Ben, has read and reread and helped edit every word, comma, sentence, image—every thought. And I'm grateful to my family, who lived with me during the time I was writing many of these stories— Mary Katherine, Lowry, and Elizabeth, whose intelligence and high critical standards were invaluable; my parents, Charles and Mary Lucy Bass, and brothers, Frank and B.J. Of the writer's need to submerge to the land of stories, the Mary Oliver phrase comes to mind: "I miss my husband's company— / he is so often / in paradise."

PUSHKIN PRESS

Pushkin Press was founded in 1997, and publishes novels, essays, memoirs, children's books—everything from timeless classics to the urgent and contemporary.

Our books represent exciting, high-quality writing from around the world: we publish some of the twentieth century's most widely acclaimed, brilliant authors such as Stefan Zweig, Marcel Aymé, Teffi, Antal Szerb, Gaito Gazdanov and Yasushi Inoue, as well as compelling and award-winning contemporary writers, including Andrés Neuman, Edith Pearlman, Eka Kurniawan and Ayelet Gundar-Goshen.

Pushkin Press publishes the world's best stories, to be read and read again. Here are just some of the titles from our long and varied list. To discover more, visit www.pushkinpress.com.

═══

THE SPECTRE OF ALEXANDER WOLF
GAITO GAZDANOV
'A mesmerising work of literature' Antony Beevor

SUMMER BEFORE THE DARK
VOLKER WEIDERMANN
'For such a slim book to convey with such poignancy the extinction of a generation of "Great Europeans" is a triumph' *Sunday Telegraph*

MESSAGES FROM A LOST WORLD
STEFAN ZWEIG
'At a time of monetary crisis and political disorder… Zweig's celebration of the brotherhood of peoples reminds us that there is another way' *The Nation*

BINOCULAR VISION
EDITH PEARLMAN
'A genius of the short story' Mark Lawson, *Guardian*

IN THE BEGINNING WAS THE SEA
TOMÁS GONZÁLEZ

'Smoothly intriguing narrative, with its touches of sinister, Patricia Highsmith-like menace' *Irish Times*

BEWARE OF PITY
STEFAN ZWEIG

'Zweig's fictional masterpiece' *Guardian*

THE ENCOUNTER
PETRU POPESCU

'A book that suggests new ways of looking at the world and our place within it' *Sunday Telegraph*

WAKE UP, SIR!
JONATHAN AMES

'The novel is extremely funny but it is also sad and poignant, and almost incredibly clever' *Guardian*

THE WORLD OF YESTERDAY
STEFAN ZWEIG

'*The World of Yesterday* is one of the greatest memoirs of the twentieth century, as perfect in its evocation of the world Zweig loved, as it is in its portrayal of how that world was destroyed' David Hare

WAKING LIONS
AYELET GUNDAR-GOSHEN

'A literary thriller that is used as a vehicle to explore big moral issues. I loved everything about it' *Daily Mail*

BONITA AVENUE
PETER BUWALDA

'One wild ride: a swirling helix of a family saga... a new writer as toe-curling as early Roth, as roomy as Franzen and as caustic as Houellebecq' *Sunday Telegraph*

JOURNEY BY MOONLIGHT
ANTAL SZERB

'Just divine... makes you imagine the author has had private access to your own soul' Nicholas Lezard, *Guardian*